The Painter

Roberta ~
ENJOY & God Bless!

Arleen Jennings

ARLEEN JENNINGS

BOOKS

BOOKS

www.arleenjennings.com

For Colleen

Thank you for believing
that my stories are worth telling
and for pushing me to
make them better!

Prologue

FIVE YEARS AGO

Claire's heart raced as she walked into the Casper Events Center. The Wyoming High School Art Symposium was her favorite event of the year and she wanted to see every exhibit. As soon as they entered the auditorium, she grabbed Tim's hand and hurried him toward the first display booth. "Isn't this so cool?"

"Claire, slow down." Tim pulled her back and flashed an irresistible smile.

Her hazel eyes met his gaze. "You know I love you, but we didn't come all this way to flirt."

"Fine, but do you really care about the art show or are you just in a hurry to see where you placed?"

She smirked. "That's not fair, you know me too well." They were close to the same height, which made it easier for her to sneak a kiss.

"There, that's more like it." He raised his eyebrows at her a few times.

"You're a dork. Now, come on . . . you want to see if your drawing won, too."

"That's true." Tim gladly followed her, and they started working their way through the maze of artwork. They thought it was fun to critique the judges' decisions, stopping often to make comments.

Turning into a new row, Tim caught sight of his charcoal drawing of a mountain lion. "Sweet, look at this." It not only had a first-place ribbon on it, the prize included a college scholarship worth $8,000 over four years. "I knew I could win but I didn't expect a scholarship for this much."

"That's fantastic." Claire pulled out her phone. "Here, stand by the ribbon so I can get a picture of you."

Tim straightened his tie. "How do I look?"

"Handsome."

He grinned and stood where both the drawing and the award were visible. After she had taken a few that he was happy with, he said, "Art school, here I come. Let's go find yours. I'm sure you won something too."

"Excuse me, Claire Patterson?" A low gravelly voice came from behind her. She swung around to see a short, balding man with a graying beard and round glasses looking up at her.

"Yes, I'm Claire Patterson." She flipped her wavy, brown hair over her shoulder. "Um, can I help you?"

"You need to come with me."

Tim stepped closer. "Is there a problem, sir?"

"That's yet to be determined."

"Can I come?"

"This doesn't concern you, young man. Now, please." The older gentleman gently pulled on Claire's elbow. "Important people are waiting to speak with you."

"But—"

"Tim." Claire put a hand on his chest. "I shouldn't be long. Why don't you catch up with the rest of our group? You can tell them about your scholarship." Claire smiled, despite the queasiness in her stomach.

She walked with the man out of the auditorium and down a long hallway until he turned into a brightly-lit conference room. Three people sat on the far side of a large table: two women who talked quietly and a man who scrolled through something on his phone. Claire's art teacher, Mrs. Hayes, stood at the far end of the room with her hands folded across her stomach. She was looking at a large painting consisting of random swirls of color.

Claire joined her and whispered, "Do you know what's going on?"

"Not yet." Mrs. Hayes motioned toward the table. "These are the judges for your age group. They want to ask you some questions."

"About what?"

"I don't know."

Claire wasn't sure if she should feel honored or worried, but then she didn't have time for either. All three judges were looking at them. The man put his phone on the table and said, "Please, take a seat."

Claire turned to thank the older gentleman, but he had already left the room, so she settled into a chair next to her teacher and wove her fingers together in front of her. She didn't understand why she would get a private audience with the judges.

The woman sitting in the middle was younger than the other two, but she seemed to be in charge. "Hi, Claire, my name is Ms. Banks." She pointed to her right. "This is Mrs. Johnson." And then to her left. "This is Mr. Turner."

Claire nodded to the judges as their names were mentioned.

"We're impressed with your painting style. You have an enormous amount of talent."

"Thank you, ma'am." Claire beamed. The knot in her stomach loosened.

"You might want to save your thanks until after you answer a few questions." Mrs. Johnson leaned forward onto her elbow and with narrowed eyes, asked, "Can you confirm that your paintings are all originals?"

The question sent a chill down Claire's spine. She knew she'd been caught, but at that moment fear overtook logic. Instead of admitting the truth, she said, "Yes. I, uh, used pictures that I took from my family's ranch and combined them to make them more interesting."

"And you used no one else's work?"

"No, why?"

The judges looked at each other before Ms. Banks answered. "We're trying to give you an opportunity to come clean about the painting with the two cowboys."

Claire squirmed a little but didn't alter her story. "For that one, I used a picture of my dad and my oldest brother."

"So you're telling me that your dad and your brother look exactly like this?" Mr. Turner asked. He reached across the table to give Claire his phone. On the screen was a painting with a different background, but the exact image of the two cowboys.

She stared at the picture but didn't speak.

Mrs. Hayes leaned over to see. Without pretense, she gasped, "Claire, what have you done?"

"You see, Claire, you have excellent taste in art and in style. I'm honored . . . but you *stole* my image."

"Which is illegal," Mrs. Johnson snapped, "and—"

Mr. Turner held up his hand to keep her from saying more. "We'll get to that in a minute. But first, I'd like to know how you added a portion of my painting to yours. You didn't just use mine as a reference; it looks like you transferred it to the paper."

Claire's heartbeat thundered in her ears. Tim had taken a piece of her watercolor paper and when he gave it back, it had the image of just the cowboys printed on it. She only used the background of the picture of her dad and brother to make the painting look like an original.

Suddenly, she understood the severity of the situation, which she had made worse by not being honest in the first place. Because she didn't want to drag Tim into it, she told the story as if she was the one who had come up with the idea and did it by herself.

When she finished, Mr. Turner said, "That is quite ingenious. You did a fantastic job of blending the edges." He reached beside his chair to get Claire's painting and put it on the table. "If you hadn't used part of a painting that we recognized, you probably wouldn't have gotten caught."

"But you are caught. Lying, cheating, and stealing." Mrs. Johnson folded her arms across her chest and glared. "This Art

Symposium has been an upstanding competition for close to fifty years. We will not tolerate cheating."

Claire hung her head and moved her hands to her knees. The pressure she applied wasn't nearly enough to keep them from bouncing.

Ms. Banks allowed her time to think about her actions before saying, "Claire, I need you to look at me."

When Claire didn't look up, Mrs. Hayes nudged her and whispered, "Don't make this any harder than it already is. Show some respect."

Claire bit her lower lip and raised her head just enough to make eye contact with Ms. Banks. A single tear inadvertently escaped.

"I'm disappointed that you didn't tell us the truth when we asked. Mr. Turner has decided not to file criminal charges, but to be clear, you are barred from entering this competition next year. The fact that you not only cheated but then lied about it will go on your school records, which means getting into the art school Mrs. Hayes mentioned to us before you came in probably won't happen."

"But—"

Mrs. Johnson spoke up, her voice now softer. "If you had just been honest, we could have lessened the punishment. There must be consequences, Claire. How else will you learn?"

Claire turned to Mr. Turner with the look of a caged animal. "Please, no! I'm sorry I stole part of your painting. I was so excited to see this idea work that I never gave it a thought that it was cheating. By the time you challenged me on it, I . . ." she shook her head, "I thought it would be easier to say I did the painting than to explain. That was stupid. I see that now, and I truly am sorry."

"Me too, Claire, but rules are rules." Mr. Turner paused before adding, "Let me give you a word of advice. Don't quit. Your other two paintings are very good. I'd hate for you to throw away this much talent. Just be sure to use your own stuff from now on. Okay?"

More tears ran down Claire's cheeks when she nodded.

"Now, Mrs. Hayes, we cannot let your actions go unpunished, either." Ms. Banks' tone became harsh. "Because you allowed a student to cheat and willingly submitted the painting, your school has been given a five-year suspension from this competition."

Claire jumped to her feet. "No! That's not fair."

"I'm not sure you're in a position to lecture us on what's fair."

"But she didn't do anything wrong. Mrs. Hayes is a terrific teacher. She deserves praise, not punishment." Claire patted her chest. "I screwed up. Please don't take it out on her. I did this painting at home. She never saw it until the day before the submissions were due."

Ms. Banks started to cut Claire off, but she pleaded with Mr. Turner. "You said it yourself, sir, if I hadn't used a part of your painting, you wouldn't have noticed it either. Please don't penalize Mrs. Hayes for something she didn't do. Think of her other students. This isn't their fault either."

Mr. Turner nudged Ms. Banks. "She makes a valid point."

Mrs. Johnson, who hadn't taken her eyes off Mrs. Hayes, spoke up. "Is this true?"

"Yes, ma'am. Claire did her other paintings during class, but she brought this one to me already completed. I had no idea that image was added until you brought it to my attention."

Ms. Banks consulted with the others before answering. "Considering your response earlier, when you seemed genuinely surprised, we've decided not to ban your school from further competitions. The effects of this event will go no further than Claire."

Mrs. Hayes blew out a long breath before saying, "Thank you. I've had students attend this event for the past twenty-six years without incident. I'm sorry for the trouble we've caused you."

She stood to join Claire. "Are we at liberty to go? I have other students here."

6

When Claire found the rest of their group, Tim pulled her aside. "Hey, what's wrong? You look like you've been hit by a train."

"Yeah, well it feels like it, too. This has been the worst day ever."

"What happened?"

"Remember the painting that you helped me with?"

"Yeah, it turned out amazing . . . what about it?"

"The part of the painting that you used was taken from one of the judges' paintings."

"For real? What are the odds."

"That's what I thought, so I didn't admit how we did it until after he showed me a picture of his actual painting."

"Wait, you busted me?" Tim stepped back.

"Seriously? I just got banished, not only from next year's competition but from our art school and all you care about is if you got busted?"

"Did you tell them that I helped you?"

Claire reached for his hands, but he shoved them into his pockets. "Wow, why don't you dump me before you even hear the rest of my story?"

"Maybe I should. It's not worth ruining my future over."

"That's comforting, and here I thought you actually loved me."

"I do, but this scholarship is my ticket out of here, and I'm taking it." Tim started to walk away.

"I should have told the judges the truth," Claire called after him, "and told them that it was all your doing. But no, I covered for you—" Her voice began to fade, "at my own expense, because I love you."

Tim turned back with a look of relief. "Hold up, you really didn't mention my name?"

"Right, but that doesn't matter now, does it?" She ran out of the room.

"Claire, wait."

Chapter 1

THE DROPPED BRUSH

Claire didn't wait, and she never looked back. Five years passed, she graduated from college with a degree in graphic design, and a good paying job awaited her in Denver. But now she was having second thoughts. Would it be a good fit for her? The company had given her two weeks to decide, so she came home to weigh her options.

Her parents, Paul and Helen Patterson, owned a beautiful, 750-acre horse ranch in the hills northwest of Buffalo, Wyoming, where they not only sold horses to ranchers but also trained them for rodeos and competitions. Her two older brothers had already moved out of the area, but she wasn't sure she wanted to follow in their footsteps. Did she really want to trade the beauty and freedom of her hometown to live in a city? Her younger brother, Trevor, had stayed and he seemed happy enough here.

Claire woke to the sound of pouring rain, leaned on her elbow to look out the window, and then let her head fall back on the pillow. *Ugh, why can't the weather cooperate?*

She hadn't had a chance to take her horse, Lexi, out for a ride since she had arrived home a few days earlier. She'd hoped spending some time outside would help her come to the right decision.

Twenty minutes later, she crawled out of bed and wandered into the kitchen where her mom was finishing up the breakfast dishes. She wore a pair of jean capris and a light blue tee that modestly covered the extra twenty pounds she'd gained since hitting her forties. Her graying hair was loosely tied into a braid that reached halfway down her back.

"Morning, Mom."

"Good morning, Sleepyhead."

"Sleepyhead? You haven't called me that since third grade, and it's not even 7:30."

"Well, you know what they say, early to bed, early to rise is the way to be healthy, wealthy, and wise." Helen laughed. She dried her hands and then poured another cup of coffee. "Want some?"

"Sure, but what's gotten into you?"

Helen grabbed another mug before saying, "Sorry. I'm just trying to keep the mood light as I deal with the fact that you'll be leaving for good soon."

"It's not like I *want* to leave you, but I didn't think I should pass up this opportunity to use my degree."

"I know, sweetie, but that doesn't make it any easier." She put the carafe back and gave Claire a hug before bringing the steaming mugs to the farm table.

Claire got a bowl of cereal and joined her. They chatted for close to an hour before she finally said, "I suppose I should start looking for apartments."

"Yes, my dear, I suppose you should. We can't postpone the inevitable forever, and I was planning on making a fresh batch of candles this morning, so I best get at it."

Claire went to get her laptop and decided to curl up on the couch in the living room where she'd be out of her mom's way.

It was close to 11:00 before Helen came to ask, "Did you see it stopped raining?"

"No, but that's exciting. Now I can go riding."

"I thought that's what you'd say. There's something magical about fresh air and sunshine; it seems to have the ability to bring clarity."

"Yeah, I could certainly use some of that. It'd be foolish to turn down a good paying job, but I can't picture myself living in a city either."

"Here, I packed you some lunch so you can take your time. Dinner's at 6:00."

"Thanks. See you later."

Wooden fences lined the fields, adding another artistic element to the already beautiful, rolling hills surrounding their ranch. The main barn was less than two hundred yards from the house. To the far side of that, they had a large arena built to make it easier to work with the horses during the harsh winter months.

No one was in sight when Claire entered the barn, so she went straight to Lexi's stall. "Hey there, girl, have you missed me?" She put her forehead between the mare's eyes and rubbed her neck. "What do you say to getting out of here?"

Lexi neighed and bobbed her head.

Claire laughed. It didn't take her long to get Lexi saddled and then they were off to visit their old stomping grounds. Her favorite places were the pond and the cabin that her parents had built about three miles up the mountain. That was where she'd spent most of her summers growing up.

Claire didn't want the afternoon to end. It was close to six when she walked through the kitchen door. "Wow, Mom, supper smells amazing. What are we having?"

"Barbequed ribs, maple baked beans, German potato salad, and cheddar cornbread with jalapeños. All your favorites."

"Ah, not trying to manipulate my decision now, are you?"

"Maybe." Helen winked. "But seriously, I hope you know I'd never stand in your way, no matter what you choose."

"I know, but that's part of what makes this decision so hard. I don't want to live here. I mean in this house. But I love you and this way of life."

10

Helen took the ribs from the oven. "Listen, the guys already came in. Go get washed up; we can discuss this over dinner."

Everyone was seated and filling their plates when Claire came back into the kitchen. Trevor was talking about something else, so she took a seat and joined in.

They were almost finished eating before Paul asked, "Claire, have you decided if you're going to take that job?"

"Not yet. It's a great offer and I'd be using my degree, but my real passion is painting."

"Can't you paint in your spare time?" Helen asked.

"Sure, but I love country living . . . and you guys. I don't think I want to move away over a job, especially to live in a high-rise."

Paul had been twisting his goatee as he listened in silence. Finally, he said, "You can always stay and work with the horses. I'd have to pay you less, but you could live here for free."

Claire ate her last bite of cornbread before voicing her concerns. "I don't want to seem ungrateful, Dad, but that's part of the problem. I'm twenty-two years old and without a full wage, I can't afford a place of my own. To move home for the long term doesn't seem like a great option."

"I hear ya there, Sis," Trevor said. "I don't need you to come back here and start thinking you're little Miss Bossy again like when we were younger." He gave Claire a playful nudge, grabbed his hat, and excused himself from the table.

Trevor had no interest in going to college and had already worked full-time on his dad's ranch for close to two years now. He had just turned twenty and wasn't too worried about getting a place of his own yet.

During the commotion, Paul had gone to get himself a cup of coffee. "Does anyone else want some while I'm up?"

"I would," Helen said. "Thanks."

"Claire?"

"Oh, uh, no, I'm good."

He came back with the mugs and took a seat before saying, "As you know, I already have a hired hand to help with the chores and the upkeep of the place. I don't need another full-time employee. I could use someone with your knowledge and skills to help Trev and me with the training of the horses, though. I realize that won't be enough income for you to get a place of your own, but you could get a part-time job in town."

"What about the cabin?" Helen asked, looking from Paul to Claire.

Claire lit up at the thought and reached across the table to give her mom a high five. "That's a great idea."

"Not so fast," Paul said. "I'll have to give that some thought. I don't like the idea of not having the cabin available at a moment's notice, especially with summer coming."

Helen nodded. "True, but with Trevor living here and Claire at the cabin, we're not tied down like we used to be. Maybe we could take a real vacation this summer."

"Huh, not a bad idea, but summer is our busy season. That's why we built the cabin, remember?"

"I do."

"But I thought you loved being at the cabin. You're willing to give up our private retreat?"

"It won't be forever, and anyway, do you want Claire to move to Denver?" She bumped playfully into his shoulder.

Claire clasped her hands together and started rapidly tapping her foot as she waited for her parents to hash things out.

"Well, the cabin *is* empty a good portion of the year. I guess we could work out a deal." Paul turned to Claire. "If you give me four hours a day, you can live in the cabin for free. I'll even pay you."

"Sweet." Claire pumped her fists. "It's a deal."

"But we also expect you to paint," Helen said.

"Oh, that won't be a problem."

"I don't mean simply for the fun of it; I mean to sell. We should register for some arts and crafts fairs this summer where you could put your paintings on display."

"Whoa, hold up. Just how many paintings do you think I can get done by the first event and then have any left for a second?"

"You must have some from college that are good enough to sell, plus, I could bring some of my homemade jams and candles to help cover the expense of the booth." The more Helen talked, the more her own excitement grew.

Paul squeezed her hand. "You drive a hard bargain there, Mama."

She laughed. "Hey, the sooner Claire gets on her feet, the sooner we get our cabin back. It's a win, win."

"That works for me." He kissed her on the cheek and then took another sip of coffee.

"Me too!" Claire said as she jumped to her feet and came around the table to give them both a hug. "Thanks. This way I can still be around family and the horses, but also pursue my painting career."

"And you won't be invading my space," Trevor called from the living room.

Claire laughed. "You're too funny, Trev."

"Hey, I was dead serious."

"Point taken." She looked back at her parents with a huge grin plastered across her face. "I appreciate you sacrificing the cabin for me so that I can have a place of my own. I'll call the company in Denver tomorrow to let them know that I won't be taking the job."

Trevor returned to the kitchen and leaned against the door frame. "When's moving day?"

"Soon, I hope," Claire said. "Most of my stuff is still in boxes. I didn't bother to unpack from college."

The cabin backed up against a wooded area and the porch faced west, offering a beautiful view of the Bighorn Mountains. To its front and east were rolling hills.

Claire's favorite place to paint had always been at the cabin. The first thing she did after moving in was to set up a permanent studio in the loft. For graduation, her mom had given her an antique wooden art desk that tipped to any angle and height she wanted.

The ladder, which looked more like steep stairs with an iron railing, was the only way to reach the loft. Paul tied a rope to the desk, and with Trevor's help, they were able to pull it up to the second floor.

Windows filled the vaulted end wall of the loft, which allowed for plenty of natural light and provided a fantastic view. The snow-capped mountains could be seen in the distance along with the neighbor's cattle roaming the hills below her. Her parents' house and barns were tucked behind a knoll of pines and out of sight. It was perfect.

The desk had not been situated, nor the art supplies unpacked for more than an hour before Claire started a new painting. By the end of her first week there, it was finished. *Nice. Now if I can keep this pace, I'll have enough to sell at Frontier Days.*

The morning schedule at the barns worked out well for Claire because she was an early riser, and the fresh air and activity always helped to get her creative juices flowing. She kept her artwork original by adding some crisp details but leaving other parts of the painting loose, sometimes not even painting to the edge. If she wasn't painting a Wyoming landscape, she'd be narrowing in on a specific part of a photo to come up with a unique perspective. In her newest watercolor, she did a close-up of some weathered and patched barn doors; the small window to the left was missing two of the four panes of glass.

She'd been painting for close to three hours when she heard a loud crash outside her window. It startled her so badly that she jumped, hitting her thighs against the bottom of the desk and causing her water jar to spill. As she tried to catch it, she dropped a freshly loaded brush, which rolled across her watercolor paper and left an unintentional trail of rust-colored paint.

Everything got wet, including herself. "What a mess; all because of a stupid noise." She quickly dabbed up the excess water, frustrated that the reddish-brown paint had already stained the paper. Watercolor is not as forgiving as other mediums, and the placement of the spatters could not be hidden. The painting was ruined.

She threw the wet paper towels into the trashcan and went to look out the window. Even though it was starting to get dark, she could still see that the leaves in the trees were barely moving, and there wasn't a cloud in the sky. *Huh, no wind. Must be a wild animal knocked something over.*

Claire didn't really care how it happened; she was just irritated with herself for dropping the brush. *Maybe I should listen to music while I paint, that way sudden noises won't make me so jumpy.*

She went downstairs to get changed and had just slipped on some dry jeans before the wind began to howl and the electricity went out. Darkness filled the room, interrupted by flashes of lightning that were accompanied by booming thunder. The windowpanes creaked and shuddered with every gust. She could hear trees snapping and crashing all around her.

Claire couldn't remember a storm of this magnitude ever starting so abruptly. Just then, another tree came down, this time scraping against the cabin. She threw herself onto the bed and buried her head under a pillow. For the first time, possibly ever, she was frightened by a storm. To make matters worse, her cell phone was still in the loft, and she couldn't remember where her mom kept the candles.

At that moment, she was glad that her brothers weren't there; they'd make fun of her for sure. Once, when she was eight, they called her 'chicken' and she hadn't shown any kind of fear since. Ranch life was hard work and keeping up with the boys made her strong, competitive, and independent. She wasn't about to let that change. *At least they'll never know.*

Close to ten minutes passed before the wind started to subside. By then, Claire had regained her composure and remembered a lantern hung by the back door. She felt her way to the kitchen and managed to light it. Now that she could see, she went back to the loft to get her cell phone.

Chapter 2

HOW?

Because she was distracted by the intensity of the storm, Claire hadn't given the ruined art any more thought until her head cleared the floor of the loft. Her lantern cast enough light across the room to reflect a small puddle of water that she had missed earlier. She groaned.

Without looking at the painting, she grabbed some more paper towels and wiped it up. *I should call mom to see if they had any of the trees come down around the house. Huh, now where'd I leave my phone?* It had slipped under a scrap piece of watercolor paper used to test colors and brush strokes. *Ah, there you are.* She snatched it up and went to sit on the futon opposite her desk before making the call. Helen didn't answer.

Then she texted Trevor.

'Is your electric out?'

'No. Why?'

'I'll call.'

"Hey, Sis, what's up?"

"Some storm, huh?"

"What are you talking about?"

"You didn't just get hit with a wicked bad storm? It came out of nowhere: high winds, rain, thunder, and lightning. At least two trees are down, probably more."

"I thought you were a painter, not a storyteller. The weather hasn't changed here all evening."

"And you didn't lose power?"

"Nope."

Claire walked to the window, cupped one hand on the glass, and leaned her face into it, but she couldn't see a thing. "Well, my electric feeds from the ranch; the line must be down between here and there. I think I'll come to spend the night."

"What? Are you afraid to sleep in the dark?" He laughed.

Claire cringed; she was no scaredy-cat. Yet if she was honest with herself, the suddenness and severity of this storm had her shaken. There was no sense in getting upset at Trevor.

"Fine, I'll see you in the morning."

"Hey, Sis, I was kidding. You can obviously come."

Instead of answering, Claire ended the call and plopped onto the futon. It didn't seem feasible that he wouldn't have at least heard the thunder or seen some lightening; as the bird flies, the cabin was less than three miles from her parents' house. But then again, Trevor had no reason to lie to her.

She clasped her hands behind her head and watched the lantern's light flicker across the vaulted ceiling. After bemoaning the fact that the electric probably wouldn't come back on, she went back to the desk. The lantern didn't cast enough light to work on a new painting, so she took a seat and mindlessly started spinning on her art stool. Around once, then twice, then wait! Something on the ruined watercolor paper caught her eye, and it wasn't the streaks and splatters from the brush she had dropped.

Claire felt sick to her stomach and wished the electric would come back on. She got to her feet, grabbed the lantern, and held it over her art desk. The painting had changed.

No way. This can't be happening.

Standing in front of the barn doors that Claire had been working on were three teenage boys. She couldn't believe her eyes and figured her mind must be playing tricks on her from all the stress.

For the second time that hour, fear gripped her. *How? No, who? The culprit must still be in the house.* "Hello? Is anyone there? Show yourself. This isn't funny."

No one showed themselves or answered. If someone was in the room, they did a great job of being invisible. Claire told herself to be brave. She picked up the lantern with every intention of looking for the intruder, yet her courage failed. She couldn't move. Finally, she sat, but kept her eyes on the ladder, while listening for any hint of movement.

Even the wind had ceased, and an eerie hush fell over the cabin. In the stillness, all Claire could hear was her heartbeat. To sit there any longer would simply drive her crazy. She turned back to the painting. The surface of the paper was dry. Though her mind raced, no feasible conclusion seemed possible. *Okay, get a grip; you were probably just seeing things because you were so freaked out earlier.*

Claire scanned the room one more time before closing her eyes. She took three deep breaths and exhaled slowly each time. When she looked again, the boys were still there.

Confident that this was a figment of her imagination, she knew the best way to set her mind at ease was to show the painting to someone. *Mom, I'll show mom. When she only sees my unfinished barn doors, I'll say nothing. No one will ever know about this ridiculous illusion . . . end of story.*

Claire left the lantern on the desk and went to get her portfolio. Once she had the painting safely tucked away, she made her way down the steep stairs. As she neared the first floor, the lights flickered a few times and then stayed on. The cabin filled with light. "Yes. Thank God."

She hurried to the couch, pulled out the painting, and winced. "This can't be happening." The boys, perfectly detailed from the grins on their faces to the spurs on their boots, were still there. "How? There's no way a dropped paintbrush and some spilled water could dry to look like this."

In desperation, she briskly rubbed her face, hoping to remove the impression of an image that wasn't actually there. When that didn't work, she left the painting on the couch and went to the kitchen where she found a half-eaten bag of chips. She sat on the floor and stuffed them in her mouth, desperately trying to think of something else. The only thing that came to mind was the high school art symposium and how Tim had transferred an image onto her watercolor paper. *That's obviously not what happened; he doesn't even live around here.*

Once the bag was empty, she looked out the back door. Downed trees and debris could be seen as far as the floodlight illuminated. "Well, the storm happened, though that doesn't solve my painting dilemma."

Waiting any longer wasn't going to change things. Either the boys would be gone, or she'd have to face the reality that they were still there. Before she reached the couch, she could see them, and her heart sank. "Now what? It doesn't make sense to try and sell a random picture of someone else's kids. I guess I could have it on display for commission jobs. No one would ever know that I didn't do them . . . or would someone?" The face of each art symposium judge crept into her mind and anxiety filled her heart.

Still lost in thought, she picked up the painting, no longer wondering how they showed up, but why? The oldest boy appeared to be seventeen or eighteen; he stood in the middle with his arms crossed, looking strong and confident. The other two boys flanked him, one to his right and the other to his left. Not to be outdone, they stood with their backs to his shoulders with their arms crossed too.

I wonder if this was a special occasion. The boys wore cowboy boots and hats, new jeans, and non-matching plaid shirts. By the detail in their faces, Claire assumed they must be brothers, but that didn't help her understand who they were or how they got into her painting.

The more she looked for something that made sense, the more her heart hurt. Was it fear? No, the anxiety that had haunted her earlier was gone. Taking a hold of her shirt, she put pressure on her chest. "What am I supposed to do now?"

On a whim, she thought of taking a picture of the painting with her phone to see if the boys would show up. They did. Without wasting another minute, she bagged up the painting again and drove to her parents' place.

"Hey, Claire, what brings you off the mountain at this hour?" Her dad asked when she walked through the front door.

"I wanted to show Mom my latest painting."

"It couldn't wait until morning?"

"No, I need her advice; it's for the art fair and it has to be right."

"Helen," Paul called, "Claire's here."

"I'm in the study, catching up on some bookwork."

Claire joined her, portfolio in hand.

"Hi, Claire, Trevor told us your electric was out. Is it still?"

"No, it came back on shortly after I called him."

"That's good. Just give me a sec to finish this entry and I'll be right with you."

"No need to hurry. I just have a question." Once the painting was propped on the empty recliner, she stepped back and started rubbing her hands together in the hopes that it would help calm her nerves.

Helen, oblivious to Claire's dilemma, saved the file and then came around the desk to look. "Oh wow. That's really good. Who's the commission for?"

"It's not a commission."

Helen narrowed her eyes. "But why did you add so many details to the boys' faces if they're supposed to be random? And anyway, I thought you were working on a painting of the old barn over at Clayfield's."

She can see the boys. Now what?

"Um, well that's what I started with. As you can see, my focus was on the doors." She pointed. "Then it just seemed to . . . evolve."

"What do you mean, evolve? It's too clean and crisp for those boys to be an afterthought." Helen knew enough about watercolors to know that it would be impossible to start with barn

21

doors and alter the painting that much without leaving traces of the changes or marring the paper.

Claire shifted her stance and skirted the question by saying, "I'm trying to build my portfolio. I thought it would be good to mix things up; you know, show people what I can do. Hopefully, this will lead to getting some commission jobs."

"Oh. That's a great idea." Helen gave an approving nod.

"Right, and if I have a diverse range of my art available, it will help me gauge what buyers are looking for. I already have a few landscapes done. Next, I want to look through the pictures I took at the Renaissance Faire last summer. If I remember correctly, I got a few from the pow-wow; those would be colorful and fun. I also have a nice photo of Dad and Trevor riding their horses across the western knoll with the mountain in the background."

"If you have time, I think you should do both. Now back to the painting of the boys. Who are they?"

Claire dropped her gaze and fidgeted with her necklace. It was now or never to admit what happened. Her words were almost inaudible. "I don't know who they are and what's worse, I didn't add them."

Helen bent down and tipped her head enough to look into Claire's eyes. "What do you mean, *you didn't add them?*"

"I'll show you." Claire quickly opened her portfolio and pulled out a picture. She gave it to her mom. "Look. This is the photo I used." Her lips quivered and her voice trembled.

"Yeah, this is the one I thought you said you were going to paint. What changed your mind?"

"That's what I'm telling you; I was over halfway finished with this painting when the electric went off." Claire proceeded to tell her the story. "At first, I thought I was just seeing things. Honestly, I didn't think you'd see them."

Helen listened with wide-eyed wonder until the last sentence, but then abruptly shook her head and said, "Oh, Claire, I know you think I'm gullible and you and your brother like to play practical jokes on me, but don't you think it's a bit late for this kind of foolishness?" She turned back to the painting. "Especially, when you did such a nice job. And if you didn't paint it, why'd you sign it?"

"But I didn't sign it." Claire turned from her mom and picked up the painting. The background was now complete, signature and all. *It's exact.* She slumped into the chair and let the painting drop to the floor. "I don't understand how this is happening."

"Enough already," Helen snapped. "Can you please stop with this charade? I might be an uneducated farmer's wife, but I don't deserve to be treated with such disrespect."

Lost in a whirl of confusion, Claire was taken aback by her mother's reaction. To find out that she carried this weight of insecurity caught her off guard. Her own dilemma would have to wait. "I'm sorry, mom. I didn't mean to upset you."

Helen stood there with arms crossed. "Well, it just seems a little late for a prank, don't you think? The only reason to make up such a story would be to have a good laugh at my expense, and I don't appreciate it."

"Wow, this is unbelievable!" Claire jumped to her feet, no longer able to keep her emotions in check. "Right, because I thought it would be hilarious to drive off the mountain tonight, especially after that horrendous storm, just to be mean to you."

"I don't even know what storm you're talking about. Now please, stop."

"I genuinely don't know how my painting changed and I'm freaking out. I needed someone to talk to, so where did I turn? To you, my mom, my confidant. I can't prove it, but I can't deny it either. If you won't believe me, who will?" Claire picked up the painting and left before Helen could answer.

Now, what am I supposed to do? She was too frightened to go home, but after Trevor accused her of being afraid of the dark and now the conflict with her mom, she couldn't ask to spend the night.

By the time she reached the end of the driveway, she remembered that her dad had given her a spare key to his office in the arena. She drove behind the barns where her SUV couldn't be seen from the house. Once inside and the door locked behind her, she grabbed the afghan draped over the back of the couch, curled up, and fell asleep.

Chapter 3

DOUBT

Claire woke early, put the afghan back where it had been, and headed home before anyone knew she had spent the night. There was no evidence of the storm until she was within a quarter mile of her house, where a narrow path was carved through the pines. The mess was more than she could deal with before work, so she grabbed her painting and went inside.

Natural light filled the rooms and made the cabin feel less creepy. With her mind set at ease, Claire put on a pot of coffee and then went to get changed.

Still anxious about going to the loft, she slowly climbed the stairs. From what she could tell, everything looked just as she had left it the night before. She scanned the room for good measure, put the painting on her desk, and then washed out her paint brushes. When she turned back to the painting, she said aloud, "Boys, who are you and why are you trying to ruin my life?"

With a heavy sigh, and for no specific reason, she put the painting back into her portfolio and brought it with her.

Forty-five minutes later Claire was at the barns saddling the mare that she had been working with yesterday. When Trevor saw her, he came to see if everything was okay. "Hey, what happened last night? Mom was really upset after you left."

"You know how we've played practical jokes on her before?"

"Yeah, so?"

"Unfortunately, she thought I lied about the painting that I came to show her. I had no idea how much our 'harmless' pranks hurt her." Claire grabbed the harness and led the horse into the center aisle.

Trevor stepped back to let her pass. "And?"

"And apparently she's taken it more personally than we realized. She felt like we were belittling her, not simply having some innocent fun."

"How'd you come to that conclusion?"

"When I told her what happened to my painting, she thought I was trying to get a rise out of her."

"Yeah, she told Dad and me your story. It sounded more farfetched than our usual pranks, but because you swore it was true, I'm not surprised she got upset."

"But it *is* the truth." Claire looked at him with pleading eyes. She needed someone to believe in her story.

Trevor raised an eyebrow at her persistence. "Come on, Sis, give it a rest."

"Fine." She stomped off with the horse at her side, calling over her shoulder, "I'll be sure to never confide in you again."

"What'd *I* do?" He dropped his hands to his hips and watched her walk away.

❖ ❖ ❖

Later that morning, Claire asked her dad if she could borrow the chainsaw. "Some trees are down at the cabin."

"Trev and I will come to help you later this afternoon. In the meantime, you need to go talk to your mom."

Claire shrugged. "There's nothing to say."

"Just apologize. There's no sense in prolonging an unnecessary feud."

"So you think I'm lying too, huh?"

"Wait just a minute, young lady." He held up a hand to stop her from saying more. "Listen, I was okay with your dramatic tale, to say your painting changed on its own was quite clever, but—"

"But it's the truth!"

He rolled his eyes. "Remember the time you told us you got lost in the woods, but you were really hiding in your tree house? You were so mad at your older brothers for tattling on you that you wouldn't speak to them for a week. We all know you can hold a grudge. Why do you refuse to admit you stepped over the line this time? It's obviously a lie, and your holding to its validity is making things worse for everyone."

Claire crossed her arms and glared at him.

"What's with the attitude? I've never seen you act like this."

"Let's just say I've—oh, never mind." Claire uncrossed her arms. She realized this was an argument she couldn't win and why should she defend something she didn't even understand herself? Straining to smile, she said, "Sure, I'll go apologize, but don't bother coming to the cabin later. I made up the storm and downed trees, too." With that, she stomped off toward the house.

I haven't lied since the art symposium in high school, and now I'm being forced to lie just to keep the peace. It's not fair. Like I wanted any of this to happen.

Claire smoothed things over with her mom the best she knew how without totally contradicting herself, which didn't help because the tension could still be cut with a knife. She walked out of the house like nothing was wrong, but she jumped into her SUV and tore out of the driveway, leaving a cloud of dust in her wake. Instead of going back to the cabin, she drove into town without a plan.

At first, she thought she would go to the local diner, but she wasn't hungry. While sitting at the red light on Main Street, she decided to pay her high school art teacher a visit. Maybe she would have some answers.

When she got there, Mrs. Hayes happened to be sitting on her front porch reading a book. Claire parked on the street under a large maple tree but didn't get out of her SUV. Doubt, along with anxiety, swept in like a flood. *Maybe I should leave before Mrs. Hayes sees me. Depending on how she responds, I could end up at odds with her too.*

Claire ran possible scenarios through her mind, all of which ended poorly. But she was desperate for a confidant, so she grabbed the painting from the back seat and headed up the walk. Before she reached the porch, she called out, "Hi, Mrs. Hayes. How have you been?"

The sound of Claire's voice caused her to jump. She covered her mouth to stifle a laugh. "Oh, my dear, you startled me."

"I'm sorry. It must be a good book." Claire grinned.

"It is. I started a new mystery novel, but at the moment the author has me stumped. Strange markings are showing up on antiques. So far, the protagonist doesn't know how to interpret them."

"How fitting," Claire said as she jogged up the steps.

"What do you mean?"

"I have my own real-life mystery. That's why I came to see you."

"Come." Mrs. Hayes stood and gestured to the chair across from her. "Would you like some lemonade or iced tea?"

"Sure, lemonade would be great."

Claire sat and then took a quick peek into her portfolio before leaning it against her chair. She wanted to be sure the painting hadn't changed. She knew her mom could see the boys, but would her teacher?

A minute later Mrs. Hayes returned with two glasses. "Here you go."

Claire took the one offered to her. "Thanks. So how is retirement treating you?"

"I love it. I have time to read and paint, and I volunteer a few hours a week at an after-school program at the community center."

"Oh, nice." Claire scooted to the front edge of her chair and took a drink. She wondered where to start.

Mrs. Hayes began the conversation for her, "So what brings you into town at this hour of the day?"

"I had a fight with my parents, and I didn't feel like going home."

"But I thought I heard that you moved into the cabin, so what's the problem?"

"Oh, um, being at the cabin scares me." Claire squeezed the glass with both hands to keep it from shaking.

Mrs. Hayes furrowed her brow. "Huh, I didn't think anything scared you, and if it did, it's not like you to admit it. What happened?"

Claire set her glass on the small table that sat between the chairs and pulled the painting out of her portfolio. "This happened."

Mrs. Hayes took the painting and looked at it for a minute before saying, "Wow, this is your best piece to date. I'm impressed." Her eyes brightened with admiration. "You were always good, but this time you've outdone yourself."

"But that's the problem, I didn't add the boys. And no, I didn't take the paper to a printer."

"Okay, now I'm confused, is this your painting or not?"

"It is, but please, hear me out." It took Claire about fifteen minutes to explain what had happened the night before. "So you see; I don't know what to do. I'm trying to get enough paintings ready for Frontier Days, but I don't know if I should have this one on display. What if someone accuses me of stealing their work?"

Mrs. Hayes looked from the painting to Claire and back to the painting, speechless.

"Do you have any idea how this could have happened?"

Then she burst into a hearty laugh. "Good one, Claire, you almost got me. You sounded so serious."

Claire winced at this unexpected reply. Her heart sank. "But I am serious."

"I've called your bluff. Let's chat about other things and finish our lemonade."

Claire took the painting back and turned it toward herself. "Why won't anyone believe me?"

"How do you expect me to believe you after you lied to the judges at the Art Symposium?"

"Because I'm not seventeen anymore, and I already apologized for lying about the painting that I didn't do. I've paid the price for that ever since. Remember? I have no reason to lie to you, especially after what happened."

"Right and yet here you are telling me that you didn't do part of this painting . . . that it magically appeared. It sounds exactly like it did five years ago, just with an *unbelievable* twist. Why?" Mrs. Hayes's usual sweet disposition vanished along with her smile. She tightened her lips and gave Claire a hard look.

Claire didn't back down. "Do you really think I would randomly waste my afternoon just to prank you? My parents are already mad at me because I won't denounce the validity of my story."

"Then why did you come here?"

"Because I'm scared. And I'm trying to be honest." Claire set down the painting, got to her feet, and started pacing the porch. She stopped long enough to ask, "Did someone break into my house? Am I the one being pranked?"

"Stop." Mrs. Hayes stood and stepped in front of Claire. "You're sounding like a crazy person. In one breath you say you did the painting and the boys showed up after a freak storm and some spilled water. Then in the next breath, you want to know if someone switched out the painting. You can't have it both ways. You either did it or you didn't."

"This is rich. I come here thinking you'd be the one person who would believe me. Instead, you're accusing me of lying and calling me crazy."

"It *is* crazy, Claire. You were always one of my favorite students and you're a phenomenal painter, but I can't figure out for the life of me why you're doing this."

"You're right, I must be going crazy because none of this makes sense."

Mrs. Hayes turned to pick up the painting. She ran her hand over the surface. Then she leaned in to get a better look at the brush strokes. Finally, she said, "How can you expect me to believe those boys showed up on their own?"

"I wish I knew." She hung her head and sat again, clasping her hands together over her knees.

"Come on, Claire, it's too perfect. I can't even see where you might have added a digital image the way you did in high school. Once the judges showed us your painting again, I could see the difference between the added image to your actual brushstrokes. So unless you got really good at covering your tracks, even that doesn't seem plausible."

Claire eventually looked up. "Can you at least let me know if you think it would be safe to have it at Frontier Days? I can't risk being accused of forgery again."

"The best advice I can give you is that if you did the painting, it'd be safe to display it because you haven't stolen anyone else's image. But if you come to your senses and admit that you had the boys printed on the paper before you started, then it's obvious that you shouldn't." Mrs. Hayes handed her the painting.

Claire looked at it for a moment before putting it back into her portfolio. "I hope you realize that I have nothing to gain by lying to you." She stood and with stoic resolve, added, "I'm sorry for interrupting your novel. I hope you figure out how the images appear on the artifacts and what they mean." With a disheartened nod, she left the porch.

Mrs. Hayes came to the porch railing and called after her, "Aside from your effort to get me to fall for that story, your painting really is quite remarkable."

Claire turned back to look at her former teacher, calculating whether a reply would be worth the effort. She decided it wasn't, but she didn't want to leave things on worse terms than they already were, so she forced a smile, thanked her and then walked away. *It seems wrong to take the credit for a painting that's not completely mine. Yet after that fiasco, maybe I should just leave it home and not mention it to another person.*

By the time Claire got home, Paul and Trevor were already at the cabin cutting wood and clearing fallen limbs. Her talk with Mrs. Hayes had only made things worse; facing her dad was the last thing she wanted to do.

Instead of helping them, she straightened the furniture on the porch and swept up the dirt and debris from the broken flower pots. Once she had that finished, she realized it was silly to be stubborn; the guys did come to help. She started dragging limbs into the woods.

Ten more minutes passed before Paul turned off the chainsaw. When she came back to grab more limbs he said, "We're fortunate that this tree didn't hit the cabin."

Claire held her tongue even though on the inside she was screaming, *do you believe me now?* But then, the conflict flared because of the painting, not the storm.

"Well anyway, it's getting late; we'll have to finish this tomorrow."

"No need, I can get it."

Trevor put the maul next to the pile he had already split and joined the conversation, "It must have been a microburst. The damage is way worse than we expected."

"Imagine that," she said, coldly.

He rolled his eyes. "How long are you going to be ridiculous? Guess you should have taken the job in Denver."

"Come on, Trev, time to go," Paul called from the truck.

Trevor got in without saying another word and they drove away.

Claire kicked at the dirt and yelled, "Ugh, this is so unfair. How is any of this my fault?" She knew they couldn't hear her, but it felt good to get it off her chest.

Once her dad and brother were out of sight, Claire walked to the pond and sat on the dock. What Trev said about Denver stung, yet maybe he was right. She got out her phone and called the firm. "Hi, Claudia, this is Claire Patterson. Is the job I turned down last week still available by chance?"

"No, Claire, we had five other qualified candidates itching for an opportunity to work here. That position was filled within fifteen minutes of your call."

"Oh wow, uh, okay."

"You were always our first choice and we'd love to have you work here. Do you want me to keep your résumé on file? I can let you know when we have another opening."

"Sure, that'd be great. Thanks."

She watched the reflection of trees and clouds dance on the pond's surface, disappointed that she had let that opportunity slip away. "I guess I'm stuck here for now, so I better get back to work."

She went to her SUV to get the painting and headed to her studio. With two steps left, she could see a jar of tinted blue water sitting on her desk. "Seriously? Now what?" She hurried up the stairs to see what had been tampered with. There on her art desk was a scrap piece of watercolor paper with blue letters painted on it. It read, 'KEEP PAINTING. This will eventually make sense - And NO, YOU'RE NOT GOING CRAZY!'

Claire picked up the paper and turned it over; the other side was filled with colorful test strokes. She flipped it back and read the words again. When finished, her eyes landed on a paintbrush that sat near the jar. The bristles were still wet. "Huh." She picked it up and started sloshing it in the water to make sure it was clean. Then she burst out laughing. "Ah, good one, Trev."

It was quite clever that he thought to prank her in this way, even though she didn't appreciate the mockery. "Now, should I play along with his prank? Show him the note and act all freaked out by it?"

Chapter 4

TREVOR

For the next week, Claire came to work but avoided any conversation that didn't have to do with the horses and left without saying goodbye. By Friday morning, Paul had had enough and was waiting for her by his pickup truck when she pulled in.

"When are you going to stop with the silent treatment?"

She shrugged and looked at the ground.

"I don't even know what we've done to offend you. That's a bit unfair don't you think?"

"Fair? You want to talk about fair?" It was like Claire blew a gasket. She didn't hold back. "You force me to lie to Mom by saying what happened last week wasn't true. That 'I was kidding.'" She gestured. "Well, I wasn't kidding. I needed someone to help me figure out what happened, and you all turned on me."

She tried to pass him, but he grabbed her arm.

"Not so fast, missy. Just because we saw the storm damage, doesn't make your painting story true."

"But why would I lie about that?" Claire yelled. She jerked her arm away. "How would I even come up with such a ludicrous idea? Let alone hold to its truth so you could all hate me if it weren't true?"

Paul took off his baseball cap and rubbed his bald head. He started to answer, but she cut him off.

"Don't bother. I'll stay clear of you, and you stay clear of me. As soon as I sell some of my art, I'm moving out."

Paul crossed his arms and with knit brows, said, "I don't know what's happened to you, but—" He stopped short of continuing that thought. "Fine, Trev and I will do your chores. For today's wages, mom could use some help in the kitchen. But, don't you dare pull out of here like you did last week!"

Without another word, Claire turned and walked to her SUV, threw her hat on the seat, and pulled a hair tie from her pocket. Once her hair was gathered into a ponytail, she closed the door and took a deep breath, pausing long enough to pull herself together. She'd always been close with her family, so this unwelcomed friction was tearing her apart. Turning, she saw her dad watching her from the barn door. A small nod was all she had to offer. Like a sentinel giving orders, he nodded too and then went inside.

No more paintings had changed. She decided it wasn't worth losing her family over the one that did.

"Hey, Mom, Dad said you could use some help."

"That'd be nice," Helen said. "My shipment of peaches arrived last night, and I need to make jam. There's fresh iced tea in the fridge; we can sit on the porch while we peel and slice them."

"Okay." Claire filled two tall glasses and took them outside, then returned to help carry the washed peaches out.

She actually looked forward to spending the day with her mom. They'd become good friends over the last few years and it wasn't fair to expect her to believe the painting story.

The morning started with more work than talk, but by 10:00, things seemed back to normal.

"How many paintings do you have done?" Helen asked.

"Two new ones." *Three if I count the boys.* "But I still have a month before Frontier Days. I should be able to get a few more finished by then. I also have eight from my college days that are good enough to sell."

"Nice, but if you weren't such a perfectionist, you'd probably have more like twelve."

"You've always been my biggest fan."

"Someone has to be." Helen grinned.

"Thanks, Mom. And if any of these sell, I can always mat some of the others for our next event."

"It sounds like you're looking forward to showing your work."

"And making some money. I've already ordered several prints in a few different sizes of my best paintings. I plan to mat them and have them available for sale."

"Oh, what a good idea. Not everyone can afford an original."

"Yeah, that's what I thought," Claire said, glad her mom wasn't holding a grudge over the fight they had a week earlier. "I'm even getting my favorites made into greeting cards with matching envelopes and bundling them into sets."

"Wow, you've really put a lot of time and effort into this. Do you think I should have your dad get us another tent to be sure we have enough room?"

"That won't be necessary. We already bought the biggest tent allowed for one slot. If we get another one, we'd have to pay for two spaces and that would chew into our profits."

"Oh right."

"Besides, I'm only matting my paintings and then covering them with a protective plastic wrap; this will keep them lighter and less cumbersome."

"And cheaper."

"That too." Claire grinned. "I also have two easels that we can set up out front. The rest of the originals will hang on the grid panels that I bought. I'll get Trevor to help me make a few collapsible V tray racks to hold the prints. That way people can flip through them without taking up so much space. If you don't mind, I thought it would look nice to disperse the card sets around your candle display cases and on the table with your jams."

"I don't mind at all. Our booth is going to be a lot of fun, I can't wait."

"Yeah, me either." Claire finished cutting the last peach. "There, do you need help with the canning? If not, I'd like to get home and start another painting."

"You've done plenty," Helen said, as they carried everything inside. "And Claire?"

"Hmm?"

"Thanks for helping. It was really nice getting to spend the morning with you."

Claire agreed. She gave her mom a hug and started for the door.

"Oh wait, would you like to come for dinner?" Helen asked.

"No thanks. Time's a-ticking and I have a lot to do; not to mention the horse I've been training is ready to sell and the new owners are coming in the morning."

"You should at least take some leftovers, then." Helen grabbed a plastic container out of the fridge. "You look like you haven't been eating enough."

The next month flew by without further incident. No more paintings had changed, and no more notes showed up on her desk. Claire still kept mostly to herself at work and always went straight home to paint or mat prints. With two more watercolors completed, she had twelve originals to sell, and a few more started for their next event.

The third Thursday in July seemed to come quickly, but Claire was packed and ready to leave for Frontier Days. Trevor wouldn't be there for another half hour, so she went to sit on her front porch with a mug of coffee. Two months had passed since she moved into the cabin, and she'd been so busy she hadn't done this yet. With a hectic week still ahead of her, taking a few minutes to soak in the early morning sunshine and the mountain views were just what she needed.

As she sat there, she couldn't get the painting of the boys out of her mind. Would someone recognize them? And if they did, would it be awkward? How should she reply? Despite the beauty surrounding her, these thoughts and many more left her stomach churning.

When her coffee was gone, she tipped her head back against the chair and closed her eyes. The melody of nearby songbirds filled the air and some much-needed peace washed over her. It was the sound of Trevor's truck that brought her back to the present, and she remembered that she wanted to bring the painted note. After retrieving it, she met him at the back door.

His truck had a cap, which would make it easier to bring all their stuff. He had already loaded the tent, tables, and a few lawn chairs. Claire was able to slide her panels and paintings onto the tables while Trevor tucked the collapsible easels, V stands, and her suitcase beside the tent.

"There, I'd say everything looks secure. Are you ready?" Trevor asked.

Claire grabbed her cowgirl hat and locked the door. "Yep. How about Mom and Dad?"

"They should be ready by the time we get back."

Frontier Days had always been a family affair, though this was the first time they were setting up a merchant's booth. Claire and Helen would run the booth while the guys went to the rodeo events and hung out at the barns. Paul and Trevor knew most of the riders and had sold several of them their horses. This event was a chance to showcase their horses and pick up new clients. The guys said they would take turns helping at the booth so the ladies could get a chance to enjoy some of the festivities too.

When they got back to the house, the camper was hooked to the truck and the boxes of candles and jams were already loaded into the back.

"Has anyone gone over my checklist?" Helen called from the kitchen door.

"Not yet. I'll do it," Trevor said. He grabbed the list and a pen, marked the things he knew they already had and asked about the things he didn't. "The only thing that's not here is your cash box."

"Oh, good catch! My credit card reader is with it. I'll go get them," Helen said.

When she came back, Trevor handed her the list. "I think we're good to go. Claire, do you want to ride with me?"

"Sure."

It took four hours to get to Cheyenne. This would give Claire and Trevor plenty of time to talk.

"So Sis, should you move back in with us?"

Claire shifted her weight toward the door and looked at Trevor with a mix of surprise and confusion. "No way. Why?"

"Ever since that freak storm at the cabin, you've been elusive, moody, and hard to talk to. I want my happy-go-lucky sister back."

"When I'm accused of lying, especially when I didn't, how do you expect me to act?"

"To be fair, how did you expect us to believe you? It's not like those boys could magically add themselves."

"Right, like I thought it would be a barrel of laughs to lose my family over it. Then to pour salt into my wound, you left this on my desk." Claire pulled the note from her vest pocket and tossed it onto the seat next to him. "It's not funny."

Trevor glanced down to see what it was. He didn't smirk, laugh, or react in any way that would suggest that he'd seen it before. This surprised Claire.

He picked it up with his free hand and asked, "What's this?"

"Come on, Trev, are you going to tell me you didn't do this just so you could prove how ridiculous my story sounded?"

"You're kidding, right? I've never seen this before. I haven't even been in your house since the day we helped you move."

"Wow, now you're the one lying. What gives?" Claire crossed her arms.

"Let me get this straight, you're saying a random note showed up on your desk and you're accusing me of leaving it?" Trevor shook his head and tossed the paper back toward Claire. "Why are you doing this? I thought this scam was ancient history."

She gave Trevor a good long look, trying to read his facial expressions. Then as if being hit by reality, she said, "Wait, you're not kidding, are you?"

"You might think I'm clever . . . or cruel . . . depending on how you want to look at it but trying to prank you with your own medicine never even came to mind."

Claire closed her eyes and started rubbing her temples. Five minutes passed before she replied, "If you didn't paint this, then who did? And you better not start laughing at me now."

Trevor threw his hands into the air, momentarily letting go of the steering wheel. "I said I didn't do it. Maybe *home* isn't where you need to move." He whistled and spun his index finger near the right side of his head.

"Ha-ha, very funny."

"I wasn't kidding."

"Ugh, there's obviously no sense in discussing this." She turned to look out the window.

"See, this is what I mean, you just flip out and clam up." Trevor sighed and turned on the radio.

Nearly half an hour elapsed before Claire couldn't take the silence any longer. In her mind, the music only served as a distraction. A cover that couldn't conceal the rawness of their emotions. The mountain between them seemed insurmountable. Yet, in the midst of this muddled situation, she yearned for peace even if there was no clarity.

"Having those boys show up in my painting has caused me more grief than it's worth. Why would I make that up?" She looked at Trevor, hoping to find a chink in his armor. "What do I have to gain from holding onto a lie? Especially after losing my art scholarship."

"That's fair . . . I've only heard mom's side of the story. Why don't you tell me yours?"

"Because you won't believe me."

"Come on, Sis, I'm trying to understand. It's not to either of our benefits to be at odds with each other, ya know."

Claire wiped her cheeks with her shoulders and turned off the radio. Then she replayed every detail of what happened at the cabin that night. Trevor listened without interruption, though he did give an occasional nod, which Claire appreciated. When she finished that part of her story, she asked, "Can you even imagine how freaked out I was, or how alone I've felt?"

He shook his head.

"Seriously, when was the last time I admitted that I was scared?"

"Never. You're tough as nails . . . sometimes too tough."

"What's that supposed to mean?"

Trevor raised an eyebrow. "You've scared off more than one boyfriend because you're too competitive, not to mention, fearless."

"Quite the observation coming from my little brother, but we've gotten off the subject. You know the storm really happened because you've seen the damage. You've seen the painting, too, but I don't know how to convince you to believe me. I would never have thought to make something like this up, let alone live with the repercussions."

"I can't say I believe you, but I can't say I don't, either. At least now I understand why you felt it best to avoid the subject."

"Since when did you get so grown up?" Claire asked, nudging his shoulder.

He shrugged, "You've been off to college; we haven't exactly spent a lot of time together over the last few years."

"Yeah, unfortunately. We'll have to work harder on that now that I'm back for good."

Trevor smiled and said, "I'd like that."

"Me too. Now, I need to tell you the rest of my story. When the boys first appeared, I needed someone to talk to. You already know that I came to show the painting to Mom. At first, I assumed they were a figment of my imagination and that no one else would be able to see them, but without me saying a word, Mom asked if I was commissioned to paint the boys. When I tried to explain what happened, that's when the wheels fell off."

"And rightfully so—"

Claire rolled her eyes. "Can you please listen?"

"Okay. Okay." His usual grin had returned.

"Here's the point: now, I not only had to deal with the reality that something paranormal happened, but also that Mom thought I was mocking her 'lack of education.' Where'd that come from, anyway? Is she jealous that I got to go to college, and she didn't?"

"I don't know. This is the first I've heard of it."

"Could she be disappointed about her life choices? I mean, she and Dad seem happy, but they got married right out of high school."

"Yeah, but that comment seems out of the blue unless she figures you stepped over the line this time by claiming your story to be true. It certainly sounds unbelievable," Trevor said.

"I know. I wouldn't believe it myself if I didn't know what the painting looked like before it happened." Claire picked up the note and waved it in Trevor's direction. "Do you still deny having anything to do with this?"

"Absolutely."

She read it out loud, "'Keep Painting. This will eventually make sense. And no, you're not going crazy.' Huh, I feel like I'm going crazy. Mrs. Hayes said I was crazy, and now you're accusing me of being crazy, so I guess this note is all I have to hang onto for now. How about we call a truce and we'll see how this all plays out. Deal?"

"Sure, but let's keep this between us."

"No worries on my end; I have no desire to ruin this festive week." Claire stuffed the note back into her pocket and changed the subject. By the time they reached Cheyenne, things were back to normal between them. Claire breathed a sigh of relief, *almost* feeling like she had a confidant.

Chapter 5

FRONTIER DAYS

This year the Patterson family came a day early to get everything set up. Claire checked in and found their vendor spot. She helped Trevor unload the truck, raise the canopy, and attach the side walls. Then they situated the tables and display shelves in a way that would make the best flow for customers.

Before they left, Trevor helped Claire set up the grid panels near the back of the booth. They would wait to hang the paintings until morning. Once they had that done, they closed the canopy sides, locked it, and drove to Curt Goudy State Park where their parents had the camper opened and ready for use. Helen had brought lunch and was setting it on the picnic table when they pulled in. This would be their only down day, so after they ate, they took advantage of an opportunity to play cards.

The next morning, they left early for the venue. Paul carried in the heavy boxes of candles and jams while Helen spread out tablecloths and started filling her shelves. He set the extra boxes under the table where they would be easy to reach, but not in anyone's way. Trevor hung paintings on the panels while Claire set the two easels just outside their booth and placed her favorite paintings on them. Then she filled the V stands with prints and spread out some of her card sets on the tables.

To help make the space feel bigger and let in more light, they removed three of the canopy walls. Once they had everything set, they walked out of the booth to take a look.

"Not bad," Trevor said.

"Not bad?" Helen retorted. "It looks amazing."

"I agree," Claire said. "Now let's hope that translates into sales. I have a lot of money tied up in the cards and prints."

"Not to mention the cost of renting this space," Paul said, rubbing his fingers together. "Half your profits are gone before you even get started."

"Now Paul, I thought we weren't going to fret over that." Helen poked him in the ribs.

"I know, but dang, it's expensive. Oh well, Trev and I are going over to the horse barns. We'll be back before the pow-wow." He gave Helen a kiss and the guys started to leave.

"Hey, Trev, be sure to bring me some lunch when you come back."

"You got it, Sis."

It wasn't long before people stopped to look. No one bought anything.

"Don't worry, Claire," Helen said. "This doesn't reflect poorly on what we're selling. I've been coming here for years as a shopper and I never bought anything the first trip around. I wanted to see what was available in this sea of options before deciding where to spend my money."

"Oh, I know. I've been with you plenty of times." Claire let out a playful laugh.

"I was serious, but I'm glad to see you're not stressing about it. How about you help me open the sample jars of jam. I have one for each flavor." Helen set out miniature spoons and encouraged those who passed by to have a taste. Sales immediately picked up.

By noon, Claire had sold six prints, one original painting, and several card sets.

44

"Not bad for your first show," Helen said, with her proud mama smile.

"Thanks. It's exciting to have people take an interest in my artwork and want to hang it in their homes." Claire moved an original from the display panel to fill the empty easel out front and hung two smaller prints in its place.

When she turned from doing that, she saw two familiar faces looking at one of the paintings out front. Her heart sank, but there was nowhere to hide, so she went to say hello. "Ms. Banks, Mr. Turner, what brings you here today?"

Ms. Banks answered, "I live in Cheyenne and I came to see Mr. Turner's latest pieces of art."

"Yeah, I have a booth a few rows over," Mr. Turner said. "When we saw your name on the list of art vendors, we wanted to see if you were the same Claire Patterson we remembered from the High School Art Symposium."

"It's me." Claire let out a nervous laugh. Not knowing what else to do, she put her hands into her back pockets and waited breathlessly to see if either of them would recognize the boys.

"We're glad to see you didn't quit painting," Ms. Banks said.

"Me too." Claire relaxed and with renewed confidence, gestured toward the booth. "I have more in the back if you'd like to take a look."

Ms. Banks did, but Mr. Turner stayed where he was.

"Your work is impressive. I always did like your style." He winked and then leaned in to get a better look at the fateful painting. Claire suddenly felt nauseous. Was he looking for a separation between the boys and the background? Would he accuse her of pilfering another one of his paintings?

After a bit, he stepped back and started rubbing his chin. With eyes narrowed, he turned to face Claire.

She had never forgotten that dreadful look. What was he thinking? Why wouldn't he speak?

Resting his index finger on his upper lip, he turned back to the painting. Finally, she broke the uncomfortable silence and asked, "Is everything okay?"

"Yes, fine. That just seems like an odd choice of background for a portrait."

"You don't like it?"

"Actually, I do. I would never have thought to put those exuberant looking boys in front of an old barn door. Do you know them personally?"

"Um, no."

"It looks like you must have done a good job showing their personalities." His expression softened. "Do you have the picture of the boys with you? If you do, I'd like to see it."

"No. What's with the twenty questions?" Claire knew she should've checked her tone, but he clearly had nothing to do with these boys and she didn't feel obligated to give him an explanation.

"Whoa, I meant no harm. Excuse me." Mr. Turner left her to join Ms. Banks at the back of the booth. The two of them started critiquing Claire's paintings as if they were judging a competition.

She knew they weren't going to buy anything, so she went to help another customer.

When they got ready to leave, Mr. Turner said, "You certainly have a bright future ahead of you, Claire. If you get a chance to take a break, you should come to see my latest pieces of art. I've gone in a different direction lately. I'd like to know what you think. My booth's back that-a-way." He pointed to his left.

"I'll be sure to stop by. And uh, thanks for your kind words."

Helen had caught only a part of their conversation and now that they were gone, she asked, "Who were they?"

"The judges that banished me from art school."

"No wonder the color drained from your face. You had me worried when you snapped at the man."

"Just nervous. He was questioning the painting that you didn't believe changed. I was afraid he would recognize the boys or, even worse, say that I stole that part of his painting. Then I'd be done for."

"I don't see why you're still holding to that silly story, so I'm going to pretend that I didn't hear you. On a brighter note, they

46

both seemed quite complimentary, considering the circumstances."

Claire wished her mom believed her, but she didn't. She didn't even mean to say something; it had just slipped out. Now all she could do was hope that it wouldn't ruin the rest of their week together.

❖ ❖ ❖

At 12:30, as promised, Trevor came with a burger and curly fries for Claire. He planned to stay and help while Paul took Helen to lunch and then to the pow-wow.

"We should be back by 2:30," Paul said.

"Take your time and have some fun; we've got this," Trevor said, taking a few fries from the bag.

"Hey." Claire swatted his hand. "I thought those were mine."

He grinned and stuffed them into his mouth. She pulled the bag away before he could take any more.

Things remained steady for the next two hours. When Helen and Paul got back, Claire and Trevor took a break and walked around the vendor booths. She wanted to see what other kinds of arts and crafts were available and what their prices were.

When they reached Mr. Turner's booth, he was busy with other customers. Claire breathed a sigh of relief. She had no desire to speak with him again, even though she was interested in seeing more of his art. Before today, she had only seen his painting of the two cowboys, which had secured a permanent spot in her nightmares. There were times when those horses would gallop off her painting with the intention of trampling her underfoot. She always woke at the last second, trembling and feeling helpless . . . like that foolish mistake would haunt her forever.

Now that she had seen more of his paintings, she hoped the dreams would cease. He had complimented her. They had both moved on and it was time for that part of her past to be forgotten.

Trevor broke her introspection. "Wow, his prices are really high."

"Yeah, well, his work is amazing, and he *is* well known in this part of the country. Let's go before he sees us."

On their way back, Claire caught sight of their mom waving for them to hurry. They did.

"Hey, Mom," Trevor called. "What's up?"

"You just missed her."

"Missed who?" Claire asked.

Helen looked to see if the woman was still in sight. She wasn't. "A middle-aged woman just stopped to enquire about the painting of the boys."

"Oh yeah? Was she interested in a commission job?"

"I couldn't tell. She asked if I was the artist and seemed . . ." Helen paused to straighten her glasses. "Actually, she seemed troubled. When I told her my daughter did it, she wanted to know if you were here. I let her know you'd be back shortly, but then she abruptly left."

"Huh, it seems like if it truly bothered her, she would've explained why."

"I was more surprised that she didn't wait."

"If it's important, she'll be back," Paul said. "There's no sense in fretting about it now."

Claire started straightening the card sets to avoid eye contact with her parents. All the uncertainty surrounding the painting made her feel uneasy, and she didn't want to talk about it. To change the subject, she asked. "Did any more of my art sell?"

"Yes, three more prints. The one of the Bighorn Mountains is very popular."

"Nice, I'll have to order more of those before our next show."

"Oh, and a different lady left her name and number. Here." Helen held out a piece of paper. "She loves your style and wants you to do a painting of their cottage on the Pathfinder Reservoir."

Claire gladly took it, thankful for the diversion. "I'll be sure to give her a call next week." She pulled out her phone and started to add the woman's contact info.

"Hey Trev, are you ready to go?" Paul asked.

"If you don't mind, I'd like to stay. Mom, why don't you go with Dad? We can run the booth and close it up for the night."

Helen raised an eyebrow, "I'm happy to stay, it's half my stuff."

"Yeah, but you hardly ever get a chance to get out. We'll be here all week; it's not like you won't have your fill of it."

She nodded at his rationale and agreed.

Paul smiled and took Helen's hand. "Thanks, Trev."

As they walked away, Claire saw her mom bump into her dad's shoulder like young lovers. "We have some pretty great parents."

"We sure do," Trevor agreed. "Now back to work." He tipped his head toward the mother and daughter who were ready to check out.

After they paid, Claire asked, "Trev, why'd you do that?"

"Do what?"

"Offer to stay."

"Because I thought it'd be easier if Mom wasn't here when that woman comes back. Anyway, I'd like to hear what she has to say."

"To be honest, I feel sick. I had no idea the painting would bother someone."

"Think about something else. Mom probably overreacted because of your story." Trevor left her to help a young couple who were taking turns smelling candles.

Business ebbed and flowed for the next two hours, and though a few people commented on the painting of the boys, no one seemed troubled by it or asked about a commission.

By 5:00, the woman still hadn't come back, and things were slowing down. It was then that Claire realized her stomach had been in knots all afternoon. "I don't know why this stresses me out so much."

"Ha, I was nervous too, and I don't even have a reason to be."

"Probably because you'll find out I wasn't lying, and you'll have to eat humble pie," she said with a wink.

"Nothing's been proven yet, Sis. You still might have to admit you did the painting and why you made up the story. You can't keep this charade going forever."

Claire threw her hands onto her hips. "Wait, I thought you said you believed me."

"No, I said I wasn't sure. The jury is still out. Come on, let's close up for the night and go hang out at the carnival for a while."

Chapter 6

SOPHIE

The next morning, Claire woke to pangs of anxiety. First, the painting of the boys, and now a woman who 'seemed to be troubled' by it, gave her every reason to believe that conflict awaited her. Yet, if truth be told, this woman could have the answers she desperately needed.

The rest of her family was still asleep, so Claire crept out of the camper and headed for a nearby stream. The sound of moving water was one of her favorite things and she hoped it would calm her nerves and help prepare her for what lay ahead. As she walked, she came to a place where the banks became a wall of rocks, which eventually opened to a narrow waterfall. It was there that she saw a teenaged girl, sitting on a rock, sketching.

When the girl saw Claire, she gave a hearty wave and said, "Isn't it beautiful here?"

"It sure is. Do you mind if I look at your drawing?"

"Of course not." With bright eyes and a broad smile, the girl thrust her sketchbook forward. "I'm Sophie."

"Pleased to meet you, Sophie, I'm—" She did a double take when she saw the drawing. "Claire." Blinking hard didn't help to dissolve the vision of three boys sitting on a log, wearing white tee shirts. The resemblance in their faces was quite impressive.

"What? Don't you like it?" Sophie sheepishly asked.

"I do like it. You just caught me off guard, that's all. I expected to see the waterfall."

Sophie flipped her sketchbook back toward herself and frowned. "But it is the waterfall."

"Oh, uh, sorry. Here," Claire reached to take the sketchbook, "let me look at it again."

The sparkle that had filled Sophie's eyes had vanished and with some reluctance, she handed it to her.

There was no mistaking the boys. The waterfall wasn't even in the drawing. Claire forced a smile and looked closer. Across the bottom of the page were the words: 'There's a story yet to be told. When you hear it, pursue.' *Hmm, either the girl can't see the boys, or she's very convincing.*

"So, what do you think?" Sophie asked as she tapped her charcoal pencil impatiently on her knee.

It was then that Claire realized her personal quandary had nothing to do with this girl. She needed to keep it simple. "You're very talented. If you don't mind, I'd like to take a picture of it."

"For real?"

"Absolutely." Claire pulled her phone from her back pocket. "I'll take two; a close up of the drawing and then one with you in it."

"Okay."

Claire took the first picture, and then said, "Here, for this one, let's move the drawing closer to your face." She repositioned the sketchbook. "Hold it right there."

Sophie complied.

"Come on now, give me a big smile."

She laughed a little and then smiled.

Claire took the picture and looked at the screen before saying, "Nice!" Then she handed Sophie the phone. *I wonder if she'll see the boys now.* With eyes fixed, she waited for Sophie's reaction. The one she got was not what she expected . . .

"Sweet, can I text these to myself?"

"Sure." Claire's thoughts went to the note still stuffed in her pocket . . . 'And no, you're not going crazy.' *Well then, how do you explain this?*

Sophie had the pictures sent and the phone handed back in no time. "Thanks!"

"Not a problem. By the way, I'm a painter and have a booth at Frontier Days. If you have time, you should stop by."

"My mom loves going to the arts and crafts fair. We'll look for your booth."

"Great. I'll see you later then." Claire smiled and started for camp. After only a few steps, she turned back to ask Sophie a question. The girl was gone. *Huh. I guess at this point, nothing should surprise me.*

Opening her phone, she looked again at the photos she had just taken. *I see boys, Sophie saw a waterfall . . . I wonder what Trevor will see.*

By the time Claire got back, everyone was up and ready for the day.

"Oh good, you're here," Helen said. "The guys have already eaten."

"Yeah, we're heading over to the barns now. If either of you needs anything, text one of us," Paul said. He kissed Helen's cheek and then jumped into his truck where Trevor was already waiting.

"Okay, see you later," Helen said. She waved and watched them pull out. "Claire, your breakfast is warming on the stove."

"I need to get changed, first. I'll be right there."

Claire was disappointed that she didn't have a chance to talk to Trevor. She knew he wasn't sold on her story, but at least she could confide in him. Not wanting to wait, she sent him a text with the picture of the boys. 'What do you see?'

A minute later he texted: 'A drawing of a waterfall.'

'Are there any words on it?'

Another minute or so passed before he replied. 'No. Why?'

'I'll explain later.' Claire added a smiley face with sunglasses to hide her disappointment. 'Thanks.'

"Are you ready, Claire?" Helen called from outside the camper. "We should get going."

"Yeah." She stuffed her phone into her pocket, wrapped her bagel sandwich in a paper towel, and locked the camper behind her.

She could hear Trev's advice from the other day ringing in her ears, "Remember, keep this to yourself." *Ha, that's not going to be a problem.*

Once they had the booth sides open, Claire put different paintings on the easels out front. She thought it best to keep the one of the boys on the back panel for now, especially if that lady was truly troubled.

The morning started much faster than it had the day before, and sales were good for both. Claire even sold the original of the Bighorn Mountains. With all the activity and excitement, she forgot about the painting of the boys, that is, until a woman who looked to be in her late thirties or early forties, came in. She walked straight to that painting.

She stood there for a moment and rapidly spun her wedding band. Then, with narrowed eyes, she leaned closer as if trying to see something that wasn't there.

That caused Claire's heart to skip a beat and a lump quickly formed in her throat. To settle her nerves, she took a deep breath and swallowed hard before going to say hello. The woman replied warmly and asked how much a commission would cost if there were only two teenagers instead of three.

Claire exhaled louder than she had intended, but to cover, she immediately gave the woman a list of size options along with the pricing.

"Oh, that much? I had no idea what a portrait of this quality would cost. I'm sorry for having bothered you."

"You're not a bother at all, thanks for asking."

The woman blushed and turned to leave.

"I'll tell you what," Claire called after her. "If you can wait until winter when things are slower for me, I'll do the portrait for half the price."

"You'd do that for me?" Her eyes brightened.

"Yes, ma'am." Claire handed her a business card. "Please write 'winter project' in the subject line of the email and be sure to attach a picture."

"I will. Thank you."

Chapter 7

THE BOYS

An unexpected calm filled Claire's heart as the woman walked away. It felt good to be generous and she was no longer consumed by what the rest of the day would bring. Not long afterward the guys came with lunch and Trevor offered again to stay.

"Okay, but only for an hour," Helen said. "I like being at the booth. It's fun to interact with the people."

As soon as their parents were gone, Trevor said, "I see you still have the painting. Does that mean the lady hasn't come back?"

"Not yet." Claire removed the lid from the piping hot cup of chili and raised it to her nose. "Mmm, smells yummy, thanks."

"Extra spicy, just the way you like it. Oh, and what was with your text this morning?" Trevor asked, as he got out his phone and opened it to the drawing.

"Just more of the 'You're not going crazy' kind of stuff that makes me wonder if I really am."

"Want to clarify?"

"Sure, but let me see the text I sent you, first."

Trevor handed her his phone.

For the first time, Claire saw the waterfall, too. *Huh, Sophie does have talent.* She quickly opened her picture app and asked, "What do you see in this one?"

"A black and white drawing of three boys. Wait. Are those the same boys that you painted?"

"Seriously, you can see them?"

"Yeah, so?"

"It's the same photo I sent you earlier."

"No way!"

"It's true. And can you see the words at the bottom?"

He stretched the image so he could see it better. "Yeah, it says, 'There's a story yet to be told. When you hear it, pursue.'"

"Yes!" Claire pumped her fist and then told him about Sophie and her early morning hike. After a few short interruptions to wait on customers, she finished with, "So it was a weird start to my day, especially when you only saw the waterfall."

"Now it makes sense why you thought your mind was playing tricks on you. But why can I see it on your phone but not on mine?" Trevor asked.

"I have no idea, but I'm thrilled that you can see it now."

"Here, text that picture to me again." This time the boys showed up. "Hold up, let me look through the rest of your pictures."

"You're not going to find a drawing of the waterfall and look, here's my first text to you from earlier. See? The boys. You received a waterfall."

Trevor shook his head. "I hope that lady comes soon. I'd like to hear what she has to say."

"Me too."

Not long after this, a slender, middle-aged woman with brown, short-stacked hair abruptly entered the booth. Without hesitation, she approached Claire and in a nervous, hurried tone, asked, "Are you the artist who painted my nephews?"

"If you mean the painting of those boys," she gestured toward the back, "I am." She smiled, hoping this would help to calm the storm, and set the woman's mind at ease. She reached to take her hand. "I'm Claire, and you are?"

"My name's Maggie. But about the painting, do you know the family?"

"No."

"Then where did you get that picture?"

"I didn't use a picture."

"Impossible. The painting is too exact."

The sharpness of her retort broke Claire's resolve and she looked away, desperate to find the right thing to say. It was then that the message on Sophie's drawing flashed before her eyes. She quickly asked, "You say these boys look like your nephews?"

"Yes, but I've never seen this picture before," Maggie said, stepping closer to the painting. "It looks like it must have been taken less than a month before the accident."

Claire seized the moment. "What accident?"

Trevor waited on other customers but kept an ear toward Maggie.

"I'm sure you don't really want to hear my story, but I'll buy the painting." With a shaky hand, she fumbled through her large handbag. "Ugh, where did I put my wallet?"

"Actually," Claire gently touched the woman's arm, "I'd love to hear your story."

Maggie looked behind her and saw the booth was mostly empty. "I guess if you have time, I could share what details I know."

"I have time." Claire nodded with a bit too much enthusiasm. *I have all the time in the world if this painting could finally make sense.*

"I still don't see how you did this; it's quite remarkable. Well, anyway, for Jonathan's thirteenth birthday," she pointed to the youngest boy, "he asked his dad if they could go kayaking. They didn't go often, but enough that they knew how to maneuver through small rapids. To make the trip special, his father took them to visit a rancher friend, who lived a few hours away. He owned land along a tributary of the Bighorn River."

Maggie stopped to face Claire, her eyes now moist. "The boys in your painting look exactly as I remembered them ten years ago. It was a wet spring that year and unusually warm. The rain and melting snow made the water higher and the current faster than they were used to, but they were strong and adventurous and thought it would be fun to ride the bigger rapids. Johnny's kayak got thrown sideways into some rocks. He was wearing a helmet but apparently went limp, lost his paddle, and never struggled to right himself. His lifejacket brought him sideways, which exposed his face to the next set of rocks. In a panic, Zac," she pointed to the boy in the middle, "who was in the lead, tried to maneuver back to help his brother. The current was too strong, so he threw himself from his own kayak and eventually got Johnny back upright, but by then, they hit a new set of rapids, and Zac got swept away. In a matter of minutes, he was out of sight.

"In the meantime, Roger, the boys' father, and Chase," she pointed to the last boy, "caught up with Johnny and struggled to get him to shore. He was unconscious and his lungs were full of water. Roger did CPR, but Johnny never regained consciousness and died before they could get help. Chase went to get back in his Kayak so he could find Zac, but his dad wouldn't let him. He figured Zac was wearing a life jacket and was a strong swimmer. He would make his way to shore at the next lull in the river."

By this point in the story, Trevor had come to listen.

Claire covered her mouth, absorbing every word as if their plight was fresh and raw. Why did real boys, with such a haunted past, show up in her painting? She finally dropped her hand and said, "That's so sad."

Claire's response brought Maggie out of her story. "Oh, I'm sorry; you don't need to know all the painful details." She reached a second time for her wallet, this time finding it immediately. "I would like to buy this painting."

"And I would like to hear the rest of the story," Claire said adamantly.

"Yeah, you can't leave us hanging," Trevor added.

"There's not much more to tell," Maggie said.

"So Zac made it safely to shore then?" Claire asked.

Maggie set her jaw and shook her head. "Roger had his phone in a plastic bag, but this happened back before there was good cell reception. He couldn't get a call out for help. Chase climbed up the steep bank and ran as fast as he could, but there weren't any roads in sight. By the time he got help, hours had passed.

"Rescue teams scoured the area; they even sent other crews further downstream. Zac never made it to shore, or they would have found him. The people helping didn't know this part of the river very well and their best guess was that the powerful current had dragged him under. Because this section of land was so sparsely populated, the kayak wasn't found until a few days later, nearly twenty miles from where Johnny died, which only broadened the search area. They even brought in helicopters but with no success. After searching for days, they told Roger they would have to wait for lower waters to look for Zac's body."

"But how far away from the water did they look? Maybe he was hurt and collapsed trying to get to safety," Trevor said.

"They were certain that if he made it to land, the aircrew would have spotted him. His body was never found."

Trevor shook his head. "Wow, I have two brothers; I couldn't imagine losing them both in one day."

Claire wiped her cheek with her shoulder and asked, "How's Chase doing? That seems like it'd be a heavy burden to bear."

"You have no idea. He lost more than his brothers that day." Now it was Maggie's turn to dry her eyes. She cleared her throat, "Ahem, but that's a whole different story and one that won't be told today. Back to the accident, these events devastated Roger. He fell into a deep depression. He couldn't work. He didn't care about anything. They would have lost everything if my sister, Michelle, hadn't called to beg us to move back to Wyoming and help her. My husband Brad and I walked away from prosperous jobs in Denver. We started working on the ranch nine years ago."

"I know we just met, but it sounds like you and Brad are amazing people. To trade your lives to help others is not a common occurrence these days," Claire said.

Maggie shrugged. "Sure, we enjoyed the city, but family is far more important than money and things. Besides, we've come to love the ranch and this way of life."

Again, the words on Sophie's drawing came to Claire's mind . . . *Pursue.* "Can I come to the ranch? I'd like to see the actual barn and where these boys grew up. Maybe learn something about them."

Maggie tipped her head and bit her lower lip. She seemed to be contemplating a reply. Finally, she said, "You can, but what would be the point? Zac and Johnny are dead."

"True, but in my painting, they're full of life. Does it capture their personalities?" Claire asked. She was intrigued by Maggie's story and determined to find out more.

"It's uncanny how you captured them exactly. Johnny was a goofball, the glint in his eye and his crooked smile are perfect. He was thin and not real strong; he would rather draw a horse than ride one.

"You have Chase, here, on his toes, which is classic. His lack of height at the age of fifteen caused some insecurity issues. Even though he was younger than Zac he always tried to keep up with him, especially when it came to his skills on a horse. Funny thing is, Chase has grown, not only taller, but he's quite the horseman."

"Does he compete?" Trevor asked.

"Not anymore." Maggie gave a slight wave of the hand before adding, "He loves going to the rodeos, though. I didn't stop back yesterday because Brad and I had already planned to meet up with Chase. It was his one day to get away from the ranch."

Apparently realizing that she had gotten off track from her story, Maggie turned back to the portrait. "Zac, here, was his father's favorite and could do no wrong. He was strong, secure, and even a bit proud, but then he was good at everything. That confident smile with his arms crossed is perfect."

Maggie concluded her story with, "Their parents are going to love this portrait. Now, are you going to tell me how you were able to do this painting without a picture?"

Claire wished she had an answer. It's not like she was trying to hide something; she just knew the truth would mirror a fairytale and destroy what good-will she had just gained. "Not today."

61

Then with a persuasive grin, she rocked onto her toes and asked, "So, can I come?"

"You're too much." Maggie laughed. "And yes, you can come. I would like to commission you to do a painting of Brad and me with our horses, so be sure to bring your camera."

"That'd be perfect, and it'd give me a legitimate reason to come."

Maggie paid for the painting and after they exchanged contact information and an address, she said, "Any day of the week works for us. You can even meet Roger and Michelle."

"That would be awkward, don't you think? Especially since I can't explain how I did the painting to anyone's satisfaction."

"Will you have an explanation by the time we meet again?" Maggie asked with a quizzical look in her eye.

Pinched lips and a furrowed brow replaced Claire's smile. She shrugged.

Trevor caught the last end of this exchange and said, "Excuse me, Sis; this young lady has some questions about your art that I don't know the answers to."

"Okay, great." Claire motioned for her to wait. "I just need a minute to finish up here. I'll be right with you."

"No worries," the younger woman said. "I'm not in a hurry." She smiled and went back to talking with Trevor.

Claire wrapped the painting in stiff brown paper. "There, that should protect it until you get it home."

"Yes, this is great, thanks." Maggie picked up the package. "I'll wait to give it to Michelle until after you come. Does next week work for you?"

"Sure. How about Tuesday evening?" Claire asked.

"Sounds good. Instead of meeting us at the house, we'll wait for you by the main barn, say 6:30-ish. I look forward to introducing you to Brad."

"I'd like that. See you on Tuesday. Bye."

"Bye."

Claire blew out a deep breath and joined Trevor and the young lady he was still talking with. "Thanks for waiting," she said.

"No problem. I just love your style. I especially like how you mix realism with some looser elements."

"Thanks. It's always nice to talk with someone who appreciates the artistry that goes into a painting. Now, what was your question?"

"I didn't have one. I'm in my third year of art school and because you were busy, I started talking to your brother. I don't know what happened a few minutes ago, but he suddenly seemed concerned for you, so I played along."

"That was really sweet of you. Thanks."

"Oh, it was nothing."

"Actually, it was," Trevor said. "We owe you big time."

"I don't see how, but I'm glad I could help. Even though I'm not in a position to buy anything right now, I did want to meet you, and tell you how much I like your art."

"Here, look through my prints, if there's something you'd like, you can have it."

"I didn't say that to get free art."

"I know, but you really did just save me from an awkward situation. This is my way of thanking you."

Chapter 8

AN ALLY

When the booth was empty, Trevor said, "Wow, Maggie's story was intense."

"And extremely sad. But it still doesn't explain why the boys showed up in my painting. Like, why do I need this information?"

"Yeah, I don't get that part either, yet hearing her story helps me believe you."

Claire's face lit up. Without warning, she flung her arms around Trevor's neck and kissed his cheek.

"Whoa, Sis." He stepped back. "What's gotten into you?"

"Sorry; it's just such a relief to finally have an ally."

"Let's not get ahead of ourselves. I'm simply saying that I can't blame you for being frustrated."

"Frustrated about what?" Helen asked, coming into the booth with Paul.

"Oh, uh, nothing. We were just discussing how to handle challenging customers," Claire said.

"Was it the woman who asked about the painting yesterday? I see it's gone."

"She came back and did buy the painting, but she wasn't a problem."

"That's good. I was kind of worried for you, especially after you said, 'the boys magically appeared.'" Helen gestured quotes and laughed a little. "I would've loved to hear your explanation."

"Me too," Paul said. "Hey Trev, did Claire finally take credit for the painting?"

Claire started to roll her eyes but quickly caught herself, knowing that would add fuel to the fire. She answered before Trevor could, "Actually, she told us her story. Now we know why she had such a strong reaction to the painting."

"So there's more to it than you simply doing an amazing job?" Helen asked.

"Way more," Trevor said. "The how isn't relevant, though it did get brought up."

"And you didn't just tell her the truth?" Paul put his hands on his hips and glared. "I don't get you."

Claire slumped into the chair next to where she was standing and started to rub her temples. *I might as well get used to it; they won't be satisfied until I renounce my story.*

"Hey, Dad, Mom," Trevor stepped in front of them, "you guys are missing the point. Two of the boys in her painting died ten years ago. That's why the woman, who happens to be their aunt, was so surprised to see the painting for sale. Anyway, now the parents will have a beautiful portrait of their sons when they were all alive. Isn't that awesome?"

Confusion lined Helen's face. "Huh, that's interesting, for sure."

At that moment, Claire realized she needed to keep her focus on Maggie's story and the possible purpose, rather than defending her integrity, so she said softly, "More like heart-wrenching. The youngest boy died in his father's arms."

Paul shifted uneasily but didn't speak.

Helen, on the other hand, seemed surprisingly cold and calculated. "Well, I for one am relieved that the painting is gone, no matter how sad the story. I'd been uneasy about it since yesterday and now it won't ruin the rest of our week." She offered a thin smile and went to set out more candles. Paul pulled a box from under the table and helped her.

Claire dropped the necklace she had been fidgeting with and came to join Trevor. "Thanks for *all* your help."

"You got it, Sis, but now I'm out of here." He gave her a toothy grin. "I'm going to hang out with Lynn."

"Who's Lynn?" Paul asked.

"She's an art student that came into the booth earlier. Claire was busy with another customer, so we chatted while she waited."

"Glad I could help," Claire said with a wink. "Have fun."

Sophie never came to their booth. At first, Claire was disappointed, but the more she thought about the morning at the waterfall, the more she wasn't surprised. Phantom, angel, or girl, it really didn't matter; she had gotten the message before meeting Maggie and now she looked forward to seeing where this adventure would take her.

The rest of the week passed without conflict or much interest. Claire sold eight of the twelve original paintings along with most of the prints and card sets. She also secured three more commission jobs, which made for a successful week.

The Beartrap Summer Festival in Casper was approaching fast, and Claire needed to start another painting. After several minutes of looking through her box of photos, she decided to paint a Native American girl who was on her horse, leaning forward on the saddle horn. She played around with a few sketches and chose to focus only on a close-up of the girl in her colorful pow-wow outfit.

She laid in a bluish-green background, and then went downstairs to unpack from Frontier Days and put in a load of laundry. Twenty minutes later she returned to the loft and found her painting half done.

The background looked the same but everything else had changed. The girl had been painted in but was no longer Native American and she looked younger, maybe three or four. Instead of sitting on the horse, she stood on her tippy toes with her arms extended to hold the horse's chin in her tiny hands. Claire chuckled when she saw the girl had her cheek against his nose. Her curly, blond hair tumbled out from under a cowgirl hat and almost reached her waist. She wore a denim skirt with a rainbow tulle bottom and a white tank top along with cute little cowgirl boots. The horse and the wood fence were not finished.

Claire bent over her desk and placed a hand on each side of the paper. "Huh, it happened again." This time she wasn't afraid. Nor did she worry about the how. Instead, she hoped this would pave the way for another opportunity to meet someone with a tale to tell.

Since meeting Maggie and hearing her story, she no longer cared if others believed her. To eliminate undue stress, she wouldn't tell anyone, well, except for Trevor. He seemed to be on board.

Too excited to wait, she texted him: 'Can you come to the cabin?'

A few minutes passed before Trevor sent a reply. 'You mean like now?'

'Yeah.'

'K, be there in 10'

'Thanks'

While Claire waited, she looked around her desk and her eyes landed on the paint tray. There in the corner was a dab of purple that she hadn't put out. Two smaller brushes lay next to the water jar, clean, but still wet. She shuddered and scanned the room; the *how* suddenly becoming frightening again. It was the sound of Trevor's truck that extinguished the momentary flame of anxiety. In a flash, she slid down the stair railing—a trick her brothers had taught her when she was twelve—and ran outside.

"Hey, Sis, what's up?"

"Another painting changed."

"Thought maybe." On their way to the loft, he asked, "Did you see it change?"

"No, but thankfully the lights stayed on this time." Claire laughed a little. "I got the painting started and then went downstairs to throw in a load of laundry while I waited for the first wash of paint to dry."

When they reached the desk, he said, "Cute little thing. What'd you start with?"

"This." Claire picked up the picture and handed it to him. "At least I didn't spend a lot of time on the painting before it changed on me."

"You're telling me you just started this painting today?"

"Yeah, after I got home from work. I didn't even have the drawing started. Here, look." She opened a wide cabinet drawer and pulled out the sketch. "Once I get the outline drawn, I transfer it to my watercolor paper using graphite paper."

Trevor looked at his watch. "Which was like less than two hours ago?"

She nodded.

"Let me guess, you wanted me to come right now to prove you didn't have time to get this much done from the time you got home. Right?"

"Exactly."

"And you've never seen this girl before?"

"Nope."

"Okay, but can you please promise me you won't tell Mom or Dad?"

"I wasn't planning on it. And like it or not, you're my go-to guy, little brother." She smacked him on the back.

Trevor laughed. "You got it, Sis. Maggie's story, though devastating, was totally worth the intrigue, and I'm glad to see that you're not freaked out this time."

"It's still a little unnerving, but then it's not like I can stop it, and who knows, there might be a connection."

"That'd be cool. But hey, I need to get back before Dad wonders where I went."

"Yes, please hurry." She jokingly pushed him toward the stairs. "And I need to finish this painting."

"Ha, good luck with that."

After Trevor left, Claire remembered she had a photo of a horse in their outdoor corral leaning over the wood fence; she could use that as a reference. When she had the painting finished, she put it on the easel in the corner of the loft and stepped back to look.

Nice. Now, if all my paintings came half finished, imagine how many I could get done. She smirked at the thought. *Except it's not nearly as fun not getting to paint the details myself and knowing I can't take full credit. Oh well.*

She put the picture of the girl in the pow-wow dress, along with the original sketch, back on her art desk. *I'll try again tomorrow.*

It had become a common occurrence these days for Claire to lose track of the time or to forget to eat. She laughed when her stomach growled in protest. Some scrounging through the kitchen cupboards revealed a can of corn chowder. As soon as she had it piping hot, she brought it to the porch to watch the sunset over the snowcapped mountains. Though the ever-changing sky was captivating, it wasn't enough to keep her thoughts from the painting of the little girl and how she reminded Claire of herself when she was that age, minus the tulle skirt of course. She chuckled.

After finishing the soup, she took the quilt that was on the back of the cushioned wicker chair and wrapped it around her shoulders. It wasn't until she woke gasping for air and gripping the quilt close to her chest that she realized she had fallen asleep. The dream was all too vivid in her mind . . . she was being swept down a raging stream but woke just before crashing into some large rocks.

Huh, maybe I don't want to hear the story about the little girl. What if she died, too?

Claire left the quilt on the chair and went back inside. It was now close to eleven, so she got ready for bed, but the dream was still too raw to fall asleep. Finally, she gave up and went to the loft.

She sat on her stool for a long time and just stared at the painting that was still on the easel about ten feet from her desk.

"Who are you little girl, and why have you appeared?" When no logical answer came, she curled up on the futon. Before slipping into slumber, she whispered, "And please don't be dead."

A loud knocking on the kitchen door woke her. "What—"

She flipped on the lights and quickly stumbled down to the first floor. The banging continued. When she opened the door, a young man leaned against the casement struggling to keep himself from falling. His clothes were burned and torn, and he was bleeding in several places. His face was mangled beyond recognition and fear emanated from his one good eye.

"Please save me," he wheezed, "I don't want to die." Unable to steady himself any longer, he collapsed to the floor. Claire tried to break his fall but without much success.

In a panic, she ran to get her phone and called 9-1-1. "Help. Please send help."

"What's the emergency, ma'am?"

"There's a severely wounded man in my house. If you don't send someone now, he's going to bleed to death." Claire quickly gave her address, grabbed some towels, and hurried back to the kitchen to see what she could do to help.

He moaned as she carefully turned him over. Claire gasped. The young man was now old and his wounds were healed into hideous scars. His one eye looked to be made of glass and he reached for Claire's hand with his maimed one. "Thank you, ma'am. I knew you'd come."

Claire, too dazed to answer, sat on the floor next to him, her hand still in his. She closed her eyes and waited for the sound of the ambulance. When she opened them, sun filled the loft. Bolting off the futon, she looked at her hands and shirt; there was no blood. "Man, what's with all these crazy dreams?"

Chapter 9

THE WOODEN BOX

"Hey, Sis, I was just going to call." Trev waved his phone toward Claire as she got out of her SUV. "You're like an hour late."

"Yeah, well I had a rough night." She joined him and they walked back into the barn together.

"What happened? You look like you've seen a ghost."

"If you count nightmares, I have. I guess these paintings and Maggie's story are affecting me more than I care to admit. I had two terrifying dreams in one night . . . who does that?"

Trevor cringed. "Did either of them include the little girl?"

"No, thank God. In the one, I felt like Zac being swept down the river. The other dream didn't make any sense at all, and I don't care to elaborate on it right now."

"You don't have time to anyway; Dad is in the arena with customers. He needs you to head there right now."

Later that day, Claire retraced her drawing of the Native American girl onto a new piece of watercolor paper and started to wash in a different color for the background.

Engrossed in the colorful detail of the girl's pow-wow outfit, Trevor's text startled her. *Geez, jumpy much?*

'Say hi to Maggie for me. Take pictures.'

Claire threw her paintbrushes into a jar of water before replying, `I will. And thanks for texting. I didn't realize it was so late.'

`Glad I could help. ☺'

She rushed to get changed and ran out the door. About halfway down her driveway, she called Maggie. "Hey, it's Claire. I'm running a little late. The GPS is bringing me through the mountain pass. I should be there by 6:45."

"Okay, but don't hurry on our account. That road is windy and steep in places. We'd rather have you get here safely."

"Ha, me too. See you soon."

Maggie and Brad were sitting on a bench to the left of the barn door reading books when she arrived.

"Hello, Claire," Maggie called with a wave for her to park closer. "You made it."

"Yes, and without incident." She grinned as she hopped out of her SUV.

Maggie gave Claire a hug before introducing her to Brad.

He was a bigger man, clean shaven with graying hair, and wire-rimmed glasses. He looked more suited to sit behind a desk than on a horse, though as he shook Claire's hand, she could tell they were calloused and strong.

"Nice to meet you, Brad."

"Likewise," he said. "Come, I'll show you around."

The outside of the barn looked nothing like Claire's painting, nor did she expect it to. She got out her phone and took a few pictures before they went inside. Brad slid the wide door along its track until it was completely opened, allowing light to flood the entrance. Maggie flipped on the lights as well and took the lead inside.

"This barn has a nice feel to it," Claire said as she entered.

"We whitewashed the interior a few years ago." Brad patted a stall door. "It not only makes it brighter in here, it helps to fight the gloom."

Claire nodded thoughtfully as they continued down the center aisle. She walked slowly, not knowing what to look for or what she hoped to find. Was the purpose of the painting solely to bless this hurting family or was there more to it?

Brad interrupted her musing. "Roger sold both the boys' horses shortly after the accident. Their stalls remain empty."

"Oh yeah? Which ones were theirs?"

Maggie walked ahead and stopped in front of Johnny's. The door was covered with pictures and laminated drawings. "He was quite the little artist."

Claire came closer and leaned in to get a better look before saying, "Impressive."

"He did a new drawing every year for his booth at the county fair. After his passing, his parents had them laminated and hung permanently on this door. As you can see by the progression, he started showing his horse when he was six."

"It's a sweet memorial."

"Yes, and a sad reminder that he's gone . . . every time we come into the barn." Maggie pointed to Johnny's seventh-grade school picture.

Claire gawked with wide-eyed wonder. The resemblance to her painting was so spot-on that Maggie had every reason to doubt that she could've done the painting without reference photos.

Brad came and put his arm around his wife. "It's not doing their parents any good either."

"More like keeping them stuck in the past." A deep voice came from behind them.

Claire turned to see a tall, young man who looked to be in his mid-twenties. He hadn't shaved for a few days, and the sleeves of his dark blue tee-shirt were ripped off exposing his muscular arms. Though he was good looking, Claire was taken aback by his dark, foreboding eyes and stern expression.

"Hi, Chase," Maggie said. "What brings you to the barns at this hour?"

"We have a sick calf." Though his answer was matter-of-fact, his eyes never left Claire. "Who's your guest?"

"I'm Claire." She smiled and reached to shake his hand.

He wiped his hand on his shirt, before taking hers. "Nice to meet you."

"She's the artist I was telling you about," Maggie said.

"Ah, the one who miraculously painted us boys without a picture."

Claire jerked her hand back as if it had been stung. She stared at him, but by his expression, she couldn't tell if he was jesting or upset. Not sure how to reply, she said, "Something like that." Desperate to change the subject, she turned to Maggie. "Where's Zac's stall?"

"Over there." She pointed a few doors down on the other side of the aisle.

When Claire looked in that direction, she realized she didn't need to ask. The door in question had several ribbons and awards mounted on it. She quickly left the group to go check it out.

Among all the awards was a laminated picture of Zac with his prize-winning Thoroughbred.

I still can't get over how exact the resemblances in the painting were, but then again, if something is going to be 'miraculous,' it might as well be perfect, too. The thought warmed Claire's heart, yet her focus remained on finding out why it happened in the first place.

When she turned back to ask Maggie if she could look inside, they were all heading toward the far end of the barn. Without waiting, she flipped the latch, slid the door open, and stepped inside. The stall was smaller than the ones at her dad's horse barn and instead of a door to the outside on the back wall, there were windows.

Someone had swept the stall clean, which gave it a sterile, lifeless feeling. In the middle of the room, propped on its side in a custom-built frame, was a large, wooden barrel. Zac's name was branded into the end of the barrel and his saddle was draped over the top. Claire shuddered at the finality of it all. She ran her fingers a few times across the seat of the saddle before looking around at

74

the otherwise empty space. It was then that she spotted a wooden box tucked in between the corner rafter and the ceiling. Abandoned spider webs helped to conceal its existence.

The box was too high for Claire to reach without something to step on so she went to ask for help. Maggie and Chase came before she reached the door. Maggie entered and stood across the saddle from her.

Chase stayed in the doorway and leaned against the frame with his arms crossed. "Can you tell me why you're here?"

"Chase, stop," Maggie snapped. "Where are your manners?"

"Just because she did the painting you bought, I don't see why that gives her permission to snoop around our barn."

"She's not snooping. I'm commissioning her to do a painting of Uncle Brad and me with our horses. I don't see the harm in having a look around first."

"Fine." Chase came forward and rested his hands on the saddle horn. "Have you found anything interesting?"

"Actually, I did."

He raised an eyebrow. "Oh yeah, and what would that be?"

"A wooden box." She pointed toward the back corner. "There, on that rafter. Do you see it?"

Both Chase and Maggie looked.

"Well, I'll be—"

"Eating humble pie," Claire said, with a little too much enthusiasm. She quickly added a smile.

He turned back with an imperious glare.

"Hey, I was kidding. I thought you were kidding earlier about my painting, but apparently not."

Without saying a word, he abruptly left the stall.

Claire cringed. "Sorry, Maggie; I meant no offense."

"I know, but can you blame him? First the painting, then you come along and find a box that none of us knew was there."

"But I thought you said you wouldn't show the painting to anyone until *after* my visit." Claire started to cross her arms but then thought better of it. To cover, she tucked some loose strands of hair behind her ears and then brought her hands back to the saddle.

"I said I wouldn't show his parents. I thought I knew Chase better than I apparently do . . . I didn't expect this kind of reaction from him. And anyway, Brad hadn't mentioned the sick calf. I didn't know Chase would be here tonight."

"I should go. It wasn't my intention to cause a problem. Thanks for letting me come."

Claire started for the door, but before she reached it, Chase came back with a stepladder. "Hey, where are you going? Don't you want to see what's in the box?"

She gave him a puzzled look. "I thought you just stormed out because you were angry with me." She started to pass him, but he blocked her way.

"Wait. That box has been there for the last ten years. If you didn't point it out, it would probably be there for another ten. It's not like anyone comes in here except my parents and that's only once a year."

"That's true," Maggie said. "I don't see how this stall got cleaned out and painted without anyone noticing it. Please stay, Claire. Aren't you curious to find out what's inside the box?"

"Of course I am, but it's really none of my business."

Chase didn't wait to see if she stayed; instead, he went to retrieve the wooden box from the rafters. Once he reached the floor, he brushed off the spider webs and blew some dust from the lid before setting it on the seat of the saddle.

Chapter 10

CARVED HORSES

Chase tugged on the lock. "Now what? I don't want to bust the box to get it open."

"Wouldn't there be some bolt cutters in the workshop?" Maggie asked.

"Yes." Chase nodded and hurried out.

"Wait," Claire called after him. "If Zac took the time to hide his box, the key could be hidden in here somewhere. Try feeling along the rafters."

"Well, aren't you clever," Maggie said with a wink.

"Not really. I have three brothers and that'd be something they would do."

Chase climbed back up the ladder and started feeling along the rafters. Maggie felt along the window sill and looked along the walls.

While they were occupied with their search, Claire thought to shut the stall door. It only took her a moment to scan the perimeter and find the key in the bottom right corner. With unfettered enthusiasm, she stood and said, "Ta-dah."

"No way! How did you know to check the door?" Chase asked.

"Think about it, how often would you be inside a stall with the door completely shut?"

He jumped off the ladder and shrugged. "Probably never."

"That's why it's a perfect place to hide a key."

"Please wait. I'm going to go get Brad." Maggie hurried out.

"Here," Chase held out his hand for the key, "let me see if it works."

Claire came closer and gave it to him. Her curiosity was peaked as she watched him wiggle and twist the key. Finally, the lock released, but Chase didn't open the lid.

While they waited for Maggie to return with Brad, Claire grabbed the bandanna she had hanging out of her back pocket and started to wipe the years of dust from the box. At first, Chase watched her hands, but it wasn't long before his gaze moved to her face.

When their eyes met, she flushed and quickly turned to shake out the bandanna. "I hope you don't mind that I touched the box."

Chase still held his gaze. "Not at all, it needed a good dusting."

The softness of his tone set her mind at ease.

"You know, at first I was annoyed that you thought it was okay to do a painting of us boys and put it out for public sale. And then for reasons I can't figure out, you assumed it'd be okay to come to our home . . . but now I'm glad you did. No matter what's in the box, we'll have another memory of Zac. So," he hesitated, "thank you."

Claire started to answer, but Maggie came rushing in with Brad right behind her. "Look, hon." She pointed excitedly. "The wooden box we gave Zac for his fourteenth birthday. Oh, I can't wait to see what's inside."

Claire stepped aside, knowing the family needed some time to share the contents with each other.

Chase lifted the lid. Inside were two carved horses, a jackknife, two carving gougers, and some sandpaper.

Maggie picked up the top horse. A tear ran down her cheek as she admired the craftsmanship. "These must have been something he was still working on or saving for a special occasion. The only other one I've ever seen is on a shelf in Michelle's sewing room with a Mother's Day card Zac gave her when he was sixteen."

Brad had picked up the other horse. "The intricate details are impressive."

"Yeah, Zac was a perfectionist," Chase said. "I'm not surprised he kept them locked and hidden away. He wouldn't want anyone to see them until they were finished."

Curiosity scurried through Claire's mind as she watched Chase vacillate between excitement and something she sensed but couldn't place. Even in this, she had no idea what she was supposed to be *pursuing*.

"Come look." Maggie waved Claire forward. "If it weren't for you, we would've never found these."

Claire's thoughts lingered as she took the horse that Maggie held out to her.

"Isn't it beautiful?"

"Impressive, for sure." After further inspection, she added, "This one must be finished. Look, Zac carved his name into the bottom."

Maggie looked and then asked Brad if the one he had was signed.

He flipped it over and said, "No, but then this one still needs work."

Chase had picked up the pocket knife and was opening and shutting the blades. He seemed oblivious to the conversation.

"Chase?" Claire ventured.

"Hmm?" He didn't look up.

"It looks like there's still something else in the box."

Every eye darted that way. Chase closed the knife and moved a piece of used sandpaper before pulling out an envelope with Zac's name on it. "It's a card from Mom and Dad."

"Read it to us," Brad said.

"No thanks, I don't care to know what it says." He dropped it back into the box, along with the knife, and walked out of the stall.

Claire shot a look at Brad. "Aren't you going to stop him?"

"It wouldn't do any good."

She ran into the aisle and called after him. "Hey, Chase. Wait!" He didn't even hesitate at her plea. Claire didn't know what to make of his abrupt departure but was struck by how the light filtered through the open barn doors and hit him as he approached them. She quickly grabbed her phone and snapped a few pictures before he was out of sight.

Without taking the time to see if they turned out, she slipped the phone back into her pocket and rejoined Maggie and Brad. "Wow, he's really upset."

Brad nodded. "Yes, but it's *not* something we can fix. Maggie, how about you read the card to us."

She set down the horse and carefully pulled the card from the yellowed envelope and ran her fingers over the cover where there was a painted picture of a bucking bronco. She held it up for them to see. It read, 'You're the BEST!'

On the inside were the words, 'Congrats to Our #1 Rider.' "Dear Zac, we know you are destined to do great things. Keep up the good work, and we will do whatever we can to help make your dreams come true. We love you so much and couldn't be prouder of you! All our love, Mom & Dad"

"And that's exactly why Chase didn't want to know what it said." Brad crossed his arms. "Even when his brothers were alive, he had a chip on his shoulder."

Maggie looked from Brad to Claire. "Some call it middle child syndrome."

"I call it poor parenting," Brad argued. "They always had more regard for Zac and Johnny. We didn't live here, but it was obvious whenever we came to visit."

"Huh, I'm sorry to hear that." Claire suddenly felt like a fish out of water and changed the subject. "Thanks for letting me come to see where the boys lived."

"And thanks for finding this box. What a wonderful discovery."

"What are you going to do with it?"

"We'll probably—"

"Keep it." Brad cut Maggie off. "Giving it to Roger and Michelle right now would make things worse for Chase. It might even send Roger back into a depression. It's not worth the risk."

Maggie hugged the horse to her chest. "You're right and it's not like we're keeping it from them. They don't even know it exists."

Brad came and put his arm around Maggie's shoulders and pulled her close.

Claire was beginning to realize there was more to this story than the deceased sons, brothers, and nephews, but she knew now wasn't the time to press for more information. In silent admiration, she watched Maggie close her eyes and lean into Brad's embrace.

He kissed her forehead and then helped her put everything back into the box, locked it and brought it with him.

Once they were all back in the center aisle, Claire slid the door shut and hooked the latch. "I should get going."

"Wait. You still need to take a picture of us with our horses, unless you can do it without one." Maggie winked.

"No, I need pictures. I'll go get my camera while you guys get your horses." Claire raced out before anything more serious could be said about how she did the painting of the boys.

When Claire came back, Maggie was brushing down a beautiful gray Appaloosa mare, so she took a few candids. Further down the aisle, Brad was coming toward her with an auburn-colored quarter horse. A distinguished white diamond stretched between his eyes and almost reached the tip of his nose. Claire got a few shots of them as well.

"It's not dark out yet; I say we start outside. I like the feel of natural lighting better, but if you're not happy with the background, we can take a few more from in here."

"Sounds good to us," Maggie said. "I'm thinking the background won't really matter because I would like the focus to be on us."

"That's easy enough. I can wash in a background color and not add any barn details if that's what you want."

"I like that idea because then it will have a different look and feel to it compared to the painting of the boys."

"You got it. Shall we go outside?" Claire led the way and found a place where there was good lighting. After taking pictures from several different angles, she scrolled through them to make sure she got what she needed. "These look pretty great." She held out the camera. "Here, take a look and see which one you want me to use."

"Surprise us," Brad said. "You're the artist, and we've already seen what you can do."

Maggie looped her arm around Brad's waist. "Yes, you choose. It'll be fun for us to have to wait."

"Great. That way I can select the best elements from a few different pictures, if need be, to make one perfect painting." Claire smiled at the thought.

Maggie must have caught the look. "What is it?"

"I guess I have Zac's propensity for perfection. I hope that didn't sound too proud."

"Not at all, and we love your style. That's why I want you to be the one to do the painting."

"Aww, thanks. Once you know where you're going to hang it, text me with the outside dimensions. Be sure to include a four-inch mat and the width of the frame. I'll wait to start your portrait until I know the size.

"We'll do that as soon as you leave."

"It was nice to meet you, Brad." Claire reached to shake his hand. "Oh, and please tell Chase that it was nice to meet him too. I hope he's okay."

"He's had a rough go of it, but he'll be fine," Brad said. "Good night, Claire."

"Good night."

Before she reached her SUV, Chase came from a smaller barn carrying a large bottle of powdered milk for the calf. "Hey Claire, hold up." He hurried toward her. "Do you need to get going?"

"I guess not, why?"

"I wanted to apologize for storming out of here earlier. It's not like any of this is your fault."

Hmm, that's interesting. Why does he care what I think? To make light of the situation, she put a hand to her chest and quipped, "You stormed out? I hadn't noticed."

"Ah, good one." The darkness that had filled his eyes when they first met, melted into soft hues of blue, matching the color of the distant mountains.

This made Claire smile. "If you'd like, I can help with the calf."

"That'd be great."

Chapter 11

CHASE

It took Claire a few weeks to complete Maggie's portrait because she was still working on other paintings for her upcoming show. When it was finished, she gave her a call. "Hey there, I have your painting done."

"Yay, I can't wait to see it! My schedule is clear tomorrow, so I'll take a ride out to your place in the morning."

"Actually, if you don't mind, I'd like to come your way. I already asked my dad for the day off because if I'm not working, I'm painting. I could use a break and a change of scenery."

"Well then, by all means. I'll make some of my famous, lemon poppy-seed scones and you can have breakfast with me."

"Sounds yummy. What time?"

"Does 8:00 work for you?"

"Yes, see you then."

The next morning, after some deliberation, Claire decided to bring the second painting that had changed. Maybe Maggie would recognize the little girl.

An hour and a half later, she parked in front of the large, blue farmhouse with a porch that ran its length. Pine trees provided extra shade and immaculate flower gardens stretched well into the lawn.

Maggie had just come out with a tray that held their breakfast. She set it on the coffee table and then waved for Claire to join her.

As Claire approached the porch, she said, "What a great place to relax, and your flowers are beautiful."

"Thanks. I'm much better with plants than I am with animals, though I have learned to ride. Come." She gestured to the Adirondack chair on her right. "Please have a seat."

They talked for a good while after they finished their scones and fresh fruit.

"Another cup of coffee?" Maggie asked.

"No, I'm good. Don't you want to see your painting?"

"Oh yes, of course. I was so enjoying our conversation that I forgot all about it."

Claire stood, but before leaving the porch, she said, "I've been afraid to ask, but I have to know. How did Roger and Michelle like the painting of the boys?"

"I say you show me our painting first." Maggie forced a smile. "I'll tell you later."

Claire didn't shroud her disappointment. "That bad, huh?"

"I admit they didn't respond the way we expected them to. I'll clear the dishes, while you get the painting."

"Okay." Claire bounced down the steps like this news didn't bother her, but it did. She couldn't understand why the parents wouldn't be thrilled to have a portrait that perfectly represented their boys' personalities and her time to get answers was running out. *How am I supposed to 'pursue' when I have no idea what I'm pursuing?*

With a quick shake of the head, she turned her focus back to the painting in hand. It brought her great comfort to know that she could take full credit for it and she looked forward to seeing Maggie's reaction.

As she returned to the porch, Maggie asked, "What's in the portfolio?"

"First things first," Claire said as she emptied her hands and started to remove the blanket that covered the painting. Then, with a sly grin, she abruptly stopped and looked up. "Are you sure we shouldn't wait for Brad?"

"No way. He won't be home for hours. Now stop teasing."

"Okay, okay." Claire slipped off the blanket and stepped away.

Maggie clasped her hands together and brought them to her chest. "Oh, Claire, it's simply beautiful. Can you bring it inside for me?"

Claire picked up the painting and followed Maggie into the living room. The mantel above the fireplace was empty.

"Here, set it by the couch. I'll have Brad hang it when he gets home."

"If you have a stool, I can do it for you."

"Even better. Wait here and I'll go get it."

Before Maggie returned, Chase walked in. "Hey, Claire, what brings you back here again?"

"I brought Maggie's portrait." She pointed toward the couch.

His eyes went from hers to the painting. "Wow. That's totally awesome."

"Now, Chase, you don't have to exaggerate. It's not like God did the painting," Claire said in jest, though in light of her recent dilemma, these words gnawed at the back of her mind.

Chase didn't seem to notice. "Touché, but still, I'm impressed."

"Thanks."

Maggie looked worried to see Chase when she returned with the stool. "What's wrong? Is Uncle Brad okay?"

"He's fine. We were heading to check on the herd when I saw Claire's SUV. Uncle Brad said that he and Justin didn't need my help if I wanted to come to say hello."

Maggie blew out a relieved breath. "Well, that's good." Then she turned to Claire with a mischievous grin plastered across her face. "And as you can see, this one's a smart one."

Chase rolled his eyes, though a smile tugged at the corner of his lips. He took the stool and proceeded to mount the painting.

It warmed Claire's heart when she realized he had come to see her. She had thought of him often since their chat in the barn and wondered if he had thought of her as well.

Once the painting was hung, Chase stepped away and said, "It's perfect."

"It's amazing how much of a difference the mat and frame make," Claire said, deflecting from the compliment.

"And what's even more amazing is how beautiful it looks hanging in its rightful place." Maggie gave Claire a hug and added cheerfully, "I love it, and Brad will too."

"I'm so glad." Claire got out her phone and took a picture before leaving the room. "Oh, I wanted to show you something."

Both Maggie and Chase followed Claire to the porch. She opened her portfolio with nervous anticipation and lifted the painting so they could see it.

"Another superb painting, Claire," Maggie said.

"Thanks, but I need to know." She steadied her voice. "Do either of you recognize this girl?"

Chase shook his head. "I don't."

"Neither do I," Maggie said as she took the painting from Claire. "Why do you ask?"

"Because you recognized the boys, I, uh, thought there might be a connection."

"But why would there be a connection?"

"Yeah, who is she?" Chase asked.

"I don't know."

"What, is this another one of your creepy miracle paintings?"

Claire's heart started to plummet off the cliff of despair. She hadn't anticipated them picking up on the correlation between the two paintings and she needed to rectify that quickly. The first thing that came to mind was Chase's parents. "Maggie, you were going to tell me how Roger and Michelle responded to their painting."

"Not favorably." Maggie flopped with a thud into one of the Adirondack chairs.

Claire couldn't help but notice the weariness knit into the lines of her countenance. Though this gave her pause, it didn't dissuade her. "Do I dare ask why?"

Chase answered, "Because they're selfish, that's why!"

Maggie gave him a sharp look. "That might be part of it, but that's no excuse for disrespect. They're still your parents."

"But—"

She held up a hand.

Flustered, he leaned against the porch railing and crossed his arms. "Fine."

Maggie gave him an empathetic nod before continuing, "Now, Claire, the truth of the matter is, they were offended that an artist had a painting of their boys for sale at a public event. To put it in their own words, they thought it was *heartless*."

"But I didn't even know they were real people or that anyone would recognize them."

"Yes, that's what you've said and even if it's true, that doesn't change the fact that it made them angry. They were confused about how you had a picture of their sons."

Claire buried her face in her hands and wished she could disappear. There was no viable explanation, yet she felt bad for leaving them hanging. Then again, what other choice did she have?

Chase came closer and touched her shoulder. "Hey, are you okay?"

"Uh, yeah, I guess so." Claire straightened and pushed her long, wavy hair off her face. "I don't have an answer for you because I don't know how it happened." She didn't try to explain. "The last thing I wanted to do was to hurt or offend anyone."

"Their pain is no more your fault than their reaction to the painting," Maggie said. "You're an amazing artist. Someday they'll be happy to have it, but for now, Brad brought it here. We hung it in the dining room."

"Won't that be a problem when they come for dinner?"

"Nope. They won't come for dinner," Chase said coldly. This time Maggie didn't stop him. "It's too bad too because my aunt is an excellent cook."

Claire smiled and gave her a thumbs-up. "I can vouch for the scones."

"Thanks, Claire." Maggie returned the smile, but then furrowed her brow. "We don't want you to take any of this personally. It's been hard on all of us."

"That's an understatement," Chase muttered under his breath. Then turning to Claire, he asked, "Do you ride?"

"What kind of question is that?" They locked eyes. "Are you asking if I know how . . . or if I'm *good* at it?"

"Wow! Defensive much? How am I supposed to know if you can ride?"

Claire smirked. "Defensive much?" She stood to join him.

Chase reddened but then quickly asked, "Well, can you or not?"

"She can certainly hold her own *off* a horse," Maggie teased. A glint of joy filled her eyes as the weight of their previous discussion abruptly lifted.

"Ahem." Claire cleared her voice to get their attention. "Let's just say my day job is training the horses on my father's ranch. Do I need to prove it?"

"I'd say that's a yes." Maggie laughed and patted Chase on the arm. "She can use my horse. I'll see you two later." Still chuckling, she went inside.

Claire grabbed her portfolio and left the porch.

"Hey, I meant no offense. I just wanted to show you something and you can only get there on horseback. Are you interested?"

"Sure, I need to put this in my car and get my clothes."

Chase walked with her. Once the painting was tucked safely behind the back seat, she slipped on her cowgirl hat and then grabbed her boots and a duffel bag.

"Oh wow, you came prepared."

"Not exactly. I never leave home without my riding gear."

"Ah, nice." When they got back to the house, Chase retrieved his brawny, black gelding and said, "I'll go saddle Maggie's horse for you while you get changed. Meet me at the barn, okay?"

"You got it."

Chase had the horses ready and was leading them outside when Claire reached the barn.

"That was kind of Maggie to let me use her horse."

"Yeah, she's a sweetheart. Are you ready?"

"Almost." Claire took the reins, but before mounting, she rested her forehead between the horse's eyes and then proceeded to rub her neck. "Hey there girl, are you ready for a new rider?"

"She should be. Aunt Maggie doesn't ride her nearly enough."

"What's her name?"

"Chicory."

"Ha, I'm not surprised. Maggie did say she was better with plants than animals. What's your horse's name?"

"Mingo," Chase said as he mounted.

"I like it." She smiled and swung herself onto the saddle. "I'm ready."

"Good, let's go." He nudged his horse to a trot. Claire and Chicory fell into stride beside them.

They traversed the rolling hills for about fifteen minutes before the landscape got considerably steeper. Eventually, they came to a barbed-wire fence and a bank of trees. Chase dismounted so he could open the gate that wasn't more than four feet wide. The path beyond was narrow and not worn with use.

Claire moved Chicory back a step. "Am I sure I can trust you?"

He looked toward the woods and then back at her. "Ma'am, let me assure you that I am the epitome of chivalry." Then he swept his cowboy hat off his head and proceeded to bow.

Claire covered her mouth to stifle a laugh.

Chase must have heard her because when he straightened, he wore a huge grin. He grabbed Mingo's reins, walked him through the opening, and waited for Claire to follow.

Once they were on the other side, he shut the gate. On his way back to Mingo, he took ahold of Chicory's bridle. "Whoa, girl." Concern etched his brow as he looked up at Claire. "You weren't serious about not trusting me, were you?"

"Hmm, let's see. You are charming and that's pretty scary." Claire's smile seemed to set his mind at ease.

"Well then, if that's all you have to fear, follow me." He let go of the bridle, mounted his own horse, and led the way into the unknown.

The trail constricted and Claire struggled to keep her horse steady.

After a bit, Chase stopped Mingo and shifted on his saddle to look back at Claire. "You can slack the reins and let Chicory find the best path. She's been here before."

"Oh, good." She loosened the reins and tightened her grip on the saddle horn. This part of the trail was not only steeper, but it was also rockier than she was used to.

They weaved their way back and forth until they came to a small opening where they could see off in the distance. Chase waited for Claire to come up beside him and then asked, "Is this worth the risk of following me?"

"Wow, that's quite the view; though I admit the climb was a little more than I bargained for." Claire patted Chicory's neck in appreciation. "But as far as *risks* go, I'll have to wait until I'm safely off this mountain before I can answer that." She gave him a playful nudge.

"Oh, so you *don't* trust me." He feigned being hurt and then laughed. "Come on, I want to show you something."

"I thought this was it."

He shook his head. "Wyoming is filled with beautiful scenery. In comparison, this isn't even that spectacular."

"I don't see how going higher will change the view that much."

"The view isn't what I want to show you."

Chapter 12

SECLUDED

Chase suddenly got quiet and an unexpected shadow extinguished the light that had filled his eyes moments earlier. "It's not much further." With a flick of his reins, he continued upward.

This abrupt change worried Claire a little, but her curiosity was peaked, and she had come too far to turn back now.

Possible destinations flitted through her mind as they rode in silence. Within three minutes she had her answer. They had come to an opening where there were no trees and large slabs of rock covered the ground. Not more than forty feet ahead of them was a small building with a black, tin roof and weathered, gray barn boards. Written across the back, in faded red paint, were these words: 'When the raging ceased, so did they . . . and yet I live.' Below this quote was the word, 'Why?' The paint was darker and looked less weathered as if it had been added more recently.

Huh, that's interesting. "I was going to ask if this was your childhood fort, but those words say otherwise."

He nodded. "I built this six years ago. Come see the other side." They tied their horses to a tree by the trail and walked to the front of the well-kept shed. Chase unlocked the doors and swung them open.

Claire's eyes widened and her mouth dropped simultaneously. A cross hung on the narrow wall to her left. A laminated picture of Chase with his brothers and their dad hung to her right; the boys looked close to the same age as they were in her painting. Mounted on the back wall were three kayaks.

"A memorial." She removed her hat and held it across her heart before turning to face Chase. "Why did you build this so far from home? Your parents must never come here."

"I didn't build it for my parents. They don't even know about it."

"But why not?"

"Like I said this morning, they're selfish. Aunt Maggie agrees with me, but she's right, I need to show them respect."

Instead of replying, Claire gave him a long look, trying to figure him out. It appeared that he was doing the same. Finally, she turned away and walked closer to the memorial. Chase joined her. "I'm confused. Why are there three kayaks?"

"They are my brothers' and . . ." He dropped his gaze before sheepishly adding, "and my dad's."

Claire pointed at the photo. "But isn't your dad still alive?"

"Yeah, he's around." Chase paused to look at the picture for a moment before turning to face Claire. "I'm not sure if Aunt Maggie told you why they came to help on the ranch."

"She did."

"Care to hear my side of the story?"

"Of course."

His response was more of a wince than a smile, but then he put his hand on her shoulder. "Wait here." He ran back to his horse and returned with a blanket. Claire helped him spread it out about ten feet from the front of the shed. Before they sat, he said, "Come look."

She followed him under the tin roof and saw that an object was placed in each of the kayaks.

He retrieved the plastic bags that protected the items from the elements and brought them with him back to the blanket. "These are my fondest memories of the dead. And of the living. I'm hoping these visuals will help put a face on what we've lost."

Claire sat cross-legged and rested her elbows on her knees. With great interest, she watched him open the first bag.

"I'll start with Johnny." Chase's tone was peppered with pain. "He had just turned thirteen. The kayaking trip is what he wanted for his birthday."

"Not a fun memory."

"No, but when someone dies young, I don't think it matters what day it is. It sucks."

A grimace followed the twinge of pain that shot through Claire's chest. She offered no words, only a sympathetic nod.

"Johnny didn't have a lot of life accomplishments, but drawing was his favorite thing to do." Chase pulled out a laminated colored pencil drawing of his horse.

"That's really good. I'm surprised your parents let you have it."

"They didn't. Aunt Maggie gave this to me. Johnny spent a few weeks every summer with my aunt and uncle and a week at winter break. While he was there, she gave him lessons. She's quite the artist in her own right."

"Oh, really? She didn't mention it."

"I'm not surprised; she's not the type to promote herself."

Claire took the drawing, suddenly curious to see if there might be another message. Since the encounter with Sophie, she knew that wouldn't be a stretch. Upon further examination, there was nothing of importance, so she handed the drawing back.

He set it on his lap and continued, "She let him bring the drawings home, but he always gave her one to keep for herself."

"Sounds like Johnny and Maggie had a lot in common."

"They were close. Aunt Maggie took his passing pretty hard, but unlike my parents, she chose to keep living."

Claire couldn't help but notice the disdain in his voice. To keep the conversation moving forward, she asked, "You said Chicory had been here before. Does that mean Maggie's been here, too?"

"Yeah, she and Uncle Brad helped me bring the supplies and kayaks up here, which, as you saw by the trail, was no easy task.

When we finally got the memorial finished, she was the one who gave me the idea of putting a keepsake in each kayak and gave me this for Johnny's." He traced his fingers over the drawing, seemingly oblivious to the fact that Claire was still there.

Time passed slowly, but Claire didn't mind. She had her own thoughts to contend with. Did Chase's story have anything to do with what she should pursue, or was she making something of nothing? Several minutes elapsed before she said, "If you don't mind me asking, what's in Zac's bag?"

"Oh, uh, right." Chase shook his head and set the drawing on the blanket. He opened the bag and pulled out a rope and a worn pair of riding gloves. "Zac was seventeen and had already competed in several high school and junior rodeo competitions throughout the northwest. I'm guessing you already knew that by all the ribbons mounted to his stall door. His trophies still sit on the mantle above the fireplace at my parents' house. Anyway, his goal was to make the rodeo circuit as soon as he turned eighteen."

"He must have been really good."

"The best in his age group."

"Can I hold the gloves?"

"Sure."

"I've learned a pair of gloves can tell you a lot about a person." Claire laid them on her knees, palms up. "I have two older brothers, but neither of them cared much for ranch life. After college, they both married and moved to different cities. My mom kept their gloves because they like to ride when they visit, which isn't often. One look at their *not-so-worn* gloves tells you all you need to know."

"That's a bit condescending, don't you think?"

"More like disappointing. But then I almost took a job in Denver, so it's not fair of me to judge."

"I wouldn't peg you for a city girl."

"Actually, that was a big factor in my decision to stay. Now, I work part-time for my dad training the horses, and I spend the rest of the day painting."

"Sounds like a sweet deal."

"It is, but I'm so sorry. We didn't come all this way to talk about me."

"No worries. I like it when you talk."

To hide her smile, she picked up the gloves and said, "Ahem . . . what was it that you were saying about Zac?"

"Zac loved ranch life. He spent all his free time either with the horses, practicing his rope skills, or working out. Not only was he able to easily lasso the calf, but he also beat most of his opponents simply because he was so quick and strong." Chase looked back at the memorial for a moment before turning to Claire. "That shows you how powerful the current was the day he got swept away. I still can't believe he couldn't pull himself to land."

"Unbelievable, for sure." She touched Chase's knee, causing him to look up. "I think his gloves and the rope are a perfect keepsake."

A small smile crept into the corner of his lips. "Thanks. I came up with that idea on my own."

"Were the two of you close?"

"Not really. I think in a way, that makes his death even harder. Sometimes I wish it had been me."

Claire dropped her gaze back to the gloves. She couldn't relate and nothing she could say would make the situation any better.

With a heavy sigh, Chase picked up his dad's bag and slowly opened it. He pulled out a Bible and ran his fingers over the cover; then he raised it to his nose and took in a deep breath of the old leather. A moan escaped as his eyes turned to a sea of glass. "Huh, I know grown men aren't supposed to cry. I should have never brought you here." He put the Bible back into the bag and started to stand.

Claire scrambled to her knees in an attempt to stop him. "Wait, can I hold it?"

Chase turned to face her. With eyes still moist, he fell back onto his heels and handed her the bag.

She took the Bible out and smelled the leather exactly as Chase had done. Then she sat and opened it; verses were underlined, and several of the pages were tattered. "Talk about how things are worn. Your dad clearly spent a lot of time reading this."

"Yeah, well, that's ancient history." His expression soured. He grabbed the gloves and rope and shoved them into the bag. As soon as he had it zipped shut, he snatched up Johnny's drawing and brought them back to the kayaks.

This time, Claire didn't try to stop him. Instead, she continued to flip through the worn pages, occasionally reading an underlined passage. Then she came upon an old family photo. Johnny was a toddler, sitting on his mom's lap. Zac leaned against his dad with his hand on his knee. Chase stood sandwiched in the middle. Everyone looked happy and full of life.

Yet now, all these years later, the picture was tearstained and torn in half. Claire wondered how much time had lapsed between the accident and Roger's not reading his Bible.

Chase returned with the horses and said, "We should probably get going."

"Not until you tell me what happened. You've obviously been deeply hurt by more than the loss of your brothers."

His gaze went not to her face, but to her hands. "What's that?"

"An old family photo; it was stuffed in between the pages." She held it out for him to see.

He dropped the reins and took the picture. "It figures."

"What figures?"

"Look where it's torn." He tossed the picture back. This time their eyes met.

"You don't really think that was intentional, do you?" Claire took the pieces and held them together. "See, look, you just happened to be standing in the middle."

"That's easy for you to say."

"Chase, please, come sit." Claire patted the blanket, not allowing the sharpness of his tone to dissuade her. "You obviously thought I was someone you could confide in, or you wouldn't have brought me here. It seems like there's something you need to get off your chest, so what is it?"

With a huff, he sat across from her and pulled his knees to his chest. "Do you have any idea how hard it is to live in the shadow of dead brothers?"

Claire shook her head.

"It's unbearable. You'd think my dad would dote on his only living son. You know, to overcompensate for his loss, but no, he's extremely harsh and critical of everything I do. When he actually looks at me, which isn't often, I see the contempt of a man who wishes I had died, instead of Zac."

Claire didn't know enough of the story to counter Chase's last remark so she only said, "I can't imagine the heartache that must come with losing two sons."

"Yet he acts as if he lost all three of us," Chase said coldly. "He wears his grief like a badge of honor, having no regard for the living, or care for anyone else's pain. I lost my brothers, too, you know." He slammed his hand against the blanket. "Why? Why'd he shut me out?"

"I wish I had an answer for you, but I'm kind of at a disadvantage." Claire tucked the picture back into the Bible and handed it to him. "Why did you choose a Bible for your dad's kayak?"

"He used to read this every morning at breakfast, but I hadn't seen him do it once since the accident, so I knew he wouldn't miss it. He even quit going to church, which is a sore spot for my mom." Chase put the Bible back into the bag before adding, "I guess I shouldn't take my dad's rejection so personally now that I think of it in the light of his attitude toward God."

"No, but that doesn't make your reality any easier. I'm sorry your dad has blocked you out of his life and even sorrier that he's blocked God out too."

"Yeah, it pretty much sucks." He got to his feet and reached to give Claire a hand. "We need to get going, I still have work to do."

While Chase put the sealed bag into his dad's kayak and locked the shed doors, Claire folded the blanket and strapped it behind her saddle. They mounted their horses in silence and started back.

Claire mulled over Chase's story as they made their way off the steep part of the trail. Her heart hurt for him, even though she knew there was nothing she could do to fix it. Once they were through the gate and back into the open fields, she said, "On a positive note, I can tell Maggie adores you. Her admonition this morning was certainly out of love for all involved."

"True. She and Uncle Brad not only saved the ranch, they treat me like the son they never had. There were times when I wanted to run, to leave this mess behind. They are the reason I stayed."

"I bet the sentiment goes both ways." Claire smiled.

"It does."

"Thanks for showing me your memorial and telling me your story."

A weight seemed to roll off Chase's shoulders and he returned the smile. "Thanks for listening. It was nice having someone to talk to for a change."

"But why did you choose to confide in me?"

"To be honest, I don't know . . . but I'm glad I did."

"Me too." They rode in silence for a while before she added, "It's interesting how we can find perspective in others' pain. Recently, I've been stuck in a misunderstanding with my parents, and unfortunately, it seems like the easiest way to handle it is to avoid them."

"Was it your fault?" Chase slowed Mingo's pace to a walk.

"Kind of. Well, not really."

"Okay, now you have me confused. What happened?"

Claire fussed with the reins and wondered if she had made a mistake mentioning it. To admit the conflict with her parents had to do with the painting that brought her and Chase together wasn't something she was willing to do at this point.

"Claire?" He held her gaze with an expression she hadn't seen before; his dark eyes looked lighter, softer, inviting even.

"I can't tell you," Claire finally blurted out and looked away.

Chase reached for Chicory's reins and brought both horses to a stop. Then he lifted her chin and softly turned her face toward his. "You can trust me."

"It's not a matter of trust." She sighed. "It's a matter of belief."

Chase lowered his hand while furrowing his brow. "Wait, are you talking about religion?"

Claire laughed a little. "Well, it does have to do with the impossible, which I guess would make it religious in a supernatural kind of way."

"I'm all ears."

"But you won't believe me, and it'll ruin . . . this." She gestured between them. In that moment of vulnerability, Claire couldn't keep from blushing, so she flicked the reins and said, "Chicory, let's go."

Chapter 13

ROGER

Chase stayed put and called after her, "Hey, Claire, I'm not leaving until you talk to me."

Without looking back, she waved and said, "Okay, I'll put Chicory in her stall." After a few more strides, when she realized he wasn't coming, she turned back. "Thanks for the ride. Maybe we can do it again some time." Then in a flash, she forced Chicory into a gallop, and they raced toward the barns.

"Seriously? Come on Mingo, two can play at this game." The gelding flew into action and they reached the barns first. With a big grin on his face, Chase jumped off his horse and gave Claire a hand down.

"That wasn't fair, you cut off the corner."

"You didn't think I would just *let* you win, now, did you?"

"Fine but wait till next time." She smirked.

Instead of replying, he leaned in for a kiss.

"Whoa." She quickly put her hand on his chest and stepped back.

"What, too soon?"

"Kind of. I like you a lot, and I'd like to get to know you better, but your emotions are all over the place right now. I'm not sure you want to kiss me for the right reasons."

"Do I dare ask what you mean?"

Seeing his disappointment, she moved closer again. "I don't want to feel like a replacement for your parents' lack of love. Your memorial and your story have touched me deeply, but I'd like to get to know you separate from the hurts of the past and it's only fair that you do the same for me. Okay?"

Chase nodded, too enamored with her to speak. It was the sound of a vehicle racing up the driveway that broke the spell. A moment later a black pickup came to a screeching halt not far from where they were standing.

"Hey," Chase called, "what's going on?"

Roger jumped from his truck and said, "Why won't you answer your damn phone?"

Chase quickly felt his pockets. "Oh, um, I must have left it at Aunt Maggie's house earlier."

Roger got right in his face. "Why aren't you with Brad and Justin?"

"Because Brad said they'd be fine without my help if I wanted to come see Claire." Chase took a step back and pointed in her direction. "They were just checking on the cattle. Is there a problem?"

"Problem? While you were off gallivanting and being irresponsible, a pack of coyotes attacked the herd."

"Oh no," Claire gasped. "Were they able to scare them away?"

Roger gave her a sharp look, "As if you care."

"Come on, Dad, none of this is Claire's fault. How bad is the damage?"

"We lost two calves that they know of and a third is down."

"Wow, there must have been several of them, if the mamas couldn't fend them off," Chase said. "I haven't heard anyone mention coyotes since April."

"Yeah, well the wretched beasts are still out there." Roger started for the barn.

Chase followed, "Hey, Dad, I'm sorry."

"It's a little late for that now, don't you think? The damage is already done."

Claire watched this interaction between the two men in silence. She felt bad that Chase was getting reamed out because of her, but she also wondered how much of this story she didn't understand.

"Brad stayed to protect Justin, so he doesn't know if the coyotes have attacked elsewhere. We need to go now."

"Right, I'll grab my rifle and head out." Chase ran to the office, where Brad kept the guns locked in a case.

Claire wasn't sure what she was supposed to do, so she came as far as the doorway and watched them from there.

Roger hurried into one of the first stalls and was bringing his horse into the aisle when Chase came back. "Do you want us to wait for you?"

"Us?" Roger snapped. "There is no us. She's not coming."

"Please, sir." Claire steadied her voice, "I've helped our neighbors drive the cattle lots of times and it sounds like you could use an extra hand."

"I think you've helped enough for one day, missy." He threw the saddle onto his horse. "So you can leave."

"Come on, Claire, let's go."

She followed Chase out of the barn and whispered, "Aren't you in enough trouble already?"

"I am, but there's no time to worry about that now." Chase strapped down his gun and mounted his horse. "Are you coming?"

She climbed onto her saddle. "Ready."

"Yeah, just do what you want," Roger yelled from inside the barn. "You always do."

"Ignore him, we need the help." Chase kicked Mingo's ribs and they took off in the opposite direction from where they had come.

Claire followed suit. When she caught Chase, she said, "Your dad is really mad."

"And rightfully so. I was wrong to leave Brad and Justin this morning, especially with so many calves in the herd."

"I meant about me coming."

"The only way he'll get over that is if you prove yourself useful." Chase picked up the pace.

"No pressure, right?"

"Right."

Claire tightened her reins and urged Chicory forward. They fell into stride beside the obstinate rider and his horse. "How in the world did I get drawn into this mess?"

"I think you *painted* your way into it."

"Ha-ha, good one. How far is the herd from here?"

"A few miles. Do you mind riding faster?"

"Of course not."

"Good."

Pushing their horses into a full gallop, fifteen minutes passed before Chase slowed the pace and said, "Without my phone, I can't call Brad to see where they are."

Claire fished hers out of her pocket. "Here, use mine."

"Thanks, but I don't have his number memorized."

"I have Maggie's."

"We're almost to Fisher's Creek; they shouldn't be too much further beyond that. If we can't find them soon, I'll call."

"What, are you afraid to talk to Maggie?" Claire asked.

"You're quite perceptive. She actually loves me, so I hate disappointing her."

"She seemed more than happy to send me off with you earlier."

"Yeah, well that's because she wishes I'd date, but because I wasn't where I was supposed to be, she'll feel partly to blame."

"It sounds like the coyotes had already done their damage before Brad and Justin got there. How is anyone to blame?"

"True, but if I was there, I could've been hunting them this whole time. The pack is most likely attacking another part of the herd because Brad and Justin interrupted their breakfast."

They quit talking while they worked their way across the creek, which was more like a small river. By the time they reached the other side, Roger had caught up to them. "Hey, I just got off the phone with—"

BAM! BAM!

Chicory reared, but Claire was quick to steady her. "Wow, that was close."

"Yes. They're just north of here."

Chase grabbed his gun and took off in that direction.

Claire waited for Roger to cross the tributary, then asked, "Are you going to help with the coyote hunt, or should we start rounding up the cattle?"

"The cattle, and I hope you were being honest when you said you've done this before."

"But why would I lie?" Claire realized her tone sounded a bit rude, but she didn't appreciate the condescension or his lack of trust.

"I don't even know who you are or why you're taking Chase away from his responsibilities in the middle of a workday."

"My name's Claire. I came to visit Maggie."

"Roger. But how does visiting Maggie have anything to do with Chase?"

"I met him two weeks ago when I took photos of Brad and Maggie with their horses."

Roger looked more confused than angry. Then without warning, he started riding to the southwest.

Claire joined him. "To answer the question you didn't ask, Maggie commissioned me to do a portrait of them. It's my day off, so I brought the painting over this morning. When Chase saw my SUV, he came to say hello."

"Huh, that was a long hello. How'd you catch his eye, anyway? To my knowledge, he's never even had a girlfriend."

"Well, for starters, I'm not his girlfriend." Claire hesitated before saying, "Yet. This is only the second time I've been here and when Chase asked me if *I could ride,* I got defensive and wanted to prove I could."

"Now you can prove it to me. Let's go." He turned his horse down a narrow embankment to the left.

"Come on, Chicory; show me what you're made of. Our future might depend upon it." Claire followed Roger, and as soon as there was room again to ride beside him, she said, "I'm sorry for the inconvenience we've caused you."

Roger glanced her way but didn't bother to answer.

Claire realized there was no reason to expect anything different from a man who had fortified walls of defense around his broken heart. He'd already talked more than she'd expected and for all she knew, her comment could've fostered fresh animosity.

They rode in silence for a bit. It was Claire who spoke first, "Look, some cattle are down near the woods."

"Finally, let's get them first. With any luck, the rest of the herd will be over that ridge." Roger pointed to a knoll not more than two hundred yards away. Then he removed a glove and used his fingers to give a loud whistle. A minute later, two dogs came running toward them.

Claire had already started to circle below the cows and was pushing them back into the open field. Together they were able to round up more cattle from the trees than they expected and found the rest of the herd grazing on the opposite hill, just as Roger had hoped.

"Do we push them, or are they used to slow and steady?" Claire asked.

"Slow, for now, they still seem kind of spooked. I texted Brad our location a few minutes ago. They should be here soon."

It was another twenty minutes before Chase and Brad came into view.

"What took you so long?" Roger's cold and metallic tone reverberated across the open field.

Claire cringed. *I don't get it. What does he have to gain from being so harsh?*

Neither man bothered to answer until they were closer. It was Brad who spoke first. "Chase got two more coyotes. We thought that was more important than coming immediately."

Roger nodded coolly. "Well, we couldn't get the cattle to head your way."

"Yeah, it's like they're still distressed from earlier or maybe it's from the sound of your successful gunshots." Claire winked at Chase.

The smile that crept across his lips was short-lived because Roger interrupted their moment. "We don't have time for your foolishness. The herd won't go near the pass, but we can't leave them here, so now what?"

"I say we work them down the west bank and cross them a mile downstream?" Chase said.

"That's not an option," Roger barked. "It's too far out of the way."

"Not really," Brad cut in. "We usually go that way when we moved the cattle to the southern pastures. At this point, it seems like our best course of action."

"Perfect. I'll head to the front and start turning the cattle in that direction." Not waiting for his dad to reply, Chase whistled and one of the dogs followed him.

"Fine. Claire, flank Chase. Brad and I will bring up the rear with Justin and the wounded calf."

Claire did as Roger ordered while staying far enough back to help form an arch. The cattle seemed more willing to move now that they were heading south, which made the drive much easier.

A few hours later they had the 1200 head of cattle across the river and were heading at a decent pace toward the designated pastures. The land was more open here, and the cattle were in less danger of being attacked again. Once the cattle were settled, Roger said, "Claire, I admit, you've certainly proven your worth today."

"Thanks. Does this mean we're off the hook for earlier?"

"You are. I'll deal with this one later." He pointed toward Chase with his thumb, looking dead serious.

"Come on, Roger," Brad said. "Two of the calves were lost before we even got there, and we saved the third, so even if Chase was with us, it wouldn't have changed anything."

"It's a matter of principle, Brad, and you know it."

"Yeah, but I'm the one who told him he could leave. It's not like he jumped ship."

"Enough already," Chase barked. "Not in front of Claire. I'm the one that was wrong, and I'll pay the consequences. We'll meet you back at the barns. Come on, Claire; our work here is done."

"Okay, just a sec." She turned Chicory so she could face Roger. "It was nice to meet you. And Brad, Chase already hung the painting. I hope you like it."

"I'm sure I will, and thanks for helping us with the drive. If you ever need a job, you have one waiting."

"Ah. Good to know." She smiled and tipped her hat to him. "Until next time, then."

With that, Claire swung Chicory around and joined Chase, giving him a playful nudge. "Are you ready to get out of here?"

"Absolutely."

It didn't take long to put a decent distance between them and the others. Once they were out of earshot, they slowed their pace and Chase asked, "What's gotten into you?"

"Whatever do you mean?"

"Ever since you helped with the cattle, you've been quite flirtatious."

Claire smirked. "I think your dad likes me. I thought my presence might soften his anger toward you."

"Ha, well you were certainly helpful. No matter what happens later, I want you to know you're worth the consequences." He reached to squeeze her hand.

"I hope you still feel that way in the morning," she teased.

"Don't you worry about me. I'm used to my dad being harsh. All I'm saying is, this time it'll be worth it."

Her smile widened. "If it's any consolation, I enjoyed our little excursion earlier today."

"So did I."

They chatted the rest of the way back to the barns. Once they arrived, Chase offered to take care of the horses and walked Claire to her vehicle. "I've never felt so connected to someone in such a short period of time. I hope we can see each other again real soon."

"I'd like that." Claire took off her hat and kissed him on the cheek before climbing into her SUV. "Maggie has my number; be sure to call."

"I will." Chase pushed her door shut and watched as she drove away.

Claire waved out her window, glad he couldn't see her ridiculous grin.

Chapter 14

THE PAINT HORSE

Three days passed before Chase gave Claire a call.

"Hey there, have you finally recovered from your beating?" Claire asked with a laugh.

"Ha-ha, real funny."

"I thought so."

"Actually, my dad wasn't even mad after you left."

"Sweet. But wait, if that's the case, why'd it take you three days to call me?"

"Uh, that'd be because I had to get up the nerve to ask Aunt Maggie for your number."

"And why was *that* so hard?"

"Because I knew she'd want details."

Claire's tone flattened. "You sound like that's a bad thing."

"Not at all. It just seems a little early to make more of it than it is. But so you know, I took to heart what you said about liking you for you."

"Oh yeah, what's your conclusion?"

"Truthfully, I'm scared. I can't get you out of my mind—"

That makes two of us, Claire thought, but she only said, "And?"

"And I'd like to come visit, to see your place and your art studio, to meet your horse and go riding with you again. I want to get to know you better."

Claire smiled at the tremble in his voice. "It's okay, Chase. I know you haven't dated much."

"It's that obvious?"

"Not really. Your dad told me you've never had a girlfriend . . . that he knew about anyway."

"Oh really? I didn't know he cared."

"Like I said before, I think he likes me." The playfulness had returned to her voice.

"Must be, but still, to tell that to someone he just met seems weird to me. Not to mention that it wasn't his place."

Without seeing his face, Claire couldn't tell if Chase was more miffed or embarrassed. "Let's not focus on your dad right now. When can you come?"

"Does tomorrow afternoon work for you?"

Claire finished her chores and sat on the wooden fence that ran along their driveway to wait for Chase.

When he pulled in, she waved and joined him at his truck. "Ah, you've made it to our humble abode. I'm so glad you could come."

"Me too, but I wouldn't call this place humble. Look at all the barns; you even have an arena."

"Yeah, well, that's because our focus is horses. We breed, train, and sell them. Several have been bought for rodeo events." She swung her hands open, "Now you know why I'm so good with the horses."

Chase laughed. "You're not going to let me live that down, now are you?"

"Not a chance." Claire smirked. "Come on."

She brought him to the arena, first. Barrels were strategically placed in the middle. Poles and other apparatus were stacked along the far wall.

"Oh wow, this place is impressive." Chase leaned his elbows on the railing.

111

"Yeah, it's a great facility, especially during the long winter months." Claire climbed onto the top rail. "Care to join me?"

"Sure."

They watched for a bit in silence as Paul wrote down critique points and shouted commands to Trevor who was riding one of the Paint Horses.

Finally, Chase said, "That's one beautiful horse."

"It sure is. Paint Horses aren't quite as good as Quarter Horses when it comes to barrel racing, but they're a popular choice because their drastic coloring makes them extra fun to watch."

"Definitely. Wait, how long has this arena been here?"

"About fourteen years. Why?"

Chase took off his hat and looked around. "This is crazy. I just realized I've been here before."

"For real? When?"

"We came here for Zac's sixteenth birthday. My dad bought him a Thoroughbred for competing and he won all his events in the high school rodeo season that year including state competitions. His horse deserved a lot of the credit."

"Now you're just trying to be nice." She leaned into his shoulder.

He nudged her back before saying, "Actually, I was dead serious. You can have all the skill in the world, but if your horse can't make the turns sharp enough, you're not guaranteed a win. Or if it doesn't get out of the box quick enough, the calf can take an extra step causing hundredths of a second difference in a tight competition of calf roping."

"Did you compete before Zac passed?"

"Yes. I held my own in my age group, but after the accident, my dad no longer supported me."

"Yeah, Maggie mentioned his depression. I'm sorry things between you and your dad went downhill after that."

"Hey, Sis," Trevor yelled from the far end of the arena. "Watch this. Dad's going to time us."

"We're ready, Trev. Make me proud," Claire called back.

Paul waved his hat with one hand while clicking his stopwatch with the other. Trevor kicked the horse into action, and they were off.

"See, this is what I'm saying," Chase said. "Look how smoothly the horse makes those turns."

Claire shrugged. "This is what we do, so I guess I didn't think much of it." Trevor finished the course and then rode over to where they were sitting. "Nice riding, Bro."

"Thanks, Sis. Hey, Dad, how was the time?"

Paul gave a thumbs-up as he walked over to join them. "I think this one's ready to sell."

"That's what I thought, too."

"Not so fast," Claire interrupted. "The horse swung too wide on the third corner. Was that your fault, Trev, or the horse's?"

"Oh, miss smarty-pants is in the house." Trevor bobbed his head as he dismounted. "Do you want to show us how it's done?"

"Sure, but first, let me introduce you to my friend, Chase."

Chase jumped off the fence and reached to shake their hands. "It's nice to meet you. I was just telling Claire that we bought a horse here about eleven years ago."

"Eleven years and you haven't been back? Must be we didn't do our jobs," Paul said.

"Oh no, sir. That horse was the best we ever owned. It's just, well, my brother died. We didn't need a show horse anymore."

"Oh, I'm so sorry, I didn't know."

"It's okay, why would you?"

Paul shrugged. "But why didn't *you* use the horse, then?"

Chase winced at the question and shoved his hands into his pockets. "It's, um, complicated." His eyes darted to Claire as if hoping for some help.

"Hey, Dad," she said as she hopped down from her perch, "Weren't you going to let me see if this horse is ready to sell?" She took the reins, mounted, and circled the arena. Slow at first, then faster. After a few sharp turns around the barrels, she road to the start.

The guys climbed onto the fence for a better view of the course.

Paul looked at his stopwatch and wrote down Trevor's time before he reset it. "Are you ready?"

"Not yet," Claire called back. She jumped off the horse, tightened the girth on the saddle and shortened the stirrups. Then she remounted and took the horse around the first barrel and back to the start. "Now I'm ready."

Paul waved his hat and she was off, masterfully making every turn and beating Trevor's time by two seconds.

"Hey, Trev, I guess it was your riding," Paul said, showing him the watch.

"Yeah, yeah, if I was as good as Claire, I'd be competing."

Claire rode over to where the guys were sitting. "So how'd we do?"

Trevor leaped from the fence and grabbed the reins. "Showoff. Way to make me look bad."

"Before you started whining, I was going to say thanks for making me look good. You've done a great job with this horse."

"Whatever Sis, you killed it." He turned to face Chase while waving his thumb at Claire. "If this one wasn't so bent on being a painter, she could've made the circuit."

"You're probably right," Chase said. "That was some impressive riding." He turned to Claire. "Can't you do both, paint and compete?"

"Not really. I love to paint, and I still get to spend time with the horses every day without the commitment it takes to run the circuit."

"That's it in a nutshell," Paul said. "But hey, it works for me because I always have a rider who knows how to push my horses to their limits."

Claire smiled at her dad. "Thanks. And I agree; this one is ready to sell. Hey, do you mind if Chase uses one of the horses? I'd like to give him a tour."

Paul started to answer, but Trevor cut him off. "He can take mine. I won't need him again today."

"Thanks, Trev."

"Yeah, thanks," Chase said.

"Not a problem, I can't imagine Claire being with a guy who can't ride." He gave them a mischievous wink.

"You're a trip, Trev."

"And hilarious," Chase added.

"Ahem, now that that's settled," Paul cut in, "the gate to the north pasture got left open, can you shut it on your way by?"

"Sure thing, Dad. See you later."

As Claire and Chase headed toward the stalls, he said, "You're one lucky lady."

"How so?"

"The way you interact with your dad is great, and the banter between you and your brother is even better. I'm a little jealous."

"Oh, I'm so sorry."

"Don't be, I think it's terrific. It reminds me of how my family used to interact with each other before the accident, that's all." He pinched his lips.

"I can't even fathom how much you've lost." Claire gave him an empathetic, yet endearing smile. "Let's hope that happier days are in your future."

"For as much as you brag about my father liking you, maybe my fortune *will* improve." His countenance brightened. "Now, enough about me; which horse is Trevor's?"

"Lightfoot, he's the dark brown Thoroughbred with his head in the aisle."

"Huh, he looks a lot like Zac's horse."

Claire slipped her hand into his. "Should we just drive to the cabin? I didn't realize we'd have so many blasts from your past today."

"But these are all good memories." He squeezed her hand before letting go. "If you don't mind, I'd rather ride."

"Works for me, and speaking of memories, Trevor loved this horse more than all the rest, even when it was a colt. My dad sold it like three weeks before his fifteenth birthday."

Chase stroked the horse's nose. "Yet, here he is. So what gives?"

"It was like you said; Lightfoot had trouble making a sharp enough right turn, which cost them those precious seconds. The owner returned him and bought a Quarter Horse instead. My dad didn't let Trevor know they returned the horse and gave it to him on his birthday. You should have seen his face."

"I bet I can picture it. For Zac, getting his horse was better than getting a new truck and the way he took care of it proved it."

Claire laughed. "What a perfect analogy. I bet Zac was possessive too. Trev doesn't just let anyone ride him so you must have made a good first impression. His saddle and the reins are right there." She pointed to the left of the stall door. "Lexi is across the aisle."

They continued to talk while they got the horses saddled but waited to mount until they were outside.

"We should close the north field gate first. It's not far out of the way," Claire said.

"Good call; I forgot about the gate already."

"Distracted much?"

"No. It's just that I'm a cattle rancher, not a horse-whisperer like you. Mingo and, occasionally Chicory, are the only two horses I've ridden in years."

"Show Lightfoot who's in control and you'll be fine."

Once the gate was shut, they fell into a comfortable trot and were able to visit as they rode. Then out of the blue, Chase asked, "Hey, seeing how Trevor mentioned boyfriends, have you had many?"

"Now you're prying." She pretended to look miffed but failed to hold back her smile.

"To be fair, your dad didn't have an opportunity to offer up personal information as mine so freely did."

"True, but it's not like *not* dating is scandalous or something. I'm actually glad to know you don't have a lot of baggage in that regard."

"And maybe I simply waited until I found the right girl."

"Ha." Claire let out a nervous little laugh and then quickly turned her horse to cross a small creek. Once on the other side, she took off across the open field.

It didn't take Chase long to catch her. "I'm not sure how to interpret your actions just now, but I've learned one thing—never start a serious conversation with you on horseback. This is like the fourth time you've taken off on me. Why are you so bent on avoiding certain questions, especially the one about dating?"

"Fine." She slowed her horse to a walk. "I've dated some, but I'll warn you, none of the guys lasted very long."

Chase reached for Claire's reins and brought both horses to a stop. He looked her square in the eyes and asked, "Is this your way of telling me you're not interested?"

"No!" She leaned forward to pat Lexi's neck. "It's just that Trev thinks I'm too competitive. He told me recently that 'I've scared off my share of boyfriends.'"

"Is he right?"

"Perhaps, but as far as I see it, a few of them were too conceited for their own good. I was stubborn enough to put them in their place."

"Kind of like how you had to prove to me that you could ride the other day?"

Claire smirked. "Guilty."

"And showed off at the arena earlier?"

"Hey, now that's not fair. I needed to prove the horse and you know it."

"Well, I'm glad I got to watch you ride, and now I see why the riding question was so provocative."

"Yeah, and yet I shouldn't have gotten so defensive."

"No worries. I accept the challenge and acknowledge that I've been duly warned." He tipped his hat to her.

"You're a dork, you know."

Chase grinned. "I hope you realize that I won't be easily scared off."

"Glad to hear it." She smiled. "But to be clear, I've only had one serious boyfriend, and that was during my junior year of high school."

"Let me guess, you humiliated him by beating him at calf roping, and he never forgave you?"

"I wish it was that simple." Claire blew out a deep breath and looked away.

"That bad, huh?"

"Pretty much. Do you mind if we save that conversation for later? It's a beautiful day for a ride, and I want to show you around."

Chapter 15

PAINFUL MEMORIES

As they weaved their way up to the cabin, Claire took the opportunity to point out some of her favorite places, including the pond, and the treehouse that her brothers helped her build when she was eleven. The knot in her stomach had dissolved, which made it easier to embellish a few of the stories. Maybe by the time they reached her house, Chase would forget about the ex-boyfriend, and she could forget about the painful memories.

"Nice place, but what's with all the broken and mangled trees?" Chase asked as they rode around to the back entrance.

"Oh, you know, just a little storm . . . with huge consequences." Claire didn't bother to give him details.

They dismounted, tied the horses to a post in the shade, and headed for the house.

"Were you here when it happened?"

"Yes."

He took another look around. "This storm certainly wasn't little, but it's nice to see that you're not the kind of person to be all melodramatic about it."

If he only knew. She looked down to remove her riding gloves as a way to hide her smirk. "Thanks, I think."

"Yes, it's a compliment. I've encountered a few drama queens in my day, and I wasn't impressed."

"Well, that's good to know." She winked and then led the way inside. "Oh, I've been meaning to ask, do you still live at home?"

"No way!" Chase looked surprised by the question. "As soon as I graduated from high school, I moved into a small apartment built onto the back of Justin's house."

"How far is it from your parents?"

"Only a few miles. It's actually a stone's throw beyond Maggie's place."

"But why didn't you move in with Maggie and Brad? Their house is huge."

His brow furrowed. "You're kidding, right?"

Claire leaned against the kitchen counter, looking equally surprised. "No. Why?"

"It just seems like a funny thing for you to ask when you have your own place."

"Okay, but at the time you were only eighteen and you seem like you get along with them really well; that's all."

"Aunt Maggie offered, but I didn't want to *actually* give my parents a reason to hate me, and anyway, I needed to find my own way in the world."

"I get that." Claire grabbed two cans of pop from the fridge and said, "Here, let's go sit on the porch." They both took a seat before she continued. "I usually get along great with my parents, but I wasn't ready to move home after being away at college for four years. They thankfully let me move here."

"And who wouldn't love this view?"

"I know, right?"

They sat in silence for a while, content just to be together.

"Do you want to see my art studio?" Claire asked, sitting forward in her chair.

"Maybe in a minute. First I want to hear about the fallout between you and your boyfriend in high school." Chase sat forward too, clasping his hands together over his knees.

"Oh man, I was hoping that wouldn't get brought back up."

"What's the big deal?"

Claire leaned back in her seat again and started drumming her fingers on the arm of the chair. "Actually, it was quite a big deal."

"I showed you my memorial. It only seems fair for you to give me a glimpse into your past."

The drumming stopped. "I hope you won't be disappointed because the boyfriend is only part of the story, but I do need to start with him. His name was Tim, and I was in love with him. He was a good-looking senior, popular, and quite creative. He wasn't raised on a ranch, but he liked art as much as I did. We got along great, and I saw my future with him . . . until that dreadful day."

"What dreadful day?"

"The day my world fell apart."

"I'm sorry, Claire. I didn't realize losing a high school sweetheart would be so devastating all these years later."

"That's because there's more to it. At the end of every school year, there's a statewide art competition that I thought I could win for my age group. My art teacher taught me a lot and always told me how much potential I had—"

"I don't get it. What does an art competition have to do with anything?"

"Actually, it has to do with everything." Claire's eyes stung. Her cheeks burned. "It has to do with the last five years. It has to do with who I am today."

"Whoa." Chase held up his hands. "I didn't mean to upset you."

"It's not you. The whole situation sucks, that's all. I showed Tim the photo I wanted to use for the art show, but he said he didn't think it was interesting enough to win, even if I did a great job with the painting.

"That's when he offered to help. I gave him a piece of watercolor paper to try his experiment on. It turned out so cool that I finished the painting and submitted it to the competition. To make a long story much shorter, when I was confronted about my piece being original, I lied to the judges."

"I don't understand. What did Tim do to your painting? You sound like you committed a crime."

"That's it in a nutshell."

"What's it?"

"I committed a crime." She looked at the mountains, mindlessly shaking her head. "I was such a fool."

He reached to take her hand. "Hey, look at me." She didn't, so he gently turned her face toward his. Her eyes were moist. "Claire?"

"Tim not only dumped me, I didn't get into art school, either."

"What did Tim do to your painting that made it illegal?"

"I claimed the painting was an original, which wasn't Tim's fault."

"Wow." Chase rubbed the back of his neck. "Am I slow or are you trying to confuse me? I have no idea what you're talking about."

"Sorry. I'm not trying to be ambiguous. It just still hurts."

"But without details, I don't see what you did wrong."

Claire blew out a long breath. "Tim took a photo of another artist's painting, whose style was similar to mine, though his skills far exceeded it."

"I can't believe that. Your paintings are amazing."

She cracked a weak smile. "Except that this happened five years ago. I've done a lot of painting since then and have gotten much better. Anyway, you're missing the point. Tim digitally removed everything except the horses and their riders from the photo. Then he took a piece of my watercolor paper to a print shop, sized the image so it would fit and had them print it onto the paper."

"Interesting. I didn't know that was possible."

"Yeah, the bigger print shops can print on all kinds of papers these days. When Tim gave me the paper back, I added the background and blended the edges so you couldn't tell that I hadn't painted the whole thing. I even added a few strokes of paint to the original image. The painting looked fantastic."

"I'm sure it did, but how could the judges tell?"

"That's where the bottom fell out. The judges called me in for a personal interview. They were all quite impressed, which of course played to my ego. Then they gave me one last chance to confirm that the painting was completely mine."

"Which I'm guessing you did."

"Right, I was young and stupid." Claire abruptly stood and started pacing the porch.

Chase sat back in his chair, cupped his hands behind his head, and watched her.

After a few passes, she stopped and threw one hand out to the side. "And get this, one of the judges did the painting that I used."

He lowered his arms and winced. "No way! What'd you do then?"

"I tried to remain stoic, though I felt like throwing up. It was so humiliating." Claire started pacing again.

"Did you explain?"

"Yes, but by then it was too late. My painting was disqualified from the competition, I was barred from competing my senior year, and as I mentioned, I couldn't get into the art school I planned on attending."

"Wow. That seems like an extreme punishment. I'm surprised that you didn't quit painting after that."

"I did quit."

"But you didn't."

"Before the beginning of my senior year, I dropped out of my art class. I didn't need the elective to graduate, and I couldn't bring myself to face Mrs. Hayes, my teacher." Claire finally sat again. "Two weeks into the school year, I was called into the principal's office. Mrs. Hayes was standing by the window. My parents were there, too. My heart sank.

"Mrs. Hayes came forward and said, 'Claire, we all know that you made a huge mistake last spring. None of us can fix that, but you're one of the best artists this school has ever seen.'

"Though I kept my eyes trained on the floor, I mumbled, 'I'm so sorry, Mrs. Hayes, you don't know how sorry.'" Claire looked at Chase with eyes of glass.

"Then what happened?"

"She was gracious and said: 'I know, Claire.' She stepped closer to lift my chin, forcing me to look at her. 'What you did was wrong, and you must pay the consequences, but those consequences don't have to include quitting art forever. I want you to come back to class.' My eyes burned. My hands trembled. I was too ashamed to say yes and too broken to say no. She must have seen the turmoil in my expression because she added, 'Please, the thought of you throwing away this much talent breaks my heart.'"

Claire wiped her cheek with her shoulder and looked back at Chase. "Ugh, this is so embarrassing."

"Why? It's not like you're the only one who has ever needed forgiveness and a second chance."

"True and I think it's pretty obvious that I took advantage of that second chance." She brightened a little.

"That's an understatement."

"Thanks. I didn't get into the art school that I wanted to attend, but Mrs. Hayes helped me get into her alma mater. They have a great art program, so I guess it all worked out for me in the end."

"Sounds like it. One more question, though. Whatever became of Tim?"

"I have no idea. We never hung out again after that."

Chase's eyes widened. "You mean he dumped you over it?"

"Yep, he sure did. He wasn't going to throw away our, I mean *his* dream college over it."

"That's lame."

"The whole time he was all in. The painting turned out so well that he told me not to say how we did it so that I could submit it to the competition. Once I got caught, he bailed on me."

"How would coming clean about the painting get him in trouble?"

"Technically, he was the one who stole the image I used."

"Oh, right."

"I explained to the judges how I got the image onto my paper but didn't tell them I had help."

"Tim didn't know this was illegal?"

"I'm sure he never thought I'd get caught. He just wanted to help me win."

"Then why did he dump you? Especially after you covered for him?"

"He assumed that I busted him and walked out before I had a chance to explain. He said he wasn't willing to risk his future over me. All he cared about was his ticket out of here."

"Jerk."

"Yeah . . . But hey, now you know that I'm not worth the risk." She forced a smile, though it looked more like a grimace. "So you might want to bail on me now."

"Not a chance." Chase's broad smile caused the concern stamped across Claire's brow to vanish like a vapor.

Hmm, seems a bit elaborate to have a painting miraculously change, simply to meet a guy . . . and a charming guy at that.

Chapter 16

FIRST KISS

On their way back to the horses, Claire said to Chase, "If you're not in a hurry to get home, we can take a different way back."

"I'd like that."

An hour later they reached the barns.

"Your parents own a beautiful piece of property. Thanks for the tour; I especially enjoyed the stories from your youth."

Claire was beaming as she removed her hat and fluffed her hair. "Yeah, I just love it here. There's something magical about this way of life—the horses, the land, and the vastness of it all."

Chase nodded. "I guess you could say it's in our blood."

"So true. I would've been miserable living in Denver. Hey, do you have time to take care of Lightfoot before you leave?"

"I'd be more than happy to." He caressed the horse's neck. "I haven't had this much fun in a long time."

"Me either. I'm glad that you could come and see a part of my world."

Once they had the horses back in their stalls, they met in the center aisle and walked out of the barn together. Neither spoke until they reached Chase's truck.

"I've enjoyed getting to know you better, Claire." He took her hands and looked thoughtfully into her eyes.

Claire's heart began to race. She assumed he was going to kiss her, and this time she wasn't going to stop him.

But to her dismay, he said, "You still haven't told me how you did such an accurate painting of my brothers and me, especially when that moment never happened."

"Wait, you guys never posed like that for a family photo?" Claire realized she sounded a bit too eager on that point, but she had supposed the painting was at least of an actual event.

"Right, so how'd you do it?"

He didn't look upset, just curious, but because she had no answer, the question stung. Letting go of his hands, she turned away.

"Claire, what is it?"

"If I knew, I would tell you, but I don't. I need to go." She started for the barn, frustrated that this got brought up after such a wonderful day together. Would the very reason they met, now be the thing that rips them apart?

"Claire, wait." Chase reached for her arm. "Hey, it's not important. I just hope that someday my parents will see your painting as a priceless treasure, instead of being angry about it."

Claire stiffened. "Do your parents know that I'm the one who painted it?"

"Not yet. After how they reacted when Aunt Maggie first showed it to them, I didn't want them to hate you before I had a chance to see where this is going."

She looked thoughtfully into his big, blue eyes. "And . . . where is it going?" Claire asked, relieved the subject was changed.

"Well, it's too early for a ring." He grinned. "But it might be time for a kiss." Without waiting for a reply, he leaned in, and this time, Claire didn't pull away.

"Does this mean I'll see you again?" She raised her eyebrows a few times before letting out a nervous little laugh and covering her lips.

"I would hope so." Chase pulled her into his embrace. "Thanks for an enlightening afternoon; even though it forced you to share some stuff I'm sure you'd like to forget." He kissed her forehead.

She took a step back and looked up at him. "Well, we're certainly getting to know things about each other that we've both kept close to the breast for a long time."

"Getting to know you for you, right?"

"Right."

After Chase left, Claire walked to the house and popped her head through the kitchen door. "Hey, Mom, do you mind if I stay for dinner?"

"Mind? Of course not, and you know me, I always make plenty."

"Thanks. I'll get washed up and then help set the table."

"Perfect, the guys shouldn't be too much longer."

A half-hour later, dinner was served.

Paul started the conversation. "This is the first we've seen or heard of Chase. How long have you known him?"

Helen's eyes lit up. "Who's Chase?"

"Claire's boyfriend." Trevor's answer was matter-of-fact as he proceeded to fill his bowl with beef stew.

"There you have it, Mom. Trevor seems to know more than I do." Claire wrinkled her nose at him.

"That was quite the kiss if he's not your boyfriend."

Claire hit his arm.

"Hey, what was that for?"

"Were you spying on us?"

"No. I just happened to come around the end of the barn and there you were. In fact, I turned back so you wouldn't see me and feel awkward."

"But it's okay to make me feel awkward in front of Mom and Dad?"

Trevor shrugged.

"Settle down, Claire, no one needs to be embarrassed. It was a simple question, which you haven't yet answered," Paul said.

"Not long. That was actually our first kiss."

"Where'd you meet him?" Helen asked.

"You know the painting that changed?"

Trevor perked up with a grin plastered across his face. "No way."

"Yes, way."

"What are you two talking about?" Helen asked, waving her hands in their direction.

"Trevor and I met Chase's aunt, at Frontier Days. She's the one who told us about the boys in my painting. Two of them died in a kayaking accident ten years ago. Chase is the boy that lived. He's twenty-five now."

Helen covered her mouth.

"So that's how his brother died, huh?" Paul said, half asking, half reflecting on their conversation in the arena earlier.

"But how did you meet Chase?" Helen asked.

"I know you and Dad won't believe me, and I'm not trying to anger you by mentioning the painting again, but I can't answer your question without that detail."

Paul crossed his arms, his brow furrowed. "So you really knew Chase all along. The mystery is solved, end of story."

"Fine, end of story. Good night."

She started to stand, but Trevor stopped her. "Mom, Dad—Claire quit confiding in you because she didn't want to upset you, but she didn't want to deny what happened either. If you don't want to hear the rest of her story, then I'm leaving too, because I'd like to know what happened."

"Please stay," Helen said.

Paul let out a heavy sigh but didn't leave the table.

"Trevor knows that I asked Maggie if I could come to see where the boys grew up. They own a ranch near Ten Sleep, and she agreed to let me come. That's when I met Chase. We didn't hit it off at first because he didn't see why I was snooping around their ranch."

"I can agree with that," Paul said, pointing his spoon in Claire's direction.

She bit back a reply and the urge to leave.

Helen patted his knee. "Can you please stop? I'd like to get to the good part, where they started liking each other." She nodded at Claire to continue.

Claire took a few bites of stew before she reluctantly told them the rest of the story, including finding Zac's wooden box and the trip to Chase's memorial.

"Poor Chase," Helen said when she finished. "He's had a rough go of it."

"And who would've known the painting changing would be the reason you two met," Trevor chimed in.

Paul abruptly stood. "So now you're telling us that you believe the painting changed too? I've heard enough."

Trevor squirmed a little, but the moment seemed too fluid for an explanation.

An awkward silence prevailed as Paul stomped out of the kitchen. When he was out of sight, Claire said, "Sorry for dragging you into this, Trev."

"No worries. The more this becomes something, the more it's worth ruffling some feathers. I'm not concerned about Dad; he'll get over it soon enough. Oh, and before I knew you had a boyfriend, I planned a bonfire for tonight."

"Why's that a problem?" Claire asked.

"Because I was going to ask you to come."

"And why can't I come now?"

"Because I invited Tim."

Claire suddenly looked mortified. "Wait, what?"

"You know, Tim, from high school."

"You're joking, right?

"Nope."

"I didn't even know he was back. Why in the world did you invite him?"

"Actually, I invited his brother, Sam. We're friends, remember?"

"Yeah, I remember."

"Well, he asked if Tim could come. What was I supposed to say? No, Claire might show up and that would be like weird?"

"We haven't spoken since . . . since the Art Symposium. He must have turned you down, right?"

"Sam said he was coming. A few of our other friends will be here too, including Tiffany, Bridget, and Josh. There's no reason you couldn't hang out with us for a while. I know they'd all love to see you."

"Yeah, but I have no desire to see Tim; and anyway, I have a painting to finish. We only have a week before the Beartrap Festival."

"Okay." Trevor excused himself from the table. "I need to get the fire pit ready. See you in the morning, Sis."

"Have fun." She started to clear the table.

"I thought you had a painting to work on," Helen said. "I've got this."

"It won't take long with the two of us." Claire put the bowls into the sink and started to rinse them. "Hey, Mom, don't you find the timing of Tim showing up a little weird?"

"Not really, why?"

"I haven't thought of him in years. And then for the first time since he dumped me, I really like someone else . . . a lot. It was painful enough earlier today when I told Chase about Tim, the Art Symposium, and that whole fiasco. Now I find out he lives in the area and is coming here tonight."

"I don't see the need for concern."

"It took me like forever to get over him." Claire bit her lip before saying, "What if he's charming?"

"Ah, good point. I think it would be fine to skip the bonfire. And Claire?"

"Hmm?"

"I still don't understand how the painting changed, but I'm sorry you had to confide in Trevor because I wasn't there for you."

"I can't blame you, Mom. If I didn't *see* it happen, I wouldn't believe me either. And Trev's more interested in the story than the painting changing."

"Well, I'd like to meet Chase; so the next time he comes, please be sure to introduce him to me."

"I will." Claire gave her mom a kiss on the cheek and started to gather her things.

Just then there was a knock at the back door. Claire shot a worried look at her mom. Helen only shrugged and went to see who it was.

Chapter 17

TIM

"Hi, Mrs. P. Good to see you again." Tim walked in without waiting for a reply or an invitation. "Hey, Claire, I thought you were coming out to the bonfire?"

"I was going to until I heard you were invited." She slipped her hands into her back pockets and stayed where she was.

"What? You're not excited to see me?" His eyes sparkled and his perfect smile caused Claire's heart to flutter. He removed his baseball cap and asked in a warm and inviting tone, "How have you been? You look great, by the way."

Heat rushed into her cheeks. *Darn, he's better looking than I remembered and as charismatic as ever.*

Tim came closer. Her better judgment told her to step back, but she didn't.

"I wanted to show you my latest pieces of art." He acted as if nothing negative had ever transpired between them.

Helen dried her hands before putting the dish towel on the oven's door handle. "I see you two have a lot of catching up to do. I'll leave you to it." She squeezed Claire's arm and left the kitchen.

They both watched her leave; the moment seemed too awkward to do anything else.

When Helen was gone, Claire said, "Um, would you like to sit?" She motioned to the bench beside the table.

"Sure." Tim sat and Claire joined him. He got out his phone, opened a file called 'art,' and leaned toward her.

For the time being, she forgot about their past and took his phone. She didn't even pull away when their shoulders touched. "Oh wow, these are really good. I didn't know you were interested in painting."

"Actually, after our experiment in high school, I realized the possibilities of mixed media."

Claire sucked in a deep breath, feeling as if she had just received a punch to the gut. "Before or after you dumped me?"

The distance that had closed between them became immediately obvious.

Tim turned to face her. "Hey, come on, that's not fair. It's not my fault you lied."

"Is that how you justified your actions? You seem to forget that my lie included covering for you. And how did you repay me?" Claire's elbow was now propped on the table with her chin resting between her thumb and forefinger.

"I, uh—"

"Got into our dream school while I got banished." Her tone matched the sharpness of her glare. "Now, all these years later, without so much as a boo, you come waltzing in here and expect me to be happy for you?"

Tim dropped his gaze and said, "I guess I thought you'd be happy about the art."

Claire still held his phone, so she started scrolling through the pictures again, glad for the diversion. Eventually, she said, "Your work is really good, but what? Am I supposed to pretend I wasn't devastated?" A tear seeped from the corner of her eye.

Tim gently whisked it away from her cheek before taking her hand. She tried to pull it free, but he wouldn't let go. "I'm sorry for how that all went down. I truly am."

"Yeah well, so am I." Claire yanked her hand from Tim's and slid further down the bench.

"Come on, Claire, that was a long time ago. Can't we move on? We're both older and smarter and have a better idea of what we want in life."

Without warning, she stepped away from the table, crossed her arms, and started rapidly tapping her right foot. "Let me get this straight, you used your art as an excuse to come see me because you want to get back together?"

A broad smile spread across Tim's face. "I've missed you."

Those words, that smile . . . they woke a distant memory in Claire. She had to look away. For a moment, time stood still as an internal war raged. *Ugh, why am I even attracted to him?* She shook her head, trying not to succumb to the emotional wooing of her first love. *Get a grip, I don't even know him anymore, and I've moved on. Yes, I've moved on.* With fresh resolve, she turned to face him. "Unfortunately for you, I'm dating a really great guy."

"It can't be very serious, based on how long it just took you to answer."

"Serious enough." Claire smiled at the thought of Chase.

"Huh, that certainly puts a wrinkle in my plans." Tim reddened. "I asked around, and no one mentioned a boyfriend."

"That's good. I've never been a fan of everyone knowing my business." No longer threatened by his unexpected solicitation, she came and took a seat opposite him and reached across the table to take his phone. After opening it to her favorite painting, she said, "Now, are you going to explain how you did this?"

Tim rubbed his smooth chin, the glint now gone from his eyes. "And just that quickly you've moved on?"

"Quickly? It's been five years."

His jaw tightened, but only for a moment. "I meant from giving us another chance . . . like now."

Everything within Claire wanted to scream. To bare her heart open. To make him understand the pain that he had caused. Losing art school might have been a little more bearable if he had been there for her. But he wasn't, so she held her tongue, both happy and sad to see his struggle.

"There's nothing as final as glaring silence, now is there?" He shook his head and then pointed to the painting on his phone. "Remember how I took a picture of another person's painting back in high—"

"Right, like I would forget." She rolled her eyes.

"Wow," Tim snapped. "Do you want me to explain or not?"

"You shouldn't have asked the question if you didn't want an answer." His presence confused her. She wished her wound was fresh so she could hate him. The fact of the matter was he broke her heart to follow his dreams. She couldn't begrudge him that. What would she have done if the circumstances were reversed?

"I'll be sure not to ask any more questions." His tone was clipped. "What I was going to say was as a senior in high school, I never gave it a thought that what we did was stealing or illegal. I use only my own photos now."

"If part of your finished art is actually a photo, how do you make it look like paint?"

"Once I decide on the part of the picture I'm going to use, I delete the rest, the way I did with yours. Then I work with it in my photo program to make it look more like a painting. Once I get it close, I print it onto my watercolor paper and paint the rest. I usually paint over some of the printed areas to give it an authentic painted impression."

This comment made Claire think of the changed painting still in her loft. *Hmm, could it be?* "It's a cool technique. Maybe you could show me the step-by-step process sometime."

"I'd like that." Tim smile returned with fresh vigor. "But what about your boyfriend? Won't he be jealous?"

"Are you kidding? I'll bring him with me. I'm sure he'd like to meet the only guy I was ever actually in love with. The guy who helped me cheat and then dumped me for it. The guy it took years to get ov—"

"We were only teenagers," Tim blurted out. "I had no idea how badly I hurt you or how much you really cared about me. You're right, I didn't look back. I regret that now." He stood and put on his baseball cap. "I don't blame you for hating me. And apparently, I'm still clueless because it was obviously naive of me to think I could come here after all these years and win you back." He started for the door.

Claire jumped to her feet, "Hold up, you forgot your phone. And I don't hate you, it just hurt a lot."

"I know, I felt it too, but I acted like such a jerk that day that I didn't, at the time, feel like I could mend the breach."

"Huh." Claire shook her head. "Well, you certainly haven't lost your charm. Maybe I better not come to see your art."

"If that's the case," Tim raised his eyebrows a few times, "then maybe you should."

Claire flushed at his fresh optimism. "I would seriously like to see your art in progress, but I can promise nothing more."

"That's enough for now. I'm renting a room from Mrs. Hayes. Stop by sometime."

"Or maybe you could bring some pieces by here. I saw her a few weeks ago and I'm not so sure she'll want to see me."

"Yeah, she told me about the painting you showed her. She didn't understand why you would say images showed up in your art that you didn't add, especially when in high school you refused to admit your piece wasn't a complete original."

"Oh, she told you?"

"Yeah. What's up with that?"

Claire stared at Tim, trying to decide how to answer. Finally, she said, "More than I care to tell you at this point."

"Okay, uh but as far as Mrs. Hayes goes, I have my own entrance in the back. She wouldn't even have to know you stopped by."

"Have you shown her any of your art and explained how you do it?"

"I have and she's quite impressed."

"Did she make the connection to my painting in high school?"

"No, but I told her that I helped you."

"You admitted it?" Claire wasn't sure if she should be happy or miffed. It's not like it would change anything all these years later. He got what he wanted, and she didn't. "What did she say?"

"She was surprised to hear that you covered for me and told me how the following fall she had to beg you to come back to art class." He stepped closer and took Claire's hands. "I know I'm about five years too late, but I really am sorry."

She squeezed his hands before letting go. "Well, like I said earlier, I'm dating someone. I don't plan on dumping Chase over the notion that you showing up and admitting your part in our past, makes everything all better between us."

"I thought you'd say that, minus the boyfriend of course." Tim kissed her on the cheek. "Good night, Claire."

"Night." She leaned against the door casing and watched him walk away. Then, as if getting a realization, she ran to catch him before he reached the bonfire. "Hey, how long have you been back in town?"

"About six weeks, why?"

"Oh, no reason."

"It was really nice to see you again." Tim's eyes sparkled in the firelight, which made him look more handsome than ever.

"Yeah, uh, thanks for stopping by."

Instead of going back into the house, Claire went home. As she drove up the long, dirt driveway, she couldn't help but wonder if Tim had something to do with her paintings changing. *His style is eerily similar to mine. If he's the one switching them, why's he doing it, and how do I find out?*

With these thoughts whirling in her head and getting nowhere, she decided to call Chase. "Hey, um, you got a minute?"

"Sure, but what's wrong?"

"Is it that obvious?"

"Kind of. Plus, I didn't expect to hear from you again today."

"Yeah, well, I didn't expect to see Tim."

"You mean ex-boyfriend, Tim?"

"Uh-huh. He showed up at my parents' house a few hours ago. I happened to still be there."

"It's no big deal, right? He dumped you a long time ago and it's over. I assume that hasn't changed or, has it?" Chase suddenly sounded worried.

"Nothing's changed, but I admit it was nice to see him again." Claire hesitated. "It's just, well, you and me . . . we're so close to the beginning of something wonderful that I thought if I heard your voice, you'd be the last thing on my mind when I fall asleep."

"Do I need to call you at 5:30 tomorrow morning to ensure that I'll be the first thing on your mind when you wake?"

"Maybe." Claire let out a little laugh. "You see, this is why I called you. Instead of getting all offended or jealous, you remain as charming as you were the day you opened the gate."

"Charming is my middle name, remember? But seriously, do you still have feelings for this guy or is there more to it?"

"He showed me some photos of his artwork. They were quite impressive . . . and a reminder that I didn't get into the same great art school. That hurts a lot, you know."

"I guess I'll have to come see some of Tim's art because I don't see how it could hold a candle to yours."

"Biased much?" Claire laughed again. "I told him that if I came to see his actual artwork, you'd be with me."

"See, there, it's all solved. Sweet dreams, Claire. 5:30 will be here before we know it."

Chapter 18

HELEN

With Chase still on her mind, Claire remembered the photo she took of him walking out of the barn the first night they met. She found it on her phone and sent it to the printer.

It didn't take her long to sketch the details she wanted and get the drawing transferred to her watercolor paper. Before going to bed, she washed in the background colors and was so excited about how it was turning out that she decided to start adding some details. Absorbed with thoughts of Chase, the chirp of her phone interrupted her musings.

Before looking to see who the text was from, she laid in the paint that was already on her brush. When finished, she plopped it into a jar of water and picked up her phone. Trevor had sent a selfie of everyone that was at the bonfire. The text said: 'Hey, Sis, look what you're missing.'

She stretched the photo to see who all was there before replying. 'Looks like you're having fun. Why's Tim not in the picture?'

'Oh, he left shortly after you did.'

'Did he say why?'

'Nope, I guess he just came to see you. Why'd you have to go and scare him off?'

'I said I didn't want to see him. You shouldn't have told him I was inside.'

'Fair enough. See you in the morning.'
''

❖ ❖ ❖

The ringing of Claire's phone woke her from a sound sleep. One glance at the time told her who was on the other end of the line. "Hi, Chase."

"Good morning, Sunshine."

"Seriously?"

"Hey, I don't want you forgetting about me or thinking of some other dude."

Claire could picture the smirk plastered across his scruffy face and laughed. "You're too much, you know?"

"I trust that's a good thing?"

"It is." She let her head fall back on the pillow before adding, "But I guess I should have mentioned last night that I didn't need to be up before 6:30 today."

"Ha, that would've been good to know. But since you're awake, when can I see you again?"

"Probably not until after this weekend's festival. I've got a lot to get done before then."

"I could come your way if that helps."

"It's my turn to come yours."

"Who's keeping track of that? And anyway, I liked being at your place and around your family. It's refreshing."

"Sweet. And I could introduce you to Tim."

"So you're still thinking about some other dude. I guess this call *didn't* accomplish its purpose."

"Actually, it did. I was thinking it would be fun to hang on your arm. You know, show off my hot and charming guy."

"Oh, so now you're using me."

Claire cringed but was relieved when she heard him laugh. Yes, she'd be *using* him, but it was the only way to see Tim's artwork without leading him on. "You have no reason to worry, Chase, and thanks for calling. It was nice to wake to the sound of your voice."

Instead of trying to go back to sleep, Claire got up and went to see her mom before work. She found her at the kitchen table reading her Bible.

"Oh, hi, Claire. What brings you here so early?"

"I was hoping we could talk. There's more to my story that I didn't want to mention in front of Dad, but it's something you should know before the festival."

Concern creased her brow. "Um, okay, have a seat." She left the table and filled two mugs with the freshly brewed coffee.

Claire sat, swung her legs over the bench, and weaved her fingers together in front of her.

Neither spoke until Helen returned with the two mugs. Claire took the one handed to her and said, "Thanks."

"I enjoyed hearing about how you met Chase."

"So you weren't mad that I brought up the painting, then?"

"A little at first, but because Chase is real, I didn't want to spoil the moment."

Claire looked at her mom with pleading eyes. "You must know this painting dilemma hasn't been easy for me either, right?"

Helen nodded. "Last night after the bonfire, I had a talk with Trevor. He explained why he trusts you."

Aww, my little brother came to my defense. To hide her smile, Claire took a sip of coffee. From over the rim, she could see that her mom wanted to believe. It was etched in the lines of her face, like a cracked vase trying to hold water. "Has his account helped or made things worse?"

"Well, none of this is naturally possible, but all things are possible with God. For now, I'm giving you both the benefit of the doubt."

Claire reached across the table to squeeze her hand. "Thanks, Mom. You have no idea what a relief this is."

"Oh, but I think I do." A faint smile tugged at her lips.

With renewed hope, Claire grabbed her phone and came to sit next to her mother. She opened the picture app and said, "Look. This is the picture I used for my latest painting."

"I've always liked this one, I can't wait to see it finished."

"Except that's going to be a problem."

Helen tipped her head to look at Claire. "Not again."

"Don't get ahead of me." Claire scrolled to the picture she took of the watercolor paper with the drawing done and the painting started. "I got this far before it changed."

"To what?"

Claire scrolled to the next picture. "To this."

"What a cute little thing." Helen took the phone to get a better look at the blond-haired girl and her horse. "Do you know who she is?"

"Not a clue. After the first painting changed, I started taking pictures at every interval. I wanted to have proof if it happened again."

Helen frowned. "I really am trying to believe you, but these pictures don't prove anything. You could have both these paintings done for all I know."

Claire's shoulders sagged. "So much for giving me the benefit of the doubt."

Without warning, Helen burst into a hearty laugh.

"What's so funny?"

"Trevor already told me about this painting."

"Why are you ribbing me then?"

"Mostly because I wanted to see your reaction."

The transformation of her mother caused Claire to smile. "Ah, now I know where Trev and I got our sense of humor."

"Don't be fooled, my dear, laughter is a front," Helen patted her chest, "because frankly, this freaks me out."

"Yeah, well, it's not exactly something you get used to." Claire took her phone. "This painting changed before I finished Maggie's portrait, so I brought it with me to show her."

"Did she recognize the little girl?"

"No. Chase was there too, but he had never seen the girl either. When they started asking questions, I changed the subject."

"Does this mean you never mentioned to them how the painting of the boys miraculously evolved?"

"What would be the point? It's not like they would believe me any more than you did."

Helen narrowed her eyes, pursed her lips, and nodded thoughtfully.

"Hey, Mom, I meant no offense. I just don't see why they need to know. At least not yet."

"I suppose, for now, it's more important to find out who this girl is."

"Right, so I guess I'll try to sell the painting at our booth this weekend and see what happens."

Helen held up a finger. "I don't think that's a good idea. What if someone buys it because they think it's a cute piece of art, not because they recognize the girl?"

"Oh, I didn't think of that."

"Maybe you should use it as a sample for commission portraits and not have it for sale," Helen suggested.

"I could do that. Does this mean you're on board?"

Helen let out a nervous laugh. "I guess I am."

Claire finished her coffee and then gave her mom a big hug before heading to work. She found Trevor in the outdoor corral. "Morning, Trev, need a hand?"

"How about two?" He removed his hat and wiped sweat from his forehead. "This horse is as stubborn as an old mule and jittery as Grandma Patterson."

"I'm sure it can't be that bad." Claire climbed over the wood fence, grabbed another lead rope off a hook, and added it to the other side of the bridle. Then she went to put her face between the horse's eyes, as she had done with Chicory, but the two-year-old quarter horse jerked its head back and started pulling against the ropes. "Whoa, girl."

"See? She's a feisty one." Trevor tightened his grip.

Claire pulled a sugar cube from her vest pocket and, with eyes locked, she held it out for the horse. "You're okay, girl." The horse bobbed its head a few times before licking the cube off her glove. In one smooth motion, Claire had her hand on the horse's nose, caressing it and moving closer. "Now there, how about you show us what you're made of."

Trevor loosened his rope and let Claire take the lead. After a bit, he said, "You really are a horse whisperer, and here I thought that was a hoax."

"Who are you kidding, I bribed her with sugar." She laughed.

"No, it's more than that. I tend to get frustrated, making the horse tense and even more aggressive, but you have the power to calm even the strongest of wills."

"Okay, Trev, what's with all the flattery?"

"What?" He threw his hands into the air while still holding the rope. This caused the horse to rear.

"Whoa, girl." Claire grabbed the bridle and slipped her another sugar cube. "If you're going to be a show horse, you'll have to get used to sudden movements."

"See what I mean?" He loosened his rope so she could remove hers. "And it's not flattery. I wasn't getting anywhere with this horse before you came."

"Thanks. I'm glad I could help." Claire grabbed her water bottle and climbed onto the fence. Trevor did the same and after they both got a drink, she said, "I stopped to see Mom this morning and found out I owe you big time."

"Not really. When I came in last night, she was waiting for me in the kitchen and asked me why I believed your story. The easiest way to get her attention was to show her the two pictures of Sophie holding her sketch, the one with the waterfall and the one with the boys. She knew we couldn't stage that, especially when the time and date on the photos were exactly the same."

"Ah, I hadn't thought of that. Way to go."

"I haven't told you this yet, but that's when I started to believe. I figured it was worth seeing where this goes."

"Now that you mentioned not being able to stage Sophie's pictures, it shoots a hole in my theory that Tim could somehow be involved."

Trevor shifted his weight on the fence and looked at her with narrowed eyes. "What does Tim have to do with anything?"

"He showed me some photos of his art last night. Our styles are almost identical."

"So?"

"The technique he uses could make it possible that he switched out the paintings."

"That sounds more farfetched than a *miracle*. Even if Tim did the paintings and somehow switched them out, I don't see how he could've gotten Maggie to come to your booth without putting her up to it. Then there's the painting of the girl; you said she doesn't have anything to do with Maggie or Chase. The plot seems too extensive for him to pull off."

"Maybe he has help."

"Yeah, but why would he, or they, even bother to attempt such an elaborate scheme? Sophie's drawings prove he couldn't be the one doing it. And anyway, I don't see how any of this benefits him, especially now that you've met Chase because of it. And besides, he always seemed too self-absorbed to me."

"My perceptive little brother strikes again." Claire smacked him on the back. "I guess I hadn't convinced myself of the probability of a 'miracle' yet."

"If everything happened the way you say, it has to be miraculous. I think it'd be better to focus your energies on *why*, not on *who* or *how*."

"You're probably right. Hopefully this weekend I'll learn more." She took another drink before adding, "Thanks, Trev. I'm thankful this is no longer a stress point between us."

"Me too. And it's been nice working with you now that we're not at odds because of the paintings." He jumped off the fence and grabbed a rope. "Do you mind helping for a bit longer? I need to get this horse following at least some basic commands."

"Sure."

The rest of the week passed without incident. Claire got the painting of Chase done in time to have prints made, along with the one of the Native American girl. With no new messages, she assumed she'd just have to wait and see if anyone recognized the little girl with the horse.

Chapter 19

THE PILFERED IMAGE

Since the Beartrap Summer Festival was a weekend event in Casper that focused on music, not rodeos and horses, Paul didn't come. Trevor, on the other hand, enjoyed the festival and came with them.

Claire had made a sign that said, *Sample ~ Ask Claire About Commissions* and mounted it above the painting of the little girl. She also added a small tray at the bottom of the easel, just big enough to hold a stack of her business cards.

Once all the art and supplies were brought into the tent, Trevor said, "If you don't need anything else, I'll move the truck and get the camper set up."

Helen took a quick look around. "I think we're all set. Thanks for taking care of the camper."

"Not a problem." He gave her a kiss on the cheek and said, "I'm hanging out with Lynn today, but if either of you needs anything, text."

"Be sure you stop by. I'd like to meet her," Helen said.

"I don't think we're serious enough to *meet the parents* yet, but we'll see."

"Or you could just stop to say hello," Claire nudged. "I bet she'd like to see my new paintings."

"No pressure, right?" He swung the keys around his index finger and left the booth.

"Enjoy the festival," Claire called after him. "I'll join you for the night concerts."

"Sounds good."

As soon as Trever was out of earshot, Helen asked, "Why's he so worried about introducing Lynn to me?"

Claire shrugged. "This is only their second date. I'm sure if it turns into something, you'll be the first to know."

"Okay then, it looks like we need to get to work." Helen waved a hand toward the two women who had come into their booth.

The crowds ebbed and flowed depending upon who was performing at the time, though business never came to a complete halt.

Helen had just finished taking payment from another customer when she said, "I guess it was a good thing that you got prints made of Chase's backside." She raised her eyebrows a few times and then busted out laughing.

"I like his face better," Claire smirked. "But hey, I'll take it. I think I sold nine or ten of them already."

"Has anyone asked about the painting with the girl?"

"Not yet. I did get a few commission jobs though."

"Oh, nice." Helen looked at her watch. "And it's only 2:30, which leaves lots of time for someone to still recognize her."

Claire sighed. "I hope so, Mama. Waiting is the worst part of not knowing, especially when I have no idea what to expect."

"Why don't you try to think about something else? There's no sense in stressing over things you can't control."

"If only it were that easy. My stomach has been in knots all day."

"How about we take a break. I think we've earned it." Lawn chairs were already set up near the back of the booth. Helen grabbed two bottles of iced tea from the cooler and held one toward Claire.

"Just set it on the table; I'll be right there." She put out a few more card sets and was on her way to join her mother when a young couple stopped in front of their booth.

"Hey, babe, look at this," a pregnant woman said, pointing at the easel.

The little girl, who held the man's hand, immediately let go and ran forward. "Mommy, Mommy, it's my horse."

The woman laughed. "It does look like your horse, sweetie, and see the little girl?"

"Is dat me, Mommy, is it?"

"It could be. She looks a lot like you, too."

She clasped her hands together and started jumping up and down while squealing, "I'm famous. I'm famous."

Claire smiled at the girl's exuberance and squatted next to her. "How are you famous?"

"Look, I'm in dat picture." She pointed and then unexpectedly gave Claire a hug.

Claire reciprocated and then stood to face her parents. "Do you like the painting?"

The man didn't seem as excited as his little girl. "Are you the artist?"

"Yes." Claire decided not to say more until she knew how things would go.

"How did you do this painting of Zoe and her horse?"

The question threw Claire off. Even though the girl *miraculously* showed up, she had used a picture of one of the horses on their farm. "I made the painting up. I wasn't trying to make the girl look like anyone in particular."

"That's quite remarkable then," the man said dryly before turning to his wife. "Don't we have a picture that looks similar to this?"

"We do, I posted it on Instagram."

Claire cringed. She wasn't prepared for it to look like a picture that was already taken and on social media. Especially after Chase said that he and his brothers had never even posed like they were in her painting.

The woman reached into her purse and got out her phone. After scrolling through the photos for a few seconds, she stopped and handed the phone to Claire. On the screen was a picture of

Zoe with her horse. Though the background was different, everything else in her painting looked the same.

Helen came to look.

"It's so exact; you must have used our picture," the woman said.

"I see how you could think that, but I've never seen this picture before."

The woman rested her hands on her protruding stomach. "It's not like we're going to report you to the police or something. Once it's on the web I guess it's fair game. I just don't see why you won't admit it."

"Or why you didn't at least change it up some," the man said. "Especially if you were trying to keep the girl anonymous."

Claire was at a loss. She'd never seen the picture before, but they weren't going to be convinced otherwise, and why should they be? The woman held proof in her hand. Now Claire's integrity was called into question for the second time, she couldn't afford another strike against her.

Zoe started pulling on her mom's leg. "Mommy, can I take it home?"

Helen bent down. "Zoe, how old are you?"

"I'm tree," She said proudly as she held up three fingers.

Helen laughed. "And a smart three at that."

"Well, that'd be because she's almost four, though we do need to work on some of her sounds," the mom said.

"That will come, soon enough." Helen stood to face her. "When are you due?"

"The middle of September."

Claire appreciated her mom's intervention, which momentarily diverted everyone's attention away from the alleged indictment regarding the photo.

Thankfully, the man got distracted by the painting on the other easel. "This is a sweet painting. Did you steal this one too, or do you know the guy?"

Claire knew better than to be miffed at that comment and happily answered, "I know him. His name is Chase."

In the meantime, Helen had asked the mom if she could give Zoe a cookie. She agreed and the three of them walked to the back of the booth.

"There's no mistaking your ability, I'm impressed." He turned back to the painting of Zoe. "Now, your sign says the painting of my little girl is not for sale. I say you give me a good price for it, and I'll take it off your hands."

Claire started to protest, but he held up a finger. "Zoe wants it, and I'll be sure this ends the discussion about you using our picture without permission."

Claire looked back at the man's wife, who was now sitting with Zoe on her lap. She was engaged in a conversation with Helen. "I can do that, but can you do me a favor?"

"I'm not sure you're in a position to get a favor but shoot."

"Can I take a picture of Zoe standing next to the painting?"

The man rubbed his hands together. "I'm pretty sure that will make my wife upset and reopen the conversation."

"But I didn't steal that picture."

"Look, I don't know why you won't come clean about the painting," he leaned closer and whispered, "but it's better to avoid conflict with my wife when she's pregnant."

Claire smiled at the warning. "Maybe you could ask Zoe. It'll make her day, as she's famous now, you know."

"But why do you want a picture of her?"

"For two reasons: one, so that I have a sample of how accurate my work is and two, she's such a cutie."

They agreed on a price and he brought the painting into the booth. "Hey Zoe, look what Daddy got for you."

She jumped off her mom's lap and hugged the painting.

"Careful sweetie, you don't want to bend it. Can you hold it like this?" He turned the painting toward Claire and knelt to help Zoe hold it. "We're going to get our picture taken. Smile."

Claire grabbed her phone and snapped a few photos before the mom could protest. "Thanks." Then she motioned to the table. "Here, let me wrap that up for you."

Five minutes later, without another word about the pilfered image, they were gone.

With trembling hands, Claire opened the bottle of tea that had been left on the table and took a big swig before flopping into the chair closest to her. "Wow, Mom, thanks for coming to my rescue. All I could think of was standing in front of the judges at the Art Symposium without a clue of how to answer. I really never saw that picture before."

"I believe you, and anyway, it wasn't rocket science to notice you needed help. I'm glad my distraction worked."

"And I'm glad that guy played along, too. I mean seriously, what made him randomly ask about the other painting?" Claire asked.

"It sounded more like he was quick on his toes in asking for a deal," Helen said.

"Maybe, but I would've gladly given it to him simply to change the subject."

"On a different note, Zoe is adorable, and her excitement was priceless."

"She's a sweetie for sure, but before we get too far off topic, do you have any ideas as to why she showed up in my painting?"

"Not a clue." Helen unhooked a painting from the back panel and moved it to the empty easel out front.

I must be missing something. Claire pulled out her phone and opened Instagram. "Mom, did you happen to get the names of Zoe's parents? The guy paid with cash, and I didn't think to ask."

Helen took a seat next to Claire. "The woman's name is Emma. She didn't give a last. Why?"

"I wanted to see if I could find her Instagram account; maybe learn something about them. Maggie had a story. Why would this painting change if there's no story?" Claire did a search but couldn't find anyone who looked like Emma. "Nothing."

"Nothing yet." Helen patted her knee. "I thought it was clever that you got a picture of them. If another painting changes, it could have something to do with why Zoe showed up."

Claire's eyes darted from her phone to her mother. "Wait, so now you think more paintings will change? I thought that whole exchange would've made you doubt me again."

"I don't see why?"

"If I could've found that picture online, why would you need to believe my story that she *just* appeared?"

"Do you remember the quote that was on our church sign last week?" Helen asked.

"You mean the one that said, 'Faith involves risk?'"

"Yes. You've risked your integrity and family relations over this. I think it's safe to say there's more than a practical joke going on here." Helen brightened. "I'm so proud of the way you handled yourself earlier."

Claire leaned over to give her mom a hug. "Thank you."

"What's with the hug fest?" Trevor asked as he walked into the tent.

"We have an amazing mom, that's what," Claire said.

"Well, of course, but . . . wait, did you sell the painting?"

Chapter 20

A NEW NOTE

Claire sold most of her originals at the festival, so as soon as she got home and had everything put away, she went to the loft and got out a shoebox filled with photos. Bringing it to the leather futon, she stuffed a pillow under one arm, crossed her legs, and started looking through them.

It wasn't long before she found a picture of an old barn with a 1958 Chevy pickup truck parked in front of it. She had taken that photo a few years ago while driving around the countryside looking for interesting things to paint.

Oh wow, this is great. I'm not sure why I haven't used it yet.

She set the box on the futon and came to her desk. That's when she saw a piece of watercolor paper leaning against her jar of paintbrushes. Like clockwork, she felt the brush tips to see if any of them were wet. None were. Her paints didn't look like they'd been touched, either. She picked up the note and read the message. `Love gained, love lost . . . calamity makes or breaks a man . . . and yet, sometimes it's both.`

"What in the world is that supposed to mean?" After reading it a few more times, she pinned it to a corkboard mounted on the wall next to her desk. The first painted note was already on the same board, along with photos of the two paintings that had changed and the picture of Sophie holding her drawing of the boys with the message at the bottom of it.

Claire took a step back and rested her hands on her hips. Several minutes passed as she pondered the significance of each note. The newest message seemed more personal . . . yet not necessarily personal to her . . . or was it?

A quick shake of the head didn't remove the concern that had suddenly clouded her mind, so she turned her attention back to the photo on her desk. "Do you have a part to play in this mystery?" She realized that not every painting had to change, but with a new message, it was certainly plausible. Not wanting to waste any more time thinking about things she couldn't control, she got out her sketch pad and roughed in the barn and truck. By the time she got it transferred, she wasn't in the mood to start painting. It'd been a long weekend and her bed seemed to be calling her name.

The next morning, Claire woke before her alarm, so she crawled out of bed and made her way to the loft. From the stairs, she could see the watercolor paper was just the way she'd left it. The painting was not miraculously half done.

"Huh, that's what I get for wishful thinking. Guess I should've stayed up and worked on this longer last night, but then why spend my time painting if it's going to change?"

Then it hit her like a splash of cold water. *What if 'love gained, love lost,' has to do with Chase and me?* She shivered at the thought but chose not to dwell on the possibility and went to make a pot of coffee.

With mug in hand, she headed out the back door, unable to shake the chill that had lingered at the thought of losing Chase. She grabbed her phone out of her back pocket and gave him a call. When he didn't answer, she listened to a saved voicemail of his, which was enough to warm her heart and bring peace to her mind.

Then on an impulse, Claire went back into the house, hurried to the loft, and grabbed the pencil off her desk. She couldn't find a piece of paper, so she ripped one out of the back of her journal and wrote:

`'If your goal is to scare me, it's not working. If this is a joke or a threat, it's not funny. If there's more for me to pursue, then please, show me what's next.'`

She reread the words. "Ugh, this is stupid." With a huff, she threw the note into the trashcan and left the loft.

Claire was tired and dirty after a busy morning at the barns, so she took a shower and threw in a load of laundry before heading to the loft. This time paint filled her watercolor paper. Her heart skipped a beat as she scrambled up the last few steps and ran to her desk. The paper she had thrown out that morning was unwrinkled and sitting next to her brushes.

She covered her mouth as she looked again at the painting and then back to the note. At the bottom of what she had written were these words:

`'Here's what's next.'`

The old barn had changed to a small log cabin with a porch that ran its length. To the left of the door was a stack of firewood, to the right, a solitary rocking chair and a table with one book on it. This was the first painting that had changed that didn't have people in it, yet smoke billowed from the chimney, which hinted at life within. The other major difference was that the '58 Chevy was now in mint condition and had a Vietnam War vet sticker on the back window. A driveway was sketched in, and the distant hills behind the barn had been replaced by pine trees.

Interesting. I wonder what kind of story will go with it.

Claire looked at the painting for a while before wetting a brush. She started filling in the trees but kept the details loose to make sure they didn't draw attention away from the cabin. With a wider brush, she laid in the hint of the driveway and was adding the final touches when she heard the sound of a vehicle.

Claire rushed to the window to see who was coming. The sight of a steel-blue pickup made her heart leap. *Chase.* She rinsed her brush, and then went outside to wait for him. He parked behind her SUV, where she went to join him. "What a fun surprise."

"I was hoping so." He jumped out of his truck and wrapped her in his arms. "I've missed you and talking on the phone just isn't the same."

Claire gave him a kiss. "I couldn't agree more! Are you hungry?"

"Starving."

"Great, because I haven't eaten yet, either."

"Are there any good restaurants close?" He looked over her shoulder toward the cabin.

"Ha, nothing's close! You should probably know up front that I'm not much of a cook. There are a few nice places in town, though. Let me grab a jacket, and I'll be ready to go."

Before they reached the main road, Chase said, "Maybe after we eat, I could take you to see Tim's artwork."

Claire tensed at hearing Tim's name. Her talk with Trevor a few weeks ago cleared up any suspicions that Tim could possibly have anything to do with changes to the paintings and the mysterious notes. They were the only reason she wanted to go see him in the first place. She slid across the seat and nudged his shoulder. "I thought you came to see me?"

"I did, but I thought you wanted to see this guy's art, and if it's important to you, then it's important to me."

"That's very considerate, Chase, but I've changed my mind. I'd rather we keep our focus on us."

"I like the sounds of that, but what made you change your mind? Is this about more than his art?"

"For me, it's only about the art, but then I realized to see Tim's art, I'd have to be in the same room with him and even though you'd be with me, he'd assume I was leaving the door open for if things don't work out with us. I don't want to play to his ego or give him a reason to keep in touch."

"On that note, I won't mention Tim or his art ever again." Chase squeezed her hand and smiled.

Claire leaned forward and tipped her head so she could look him in the eyes. "The fact that you were willing to do something you didn't want to do just to make me feel comfortable, means so much to me."

"Thanks! I quit trying to earn my parents love a long time ago, and I think it's made me selfish. A trait I'm not proud of but being able to care about someone who appreciates my efforts helps me realize I haven't become a total loser."

"Oh, Chase, you're not a loser." Claire sat back and leaned against his shoulder. "These admissions do make me sad though."

"Why?"

"Because the scars of your past cover more of your heart than I realized."

"On a positive note, though, you have the ability to bring out the best in me and I like what I see."

"I do too."

Claire was busy the next two weeks getting things ready for their last event of the summer. She didn't have enough original paintings left to go to the week-long State Fair, so Helen suggested they give the festival in Thermopolis a try. Claire agreed because she didn't know of any other way to get the painting of the cabin out where it could be seen.

The guys helped Claire and Helen load up the truck the night before, and they were on the road by 5:00 a.m.

Close to an hour passed before Claire mentioned that another painting had changed.

"So it actually happened again. What showed up this time?" Helen asked. She listened in silence and gave only an occasional nod as Claire explained. "I'll do what I can to run interference again if it's necessary."

"Thanks, but I'm hoping there'll be another story. Here." Claire pushed the manila envelope that was on the seat toward her mother. "Open that."

Helen pulled out the piece of watercolor paper and ran her fingers over the painted words. "What's this?"

"A message that was left on my desk the day before the painting changed."

"'Love gained, love lost, calamity makes or breaks a man, and yet, sometimes it's both.' This certainly sounds interesting. I just wish we knew why it's happening."

"Yeah, I can't help but wonder if we missed something with Zoe and her parents. Every day since this note showed up and especially after the latest painting changed, I've been praying for direction. That we wouldn't get distracted by a barrage of questions about the *how* and keep our focus on the *why*."

"I wish you would've told me sooner." Helen tucked the note back into the envelope. "I could have been praying too."

"Sorry, I didn't think of that."

Once they had their booth up and their merchandise set out, Helen started opening the sampler jars of jam. Claire finished the final touches by putting an easel on each side of the entrance. On the left, she placed her new painting of the Bighorn Mountains, and to the right, the painting of the cabin.

Business was good right from the start, better than either of them expected.

By mid-afternoon, Claire had sold all but two of her originals. The painting of the cabin was still out front, but the other easel was now empty. Instead of moving the last original, she fished through the prints and set her favorite on it. Then she rearranged the panel in the back of their booth and used more prints to fill in the empty spots. "There, that should help draw people inside. Good thing I have a bunch of prints and card sets left."

"Actually, there are only a few card sets." Helen held up the last handful before she set them on the table. "I think it's wonderful that you're doing so well."

Suddenly, the delight in Claire's voice dissipated. "Except we still have the only piece of art that I truly care about. Not one person has even asked about the cabin, let alone offered to buy it."

Helen walked to the front of the booth and looked both ways before saying, "I wouldn't lose heart. Lots of people are still in the park. Oh, and here comes a couple now."

Chapter 21

THE PICTURE

The man and his wife appeared to be in their early forties. The woman came in and looked around for a moment before walking to the stand of candles. She picked one up, read the label, and then lifted it to her nose. Helen joined her, and they immediately struck up a conversation about the process of candle making.

The man, on the other hand, stayed out front and stared at the painting of the cabin. He straightened his glasses and leaned in to get a better look.

A mixture of excitement and fear made Claire's heart race. She took a deep breath and exhaled slowly before joining him. "Hello."

He stepped back. "Uh, hi. Who did the artwork?"

"I did." She reached to shake his hand. "My name's Claire."

"I'm Luke. Your paintings are fantastic."

"Thanks. Others must agree with you because I only have two originals left. There are a wide variety of prints available inside." Claire pointed. When he didn't look, she added, "Are you interested in purchasing this one?"

"Actually, I'm confused." He started to rub his chin. "How do you know old man Wagner?" He pointed to the empty rocking chair.

Claire turned an ear toward him. "Old man who?"

"Frederick Wagner. People call him Freddie. You couldn't have done this painting without knowing him."

"Um . . ." She dropped her gaze and stepped back. "Hey, Mom, do you know a Frederick Wagner?" She hoped this diversion would give her enough time to figure out an answer.

Helen joined them. "No, why do you ask?"

"Because this is his place," Luke said. "Only a handful of people even know where it is; so I don't see how you would've gotten to take pictures without his permission."

Claire decided on the truth, leaving out the part about how some of the details added themselves. "Fated fortune, I guess, because I combined a few photos of mine and improvised on the rest."

"That seems highly unlikely; this looks exactly as I remember it."

Claire deflected by asking, "Where does this Mr. Wagner live, and how do you know him?"

He took the bait. "It's kind of a long story."

His wife had already come to join them. "Oh Luke, I haven't heard this story in years and it's not like we need to be somewhere else."

"But Brenda, these ladies are trying to work."

"You've already peaked our interest," Claire said with a grin. "So I guess you'll *have* to tell us now."

"Yes, and we can work around you if necessary," Helen added eagerly. She gave Claire a nod as she pulled up a chair.

"All right, but to understand the situation, I need to give a bit of the backstory. Mr. Wagner lived about thirty miles from town. I mean it was out in the middle of nowhere. Rumor had it that before he was drafted into the Army in 1970, he was quite the cowboy—strong, good-looking, and he even had a beautiful girlfriend. They got married just before he left for Vietnam, where he spent three years as a medic.

"One day, near the end of the war, Freddie was traveling with a small convoy when the vehicle in front of his hit an IED. It blew up and killed everyone inside. Debris and fire from the blast hit the truck Freddie was in, killing the driver and the other man in the front. It's a miracle that Freddie and the rest of the guys lived. Months passed before he got out of a hospital in Japan and was able to make the trip back to the States. When his wife saw him, she couldn't bear to look at him and told him it was over."

Helen's eyes had widened when Luke mentioned the explosion, but now she looked downright distraught at the wife's reaction. "Oh, my, that was heartless."

"Yes, ma'am, but not unexpected. It's not like they had social media or a way to keep in touch, and she was young. The realities of war take their toll. This was just another cruel blow for Freddie. He was one messed up guy. Anyway, his parents gave him a piece of land, and they, along with his younger brother, helped him build a small cabin."

"Where he could basically hide from society?" Helen asked.

"That's it in a nutshell. At first, his mom did his shopping for him, but after a few years, she realized this wasn't helping him get better."

Claire leaned against the front of the table and started twirling her necklace around her finger. "If Mr. Wagner was such a recluse, how do you know him?"

"Good question. When I was fifteen, my family moved to the town where he did his shopping. Because I was new and gullible, a few of the *cool kids* tricked me into a dare. If I did what they said, I could be a part of their group."

Just then a boy and his mom came into the booth, so Helen got up and went to help them.

"Actually," the woman said, "if you don't mind, my son and I would like to hear the rest of this man's story." She tapped her son's shoulder. "Thad is only eight, but he loves to read, and his dad is always telling him about some far-away adventure." She looked at Luke. "He heard you talking and pulled me in here."

"Claire, we're blocking the entrance to your booth." Luke swung a hand toward the midway. "Do you want us to move?"

"I'd like to keep listening, so please stay." She didn't mind the growing crowd, she just hoped there wouldn't be too many more delays.

"Now, where was I?"

"The dare," Thad yelled.

Everyone laughed.

"Right, the dare," Luke said, giving the boy a high five, which he enthusiastically returned. "Over the years, people forgot about the war and the sacrifice Mr. Wagner made for his country and only saw his scars and his deformed face. The women would gossip about his odd behavior. Children would hide behind their parents. Teenagers would call him names. Anyway, these guys thought it would be hilarious to make me go get pictures of his property. I didn't know these details when I was given the dare; all I cared about was fitting in."

"Is that your picture?" Thad asked, pointing at the painting.

"Son, if you'd quit interrupting, he'd tell us," the woman said.

"No, that's not my picture. I never got a picture."

"Why not, were you scared?"

"Thad!"

"It's okay, ma'am." Luke held out his hand to stop her correction. "And yes, Thad, I was really scared. So were the boys who gave me the challenge, though I didn't know that at the time. I talked my younger brother into coming with me. He was the one who noticed the driveway followed along a small stream with deep banks and suggested we walk up the creek bed so we could get closer without being seen. I parked the car and we started following the stream for about half a mile before we saw smoke and knew we were getting close. With some effort, we made our way to the top of the ravine and cut through the woods. To our dismay, Mr. Wagner had a dog that began barking and pulling on his chain. My brother begged me to leave but a few more steps and I would've had a clear view of the cabin. We had come this far; I wasn't about to leave without my picture.

"Freddie the freak, as the boys in town liked to call him had different plans. Bam . . . bam," Luke said rather forcefully.

Thad jumped and grabbed his mother's waist.

"I never got another step closer."

"Hey, Luke, that wasn't funny," his wife scolded. "You frightened the poor boy."

"How do you think I felt?"

"Scared?" Thad asked in a small voice, still clutching his mom's shirt.

"Terrified! My brother and I both hit the ground and covered our heads."

"Did you get shot? Is your brother okay?"

"The bullets whistled over our heads to the left and to the right. He wasn't trying to hit us; he was just running us off his property. It worked. We scrambled to our feet and ran as fast as we could away from the cabin. We must have looked like scared rabbits. I wasn't paying attention to what was in front of me, and my foot got caught in a tangle of rusty barbwire. I twisted my ankle and fell hard. My camera went flying, but instead of trying to find it, I worked my foot free, got to my feet, and ran. I could hear him yelling, 'Can't you read? This is private property.' He shot three more times, always hitting something close to where we were, but far enough away so as to not hit us."

"I'm glad you lived." Thad let go of his mother and smiled.

"Me too! But because of the wire, I also tore my jeans and cut my leg. There was no keeping this adventure from my mom. I had two choices: I could make something up and go back to find her camera or tell her the truth."

"I hope you chose the truth," Helen interjected. "Between the dog and the crazy man with a gun, going back alone wasn't going to be very plausible, was it?"

"No, ma'am." Luke gave her a knowing look and turned back to Thad. "I did opt for the truth, in hopes that I could 'work off' the cost of the camera."

"And what about the dare? Did those popular guys rib you and call you chicken?" Claire asked.

"Yeah, they showed no mercy. I decided if that's the way it was going to be, I didn't need to be friends with them. Anyway, I finally got up the nerve to tell my mom what had happened. As soon as I mentioned the gunshots, she got my dad involved. At first, he was furious, but then he realized no harm had come to me. Guess what he did, Thad?"

By now, Thad was rolling the bottom of his shirt into a knot. "Gave you a good licking and extra chores?"

"Ha, I wish. Actually, he made me go back to apologize and get the camera . . . all by myself!"

"Seriously?" Helen shook her head in disbelief. "I have three boys but would never have sent any of them back alone."

"I know, right?" Brenda chimed in with wide eyes and a bright smile.

Luke nodded. "It did seem dreadful at the time. My dad told me to drive right up to the cabin and walk confidently to the door. Then he added in his deep voice, 'You'll be fine, son.' I did wait until the next day because, for one, I had to get up the nerve to go alone and for two, I was hoping time would help Mr. Wagner cool off.

"My mom is quite the cook, so she made a pot of beef stew with dumplings for me to take as a peace offering.

"I didn't find out until later that my dad had followed me with a shotgun of his own."

By now, others had gathered around the booth and were listening to the story.

A boy, who looked to be about ten or eleven, with big inquisitive eyes, belted out, "Did he shoot at you again?"

Luke laughed. "No, he didn't shoot at me, but he was sitting in a rocking chair on the porch with his gun on his lap." He pointed to Claire's painting. "Just like this."

"Hey, mister, how'd you do that?" Thad pointed excitedly.

"Do what?"

"Add Mr. Wagner to the painting."

"What do you mean? He's been in the painting the whole time," Luke said without skipping a beat, though he seemed confused as he looked at Claire. She looked as surprised as Thad.

"No, he wasn't."

Thad's mom squeezed his shoulder. "Hush now, it's not polite to argue."

"Claire, what is it? You look like you've seen a ghost."

The man that was now in her painting looked exactly like the man she had seen in her dream. *Luke's story finally makes sense. I need to meet Freddie.*

"Claire?"

"Huh? Oh, uh, it's nothing. Your story is quite captivating. Can you please tell us the rest?" She forced a smile, though her eyes never left the painting.

Helen stared at the painting too, while a murmur reverberated through the crowd.

Luke wanted to press for answers, but for the sake of the two boys, who were now sitting cross-legged in front of him, he continued with his story. "Ahem. When I got out of my truck, Mr. Wagner stood and came to the steps." Luke moved his hand to gesture holding a rifle. "And, yes, he brought his gun with him.

"He called to me, 'What, ya come back for more?'

"His curt words didn't keep me from gawking at him. Before I could answer, he bellowed, 'Just because I'm ugly, that doesn't make me a fool's prey.'

"It was true; the man's features were grossly deformed, and they did make him ugly, but that's not what I was thinking. I was scared and didn't know what to say so I reached into the car to get the stew. I heard him cock his gun, so I yelled, 'Please don't shoot. I've come to apologize for trespassing, sir.'

"When I came forward holding the stew, he said, 'I don't need your charity, boy.'

"For those of you who joined this story late, I was only fifteen at the time. All I wanted to do was jump back into my vehicle and disappear, but I knew I couldn't leave without my mom's camera, so I said, 'I meant you no harm, sir. Do you mind if I go find my camera?'

"By now his tone had softened. 'I'll tell you what,' he says, 'you give me a hand splitting and stacking this pile of firewood, and then we'll see about your camera.'

"Long story, short, I helped him with his firewood. At first, neither of us spoke. I worked as hard and as fast as I could because I wanted to get out of there. After a bit, he offered me some iced tea, and we took a break. Next thing you know, we were talking like old friends. The funny thing was, I was gone for so long that my dad actually came to see what was going on. I introduced him and we helped Mr. Wagner finish stacking the wood."

"Did you find your camera?" the older boy asked.

"Mr. Wagner had already found it for me, and yes, he let me have it back. After that day, I went to visit him a few times a month until I graduated from high school."

"That was quite the story, Luke," Helen said.

"Thank you, Mister, for letting us listen."

"You're welcome, Thad, and boys—if you're ever given a dare that includes trespassing or mocking others because they look different, I hope you'll act like men and not as silly boys the way my brother and I did when we were young."

"Yes, sir," the older boy said, "and we learned we don't have to be afraid of people like Mr. Wagner. I'm glad you're his friend."

Luke smiled and patted both boys on their shoulders. "Me too. Enjoy the rest of your day."

After the others left the booth, Luke and Brenda joined Claire. She was standing in front of the easel gnawing on the back of her index finger.

"Claire, what are you not telling us?" Luke asked.

"You won't believe me if I tell you, so if you don't mind, we need to get back to work."

"But I do mind. I've known Freddie a long time and he never once let me take a picture of him or his place. If you've never been there, how is the painting so perfect?"

Chapter 22

SOMETHING MYSTERIOUS

Claire wanted to leave, to flee the conflict, but it was her booth and there was nowhere to hide. Looking overwhelmed and tired, she said, "As you can see, I'm a painter. What you don't see is my dilemma."

Luke threw his hands up. "What's with all the theatrics? It's a simple question. All I want is a truthful answer."

Just then Claire came to the realization that it didn't matter if the couple believed her. If she wanted to meet Freddie, she'd have to explain and let the chips fall where they may. Finally, she blurted out, "This is the third painting of mine that has changed from what I started with this summer."

"So you made changes. What's the big deal?"

Brenda took Luke's hand. "Hon, I don't think that's what Claire means. Let's hear her out."

Claire gave Brenda a thankful nod and then held up a finger as she went to open her portfolio. "Here, look for yourselves." She held out the photo of the abandoned barn and an old pickup truck. "This is the picture I started with. When I got home from my other job about a week ago, my painting had changed to the cabin."

Luke balked at Claire's explanation. "Yeah, right."

"See, this is exactly what I'm talking about. No one believes me. Can you please leave?"

Helen had come to look at the photo. "I think it's cool how you had to start with something close." Then she turned to face Luke and Brenda. "I just found out another painting changed on our way here this morning. Not that we owe you an explanation, but the first time this happened I didn't believe Claire either. I thought she was teasing me, you know, like a practical joke. I was so mad that she wouldn't admit she was lying that it caused a rift between us for weeks."

"And what? Now you're in cahoots? I don't get why you're treating us like children." Luke barked and started to walk away.

"Hon, wait." Brenda grabbed his arm. "Something mysterious is going on here, and it's obvious they've never met Freddie. Claire's painting couldn't be this accurate without some kind of supernatural help."

"And here's the thing," Helen said, "the changed paintings seem to have a purpose. Claire met people who knew something about the other two paintings, also. None of this can be a coincidence. Even if she did the paintings, how did she get you and the others to come to our booth?"

Claire slumped into a chair and buried her face in her hands.

Helen glanced her way but continued without hesitation. "And there's one more thing, crazier than all the rest. The man in the rocking chair was not in the painting when you started your story."

Brenda felt Luke's arm tense and quickly said, "Honestly, I didn't see Freddie either, until you pointed at the painting."

Claire's head shot up. Helen's eyes widened.

Luke leaned back and glared at Brenda. "But why didn't you say something sooner then?"

"Because you were giving the boys an important life lesson, and I didn't want to ruin the moment. It's such a great story."

"Fine, but you could have said something after they left." Luke pulled his arm out of hers. "So why didn't you?"

Brenda didn't back down. "Because Claire and Helen both looked as shocked as Thad and the rest of the crowd. I wanted to hear their explanation first. You were so adamant about Freddie being in the painting all along that I didn't want to cause a scene."

Luke's expression softened at these words. "But he's been right there the whole time." He pointed to the man in the rocking chair.

"I believe for you he was, but for the rest of us, he abruptly appeared. It doesn't really matter who's right. We *all* see him now."

Claire sat back in the chair and gestured toward the painting. "That means you saw the same thing we did?"

Brenda nodded. "Yes, it was actually quite freaky."

Luke bent closer to get a better look at the painting. "Can someone please explain what's going on? I'm still confused as to how the details are so accurate. Freddie's place is off the beaten path and on private property. It's not likely you would even have known about it, let alone been able to find it."

"But that's the point! I didn't find it. I don't even know where it is." Claire stood, fluffed her hair a few times and gave Luke a tired look. "And I can't explain it because I don't know how the paintings are changing. None of this makes any sense and so far, it's not been worth the headache. I wish it would all stop!"

"Don't say that, sweetie." Helen wrapped an arm around Claire's shoulder. "I'm sure there's a purpose. Just don't quit before you find it."

"Right, like I have any choice in the matter," Claire countered. A small smile touched her lips when her mom laughed and pulled her closer.

"You make a valid point, my dear. And for now, I'd say that's a good thing."

Brenda jumped back into the conversation. "I'm not sure why Luke could see Freddie all along, but maybe having him show up partway through his story was a way for the rest of us to believe."

With a look of pride, mixed with relief, Helen said, "I know it solidified my trust in Claire. So now what?"

"I want to buy the painting," Luke reached for his wallet.

Claire held up a hand. "Um, sorry, but it's no longer for sale."

"Why not?"

She came and stood in front of the painting. "About a month ago, I had a nightmare that was so real I thought I was awake." She explained the dream. "After calling 9-1-1, I carefully lifted the young man's head. Not only was he old, he looked exactly like this." She reached out to touch Freddie's scarred face. "He said to me, 'I knew you'd come.'"

Luke and Brenda both stood there slack jawed and speechless.

Helen moved a hand to cover her lips. "Incredible."

"Because Freddie wasn't in my original changed painting, I didn't think the dream had anything to do with anything. Now, I know I have to go see him, and I'd like to be the one to give him the painting."

"How about you give me your number," Luke said. "I think I should check with him to make sure he doesn't mind."

"That works." Claire grabbed a business card from the table and held it out, but then abruptly pulled it back. "Wait, how do I know you'll call me back? You seem overly protective."

"Though he's not technically a recluse anymore, that doesn't mean he wants strangers invading his privacy."

"Fair enough, but can you give me your number so in case you don't get back to me I can call to find out why?"

"Luke will call you back. I'll make sure of it," Brenda said confidently. "Hey, it would be fun to meet you in town and then drive out to Freddie's place together."

Luke was quick to keep his wife's optimism in check. "Let's make sure Freddie doesn't mind before we start making too many plans."

"Fine." Brenda grabbed a business card off the table and wrote her number on the back. Then she handed it to Claire with a big grin on her face. "Here, to secure our promise."

"Thanks." Claire returned the smile and gave her the card that was still in her hand. "I look forward to hearing from you soon."

"We'll get back to you because I want to see how this plays out," Luke said. "Enjoy the rest of your day." He took Brenda's hand and they left the booth.

"That was certainly eventful," Claire said.

"Yes, it was, especially after the painting of the little girl seemed rather pointless."

"Exactly. This sounded more like the story that Maggie told Trevor and me about the boys."

"And look, we have new customers," Helen said. "Even that was amazing how we didn't get interrupted during Luke's story or while we hashed things out."

While her mom went to assist the ladies, Claire took the painting of the cabin off the easel and brought it to the back of the booth. *No way.* Freddie had disappeared. Not wanting to cause a fresh scene, Claire set the painting behind the table and found a print to put in its place.

When the booth was empty again, Claire said, "Mom, you need to come see this." She picked up the painting and pointed to the rocking chair.

"Oh, my. This leads me to wonder if Freddie was ever in the painting or was he simply a figment of our imaginations."

Claire shrugged. "I suppose we'll never know, but now you can see why I was so freaked out the first night when the boys showed up. I assumed you wouldn't be able to see them, and my struggle would be over. When you could see them, I was at a loss."

Helen came around the end of the table and gave Claire a hug. When they parted, she said, "I know it took a while for me to come around, but I hope you know I'm here for you now."

"I do, and I'm incredibly grateful that you've been here to help me face the challenge of skeptical customers. I don't think I could have done it alone."

"You're a strong woman, Claire. I think you would've been fine without me, but I'm excited to learn more about Freddie. Remember the message you showed me this morning about calamity? It sounds like it has to do with him."

"Could be. I hope he lets me come so I can find out."

"After such a vivid dream, I'm sure he'll say yes."

Helen's words of affirmation warmed Claire's heart. The conflict over the first painting that had caused such a separation between them had now become the very thing that was making them closer than ever.

Claire was working on one of her commission jobs the next evening when Brenda called. "I have good news."

"Did Freddie say I could come?"

Brenda laughed. "Yes, after Luke told him about our encounter with you, he said he would be happy for the company."

Claire pumped her fist. "That's great. Where does he live?"

"The closest town is called Shell. I already looked; it's about two and a half hours from Buffalo. Is that too far?"

"Not at all. With the way my painting changed, and the dream that I had with Freddie in it, no distance would be too far to find out why I need to meet him." Claire knew it would add some time to her drive if she went through Ten Sleep, but she hoped Chase could come with her. "Do you mind if I bring a friend?"

"Hang on a sec, and I'll ask Luke . . . Hey, Claire?"

"Yeah?"

"Luke said that'd be fine. Now, I know its short notice, but does tomorrow night work? We're only here until Tuesday morning and we'd like to bring you to Freddie's place."

"That works for me but let me check with Chase. I'll call you back in a few."

"Okay. I don't know if this will make it harder for your friend to come, but we were hoping you could get here by 5:30."

"Good to know. Bye." She started to pace the loft floor while waiting for Chase to answer. "Hey there, are you free tomorrow mid-afternoon into the evening?"

"Could be, why?"

"I'm going to meet a Vietnam War veteran who lives near Shell. I'll come your way if you're interested in tagging along."

"For a chance to spend time with you, I'd love to come!"

"I was hoping you'd say that." Claire smiled at the thought of him smiling. "I'll call you back."

"Okay."

As soon as she hung up, she called Brenda. "Chase can come."

"Nice. Now if it's okay with you, we'd like to meet at the local diner. We could have supper together before taking you out to Freddie's place. That way you can introduce us to Chase, and we can visit for a bit first."

"Sounds like a good plan. Thanks for making this happen."

Chapter 23

FREDDIE

Claire and Chase got to the diner a bit early, so they went inside to have a look around. To their right was a quaint gift shop, but instead of spending time there Claire headed to the dining area where a large variety of artwork hung around the room. Wooden booths lined two of the walls, and square tables filled the middle.

They weren't there long before Luke and Brenda came in and the waitress seated them at one of the tables. After introductions were made and dinner ordered, Luke said, "Even though Freddie agreed to let you come, he seemed apprehensive about the painting."

Claire choked on a drink of water and coughed a few times before she was able to speak. "Wait, you told him it changed?"

"I had to because he didn't see how you could've done a painting of his place without a picture, especially when you've never been there."

Chase leaned one elbow on the table and tipped his head toward Claire. "Is there something you're not telling me?"

Claire was caught off guard; she hadn't considered that this would be the time or place to tell Chase what was going on. "Um, I'll answer that in a minute." She pointed at the waitress who had come with their food.

The subject was momentarily changed, and everyone began eating.

After taking a few bites, Chase said, "Come on, Claire, you keep avoiding this question. What's this about not having a picture and a painting changing?" He looked at Luke and Brenda. "Do you know something that I should know?"

Luke started to answer, but Brenda nudged him. "Can you please pass me the ketchup?"

"Wow, this is ridiculous." Chase slapped his hand against his thigh. "Why won't anyone tell me what's going on?"

Claire didn't want to cause a scene at the diner, so she put a hand on his knee and said, "Yes, something inexplicable has happened to three of my paintings. The one with you and your brothers was the first."

Luke dropped a fry and Brenda's eyes widened at this revelation.

Chase only set his jaw and stared.

"I didn't tell you because it's naturally impossible. These two pressed the issue on Saturday and because I wanted to meet Freddie, I had to explain."

"Well then, explain it to me."

"Both the paintings had elements appear that I didn't add."

"I don't understand. Do you mean like magic?"

Claire bobbed her head. "I prefer to think of it as miraculous. Luke, remember how you saw Freddie the whole time in his painting?"

He nodded.

"And Brenda, you said you didn't see him until the boy in the booth pointed him out, right?"

"Right."

"Well, before or after doesn't really matter because, either way, Freddie wasn't in the painting when I brought it to the arts and crafts fair. Then we all saw him."

"We've been over this; so what's your point?" Luke asked, now drumming his fingers on the table.

"You need to look at my painting again. After you left on Saturday, Freddie disappeared."

"Huh, I wonder if *I'll* still be able to see him."

"I kind of hope you can't, because then you'll believe me." Luke scowled, but Claire ignored him and turned back to Chase. "A few months ago, I was working on a painting of old barn doors—the one you're in and—"

"We just appeared? That's ludicrous." He sat back, crossed his arms, and started rapidly tapping his foot on the weathered linoleum floor.

"If you calm down, I'll try to explain." Claire knew she had to give it to him straight because she'd avoided the truth far too long. Now she hoped it wouldn't ruin the rest of their evening. "You said it yourself that you and your brothers never posed like how you were standing in my painting. I'm a good painter; you know that because you helped hang Maggie's portrait. I took pictures of them with their horses, but I didn't have a picture of you guys or any idea at the time that I would meet your aunt."

"To be fair, Chase," Brenda cut in, "Claire gave us the same story with the painting of Freddie's place, but I had an advantage. I saw the painting change before my eyes. Even if she had a picture, she wouldn't have been able to do that."

Chase had stopped tapping his foot and started rubbing his chin. "But how is this possible?"

"It's not, so I say it has to be supernatural. It was actually quite fascinating to watch . . . after the initial shock, that is." Brenda let out a little laugh.

He held her gaze but didn't join in her merriment. Then with a quick shake of the head, he looked at Claire. "Why didn't you tell me?"

"I tried a few times, but how it happened is so unbelievable, I was afraid that if I held to its validity, it would end things between us." She reached for his hand, but he pushed his chair back and stood.

"What? Did you think if I found out here with strangers present that it would make it easier? Because it's not!" Chase grabbed his hat and even though Claire tried to stop him, he stormed out of the diner.

Now what? She dropped her head into her hands and started massaging her forehead. Her heart wanted to rush after him, but her instincts said to wait . . . to give him a minute to cool off.

The chime of the front door opening caused Claire to look up, but the man who entered wasn't Chase. Then in one swift motion, she put a hand on the middle of the table and said, "Wait right here, we'll be back."

Not worrying about what the other patrons thought of their disturbance, Claire jumped to her feet and rushed out of the diner. "Hey, Chase, where are you going?" He had already reached the far side of the parking lot.

When he heard her voice, he turned, kicking some loose gravel and watching the dust swirl around his boot before saying. "Well, I was going to leave, but you're my ride."

"Can we please talk about this?" The deep crease in his brow gave her pause, and yet, the glaze that covered his eyes caused her to run to him. There was no time to brace herself for what might come next. "I meant you no harm."

"I know. I'm not even upset about the improbability of your paintings miraculously changing."

"For real?" She threw her arms around him, but then abruptly stepped back. "Wait, so what's wrong?"

"Oh, I don't know, how about the premise of our relationship starting because of a supernatural happening. Do you even care about me, or am I just a prop in some freaky charade?"

She reached for his hands and was relieved when he didn't pull away. "It's true that I met you because of the painting, but I'm falling in love with you because of your fun and thoughtful personality . . . and that you can ride almost as good as me." She smirked, hoping that last comment would help ease the tension.

The crease in his brow did soften a little, despite the fact that his smile was still missing.

"Seriously though, remember the day that you showed me your memorial and I said I wanted to get to know you for you?"

He pinched his lips and gave her a small nod.

"Well, I didn't want to make it about feeling sorry for you because of your past or the fact that we met because of my painting—both of which were outside of our control."

Chase squeezed her hands. "Now on that score, I do believe you. But *why* is this happening?"

"I wish I knew. Actually, I was hoping we'd get some answers when we meet Freddie. How about we finish our supper and I'll tell you more on our way to his house?"

"Okay, sure."

Relief washed over Claire as the conflict seemed to be diverted at least for the time being. Without further discussion, they went back inside.

When they reached the table, Chase said, "Sorry about that."

"No worries," Luke said. "We were taken aback by the news of these paintings too."

Chase and Claire took their seats, and everyone finished eating without much conversation. It seemed as if no one wanted to risk upsetting the apple cart again.

After dinner, they all walked to Claire's SUV. She opened the back hatch and removed the blanket that covered the painting. "Luke, come take a look. Can you still see Freddie?"

Brenda joined them. "Oh, Claire, that's beautiful. We didn't know you were going to add the glass and frame it first."

"It's a gift. I wanted it to be done right."

Luke wasn't listening to them; instead, he leaned closer to look at the rocking chair.

"Hon, can you see Freddie?" Brenda asked.

He stepped back and shook his head. "The chair is empty. So this is what the painting looked like before I started my story?"

"Yes. What do you think?"

"I like it better this way."

It took them about half an hour to get to Freddie's place. The last twelve minutes were on a dirt road that wound up along a ravine and into a patch of woods.

"Now you can see why Luke was so surprised I had a painting of Freddie's place," Claire said to Chase before they even reached the cabin.

"Yeah, it's not exactly a tourist hot spot."

Eventually, they came to an opening where a small area of trees was cleared. To their left was the cabin with a porch and a single rocking chair. To their right was a good-sized garden with vines covering a woven wire fence, and in front of them, sat the 1958 Chevy pickup with the Vietnam War sticker in the back window. Claire parked behind Luke and started shaking her head. "I know nothing should surprise me by now, but this is freaky."

Chase sat forward and put his right elbow on the dash. "And you've never been here before?"

"Never."

"This is beyond freaky. I'd say it's even beyond incredible."

Claire laughed. "Yup, pretty much. Come on, let's go say hello."

They joined Luke and Brenda and started walking toward the cabin when they heard a voice call to them from the garden.

"I'm over here." Freddie waved to them. He was wearing a baseball cap and a long-sleeved, burgundy tee-shirt.

A German shepherd came bounding out of the garden and jumped on Luke. "Hey there, Shadow." He gave the dog a pat on the head, and then Shadow ran onto the porch and lay down by Freddie's rocking chair.

Claire didn't see it at first, but beyond the cabin was a small barn and a larger area fenced off for a variety of farm animals. *A garden and animals; way to be self-sufficient,* she thought as Freddie came toward them.

He removed his gloves and said, "Welcome."

"You have a beautiful place here, Mr. Wagner." Claire had purposed not to grimace or stare when she saw his war-torn face gouged with hideous scars. "Thank you for letting us come."

"Please, call me Freddie and you are?"

"I'm Claire and this is Chase."

He took Chase's hand with a curious expression that suggested more than Claire could read at the moment. "It's nice to meet you, young man."

Chase apparently didn't notice because he only said, "Likewise, sir."

"Come, let's go inside before the mosquitos start eating us alive."

"We'll be right back," Claire said. "We need to get the painting."

Chase willingly came with her and once they were out of earshot, he whispered, "Wow, Freddie's face is more messed up than I expected."

"Yeah, it's pretty sad but he seems like a really nice guy. We need to make sure that we don't treat him differently. I would feel awful if we upset him or made him feel uncomfortable in his own home."

"You don't have to worry about me, Claire. I'm good."

"Me too. Let's go visit and see if we can learn anything of significance."

They found the others in Freddie's living room, which smelled of vanilla cream pipe tobacco. Luke had brought two chairs from the kitchen so there would be enough seating.

It was a cozy room with a stone fireplace and hardwood floors. A worn recliner and couch flanked a coffee table that held a few magazines and a large crossword puzzle book. Freddie's pipe and a lamp were on an end table and a floor-to-ceiling bookshelf filled one wall. Several beautifully carved pieces were displayed on a rough-cut, wooden beam above the fireplace.

Chase propped the painting in between the two chairs and sat down on the one closest to the fireplace. Claire took the other one, while Luke and Brenda got comfortable on the couch.

When everyone was seated, Freddie moved to the front of his recliner, rested his elbows on his knees, and clasped his good hand over his mangled one. "When do I get to take a look at that painting, Claire?"

"Oh, um, I guess we could do it now." She wanted to talk about other things first and hoped this wouldn't end the conversation before it even got started. "Chase, give me a hand."

"Okay." He got to his feet and steadied the painting while Claire removed the blanket. Then they both took a side and held it in Freddie's direction.

Silence pervaded the room as they all watched for his reaction. Claire was surprised when a tear slid down Freddie's left cheek.

Luke and Brenda quickly looked from Freddie to the painting. Their mouths dropped simultaneously.

Confused, Claire let go and stepped in front of the painting.

Chase quickly tightened his grip, barely keeping it from crashing to the floor. Once he had adjusted his hold, he leaned over the top of the frame so he could see what everyone else saw.

The cabin was gone, replaced by open fields and a well-kept barn. Leaning against the newly refurbished 1958 Chevy pickup was a handsome young man with his sleeves rolled up and a pack of cigarettes in his pocket. His hair stuck out at weird angles from under a worn baseball cap, and his grin brought the painting to life.

Claire's lip started to quiver. It was an effort to suppress her own rush of emotions. "Is it safe to say this is you, Freddie?"

He came to stand by Claire. "Yes. My dad gave me this truck when I graduated from high school."

"That was quite a gift."

"It sure was, and you are quite the painter. I appreciate that you left Patty Anne out of it." He turned to Luke and Brenda. "She's in the original picture. I don't mind looking at it sometimes when I'm feeling extra sentimental, but I wouldn't want to see it every day." He turned back to face Claire. "And though I don't think of myself as being a proud man, it's nice to be reminded that I was good looking once."

"You most certainly were." Claire gently nudged his arm and smiled, relieved that he didn't ask where she got the photo. "And you looked so full of life. I'm sorry the war stole that from you."

"Me too, but then again, I lived. This isn't the life I'd hoped for, but it's more than the 58,000 soldiers got that came home in body bags."

Claire winced at the thought.

Chase set down the painting. "If you don't mind my asking, could you tell us what happened and how you survived?"

Chapter 24

THE EXPLOSION

Luke scooted to the front of the couch. "Excuse me, Freddie; I don't think that's such a good idea. How about you just tell us what you've been up to lately."

Freddie sat and lit his pipe. He took a few puffs to get it going, and then said, "That was over forty years ago, Luke, and I'm happy to say that I haven't had flashbacks or nightmares in years."

"Oh, I didn't know. That's wonderful news."

"Yes, I'm very grateful." Though the right side of Freddie's lips and cheek were partly missing and permanently set into a frown, the left side curled into a small smile. He turned to look at Chase. "My story has to include some of the realities of war, but for the ladies' sakes, I'll need to leave out the more horrific details."

Brenda scooted closer to Luke. "I've learned bits and pieces of your story over the years. I'm up for hearing more."

Freddie nodded and took another puff on his pipe. "How about you, Claire?"

"My dad's a history buff. I've watched several documentaries on the Vietnam War with him, so even though hearing your story will make me sad, I can handle the truth."

"Chase, you were the one who asked," Luke said, "yet now you look like you're having second thoughts. Is everything okay?"

"To be honest, I've had my share of loss, so even though I'd like to know what happened, I don't need *all* the details."

Claire noticed that Freddie's expression had changed to the same quizzical look he gave Chase when they were first introduced. She couldn't help but wonder what he was thinking. *Maybe he reminds him of himself when he was young. When comparing him with the painting, they do look quite a bit alike.*

"Well then, young man," Freddie said. "I'll keep that in mind as I explain. I was drafted shortly after high school into the U.S. Army. My grades were good in math and science, and I wanted to become a veterinarian. Because of this, they sent me to medical school for a crash course to become a medic. My superiors told me that even though I would have to care for the wounded, being a medic was one of the safest jobs to have. Safe sounded good, but after a few months of watching men die because they didn't get to us on time, safe wasn't my biggest concern. I volunteered to go with a unit so I could try to save some of the guys that wouldn't otherwise make it."

Claire leaned forward, her elbows on her knees with her hands clasped together in front of her. "Wow, that's amazing, Freddie!"

He grimaced at her praise. "Well, I wasn't in immediate harm, so I'm no hero, but I did save my share of soldiers. Sadly, some of them ended up back on the front lines, and I never saw them *alive* again.

"Anyway, I'll move ahead a few years to how I was hurt. My tour of duty was coming to an end, almost parallel with the war. I was with a convoy heading back to the main camp. The M35 in front of the one I was in hit an IED, killing everyone inside. The blast was so sudden and severe that we drove into the fray before our driver could stop. He and his buddy in the front seat were killed. The rest of us were wounded and badly burned, but thankfully there were other vehicles behind us, and those guys were able to get us to safety.

"I was hit with pieces of shrapnel and suffered second and third-degree burns over much of the upper-right side of my body. I even lost most of my fingers." He held up his right hand and wiggled the stubs that remained. "Because I was unconscious, the details of the blast were given to me later by one of the guys who helped rescue us."

"How long was that?" Chase asked.

"I think it was about two weeks. When I first gained consciousness in Vietnam, I was in so much pain that they put me into an induced coma. All I remember is waking up in a Japanese hospital. I was there for about three months before they felt I was stable enough to return to the States. On top of my obvious wounds, I lost sight in my right eye, hearing in my right ear and I have a six-inch scar on the side of my stomach. It's a miracle that gash didn't kill me."

Freddie paused to take another puff on his pipe before continuing. "Patty Anne came to see me while I was in the hospital in California. One look at me was all it took for her to bail on the commitment we made to each other."

"Were you engaged?" Chase asked.

"Actually, we got married before I left. That way if I died, she'd be taken care of. I guess neither of us thought about this option." Freddie pointed to his face.

Chase shook his head. "That's just wrong, man."

"Wrong or not, she was young and beautiful and though it broke my heart—one look in the mirror reminded me not to hate her for it."

"But your looks don't mean you changed as a person," Brenda said emphatically.

"Unfortunately, the expression that beauty is only skin deep, was true in our case. But on to the rest of my story.

"Because I needed several skin grafts, I was in the hospital for another four months. The days passed so slowly it felt like years. My head ached and my heart burned with a consuming fire long after my body healed. I can't even count how many times I prayed for God to take me, but now I'm glad that was a prayer He didn't answer."

Claire, who never chewed her nails, was gnawing on the back of her index finger. She pulled it away long enough to say, "Your story is more heartbreaking than gruesome."

"You're right and the grief didn't end there. By the time I was well enough to leave the hospital, the Army had given me a medical discharge. Not having anywhere else to go, I came home to Wyoming. The explosion happened in October of '73; I never made it home until May of '74. A month after I got home, I received the divorce papers from Patty Anne's lawyer.

"I not only lost my wife, the town's people and tourists cringed every time they saw me. I quit going to town and fell into a deep depression." His voice trailed off as he closed his good eye and took another long draw on his pipe.

Luke looked at Chase. "Let's just say he wasn't given a hero's welcome and was often met with disrespect, even years later."

"Yeah, Claire told me how the two of you met."

"Because Shell is so small, Freddie had to do his shopping in Greybull, the town where I went to high school. That's where I met the guys who gave me the dare. Regrettably, I became one of those jerks."

Freddie opened his eye and looked at Luke. "That's ancient history, my friend. Anyway, these things paled in comparison to the pounding headaches, especially when you combine them with the endless flashbacks and nightmares from the war. Here I was, a twenty-two-year-old guy that had lost everything, except my life, and no one seemed to care."

"Is that why you built this place out here in the middle of nowhere?" Claire asked.

"Yes. It was supposed to be temporary, but the years got away from me. As you can see, I poured myself into reading." He pointed toward the overflowing bookshelf. "I'm sure I didn't feel as lonely as I actually was. Meeting Luke and his family helped improve my interactions with people, but not enough to want to join civilization, so I built this addition."

"I got my dad and brother to come out and help," Luke said, beaming with pride. "My mom brought meals, and she and my sisters helped too."

Freddie patted Luke's knee. "This young man got me through some dark days, and it's true, his family was such a blessing to me at the time. It's too bad that you all moved away and didn't keep in touch."

Luke's expression soured. "Hold up, that's a bit unfair, don't you think? You had no phone or mailing address until recently, and I went to college in Nebraska, got married, and spent the last twenty years in Oklahoma."

"I know, but that didn't make your absence any easier."

"Well, we've reconnected now, and I'm so glad we have."

"I'm glad too," Brenda said cheerfully. She turned to Claire. "Freddie's made such a positive impact on Luke's life that we named our son after him."

"Aww, that's so sweet!"

In the meantime, Chase had gone to the fireplace and picked up a carved German Shepard from off the mantle. When there was a break in the conversation, he said, "These are impressive."

"Thanks. Whittling is a hobby of mine. I did most of them. Jack did the one that looks like my 58 Chevy."

"Who's Jack?" Claire asked.

"Jack Hendrickson, he's—"

"Wait, are you talking about the guy who's new to the rodeo circuit this year?" Chase asked with fresh enthusiasm.

"Yes, he's quite the horseman. He works on my brother's ranch."

"He's fun to watch and really good, especially at calf roping."

Chase took a seat and the two men got caught up in talking about Jack and the rodeo.

Claire listened for a bit, but lost interest and walked to the mantle where she picked up several of Freddie's pieces, turning them this way and that with great admiration. Then she picked up the truck and ran her fingers over it. Lost in thought and not paying attention to the guys, she turned the carving over. Jack had carved his name into the bottom. She gasped.

Everyone looked her way.

"Are you okay, Claire?" Chase asked.

"Oh, uh, it's nothing." She put her finger to her mouth and then looked at it. "I just got a sliver, that's all. Hey, Freddie, do you mind if I take some pictures of your carvings? The details are impressive."

"Of course, you can, my dear."

Claire set the truck back in its place and got out her phone. The guys were still occupied with the stories about Jack, so she took several pictures, more than she probably needed. "Thanks, Freddie."

"No, thank you. I love my new painting. Are you sure I can't pay you something for it?"

"It's my gift, and anyway, I feel like I've already been paid by the privilege of making your acquaintance."

"You're too kind, my dear." Freddie's smile reached further than his face could physically allow.

It warmed Claire's heart and she smiled too.

"How about you take one of my carved pieces from the mantel? It can be my gift to you."

"For real? I'd love one!"

He joined her and Claire looked at all of them again before choosing the buffalo. "This is great. Thanks, Freddie. Hey, do you ever go to the rodeos?"

"Not usually. I did go to the one in Greybull in June, but that's my limit on travel and there won't be a rodeo there again until next year."

"You could join us at the one in Ten Sleep this coming weekend," Chase offered.

"Yeah, that's only an hour and a half from here," Claire added. "Chase lives in Ten Sleep. We could even meet you early and show you around."

"And maybe you could let me drive your 58 Chevy." Chase rubbed his hands together with the excitement of a kid at Christmas. "That's a sweet looking ride."

Freddie laughed. "You two have a way of making an old man step out of his comfort zone, don't you?"

Claire squeezed his arm. "Does that mean you'll come?"

"I guess I could if you promise to meet me there."

"It's a deal."

They worked out the particulars of where and when they would meet and then Chase asked, "Do you think you could introduce me to Jack?"

"I'm sure that could be arranged."

"Great. Thanks."

"Chase, we should probably get going. I still have a long drive ahead of me."

He agreed and everyone walked out to the porch together.

"Thanks for letting us come, Freddie." Claire gave him a hearty handshake.

"The pleasure was mine, my dear. I haven't had this much fun in years. Until we meet again."

"Until we meet again."

"We'll be right back, Freddie," Luke said. Then he and Brenda followed Chase and Claire down the stairs and onto the driveway. As soon as Freddie went back inside, he asked, "Am I the only one still freaking out about the painting completely changing this time?"

"I guess so," Claire said. "Freddie had such an amazing story, I forgot all about it."

"Me too," Brenda said. "It must be a God-thing because Freddie was so taken with the painting that he didn't even focus on the how."

"Yeah, I was relieved that it wasn't brought up."

Chase nodded. "I think we can all agree on that. And Luke, thanks for dinner and bringing us here."

"It was our pleasure, and the evening went smoother than I expected."

"That's for sure," Claire agreed. "Let's keep in touch."

"We will. Good night."

"Chase, here." She tossed him her keys. "You can drive."

Their conversation immediately went to all that had transpired. "To be honest, Claire, the way the painting changed from what it looked like at the diner did freak me out, but it also gave me a greater respect for you, and an appreciation for how that miracle blessed Freddie."

Claire leaned onto the console and took Chase's free hand. "And I'm relieved that the paintings are no longer a secret or a point of contention between us."

"But so you know, I can't blame you for not wanting to tell me. Even after seeing the change, it's still hard to comprehend why it's happening."

"Yeah, I don't get that part either, but Freddie is a really nice guy."

"For sure and I think it's cool how he knows Jack Hendrickson. I can't wait to meet him."

"I didn't think of it earlier, but there's a good chance Trevor and my dad know him. As you know, show horses *are* a big part of our business."

Chapter 25

THE CARVED TRUCK

It was after 10:30 by the time they got back to Chase's house. "We should ask Aunt Maggie if you can spend the night. I'd feel a lot better about you not having to drive through the mountains at this hour."

"It seems a bit late to be asking for such a favor, don't you think?"

"Not really. She already has the guest room set up and I know she'll be more than happy to play host." Chase jumped out and made the call before she could dissuade him.

Truth be told, Claire welcomed this protective gesture. She came around the front of her SUV to join him.

"Okay, thanks. She'll be there shortly." Chase slipped his phone back into his pocket. "You're all set."

"Nice. And hey, thanks for coming with me tonight. It was fun."

"And enlightening! Even though our story includes creepy miracle paintings, you're worth it to me."

"I'm actually happy about the miracle part. To me, they don't even seem creepy anymore, especially now that you and Luke have seen one change."

"Fine, but I still retain my right to say they're creepy." He winked before leaning in to give her a parting kiss. "See you in the morning."

"That's the real reason you wanted me to stay, right?" Claire gave him a playful nudge.

"Now you know that I'm not only charming, I'm smart, too." He opened the door with a big grin plastered across his face.

"Good night, Chase." She climbed onto the driver's seat and beeped as she pulled out of his driveway.

It took less than a minute to get to Maggie's place, where the porch light was already on. She was waiting by the front steps.

"Hi, Claire. What brings you here at this hour?"

"Chase and I just returned from an adventure."

"Oh yeah, and where did this adventure take you?"

"Shell. Were you heading to bed, or do you have time to talk?"

"We never go to bed before 11:00. Brad's watching a show, so let's go to the kitchen. Would you like something to eat or drink?"

"Um, sure. Whatever you have will be fine."

"Okay, I'll put the water on so we can have tea."

Claire slumped into a chair, propped her chin on her left hand, and started drumming her fingers with her right.

At first, Maggie was too busy to notice, but after the kettle was filled and the burner on, she heard Claire and turned to see what was going on. "Is something wrong?"

"I don't think so . . . well maybe." Then, throwing caution to the wind, she blurted out, "I need to see Zac's wooden box. You brought it to the house, right?"

"We did, but what's this all about?"

"Do you mind if I have a look first? Then I'll explain."

Maggie left the kitchen without a reply.

Claire was too preoccupied with her own thoughts to follow her. *What if my hunch is right? What should I do then?*

Maggie returned a minute later with the cleaned and polished box. She set it on the table with the key. "Here, you open it. I have no idea what you're looking for."

"Thanks." Claire moved her hand over the lid. "Wow, this looks really nice."

"A simple gesture to honor the dead, that's all." She smiled and went to get their tea.

Claire quickly removed the lock and opened the lid. She rummaged through the contents only to discover what she wanted wasn't there. In a panic, she asked, "Where's the other horse?"

Maggie came to the table with a tray that held two mugs of tea, a cup of cream, and a small plate of chocolate chip cookies. "Are you talking about the one that's finished?"

"Yes. Do you have it here?" Claire jumped to her feet and started rubbing her hands together. "I need to see it, like now!"

"Whoa, what's gotten into you?"

"The horse. Where's the horse?"

Maggie furrowed her brow. "Settle down and I'll go get it." This time, when she left the room, Claire followed hard on her heels. "It's on my bedroom dresser. I didn't see the point of leaving it in that box where it couldn't be seen or appreciated."

Claire halted at the door, resisting the urge to rush into Maggie's room and seize the horse. Instead, she started pacing in the hallway.

Maggie returned a moment later and handed the horse to Claire. In one swift motion, she flipped it over. "Can it be?" she whispered.

"Can what be?"

Claire grabbed her phone and scrolled through the pictures she took at Freddie's house until she found the one with Jack's name carved into the bottom of the truck. Then she stretched the photo so only the name showed and looked again at the bottom of the horse.

"Claire, what is it?"

"I can't tell you . . . not yet anyway." She met her gaze with a mix of excitement and fear.

"Oh no, missy, that's not fair. You can't barge in here and discover something that causes this much emotion and think I'll let you keep it to yourself."

Hoping to calm her nerves, Claire drew in a deep breath and exhaled slowly. She looked from Maggie to her phone and back again before asking, "Can we please go sit first?" She hustled toward the kitchen, without waiting for an answer.

Maggie followed but didn't bother to sit. Instead, she crossed her arms and said, "Claire?"

"Okay, fine; I have a hunch. Yet because it's not been confirmed, I didn't want to get your hopes up until I had time to see if I was right."

"Well, you have me hooked and it obviously has something to do with Zac, so not telling me will be as hard as knowing."

"Yeah, I didn't think this through very well, did I?"

"Not at all." Maggie uncrossed her arms and rested her hands on the back of a chair. "Now, I'll make you a deal. You tell me what's going on and I promise it won't leave this room."

"Alright, but it's not fair. How was I going to see the horse without you knowing?"

"Maybe you could have tried to be a bit more inconspicuous." Maggie quipped as she took her seat.

"Ha-ha, very funny."

"I thought so, but seriously, you were stressing me out. Now, tell me what's got you so worked up."

Claire came around the table and set the horse and her phone in front of Maggie. "Here, what do you see?"

Maggie didn't answer right away. After a moment, her eyes widened. "The A and C carved on the bottom of the horse match the letters in your picture. Claire, what's going on?"

"That's what I need to find out." She took a seat and put a few cookies on her plate, suddenly feeling the urge to eat.

Maggie picked up the phone to get a better look. "I'm all ears."

"Okay, but I need to ask you to have an open mind about what I'm going to tell you because my story is unbelievable. Yet, to me, it's finally starting to make sense."

"What in the world are you talking about?"

"All the craziness started with the painting of your nephews. I didn't add them. They just showed up."

"I'm not following. Care to explain?"

It took Claire about fifteen minutes to describe the storm and how the boys supernaturally appeared. "No one believed me, so I decided to have the painting on display at Frontier Days, hoping for answers. That's when you showed up and told me your story."

Maggie had been rubbing her chin, cheeks, and lips almost from the start. With narrowed eyes, she finally asked, "So is this why you wouldn't tell me how you were able to make the painting so accurate?"

Claire nodded. "Here, let me have my phone." She scrolled to the picture of Sophie's drawing and handed it back to Maggie. "When I met this girl, she was sketching a waterfall, but what I saw was the boys, so I asked her if I could take a picture."

"Oh my, this is a nice drawing too." Maggie looked up. "But how can you confirm that you didn't do the drawing and then have that girl hold it for you."

"See, this is why I didn't say something sooner." Then Claire remembered she had the picture Trevor sent back to her. "Here, look at this, Sophie is holding the drawing of the waterfall. Her face looks exactly the same as it does in the one of the boys. Now, look at the time stamp on both pictures."

"It's the same."

"Right, and if that's not convincing enough, please read what it says at the bottom of the one. I'm not clever enough to come up with all of this on my own."

Maggie read it aloud, "'There's a story yet to be told. When you hear it, pursue.' Is this why you were so eager to see Roger's ranch?"

"Precisely. And then to find the wooden box. How could I have staged that?"

"You couldn't have; we didn't even know it was there."

"Then, as you also know, Chase and I have become close, so I thought that was the end of it," Claire hesitated, "until another painting changed and then a third."

"You're telling me this has happened three times?" Maggie now sounded more intrigued than skeptical.

"Yes, but until today, I didn't think the paintings had anything to do with each other. Chase and I just got back from meeting Freddie, the man who showed up in my third painting. A friend of his told me part of his story at my last arts and crafts fair, so I *pursued*." Claire gestured quotes. "I not only wanted to give him the painting, but I also wanted to find out why I needed to meet him."

"But what does any of this have to do with Zac?"

"I'm not sure yet. On Freddie's mantel were a variety of carved objects. They were fantastic and when Chase asked who did them, he said he did most of them, but that Jack had done one. I happened to turn it over and about dropped it when I saw the A and C. I immediately thought of Zac's carved horse. I was planning on coming here after I dropped Chase off at his place so I could compare the letters. I thought it was cute that he suggested I spend the night because he didn't want me driving through the mountain pass at this hour."

"Claire, where are you going with this?"

"Now that we see the signatures are similar, I want to go back to Freddie's place and find out how he met Jack."

"Wait, do you think this Jack guy could actually be our Zac?"

"The possibility would have never crossed my mind except for the fact that I didn't add the images of your nephews or of Freddie's house to my paintings."

They both sat in silence for a while, drinking their tea and eating cookies.

After a bit, Maggie picked up the horse and looked again at Zac's name. "Did you say this guy lives in Shell?"

"In that vicinity. He's a Vietnam War vet and lives out in the middle of nowhere."

"Huh, that does make your story more viable. Roger's rancher friend lives over that way. It's where the accident happened."

"Oh, yeah? Chase didn't mention it."

"So even though this story sounds farfetched, you have too many connecting details for it all to be a coincidence."

"That's what I'm thinking, but it's also why I didn't want to tell you. If I'm wrong, you'll bear the burden of needless pain."

"Oh, don't you worry about me. I'm tougher than I look and like I said, I won't mention this to anyone."

"What about Brad?"

"He knows you're spending the night and won't think anything of our staying up to visit. And anyway, with the TV on he wouldn't have been able to hear our conversation."

"Good." Claire stood. "It's been a long day so if you could show me to my room, I'd like to call it a night."

"You got it, kiddo. We're close to the same size, so I'll grab you something to wear to bed."

Maggie found some yoga pants and a tee-shirt and then showed Claire to her room on the second floor. Before saying goodnight, she said, "You're a strong woman, Claire . . . and brave, too. I've done some painting over the years, but I can't imagine how frightening that must have been to have extra images show up."

"Terrifying, which is ironic, because before this summer, nothing scared me." She let out a little laugh. "If truth be told, I thought I was going crazy until others started seeing what I saw. I wouldn't have even thought of a possible connection between Jack and Zac if it weren't for the paintings, and the fact that I was the one who found the box with the horse in it."

"It certainly seems like a long shot because I don't understand why Zac wouldn't let his parents know that he's alive."

"Maybe he has amnesia. Why else would he go by Jack?"

"Could be. All I know is that I won't sleep a wink tonight."

"I think it's safe to say that neither of us will have any peace until we know for certain. I'll call Freddie in the morning to see when we can come."

Maggie's eyes sparkled with anticipation. "Does that mean you want me to come with you?"

"Of course. I'm not going alone. Oh, and Chase doesn't know about my hunch, so when he stops in the morning, please don't mention it."

Chapter 26

FREDDIE'S SECRET

Claire called Freddie the next morning, and he agreed to let them come without Luke, as long as she forewarned Maggie of his scars.

Once she knew they could come, she called her dad, "Hey, um, I need the day off."

"It's kind of short notice, don't you think?"

"I know, but something's come up and it can't wait."

"Judging by your tone, it sounds serious."

"Very!"

"I guess nothing's pressing for today, so I'll see you in the morning."

"Thanks, Dad. You're the best."

During the hour and a half drive, Claire told Maggie what she knew of Freddie's experience in Vietnam and about the IED. "He's close to 70 now and to think that after all these years he still asked me to warn you about his face."

"What a sad and lonely existence. Is he hard to talk to?"

"Not at all. He's good-natured and has poured much of his life into learning. That, along with his self-sufficient work ethic, you'd never know he was a recluse. Luke and his family helped him for a few years, but after they moved away, I don't know what

201

happened. He told us that Jack works for his brother, so maybe that's how they met, but yeah, he's not had an easy life. It's really too bad, too, because he's such a nice guy."

Shadow was lying on the porch next to Freddie, who was sitting in his rocking chair reading when they arrived. The dog jumped to his feet and started barking. "Settle there, boy, it's okay. These ladies are our guests."

"Good morning," Claire called and waved from her open window.

The sunlight danced through the trees and hit her face. "You're like a ray of sunshine, Miss Claire."

"Aww, thanks." She jumped out of her SUV and waited for Maggie to join her before they walked to the porch.

Freddie set down his book and came down the steps; his dog hard on his heels. "Long time, no see."

"Yeah, like less than fifteen hours. We might not want to make a habit of this. The town's people will gossip."

"Oh, we wouldn't want that to happen now, would we? But then I won't tell if you don't." Freddie winked with his good eye, and they both laughed.

"Freddie, this is Maggie. Maggie, Freddie."

"How do you do, ma'am?"

"I'm well. Thanks." She smiled and held up the container she was holding. "I brought freshly baked blueberry scones. Are you hungry?"

"I don't know what a scone is, but I bet it'll be delicious. Please, come in; the coffee is a-brewing." Freddie already had the mugs, and cream and sugar on the ornately carved wooden table, along with a vase of freshly cut wildflowers. "Have a seat, ladies. I'll grab some plates."

"Oh wow, look at this table," Maggie said as she ran her fingers over the surface. "Where'd you get it?"

"I made it."

"Impressive. It must've taken a long time to add all these intricate details."

Freddie set down the plates and then turned his head so he could see Maggie better. "It did, ma'am, but then *time* is something I've had a lot of over the years."

She blushed and dropped her gaze back to the table. "Well, it's absolutely beautiful."

"Thanks."

The kitchen was small. A dated light fixture hung from the ceiling. On the wall to the left, a cookstove was tucked in-between handcrafted cupboards with butcher block countertops. The counters continued into the corner and ran the length of the wall opposite the door with the sink in front of the only window. To the right was the opening to the living room. It must have been widened when they built the addition because some of the floorboards were a different color.

A few minutes later, everyone was situated at the table and Maggie dished the scones.

"This is really good," Freddie said after he took a few bites. "Maybe you could give me the recipe. I make my own bread, but it would be fun to mix things up in the summer when I have fresh fruits available."

"I have the recipe memorized so I'll write it out for you." Maggie pulled a pen and notepad from her handbag and jotted it down while they finished their breakfast.

"Thanks. Do you mind if I light my pipe?"

"Not at all. I like the smell of pipe tobacco."

"Great. Now, what is it that you ladies wanted to talk to me about?"

Claire laced her fingers around her mug and said, "Jack. We'd like to know how you met Jack."

The glint that had taken up residence in his one good eye ever since the compliment about his table vanished and his brow furrowed. "Um, I, uh, don't remember."

"You don't remember?" Claire leaned to her right. "I don't mean *when* you met him, I want to know *how* you met him. Is he a friend of the family or another boy like Luke who you took under your wing?"

Freddie took a long draw on his pipe, turned toward the window, and started blowing smoke ringlets into the air.

Claire glanced at Maggie and saw her waiting with breathless anticipation. Ten years of assuming the worst must have made his hesitation seem like an eternity. To their dismay, he didn't answer. Instead, he pushed his chair from the table and asked, "Do either of you want more coffee?"

"No thanks." Claire tipped her cup. "I still have some."

Maggie didn't answer, though her gaze was fixed on Freddie.

"Okay, suit yourselves." He picked up his own mug and walked to the counter.

As soon as he turned, Claire brushed Maggie's arm with the back of her fingers and bobbed her head toward Freddie.

She must have caught Claire's meaning because she grabbed her mug and joined him at the coffee pot. "I'll have more, please." When he didn't acknowledge her, she moved to his left side. It was then that she noticed his breaths were short and choppy. Gently touching his arm, she asked, "Freddie, are you okay?"

Without looking her way, he said, "I'm fine. I just don't want to talk about Jack, that's all."

"You know, on our way out here this morning, Claire told me that you're a master whittler. I'd love to see some of your carvings."

Freddie set his pipe on the counter and his countenance brightened. "Well then, follow me." He started for the living room. "Hey Claire, are you coming?"

"Of course. I'll be there in a sec." She took another sip of coffee, giving them time to leave the kitchen. Then she scooped up Maggie's handbag, got out Zac's carved horse, and brought it with her.

Freddie had already flipped on the light and walked to the fireplace. Claire's painting hung above the mantle. "Isn't this portrait amazing? Claire gave it to me yesterday."

"It's beautiful," Maggie said. "We love the two she's done for us."

"Thanks, guys, but I thought you came to see Freddie's art, not mine," Claire said as she joined them.

"That's true, but Maggie hadn't seen it yet and I can brag about it if I want."

Claire felt awkward about the praise because she hadn't done any of this painting. To deflect, she said, "Well, I'm glad you like it so much. Now, how about you tell Maggie about your carvings."

"These are some of my favorites. Feel free to take them down if you want a closer look."

Maggie picked up a few different ones and admired the craftsmanship. "Claire didn't exaggerate one bit. You know, you could make good money selling these."

"Thanks, but I don't do it for the money. Years ago, when the flashbacks and nightmares of the war were at their worst, I took up whittling. When I couldn't sleep, focusing on the minute details helped me to forget everything else. Now I make them for the fun of it. I have boxes filled with them in the closet."

"What a great outlet." Maggie pointed to the truck. "Is that one of your first?"

"No, Ja—, someone else made that one."

Maggie pulled the truck off the mantle and turned it over. Seeing the name, she said, "I don't understand. According to Claire, you didn't have any problem talking about Jack last night."

Claire held out Zac's horse before he could answer. "Here, Freddie, take a look at this."

He took it from her. "Wow, that's a fine piece of carving right there."

"It sure is. Now turn it over." Claire reached to help him, but he pulled away.

"Whoa, what's the hurry? I can do it." He looked. "Who's Zac?"

"He's my nephew," Maggie said. She quickly flipped over Jack's truck and held it in front of Freddie. "Look at how Jack signed his name."

He took the truck and brought it closer to his good eye. "What's this about?"

"See, the A and C match on both carvings. Do you know how that's possible?"

Freddie stared at the letters for a long time. Finally, he held out the horse and asked, "How old is this?"

"Zac carved that over ten years ago before he disappeared. We thought he drowned, but maybe he didn't?" Maggie dipped her head and looked at Freddie with pleading eyes.

To her surprise, color drained from his face and his lips began to quiver. The tremor in his voice grew with each word, "But I, I, didn't know who he was. He couldn't remember his name. He had no ID on him." Freddie dropped into his recliner and started rocking back and forth like a frightened child fearing the punishment of an abusive father.

Maggie quickly knelt in front of him. "We're not blaming you, Freddie. We just need to know if our Zac could actually be alive."

"Hey Maggie, didn't you bring his picture with you?" Claire asked.

"I did." She scrambled to her feet and rushed to the kitchen, dug through her handbag until she found her wallet and pulled out the picture. Hurrying back, she held it out with a shaky hand. "Here's Zac's school portrait from the fall before the accident."

Freddie had stopped rocking. He took the picture and gently touched Zac's face with the back of his maimed hand. With a nod, he said, "Yes, this is the boy I pulled from the river."

Maggie dropped to the floor and offered a prayer of thanksgiving to the Lord. But then, as if being hit by the reality that Zac was alive, she buried her face in her hands and burst into tears.

Claire sat on the floor next to her and pulled her close. Years of pent-up emotion gave way like a fault line that could no longer hold the bank against a raging stream. There were no words, so they just held each other for a long time.

Eventually, Maggie got to her knees and sat back on her heels. She looked at Freddie with her palms turned upward and choked out the words, "But why? Why didn't you take him to the hospital? Why didn't you tell someone that you had him?"

Freddie was rocking again and had a death-grip on his hands, squeezing them so tightly that his knuckles were white. "I, I thought when he came to, he'd be able to tell me his name and where he lived. The idea that he'd have permanent memory loss didn't seem likely." The tremble in his voice turned to a deep regret, "I'm so sorry, Maggie, I truly am." He stood and extended his good hand to help her up.

Once she got to her feet, she wiped her eyes with the back of her hands, which caused her mascara to smudge in blotchy angles across her cheekbones. "Ahem. You said you pulled Zac from the river, but you don't live near one. Can you tell us how you found him?"

"Yes, I think it would be helpful for you to understand why I handled things the way I did. Why don't you ladies have a seat and I'll grab some tissues."

Maggie drew in a deep breath, straightened her shoulders, and went to the mantle to get Zac's carved truck before taking a seat next to Claire on the couch.

Freddie returned from the kitchen and set the box of tissues on the coffee table in front of Maggie. "Thank you."

While she blew her nose, Freddie sat near the front of his recliner and lit his pipe. He took a few puffs before starting. "I'm sure you remember that we had a harsh winter that year with record snowfalls."

Maggie nodded.

"What made the conditions even worse was the fact that we had a very warm and wet spring. I knew the water would be too high and roily to go fishing, but I was tired of being cooped up, so I got out my Gator and drove to my favorite spot. It's about eight miles from here. Anyway, when I arrived, the river looked just as I expected. Because I had nowhere else to be, I stood by the shore for a while mindlessly watching the rushing water.

"I remember the sun popped out just long enough for me to notice something reflective tangled in the limbs of a downed tree, so I went to see what it was. As I got closer, I realized it was a life jacket and I couldn't tell if the person wearing it was alive or not.

"Suddenly, I found myself along the banks of a Vietnamese River, trying to rescue soldiers that had been blown from their boat further upstream."

Claire shuddered at the thought. "That must have been awful to have a flashback at that very moment."

"I believe it helped because my military training and medic experience kicked into overdrive." Freddie sat back, his hands now moving in animation with his words. "The life jacket and helmet kept the boy's face mostly above water, so I knew there was hope. Getting him to land was going to be the tricky part. The tree that held him gave me something to grab onto, but one wrong step could prove fatal for both of us. I quickly found a sturdy limb closer to land to use as an anchor. Once I had my belt looped around it, I wrapped the other end around my left wrist, which gave me enough length to reach the boy without getting swept downstream myself. With some effort, I was able to thread my right arm through the straps of the life jacket and drag him to safety. As soon as we were back on land, I started CPR.

"Even though he didn't regain consciousness, he did spit up mouthfuls of water and started breathing on his own. The gash on his left cheek bled like a sieve so I used my bandanna to stay the flow enough to get him back to my place."

"That's an incredible story and very heroic. We are forever in your debt." Though Maggie's smile seemed sincere, the softness in her tone suddenly became sharp. "But I'm still confused, once you had Zac stabilized, why didn't you take him to the hospital?"

Chapter 27

HYPOXIA

"The war, ma'am. In my mind, I was still back in 1972," Freddie said. "All I wanted was to get my buddy away from the enemy and back to safety. As I said, my instincts took over. Everything else disappeared."

"I suppose that makes sense." Fresh tears welled in Maggie's eyes. "But once things settled down and your mind returned to the present, why didn't you let someone know you had him?"

Freddie set his pipe on the end table and started rubbing his stubbed fingers against his scarred cheek. "I'm sorry that I can't tell you what you want to hear, Maggie. The truth of the matter is, ten years ago, I had no phone and very limited contact with the outside world. Taking him to a hospital was never even a consideration, especially after I knew he had no major injuries. Once I got him dry, I stitched up his face and then I checked his clothes for some ID but he didn't have any. I figured when he woke up, he'd tell me who he was, and I could bring him home.

"For the next three days, he was in and out of consciousness. He couldn't speak coherently and wasn't able to eat, but I did get him to drink a little water. When he finally came to, he was suffering from memory loss. He was also very weak, and his movements were clumsy and disjointed."

"Ugh. All you had to do was take him to a damn hospital." Maggie slammed the carved truck on the coffee table.

Claire cringed and grabbed her hand. "Please stop. Getting upset about it now won't change the past. Zac's alive! We should be grateful for that."

"But I am grateful." She crossed her leg and started bobbing her foot. "I'm sorry, Freddie. It's just that I thought you said Zac had no noticeable wounds. His helmet should have protected his head."

"From what I found in my medical books," he pointed to the overflowing bookshelf, "his condition was from a prolonged period without enough oxygen. The medical term is hypoxia and usually results in 'short-term' memory loss. So I cared for the boy. I taught him to talk again and helped him with his coordination. His words eventually became less slurred and his thoughts more cohesive."

Freddie paused and turned to make eye contact with Maggie. "I hope you realize that I never meant to hurt anyone. In hindsight, I should have taken him to the hospital, but at the time, I had no idea how many days had passed. He was getting better, and I assumed that any day now, he'd remember who he was."

"But apparently he didn't," Claire said, still holding Maggie's hand.

"Right. Before I knew it, over two months had passed. Every day I would ask him questions. Some he knew, most he didn't. To make it easier, I started calling him Jack.

"As you know, I like to whittle. Once more of Jack's hand-eye coordination returned, I gave him a knife and a block of wood. His objects were crude at the beginning, but in time he became good at it. After seeing the carved horse that you brought, it makes sense why he asked if he could use some of my other tools like the different-sized gougers."

Freddie picked up the truck and looked thoughtfully at the name carved into the bottom. "It makes sense that Jack would belong to a family, but in my isolated state, that thought never crossed my mind."

Claire felt Maggie's hand tense, so she gave it a quick squeeze. That must have helped because even though a sigh escaped Maggie's lips, she held her tongue.

Oblivious that his words stung, Freddie continued, "Anyway, by then another two months had passed. Fall was coming to an end and winter was approaching fast, so we went to town to get fresh supplies. We only saw a few folks that day, none of which bothered to ask who the boy was. Jack seemed content to stay with me, and I admit, I enjoyed having the company."

This time Maggie pulled her hand from Claire's and said, "You mean to tell us that you saw no people for over four months?"

"That's correct. My mom was old and didn't live nearby. My brother was busy with his ranch and his own family. It's just the way things were.

"Anyway, by the following spring, Jack was strong and eager to be outside more. He said he missed riding, so I brought him over to my brother's ranch where he proved to be good at it. My brother needed another hired hand, so he gave him a job and Jack moved to the ranch."

"I don't get it. How can Zac remember how to ride but not remember his name or his family?"

"I'm only giving you the facts, ma'am. But that reminds me, sometimes at night, during the ten months he lived with me, he would wake up screaming the name, Johnny. In the morning, I would ask him who Johnny was. He'd always say he wasn't sure. After this happened the fourth time, he said he remembered being in the river and trying to save Johnny. Then he would draw a blank. It was so strange that he could never remember more . . . before or after."

"Hmm, that is interesting," Claire said. "Maggie, why don't you tell Freddie what happened?"

Maggie shifted her weight and tucked one foot under her before beginning. "Johnny was Zac's youngest brother. They were kayaking with their dad and the current was too strong for Johnny to handle. Before anyone had realized that he lost his paddle, they hit another shoot of tight rapids with protruding boulders. Johnny got thrown into the rocks and tipped over. He must have been knocked unconscious because he never tried to right himself. Roger yelled to Zac who was in the lead, so he got to him first. He couldn't get Johnny's kayak upright from his own, so he jumped out, trying to save his brother. He lost his footing and got swept away by the current. Thank God that you came along when you did."

"But what happened to Johnny?"

Maggie grimaced. "He died in Roger's arms shortly after he and Chase got him to land."

Freddie wiped a tear from his cheek. "Oh, Maggie, I'm so sorry. To lose two family members in one day must have been devastating."

"You have no idea. Roger's not been right since and has taken much of his grief out on their brother, Chase."

"You met Chase, yesterday," Claire said. "Now you know what he meant when he said, 'I've had my share of loss.' For him, that not only included his two brothers but his parents also."

Freddie flipped his palms upward and said, "I'm not following."

"That's an added pain to their complicated and broken past . . . but on a positive note, Chase was quite excited when you said you would introduce him to Jack Hendrickson at the next rodeo."

Maggie grabbed Claire's arm. "Wait! You're telling me that Zac is Jack Hendrickson?"

"Yup." Claire grinned.

"How did we not recognize him? Or better yet, how is it that his own father didn't realize who he was?"

"No offense, ma'am," Freddie said, "but why would you even be looking for a person you assume to be dead, especially with a different name?"

Maggie shrugged.

"Freddie, you must have a current picture of him, right?" Claire asked.

"I do." He disappeared into his bedroom.

Maggie got to her feet. "It's going to seem weird seeing a picture of Zac after all these years. I still can't believe he's alive."

"I'm pretty sure that's about to change." Claire joined her in the middle of the room.

A moment later, Freddie emerged with a 4x6 photo and handed it to Maggie. "This was taken about a month ago."

Zac had a rope slung over his left shoulder and was holding a trophy in his right hand.

Maggie looked at the picture for a minute before saying, "No wonder we didn't recognize him. With the beard and sunglasses, it's hard to tell this is Zac. Do you have a picture of him when he was younger?"

"Let me look, I must have at least one." Freddie went to the bookcase and pulled a box from the bottom shelf. He brought it to the couch and took a seat. The ladies joined him, one on either side.

Random things were in the box, including his certificate for the high school national honor society, four varsity letters for baseball, and a silver chain holding his army dog tags along with two wedding bands.

Claire lifted the chain and said, "So you kept the rings?"

"Yes, I put them with my tags, seeing the war is what tore us apart."

As they talked, Maggie picked up a small pile of pictures that were bound together with a piece of burlap string. "Excuse me, who is this?"

"Oh, that's Luke."

"But why don't you have one of these framed and out where you can see it?"

Freddie shrugged. "This is a box of my favorite memories. Even the ones of Patty Ann are worth remembering. We had some good times before the war, and I was crazy in love with her. Every once in a while, I get this out and spend time reminiscing."

"Aww, that's so sweet."

"Luke's the one who introduced me to Claire and Chase."

"Does Luke know Jack?" Maggie asked.

Freddie shook his head. "No, Luke's family moved away decades ago. I lost track of him until recently when he paid me an unexpected visit. What a fine young man he turned out to be."

Maggie smiled and continued to sift through the pictures. She stopped when she saw the one she was searching for. The scar looked worse, but the young man didn't have a beard and wasn't wearing sunglasses or a hat. "Oh, my." She put her hand over her heart. "It's really him."

"Yes, ma'am."

She held out the picture for Claire to see. "When was this taken?"

"Not sure, maybe six years ago? It was a few years after he started working for my brother."

Maggie hugged the picture to her chest. "What glorious news we have to share with Roger and Michelle. Can you tell us where Zac lives now?"

"I can, but I should warn you, he's very shy and most likely won't recognize you. Just because you tell him you're his aunt, doesn't mean he'll have open arms and be all gushy."

"Way to steal my thunder." Maggie lowered the picture to look at it again. "There must be something we can do."

"How about you let me borrow his carved horse. Maybe when he sees it, it'll jog his memory."

"And if not?"

"Patience my dear. It's been ten years. It might take some time for him to warm up to the idea that he has a family. I said he's shy, not calloused or mean-spirited."

"Right. Can I borrow this picture of Zac so I can show it to his parents?"

"Of course, and you can take the one of him holding the trophy too," Freddie said.

Without warning, Maggie wrapped her arms around him and kissed his scarred cheek. His shocked expression turned to joy as she whispered, "Thank you for saving Zac and taking such good care of him."

"Huh, well I didn't expect that. So, does this mean all is forgiven then?"

"I can't guarantee that. His father, barring a miracle, will be furious."

Claire's thoughts went to the last message she got. 'Love gained, love lost; calamity makes or breaks a man and yet, sometimes it's both.' *Hmm, maybe this has more to do with Roger than with Freddie.*

Maggie, unaware of Claire's contemplations, continued, "We'll just have to pray for God to soften Roger's heart. That all the years of heartache and loss will be forgotten."

"And please don't tell him where I live."

Claire bit back a laugh when she realized Freddie wasn't kidding. "Ahem, sorry."

"I've had more than my share of heartache and loss too, you know." Freddie rubbed the stubs on his right hand. "Jack has been a bright spot in my lonely existence. He gave me a reason to live and coaxed me out of my shell by his vibrant enthusiasm for life. He used to come to see me, but these days it's easier if I drive over to the ranch to see him. I see my brother and his family a lot more often now, and I've even made a few good friends in town. It took a while, but I've learned to ignore the fools who stare."

Tears again ran down Maggie's cheeks, but this time they were tears of joy. "That's such a sweet story, though it sounds more like Chase. Zac used to be proud and self-centered."

"Must be he lost his self-centeredness with his memory because even when he wins an event, I don't see any pride."

Claire listened to this exchange with a sense of wonderment. Would the two brothers become friends? Once there was a pause in the conversation, she said, "You finally make sense to me, Freddie, because you're not at all like what I pictured a recluse to be."

"Not anymore. It was like God brought me to the river that day in time to save Jack; when in reality, *He* brought Jack along in time to save me." He turned to face Maggie. "I'm so sorry that I couldn't help him find his way home."

"It's all right. Like Claire said, 'we can't change the past' and now that I've heard your story, you have nothing to be sorry for." She patted his arm and gave him an endearing smile.

The lines of strain and grief that looked permanent earlier, melted from Freddie's face like butter on a warm summer's day. "Thank you, ma'am."

Claire stood. "Maggie, don't you think we should get going so we can share this amazing news with his family?"

Maggie nodded in agreement. "But what about meeting Zac?"

"We've already made plans to introduce Jack to Chase at the rodeo in Ten Sleep," Freddie said.

"Oh, nice. His parents will be there too." Maggie got to her feet. "I'll start praying that Jack remembers."

"I will too, and the delay will also give me time to show Jack the horse and tell him your story." Freddie went to get a piece of paper and a pen and handed them to Maggie. "Here, put down his parents' names and a few childhood memories."

"Good idea." Maggie sat at the kitchen table and started writing down as many things as she could think of. "Oh, Claire, can you hand me my bag? I'm sure I have an old picture of the whole family." She found the one she wanted and gave it to Freddie. "Their names and ages are on the back."

"Perfect! All these things should be good reminders. Hopefully, they'll jog his memory."

Chapter 28

THE NEWS

They had barely pulled away from Freddie's cabin before Maggie said, "I can't wait to show this picture to Michelle. Her whole world will brighten when she learns that Zac is alive."

Not sure how to reply, Claire kept her eyes fixed on the narrow, winding road in front of her. There was more at stake here than simply gaining a son or a nephew. Of course, she was happy for the family, but all she could think of was how this news would affect Chase.

As Maggie chattered on, her hands rose and fell like a conductor in the middle of a symphony. Several minutes passed before she realized something was wrong. "Claire, what is it?"

"Don't you think Chase should be forewarned? I can't imagine him getting this news from his parents with no time to process it."

"You really like him, don't you?"

"Yes, but that's beside the point. Once Roger has his beloved son back, especially after he finds out that Zac is 'Jack Hendrickson,' I don't see things getting better for Chase. More than likely, they'll get worse."

A deep crease settled across Maggie's brow. "Don't you think Chase will be happy about this?"

"For sure, thrilled even, but I also know it'll be bittersweet for him. We've had long talks about his dad and how nothing he does is ever good enough. He even showed me his memorial."

Maggie did a double take. "Oh my, you two are closer than I realized. I thought Brad and I were the only ones who knew about that."

"And you and Brad are the only ones who truly know how hard Roger's been on him all these years. I have a feeling that he'll need you guys now more than ever."

"You're a perceptive young woman, Claire. I appreciate your candor." Though Maggie sounded pleased, she turned to look out the window. Nothing more was said for a long time.

Claire wasn't sure how to interpret the silence and finally asked, "Can you please think out loud? If I stole your thunder, I didn't mean to."

"No, that's not it." She turned to face Claire. "The fact of the matter is, what you said about Chase is true. Do you think I should wait to tell Michelle?"

"Not necessarily. You just might want to tell Chase first, or I can. Do you know if he'll be at the barns when we get back?"

Maggie shook her head. "I'm not given an update on the day to day activities of the ranch; I have no idea. Do you want me to text Brad and find out?"

"No thanks. I don't want Chase to know that I'm still here. If you don't mind, I'd like to be the one to give him the news."

"I'd have it no other way. You are, after all, the one who set these events in motion . . . well, sort of." Maggie chuckled.

Claire laughed briefly, too, before her expression changed into something between a grimace and a grin.

"We are forever indebted to you. The result of your persistence, against the strangest of odds, has been incredible."

"In more ways than you know."

Maggie leaned forward and tipped her head toward Claire. "What do you mean?"

"Remember how I told you on the way that three of my paintings had changed?"

"Yes, you said you didn't think they had anything to do with each other, but then two of them did."

"Make that all three."

Maggie's eyes widened. "Seriously? How do you know?"

"Do you recall the painting of the little girl that I brought with me the day I gave you your portrait?"

"Vaguely, but I didn't recognize her."

"And knowing what I know now, you wouldn't have." Claire fished her phone from her pocket and handed it to Maggie. "Here, open my picture app."

She did.

"Now, find the painting of the little girl."

"Here it is, but what about it?"

"That cutie pie is your great niece. Her name is Zoe."

"No, that can't be; Freddie didn't say anything about Zac being married."

"So it didn't get brought up. It's not like we asked."

"Okay, fine, but what got said that proves this girl is Zac's daughter?" Maggie asked, still looking at the phone.

"When Freddie showed you the picture of Zac with the trophy, I about jumped out of my skin. He came to my booth a few weeks ago with his wife and Zoe . . . just like you and Luke did when I had your paintings on display."

"Oh, my."

"Scroll to the next image and see how excited Zoe is. I took a picture of her holding the painting."

Maggie did and immediately covered her mouth. There before her eyes was the picture of Zac kneeling by Zoe with the painting in between them. "Oh, my. Zac's not only alive, but he also has a family."

"If you stretch the picture, you will see his pregnant wife, Emma, in the background."

Maggie sat there shaking her head. "This is incredible. Only God could've orchestrated such a beautiful conclusion."

"It *is* a bit overwhelming, to say the least." Claire agreed, now drumming her thumbs on the steering wheel.

"I can't even imagine the rollercoaster of emotions that you've been riding this summer . . . especially after how Roger and Michelle reacted to your painting of the boys."

"And how my dad still doesn't believe me; so you're right, it hasn't been easy. But hey, I've met some amazing people and if this doesn't somehow blow up in my face, I just might be a part of your family someday." A grin tugged at the corner of her lips.

"I, for one, would love that." Maggie beamed as she patted her arm.

"Me too. Hey, why don't you text those pictures to yourself so you can show Michelle."

"Oh, good idea. Do I tell them you're the artist?"

"Um, I guess you can. Just don't tell them I'm the one who did the painting of their boys. I haven't met Michelle yet, remember?"

"They're going to love that painting, and you, now," Maggie said.

"But I don't want them to love me for any of these reasons. I want them to get to know me and come to love me because of Chase."

"On that note, I won't tell them it was you."

"Thanks."

Twenty minutes later, Claire pulled into the driveway. She reached to squeeze Maggie's hand. "Please keep in mind that you've been given a gift to be the bearer of this amazing news. I only ask that you not lose sight of Chase and the adverse effect this could have on him."

"I can't control how his parents will act going forward, but I do agree Chase should get the news first. How about you go tell him and I'll wait to hear from you before going to see Michelle."

"Perfect. Chase and I will come here as soon as he's ready."

Claire stopped by the office. "Hey Brad, do you know where I can find Chase?"

"Yeah, he's changing a tire in the workshop."

"And," Claire held out her hands, "where's the workshop?"

Brad looked up and chuckled. "Oh right, why would you know? Take the center aisle to the back; once you're outside, it's the first building on your left."

"Got it, thanks."

Without waiting for her to leave, he turned his attention back to the receipts on his desk.

Claire stayed put and looped her necklace around her index finger. "Um . . . Brad?"

"Hmm?"

"You need to go talk to Maggie. The paperwork can wait."

His head shot up. "Is something wrong?"

"Not exactly. There's news, and you need to hear it from her—like now."

Brad dropped his pen, grabbed his hat, and left for the house without another word.

Claire found the workshop. The building was newer than the horse and cattle barns and looked more like a large garage with four bays. Different sized ATV's and tractors filled three of the bays; the fourth was larger and set up like an actual workshop. The doors were open, filling the room with light. Claire crossed her arms and leaned against the left side of the entrance to watch him work.

When Chase reached for a tool, he saw her. "Hey, Claire. I didn't know you were still here." He grabbed a rag and started wiping grease from his hands. "Why didn't you come to find me sooner?"

She stepped away from the building. For reasons she couldn't explain, she felt like being outside would somehow make her news easier. "Well, that'd be because Maggie and I just got back from Freddie's place."

Chase tossed the cloth on a table by the door and joined her on the gravel driveway. "But why'd you need to go back?"

"I had a hunch and needed to see if I was right."

"Does this hunch have something to do with your paintings changing again?"

"No." She smiled at the thought. *I guess it would be hard for him not to believe now that he's seen it happen.* "It has to do with Jack's carved truck."

"Jack's truck? What does that have to do with anything?"

"Actually, it has to do with everything!" Unsure of how to break the news, she turned her attention toward the fields.

Chase reached for her hands. "Hey, what are you not telling me?"

Claire bit her lower lip and ventured a look into his dark eyes. *'Calamity makes or breaks a man'* flashed through her mind. "I finally figured out the purpose for the paintings." She let go of his hands so she could wrap her arms around his waist. Leaning her face against his chest, she wouldn't let go.

"Okay, now you're scaring me." He pulled back. "What's going on?"

"Do you have time to take a walk?"

"Sure, but you better start talking."

She started toward a large beech tree that was about forty yards away. "I guess I'll give it to you straight, and then we can talk about it."

"This is about Tim, isn't it?"

Claire laughed a little and nudged his shoulder. "You're too funny. How did you get from Jack's truck to Tim? And anyway, if I was breaking up with you, I could've called, or worse, sent you a text."

He pulled her toward himself and raised his eyebrows a few times. "That's good to know."

She punched his arm. "Can you please stop? I love this flirtatious side of you, but I have serious news, and I don't know how you're going to take it."

"Well, how am I supposed to take *it* when you won't tell me what *it* is?"

"Okay, fine. When we were at Freddie's yesterday, I picked up the truck that Jack carved. Not thinking anything of it, I turned it over. That's when I noticed the signature looked a lot like Zac's."

"A crazy coincidence, right?"

Claire bobbed her head. "Yes and no."

The color drained from Chase's face. He shifted his stance but didn't speak.

"I took a picture of it when you and Freddie were talking. When I got to Maggie's last night, I looked at Zac's carved horse. The letters A and C were almost exact."

"No way. That's impossible."

"That's what I thought, but with how my paintings changed, I figured there could be a chance. Maggie and I drove out to Freddie's place this morning and after some coaxing, he admitted that he was the one to pull Zac from the river."

While Claire got out her phone, Chase started rubbing the back of his neck. Finally, he asked, "But how do you know it was Zac?"

"Because Freddie gave Maggie a few pictures to show your mom. Here, look at these."

Chase took the phone. "So you have a picture of Jack holding a trophy, how does that make him my brother?"

"I know with the beard, hat, and sunglasses, you can't see him very well, but scroll forward one."

He did.

"Freddie thought that picture was taken when Zac was around twenty-one."

Chase stretched the photo so he could see his face better. "But how?" Pain emanated from his eyes. "And why didn't he come home?"

"It's kind of a long story." Claire tugged at his elbow. "Let's go sit, and I'll explain everything."

They walked in silence as Chase stared at the beardless photo of Zac.

When they reached the tree, Chase sat with his back against the trunk. Claire sat cross-legged opposite him and took the next half hour or so to explain the things that led up to the discovery, how Freddie rescued Zac, and why Zac didn't come home.

Chase's expression never changed once throughout the duration of Claire's story. She had no idea what he was thinking or how he was feeling. Either way, she knew he needed some time to process the news, so she joined in the silence and started braiding strands of grass together. Several minutes passed before she tossed the braid away and asked, "Hey, are you okay?"

"Do my parents know?"

Claire thought this might be his response and had her answer ready. "Not yet. I asked Maggie to let me talk to you first. I sent Brad to the house before coming to find you. She's telling him now."

"Hmm, that's going to be interesting."

"Can we forget about your parents for a minute? I want to know how *you're* taking this news."

"Me?" He shook his head. "I, uh . . . I don't know how to feel. I mean, of course, I'm elated that Zac's alive, but it doesn't sound like he'll remember us."

Without warning, he got up and strode toward the barns.

"Chase, wait." Claire scrambled to her feet and ran after him. "You didn't answer my question."

He swung toward her and threw his hands onto his hips. "What do you want me to say?"

"I want to know that you'll be okay."

"I'm great. Now my dad can fawn over his favorite son, and I won't feel obligated to stay here anymore." With that, he took off again.

"Chase, slow down; running away won't solve anything."

This time he glared at her, with a look that vacillated between bitterness and betrayal. "Oh, like *miracle* paintings make you an expert on what I should do? It sounds like I wasn't even supposed to be a part of your ridiculous story. You just used me to get information."

"That's not true and it's certainly not fair! How could I possibly know that these changed paintings had anything to do with your *dead brother*? I was just thankful that one of them brought me to you."

"But this changes everything," Chase protested.

Claire stepped in front of him. "Not everything. It doesn't have to change us."

She reached for his hands, but he crossed his arms and snapped, "Do you have any idea how insufferable my dad will be when he finds out, not only that his son is alive, but that he's the *famous* Jack Hendrickson?"

"I'm sure I don't. But I knew you'd need some time to work through the rawness of your emotions, so go ahead and take it out on me." Claire forced a smile. "Just remember, none of this was Zac's fault. You can't blame him for how your dad treated you or even how he will treat you going forward. I hope his actions won't cloud your judgment toward Zac."

Chase sighed. "And it shouldn't cloud my judgment toward you, either." He swung his arms open. "Come here, you."

Claire willingly moved into his embrace and nestled her cheek against his chest. His heartbeat raced, but the longer he held her, the more it slowed. She closed her eyes and let him hold her.

After a bit, he stepped back and lifted her chin. "This news is still overwhelming, but I'm glad you were the one who told me."

Claire smiled.

"When Trevor said you were fearless and tough as nails, he wasn't kidding. I don't know anyone who would have pursued these stories; especially after all the grief you were given."

"It's been worth it."

"Yeah well, I'm sure you didn't always feel that way. Thanks for not taking my initial reaction personally. You truly are an amazing woman, Claire Patterson."

"And you just made a smart decision," Claire said with a glint in her eyes.

"Oh yeah, what's that?"

"Not giving up on us. Even though this wasn't a conventional way to meet, that doesn't change the chemistry between us."

"And who knows, that could be why you were the one chosen to be the messenger."

"My thoughts exactly." She squeezed his hand. "Now, if you're ready, we should probably go see Maggie and Brad. They wanted to know how you're doing before they go to tell your parents."

Chapter 29

REMEMBERING

They walked hand in hand toward the house where they found Maggie and Brad waiting for them on the front porch.

Claire called from across the lawn, "Hey Brad, some news, huh?"

"Absolutely! Beyond incredible." He stood to join them as they came up the steps. "How about you, Chase, are you okay?"

"If you mean because of my mom and dad, only time will tell. But as far as Zac goes, I can't wait to see him and have him back in our lives."

"Maggie and I talked it over; we won't tell your parents until you're ready."

"You can go tell them now. It's not fair that they should have to wait for the best news they'll ever receive, especially on my account. I just hope Zac's life will bring them some much-needed joy."

Maggie stood and wrapped Chase in her arms. "No matter how they act going forward, we hope you know how much we love you and that won't ever change."

She kissed his cheek and then took a step back, leaving room for Brad to put his hand on his shoulder. "You've become a son to us, and we have no plans of leaving the ranch."

333

THE PAINTER

A smile crept into the corners of Chase's lips. "Thanks. You've been my lifeline, and this means more to me than you know." He pulled them into a group hug. "I love you guys."

When they separated, Brad asked, "Are you sure you're going to be okay?"

Chase shoved his hands into his pockets. "It can't get any worse than it already is, right?"

"Right. All we can do is hope for the best."

Maggie gathered up the carved truck, the two pictures, and her phone. "Well then, there's no time like the present; do you two want to come with us?"

"Oh, uh, no thanks. I need to get home." Claire said.

"How about you, Chase?"

"I'll pass. It'd be better for me *not* to see their reaction. And anyway, this is a moment my parents need to enjoy without having to feel bad that they've treated me like crap all these years."

"Chase!" Brad shot him a stern look.

"Sorry. Just because this is a good day, doesn't eliminate our reality, which includes how they've treated *you* over the years."

"We know. We all want them to start treating us with more civility, but that doesn't mean we don't need to improve our own attitudes."

Chase gave a quick nod. "Yes, sir. I'll work on that. Now go; you have wonderful news."

Chase came and stood behind Claire and put his hands on her shoulders. Together they watched Maggie and Brad climb into his truck and drive away.

After they were out of sight, Claire asked, "Do you want to come to my place for the rest of the day? My mom wants to meet you, and you can talk rodeo stuff with my dad and Trevor over dinner."

"Sounds tempting, but I probably shouldn't."

228

"Come on, your dad can't begrudge the fact that you will need some time to absorb the news. Let's go." Claire grabbed his hand and pulled him off the porch.

"Okay, but I'll drive separately; I need some time alone. You get that don't you?"

"Of course. And anyway, then I won't have to bring you back later. Jump in and I'll drive you to your place."

An hour and a half later, they pulled into the Pattersons' driveway. An unfamiliar truck and horse trailer were parked by the arena.

Chase parked behind Claire. She had already gotten out of her SUV and was coming toward his truck before he got out. "Hey, do you mind if we go check out who's in the barn? I want to see which horse we're selling."

"Sure."

As they walked toward the building, Claire said, "I talked to my dad this morning. I'm surprised he didn't mention we had a customer coming today."

"What's the big deal? It's not like you knew of every transaction while you were at college."

"True, but I spend four hours a day training the horses now. I want to be sure the customer is happy, that's all."

When they walked in, everyone was at the far end of the arena. One man was on a horse in the box behind where Paul stood. Trevor was a few feet away, by a second box. He nodded to his dad and then released the latch; a calf shot out. Paul let it get a head start before opening the chute. When he did, the rider kicked his horse into action and within a few seconds, he had the calf lassoed, down, and its feet tied.

"Impressive," Claire said.

Chase agreed. "His style is a lot like Jack's." As he leaned over the wooden railing, he abruptly blurted out, "No way!"

"What?"

"Look." He pointed to the guy who was now untying the rope to let the calf go free. It bounded to its feet, kicked its back legs and took off.

Claire stepped onto the bottom rail and pulled herself up. "Well, I'll be—"

"Hi Sis, nice of you to join us." Trevor's voice cut through their amazement. Wearing his usual grin, he held out his hand to Chase. "Good to see you again, man."

"You too. Hey, is that Jack Hendrickson?"

"It sure is. His horse came up lame during practice this morning, so he gave us a call to see if we had a horse show-ready. I don't know if we have what he wants, this is the third horse he's tried."

"The first day I came here, when you were timing the Paint Horse, I told Claire, you can have all the skill in the world but if your horse can't make the turns quick enough—or in this case, get out of the box—you're not guaranteed a win."

"That's true."

Jack remounted the horse, and they watched as he maneuvered her around the barrels and over some of the jumps set along the far side.

"Come on, I'll introduce you." Trevor strode toward the people at the far end.

As they followed, Claire whispered, "Chase, are you okay?"

"I think so. We'll just have to see how it goes."

When they reached the group, the older gentleman was speaking to Paul. Trevor let him finish before saying, "Excuse me, Claire, this is Robert Wagner."

She nodded. "Nice to meet you, sir."

"You can call me, Bobbie, everyone else does." He pointed to his right. "And this is my granddaughter, Emma."

Claire smiled. "Nice to see you again, Emma."

Paul jerked his head their way. "You two know each other?"

"Sort of. We met at the arts and crafts fair a few weeks ago."

Then, a little girl with long blond curls stuck her head out from behind her mother's legs and said, "Mommy, I know her."

"Yes, you do, sweetie."

Claire knelt and held out her hands. Without hesitation, Zoe ran and jumped into them. In one smooth motion, Claire swung her onto her hip and said, "Hi Zoe, how have you been?"

"I'n good. Look, my daddies on a horse."

"Do you like that one?"

"Uh huh, it's beautiful."

"It sure is." Claire gave Zoe a hug and set her down.

Jack joined the group and Bobbie asked, "So what do you think of this one?"

"I like it." He hopped down and patted the horse's neck. Then he saw Claire. "Well, well, if it's not the picture thief. What are you doing here?"

"Ha-ha. Actually, I'm the one who trained that horse. Zoe likes it best, and she ought to know." Claire smirked.

"So you work here?"

"Yeah, Paul's my dad, Trevor's my brother, and this is Chase, the guy in the painting that I 'didn't steal' the picture of."

"Hi, Chase, it's nice to meet you." He pulled off his glove and reached through the fence to shake his hand.

"The pleasure is mine. You've become our favorite rider since you joined the circuit."

"Thanks." Jack nodded. "I'm glad to hear it."

"Now, Claire, what's this about a painting?" Chase asked.

"Oh yeah, I haven't shown it to you yet. Your backside has been a good money maker for me." She playfully nudged his shoulder.

"Uh, I have no idea what you're talking about."

"Chase, you didn't give Claire permission to paint you?" Jack asked with a touch of sarcasm in his voice, but then a smile curled across his lips.

"You two are a trip." Claire fished her phone from her back pocket, found the picture, and handed it to Chase. "I took this the night you walked out of Zac's stall." She nodded to him as he took it, hoping he would help with the narrative.

"Oh, so now you're using me to make money? I can't wait to see the actual painting."

"It's really good," Jack said. "Here, let me look."

Chase handed him the phone.

Jack's expression became serious as he stretched the picture and moved it back and forth on the screen. Without looking up, he said, "I don't know why, but I feel like I've been in this barn before."

"That's because you have." Chase looked straight at him.

Their eyes met.

Emma stepped closer and looked at the two men. "But how do you know that?"

Chase pulled his gaze from Jack just long enough to say, "Because it's where he grew up."

Emma gasped and covered her mouth. Bobbie quickly put his arm around her shoulders to help steady her. They watched in silence, as Claire realized they must be hoping Jack would remember who he was.

Jack let go of the horse's reins and quickly climbed over the fence to stand face to face with Chase. A moment later, he grabbed his arms and cried out, "You're my brother!"

Chase threw his arms around Zac and wouldn't let go. They both cried and laughed and smacked each other on the back.

Once Chase regained his composure, he said, "We thought you were dead. I only found out a few hours ago that you weren't and look, here you are."

"But how did you make the connection?"

"That would be Claire's doing."

With a priceless smile, she said, "Your Aunt Maggie and I drove out to Freddie's place this morning. He's the one who told us of your rescue."

"Now I'm really confused. How in the world do you know about Freddie?"

"It's kind of a long story. How about you guys work out the details with the horse, and I'll go help mom make enough food for everyone. We can talk about it over dinner."

"We'd appreciate that," Emma said sniffing. She started to wipe her nose with the back of her hand, but Bobbie grabbed a bandana from his pocket and handed it to her.

"Here, use this."

"Thanks, Gramps. Claire, can Zoe and I come help?"

"Of course. Follow me."

"Wait." Chase reached for Claire's hand. "Before you leave, I have a question." He turned to Zac. "How is it that you remembered me so quickly?"

"Yeah, Freddie was afraid you wouldn't recognize your family," Claire said. "You know, with the memory loss and all."

"Actually, it's the strangest thing . . . ever since I saw the painting of Chase a few weeks ago and you mentioned his name, I started having flashbacks to when we were kids. Which didn't help me any, because I couldn't remember my real name, or where we lived." He turned to Emma. "This is an answer to all our prayers."

"It sure is!" She threw her arms around him and added, "I'm so happy for you . . . for us . . ."

"For all of us," Claire said. "What an amazing turn of events, which includes the painting of Zoe. I'll explain over dinner."

Before she started toward the house, Chase squeezed her hand and whispered, "Thank you."

Helen was in the living room crocheting an afghan. "Hi, Mom. You remember Emma, don't you?"

"Of course, I do. What brings you here today?"

"We're buying a horse."

"It's beautiful," Zoe said as she brushed the curls off her face. "But Mommy, why was Daddy crying?"

Helen looked from Zoe to Emma. "Is everything okay? It looks like you've been crying, too."

Zoe put her hands on her hips. "I didn't cry."

Claire picked her up and kissed her cheek.

Without pretense, Zoe wrapped her little arms around Claire's neck and said, "I wuv you."

Now Claire's eyes were moist.

"Can someone please tell me what's going on here?" Helen put down the blanket and got to her feet.

"The short version is that Emma and I have come to help you cook. We have five extra people for dinner tonight."

"It's kind of short notice, don't you think?"

"Oh, but it'll be so worth it." She squeezed Zoe and spun her in a circle. Zoe giggled. When they stopped, Claire said, "Remember Emma's husband?"

"Sort of. Why?"

"He's Chase's brother."

Helen's palms sailed upward as her eyes widened.

Claire grinned and threw an arm around Emma's shoulder. "Turns out, Zac is very much alive."

"Oh, my. When did you find this out?"

"About twenty minutes ago," Emma said with a glint in her eyes. "Jack has finally found his family."

Helen looked at Claire.

"Jack is the name he's been going by for the last ten years."

"Ahh." She nodded. "Jack works . . . and we better get to work too. What shall we have for dinner?"

"Sketti," Zoe yelled, throwing her hands into the air.

Emma laughed. "If you couldn't tell, spaghetti is her favorite."

"Perfect. That's easy enough to make for a lot of people."

They all walked to the kitchen, and Claire set Zoe on the bench by the farm table. "Wait here; I'll go get you a coloring book."

Zoe got onto her knees and leaned her elbows on the table. Helen gave her a cookie. "Tank you."

"You're welcome, Zoe." Helen patted her head and then went to get out the pots and pans and directed Emma on how she could help.

Claire came back and got Zoe situated. "So, Mom, do you think Dad will believe me now?"

"It'd be hard not to, but how did you make the connection?"

"I'll save most of the story for when everyone's here. But because you knew I went to visit Luke's friend Freddie, I'll tell you this much. Freddie is the one who saved Zac's life."

"But why—"

"Later Mom, the guys will be here shortly, and you haven't even met Chase yet."

"Chase is here, too?"

"Yes, ma'am," Emma said. "That's why we were crying earlier. The brothers reunited after all these years. It was a beautiful sight."

Chapter 30

AN APOLOGY

Between Claire, Trevor, Helen, and Chase, it took all of dinner and then some to explain the events of the last two months. Helen got everyone a cup of coffee, and they moved to the living room.

Once everyone found a seat, Claire turned to Jack and said, "So for all the ribbing you gave me about stealing Emma's picture, these events are undeniably an answer to your own prayers."

"It seems more elaborate than necessary, but hey, I'll take it. I can't wait to be reunited with my parents."

Claire felt Chase stiffen at this comment. "You've heard our story; how about you tell us yours."

"Well, as you already know, Freddie pulled me from the river. He's such a great guy. I owe my life to him, not only for saving me but also for the painstaking effort he put into helping me get better. Even after I moved to Bobbie's ranch, he would come to visit with new questions and bring up things I said just after becoming conscious. Gradually, I began to remember more."

"But it's weird how you couldn't remember your name or where you lived," Chase said.

"Yeah, I looked it up online. The articles I read said that it is an anomaly and very rare that memory loss at my age would be permanent. But then again, it's a miracle that I'm alive, and for the amount of time I went without oxygen, that I'm mentally well at all. Anyway, since Zoe was born, and even more so now that

Emma's expecting again, we've started praying for my memory to return. Zoe has grandparents and great-grandparents on Emma's side." He nodded to Bobbie, who gave him a thumbs-up. "But I wanted my wife and kids to be a part of my family. To know my parents and now that I remember, to know you, Chase."

"Aunt Maggie and Uncle Brad went to give Mom and Dad the news at the same time we left to come here earlier today."

"So they already know too, huh? That's great. I'm sorry that I couldn't save Johnny and that you lost both your brothers in one day."

"And I'm sorry Dad wouldn't let me come after you. He thought you were strong enough to make it to land. None of us could believe, as we thought at the time, that you drowned."

"Yeah." Jack unconsciously rubbed the scar on his left cheek. "I don't remember any of that, even now."

"I should probably give you a heads-up, though. That day destroyed our father. Mom has spent the last ten years catering to him, pushing him to find joy in life again. To appreciate the s—" Chase bit his lip to keep it from quivering, abruptly stood, and walked out.

Jack shot Claire a look. "Whoa, did I just miss something?"

Claire got to her feet. "I need to go, but what he was going to say was, appreciate the *son he still had*. Excuse me." She ran out the door and caught Chase at his truck. "Where are you going?"

"It's great seeing Zac, and I appreciate the miracle of it, but every time my parents get mentioned, it makes me sick. I know I have to get over it, but please don't expect that to be today."

He jumped into his truck and spun out of the driveway. Claire stood there until his truck was out of sight. *Dear Jesus, please touch Chase and comfort him. I don't know what else I can do.*

Claire walked onto the porch and looked through the screen door before entering. Jack had his hands locked in front of him, staring at the floor. Emma was rubbing his back, while the others talked quietly.

Every eye shot her way when she entered the room. "Um, sorry about that."

Jack stood. "I don't understand what just happened."

"Nothing *just happened* . . . this has been ten years in the making."

"What's been ten years?" Emma asked, her hands now resting on her protruding stomach.

"Ten years of being either invisible or the one to take the brunt of Roger's anger. He told me recently that there were times when he wished he'd been the one to die."

"So what you're saying is that my dad took that kayaking accident out on Chase?"

"Pretty much. Your Aunt Maggie told me that it was so bad in the early years that she and your Uncle Brad had to come to save the ranch. They've lived there for nine years now."

"Huh, I had no idea."

"Why would you?" Helen asked. "None of this is your fault. You did what you could to save Johnny."

"Right." Claire nodded. "But to be clear, things have been incredibly difficult for Chase and you being back is not going to solve everything overnight. So please, don't take any of this personally. You saw his response earlier when you recognized him."

"It was such a sweet moment," Emma said.

"Exactly. Chase is thrilled to know you're alive and back in his life. What's yet to be seen is if things get better or worse for him once you're back in your parents' lives."

Jack massaged the back of his neck. "Thanks, Claire. I'll be sure to keep that in mind. Well, with a three-hour drive ahead of us, we should get the horse loaded and head for home. Thank you for dinner, Mrs. Patterson. We appreciate your hospitality, especially on short notice."

"You're welcome, Jack. And I know we're not related yet, but—"

"Mom!" Claire swung toward her, looking mortified.

"Come on, Sis. It's obvious that you and Chase are crazy about each other, and we're happy for you."

Though Claire smiled, she still punched Trevor's arm.

"Ahem," Helen said loudly, "What I was going to say is, I hope we'll see more of you and your growing family."

"That's very kind of you, ma'am," Jack said, helping Emma to her feet. "I'm sure we can make that happen." Then he scooped Zoe out of the chair she was sleeping in and turned again to Claire. "Even if we don't end up related," he winked, "thanks for finding me. We are forever in your debt."

Before they left the house, Claire and Jack exchanged phone numbers, and then Paul and Trevor went with them back to the barn.

Once their guests were gone, Claire started helping her mom clean up the kitchen.

"Things should get better for Chase, right?" Helen asked, sounding less confident than she meant to.

"I would hope so." Claire glanced at the wall clock that hung above the door to the living room. "Chase won't be home yet, but I'll call him later to make sure he's okay. The time alone in his truck should give him a chance to cool off and to think rationally about everything."

They cleaned in silence and were almost finished with the dishes when the guys came in. Paul took off his hat and put it on the hook. "Claire?"

"Hmm?"

"I still don't understand all the ins and outs of this story, but I want to apologize for not believing you . . . especially after your mom and Trevor both started to."

Claire dried her hands and went to give her dad a hug. "Thanks." She took a step back. "And thanks for giving me the morning off."

"Yeah, when you said something came up that couldn't wait, you meant it."

"Well, there didn't seem to be a bigger purpose or anything to connect the paintings until after we met Freddie last night."

"It is amazing how quickly everything fell into place," Helen said.

"I know, right? And yet, with everything else being miraculous, I'm not really surprised."

Trevor, who was leaning against the doorway to the living room, jumped into the conversation. "Do you want to know what's really weird?"

They all looked his way.

"How much Jack and Chase acted alike, especially after ten years apart."

"Really?" This news came as a surprise to Claire. "Chase told me that Zac was quite cocky before the accident and that they didn't really get along."

"Huh, I didn't detect that at all."

"Neither did I," Paul said. "Even when he was fussy about what horse to buy, he didn't seem proud or condescending."

Helen took a seat at the farm table. "I read recently that severe brain injuries can alter a person's personality. Maybe that has something to do with it."

"Or he's just so thankful to be alive that he treats each day as a gift," Trevor suggested.

"Either way, I hope that works in Chase's favor." Claire gathered her things. "I'm going home. I want to give him a call."

Claire dimmed the lights, stuffed a sofa pillow under her left arm, and got comfortable before making the call. "Hi, Chase. How are you holding up?"

"Yeah, uh, sorry for taking off like that. I cried and screamed and cried some more the whole way home . . . I'm not sure it helped."

"Let's hope it did," Claire said as cheerfully as she could. Chase needed time and space to deal with this new reality, so she wasn't surprised that his emotions were all over the place and being miffed at him wasn't going to help.

"Did Jack think I was a jerk for leaving without saying goodbye?"

"No, he was more confused. I briefly explained how things have been with your dad and do you know how he replied?"

"That bad, huh?" Chase asked, barely above a whisper.

Claire could hear pain oozing through each word and she wished she could hold him. "Actually, he sounded empathetic and seemed genuinely disappointed that you've had such a rough go of it. He also said that he'd keep this in mind when he sees your parents. I know we just met him, but I feel like he'll have your back."

"If you'd been wearing my shoes for the last ten years, you might not be so optimistic."

"I was hoping my optimism would be something that could help you realize that you have a lot to be grateful for . . . especially in your recent past."

"Right as always, aren't you?"

Chase's words sounded pert and laced with sarcasm. Yet, without being able to see his face, Claire wasn't sure if she'd interpreted him correctly. It'd been a long day and she suddenly wasn't in the mood to coddle him. "Hey, how about you give me a call sometime tomorrow. Goodnight." Not waiting for an answer, she hung up.

Claire pulled the pillow from under her arm and buried her face in it. *Ugh. I probably shouldn't have done that, but he's not in a good place right now, and apparently, there's nothing I can say at this point that will help.*

Claire got ready for bed and then decided to call Maggie. "Hey there, I was wondering how Roger and Michelle took the news about Zac."

"It took them a while to get over the initial shock. Then they hit me with a barrage of questions. Eventually, they both broke down and cried."

"Did they seem okay by the time you left?"

"Believe it or not, Michelle invited us for dinner and Roger didn't object. We had the best time together. I'd say a mending of hearts has already begun, and they don't even know if Zac will remember them."

"That's great." Claire smiled despite the unsettled feeling in the pit of her stomach. "Now we need to pray for a healing of hearts all the way around."

"I presume you're talking about Chase. How's he doing?"

"I guess I don't know enough about his past to understand what he's going through. His emotions are all over the place, especially when it comes to his dad. As you know, I only met Roger once; he seemed nice enough to me."

"Has Chase told you about trying to follow in Zac's footsteps by competing in the high school rodeo competitions?"

"Not yet. Why?"

"In your painting of the boys, Chase was on his tiptoes, trying to look taller. Remember?"

"Yeah, so?"

"To me, it represented his struggle to fit in . . . to be noticed. That fall after the accident, Chase competed . . . he even used Zac's prize-winning horse, but he came in fourth place."

"That's not bad," Claire said. "He must have been one of the younger guys competing if I have the timeline right."

"True, but that didn't matter to Roger. When Chase got home, he reamed him out and told him he'd never compete again. The next day, Roger sold Zac's horse."

"Oh no, what an awful thing to do."

"That's not even the worst of it. He told Chase he wasn't worthy to be his son. That he wished he had died and not Zac." Maggie sighed, long and loud.

"Wait, Roger actually said that to him?" Claire couldn't believe her ears.

"That's what Michelle told me when she called to say how bad things were getting."

"I'm sure Roger was just disappointed and didn't really mean it."

"Mean it or not, he never apologized. I can't even imagine the depth of that blow. To be honest, I took it personally for a long time because Brad and I weren't able to have any children of our own. When Michelle called again the following spring and begged us to come help at the ranch, we did, mostly for Chase's sake."

"So you and Brad are the reason Chase turned out to be such a great guy?"

"We did what we could."

"Your love for him has obviously helped. He speaks very highly of you both."

"Yeah, he's pretty special to us, too. And Claire?"

"Hmm?"

"You should know that Chase's not competing has always been a sore spot for him. Now that Zac's not only alive but made the rodeo circuit, it could cause yet another wound to fester."

"Thanks, Maggie. This conversation has been enlightening, though it leaves me at a disadvantage. I tried to cheer him up earlier, but because I can't relate, my words seemed to ring hollow."

"Please don't take any of this personally. I'd hate for his mood swings to come between the two of you. Normally, he's pretty solid, but these have been far from normal circumstances."

Chapter 31

BITTERSWEET

The next morning when Claire got to work, Trevor and Paul were coming from the house. She hailed a "good morning" and went to join them.

"Morning, Sis. I'm sorry Chase up and left like that last night. Is he okay?"

"I think he will be, but at this point, it's hard to tell. He wasn't in the mood to talk when I called him so I figured I should give him some space."

"Just be sure not to give him *too* much space," Paul admonished. "I'm guessing with all that's happened he'll need you to be there for him."

"Yeah, but Dad, that's part of the problem, I don't want our relationship built on top of all the baggage from his past, which makes his brother's return bittersweet. It's not like we have a sure foundation to build on yet, and because of the miracle paintings, Chase figures he wasn't even supposed to be a part of this story."

"But why not?" Trevor asked. "He is Zac's brother."

Claire looked down at her work gloves and saw she had them wound tighter than a spring. She let go of the one end and watched them slowly unwind. It was then that she realized there was more to it. "I mean a part of *our* story. He feels like he should have never fallen for me. That everything is weird now because of how and why we met."

"Yeah, but why can't that be just another part of this cool story?"

"That's what I thought." She shifted her weight and started winding her gloves again. "But it takes two and if he doesn't agree, it doesn't really matter what I think."

"I wouldn't lose heart, my dear," Paul said. "Think about it, if you weren't with Chase, he wouldn't have shown up here yesterday. I'd say it all played out perfectly."

"That was pretty great, wasn't it?" Claire finally smiled.

"It sure was." Paul nudged her shoulder and bobbed his head toward the barns. "Come on, we have work to do."

Claire got home about 12:20, got some lunch and then went to the loft. Even though she didn't expect to find a new message, she really hoped there would be one. With her hands shoved into her back pockets, she started rocking from heel to toe as she looked around her desk. There was no note, and nothing looked out of place. *Oh well.*

The box that held her collection of old photos still lay open on the futon, so she took a seat and started looking through them. Nothing jumped out at her as something she really wanted to paint. After a few minutes, Claire put the box down and stared out the window. They hadn't signed up for any of the fall arts and crafts shows, so there was really no reason that she would have to start something new today. And if she was honest with herself, she wasn't in the mood to paint.

All she could think about was Chase. She wished that he would call or text. Because of the strain left from last night's call, she didn't feel it was her place to contact him first. Yet, her dad's words echoed in her ears, 'Just be sure not to give him too much space.'

Anxiety came in like a flood, washing her confidence away and causing her to wonder how much she should push or if she even wanted to. With a heavy heart, she walked to the loft window and watched the clouds race over the distant mountains. *Oh Chase, why can't you look past the circumstances of our meeting and see me. I love you.* A small laugh caught in her throat. *It's not like I'd dare to call and tell him that.*

But she did need someone to talk to . . . someone who would understand, so she grabbed her phone from her back pocket and called Maggie. "Hey, um, hi. Do you happen to know how Chase is doing today?"

"So that means he's not talking to you either, huh?"

"Not since last night, before I talked to you."

"I guess that makes sense. I spoke with Brad at lunch, and he said Chase did come to work but stayed to himself. When he tried to approach him, Chase just said, 'Please, not now,' and walked away."

Then as if a light came on, Claire asked, "Do you mind if I drive out to your place? I have news."

"What news?"

"News I'd rather tell you in person."

"Oh, okay. Why don't you plan on coming for dinner?"

"Sounds great. I'll leave shortly."

Claire went to get changed and had just grabbed her jean jacket off the hook by the kitchen door when her phone rang. She scooped it up in a hurry, hoping it was Chase. To her disappointment, it wasn't. But then again, it was someone who might have info. "Hello?"

A cheerful little voice was on the other end. "Hi Cwaire, tis is Zoe."

"Hi, Zoe, I'm so glad you called."

"I'n a big girl cuz I'n on the phone."

"Yes, you most certainly are."

She giggled. "My daddy wants to talk to you."

"Okay, thanks for saying hi."

Jack took the phone. "Zoe adores you."

"That's because I've made her famous, remember? You know the whole stolen painting and all."

"Oh snap. You'll never let me live that down now, will you?"

"Not a chance, but I do think it's fun how she's taken to me."

"Take it as a compliment, she's usually quite shy. Hey, um, how's Chase doing?" Concern abruptly dogged Jack's tone. "I've tried to call him a few times, but he won't answer."

"I can't help you there because I haven't talked to him since last night, either."

"I'm sorry to hear that."

"Me too, but is Chase the only reason for your call?"

"No. I paid Freddie a visit this morning."

"Is there a problem?"

"I don't know; that's why I wanted to talk to Chase. Freddie fears my dad will be furious with him for not taking me to a hospital."

"I talked to your Aunt Maggie after she told your parents that you were alive. It seems their biggest concern is that you won't recognize them."

"On that front, Freddie showed me the picture of my family when we were all younger and my memories seem to be returning rather quickly."

Claire pumped her fist. "That's fantastic, Jack."

"It sure is, but should I pretend to not remember them to keep their focus on that, instead of on Freddie?"

"No, I think that would make things worse."

"How so?"

"Because when they realize you recognize them, they should be so overjoyed that it won't matter. But also, if they still end up being mad, you'll be able to defend Freddie."

"Oh, good call. I didn't think of that. Freddie also mentioned the plan was to meet at the rodeo at Ten Sleep, but now that I've seen Chase, I'm not sure I want to wait till then to see my parents."

"Nor should you have to. I'll text you with what info I have."

"Thanks, Claire. Our family owes you a debt of gratitude."

"No one owes me anything, and anyway, this was all set up by things clearly beyond my control."

"True, but if you didn't sell the paintings or pursue the stories, despite the flack you got for them, this reunion wouldn't be possible."

"I am truly happy for your sakes." Claire's tone betrayed her.

"I know we haven't known each other long but something seems off. Are you okay?"

"Oh, um . . . I'm fine."

"Claire?"

"I met your brother because of the paintings, but he didn't know about them until the other day when we met Freddie. Now he feels weird about being with me."

"But why would that change things between the two of you? He seemed okay with the paintings yesterday." Jack sounded more confused than concerned.

"I don't think it's the paintings, it's more like he thinks that I have an unfair advantage and that our relationship was built on a false pretense. He became snarky with me last night when I tried to give him some positive feedback. Apparently, the wounds from his dad are deeper than I realized. Paintings or not, I can't relate. So even though my heart hurts for Chase, all he can see is me being someone who thinks I have all the answers without having a clue."

"I'm sure once the dust settles, Chase will see you for the gem you are."

"I hope so because, at the moment, I'm not in a position to help him see things clearly."

"Neither am I," Jack said. "He's not answering my calls either, remember?"

"Right. And Maggie said he avoided Brad all morning, too. I know this is off subject, but Chase really is a great guy. I hope the two of you will become the best of friends."

"I'm looking forward to that."

"And maybe . . . eventually . . . you could encourage your parents to give Chase a chance."

❖ ❖ ❖

Claire arrived around 3:00 and found Maggie in her vegetable garden.

"You made it. I was expecting you a while ago." She tossed a handful of green beans into her basket and kept picking.

"I was delayed because I got a call from Jack."

Maggie sprang to her feet. "Jack talked to Freddie? Does he remember?"

"Slow down with the questions and I'll tell you, but first, where do you want me to pick?"

"We won't need more than the row I'm in, so you can start at that end."

Claire ate a bean and they both started picking before she continued, "You'll never guess what happened."

"You're right. Now stop with the suspense already! Does Jack remember his family or not?"

"When I spoke to you earlier, I said I had news. Well, that was *before* Jack called me."

Maggie leaned back on her heels. "I'm not following . . . what could be more important than Jack?"

Claire grinned. "You're taking all the fun out of my story."

"I'm sure it'd be more fun if you'd share with the class."

"Chase needed time to think after he found out that Jack was alive, so I invited him to my place. He hadn't met my mom yet, and I thought it would be a good distraction. When we arrived, a truck and trailer were there that I didn't recognize so we went to the arena first. To our great surprise, there was Zac buying a horse."

"Oh my." Maggie put a hand over her heart. "Was that awkward?"

"A little at first but because I had met him a few weeks ago, it opened up the conversation. It went in such a way that Jack remembered Chase. They embraced and cried. It was truly beautiful, and they hit it off really well."

"That's wonderful and it means that Zac should remember his parents, too." Maggie waved her hands in the air with the excitement of a young child running through a water sprinkler. "What glorious news!"

Claire wasn't sure if she should interrupt this reverie, so she waited a bit longer before saying, "Um, have you heard enough, or would you like me to finish my story?"

Maggie burst out laughing. "Oh, sorry." She rolled a hand in Claire's direction. "Please, continue."

"Are you sure? It's kind of important, and I don't want to squelch your joy."

Suddenly, Maggie became serious. "Isn't everything okay?"

Claire bobbed her head. "Yes and no. We invited him and his family to join us for dinner. That way the boys had more time together, and we could explain how we met Freddie and all the pertinent details."

"You mean to tell me, you saw Jack before he even talked to Freddie and he still remembered?"

Claire nodded.

"That's great . . . but wait, why is Chase all out of sorts then?"

"That's the part of my story that's not okay. Chase was engaged in listening and answering questions. Things were going well until Jack started asking about his parents. Chase let him know that *that day* changed everything, how it destroyed their father. How their mom has spent the last ten years catering to him, pushing him to find joy in life again. Then he said, 'and to appreciate the—' he quit midsentence and left without even saying goodbye."

"The son they still had," Maggie whispered and then got to her feet. "Oh, Claire, after seeing how giddy Roger and Michelle were last night, it'll be interesting to see how this all plays out."

"That brings me back to Jack's phone call earlier. He visited Freddie this morning and doesn't want to wait until the rodeo to be reconnected with his parents. I didn't have their info, but I gave him your number and address."

"Do you think he'll show up without calling me first?"

"If he hasn't called you already, he might. He sounded like it was his top priority."

Maggie felt her pockets. "Shoot, I left my phone in the house. I'll go check it."

"Okay and I'll finish picking the beans."

"Here, put yours in this basket. I'll be right back."

Maggie never came back to the garden, so when Claire knew she had more than enough beans, she started for the back door. It was then that she heard a voice calling to her from the front corner of the house.

Chapter 32

TEXAS

"Hey, Claire, what are you doing here?" Chase rode closer before dismounting Mingo.

She started caressing the horse's nose. "I hadn't heard from you, so I came to see Maggie. I thought she should know we met Jack."

"Couldn't you have told her that on the phone?"

Claire's shrug quickly turned into a flirtatious smile. "Actually, I used it as an excuse to come see you."

"But why didn't you call me first?" He stepped closer.

"With the way we left things last night, I didn't want to push." Then she sheepishly laughed while turning three shades of red. "Like coming to see you without an invitation isn't pushing, right?"

Instead of answering, he pulled her close.

She willingly leaned into his embrace and said, "See, things make more sense in person."

"And this is why I don't want to lose you."

Claire jerked back and looked him in the eyes. "But why do you think you'll lose me?"

"Because, I've made up my mind," he reached to tuck some loose strands of hair behind her ear, "after Jack reconnects with our parents, I'm moving."

"Moving where?"

"A friend of mine from high school went to Texas a few years ago to work on his uncle's ranch. He told me if I ever needed to get out of here to give him a call, so I did. He said this was great timing because one of their ranch hands is retiring at the end of September. He's already put a good word in for me to be the guy's replacement."

Claire forced a smile but then looked away so he wouldn't see the concern etched in her brow. *He can't be serious, can he?* She needed time to process this and think through the ramifications of such a move.

"Hey, how about we take a walk so we can plan out our future." He reached for her hand, which she tentatively offered. They led Mingo to the barn, but before he removed the saddle he asked, "Would you rather I get out Chicory and we go for a ride, instead?"

"No, it's easier to talk when one of us can't take off like the wind as soon as we hear something we disagree with."

"Is that your way of saying you already disagree with me?" Chase asked. When no answer came, he removed the saddle and got Mingo back into his stall.

Claire sat on a bale of straw, crossed her legs, and tried to brace for what was coming next. It wasn't until he slid the door shut that she said, "I'm not in the mood to walk either."

"Ah, okay." Chase took a quick look around and saw an empty bucket that he could use for a seat. He flipped it over and set it in front of her. "So, I know we haven't dated long, but I really think we could make a go of it. I'd like you to come with—"

"Chase, stop! You're not moving anywhere; at least not anytime soon."

His expression soured as light vanished from his eyes. "I know it's not ideal, but I can't stay."

Claire started to answer, but he reached to put a finger on her lips.

"Please, just hear me out. My dad called last night after I got off the phone with you. You should have heard him; it was like he won the lottery or something."

Claire didn't let him finish. "What did you expect? This news is better than any lottery, and don't forget, you've gained a brother. I think the two of you could become good friends."

"Well, sure, but this isn't about Jack, it's about me finally feeling like I can leave this dreaded place. Dad will have his one and only son back, and no one will even miss me."

Claire shook her head. She wondered if he heard the words that were coming out of his mouth.

"What?" Chase snapped.

"I had no idea you were this selfish."

"Selfish?" He got to his feet, threw his hat, and kicked the bucket that he was sitting on down the aisle.

Claire flinched as it banged off a stall door two down from where she was sitting. The horses reared and neighed.

He glared at her with the same disdain she knew he held for his father, but not with the same reserve. He flailed his hands at her as he yelled, "I've stayed. I've worked countless hours without one bit of gratitude. I've put up with *his* condescension and have given up trying to accomplish my own dreams, just to keep the peace. How is that selfish?"

"And what about your mom? What about your Aunt Maggie and Uncle Brad? What about Jack and his family? I won't even include me in the questions for argument's sake." Claire got to her feet. "Just because you're at odds with your dad doesn't mean the rest of your family deserves to lose you. Not now. Not after what all of you have gone through."

With clenched teeth, he folded his arms across his chest. Claire had never seen his eyes this dark or foreboding before. It scared her a little, but she had no intentions of backing down now.

She walked toward him, her voice steady and inviting. "I know you've been hurt and none of us expect you to pretend the pain isn't real. Come, let's sit." As she untucked his brawny arms, she could feel his muscles relax a little, so she took his hand and led him back to the bale of straw.

This time they sat together. Chase leaned against the stall, crossed his arms again, and started rapidly tapping his foot. Then, without warning, he dropped his head into his hands and dug his fingers into his scalp. "It's not fair. None of this is fair."

"Fair is not the point, just look at Freddie. It's how we deal with our problems that makes or breaks us."

He shot a look her way and snapped, "Freddie has hidden from his problems for over forty years, so if that's your logic, why's it not okay for me to run?" Without waiting for a reply, he went back to staring at the floor.

The image of Chase lost on a raging sea flashed into Claire's mind, yet because her example backfired, she had no idea of how to get him safely to land. Not knowing what else to do, she started to massage his back in hopes of dissolving the tension between them.

The only sound that could be heard was the random movements of a penned calf. Several minutes passed before she leaned forward and whispered into his ear, "I love you . . . no matter what you choose."

Chase sat back.

Claire met his gaze with a hopeful smile. "And, just so you know, I understand more of your situation than you realize . . . Maggie told me what your dad said to you after your first rodeo, and why he sold Zac's horse."

Chase winced at these words. "She knows about that?"

"Yeah, your mom called her back when it happened. According to Maggie, you're the biggest reason she and Brad came to the ranch and the only reason they've stayed all these years."

Just then the sun found a break in the clouds and beamed through the stall windows, which caused light to invade Chase's eyes as the reality of her words seemed to soften his heart. "Huh."

"Exactly. You're loved more than you know, and if you think running away won't shipwreck this family again, then yes, you're selfish." Claire nudged his shoulder.

"Way to throw in a zinger right when I was starting to feel better."

"Well—"

"Okay, I get it." He nudged her back. "Thanks for setting me straight. I still have a few things to get done. Do you want to help or go visit with Maggie?"

"Actually, because you didn't answer Jack's calls earlier, he got ahold of me about coming to meet your parents, like soon. I want to go see if Maggie's heard anything."

They got to their feet, and Chase retrieved his hat before saying, "Maybe I should come with you then. It's not like any of this is that important in the scheme of things."

When they reached the house, Maggie was making pies.

"Whoa, a half hour ago you were picking beans, and now you're in full baking mode," Claire said. "What's going on?"

"We're having company."

Chase put his hat on the hook and leaned against the counter. "Does that mean Jack got a hold of you?"

"Yes. He wanted to know the best way to go about seeing his parents. After we talked for a few minutes, I gave him both his parents' cell numbers. Then out of the blue, he asked if we could meet here, so we worked out a plan."

"That's interesting," Chase said.

"He mentioned seeing you already and hoped that Brad and I could run interference, depending on how things went down."

"See, Chase, even your long-lost brother cares about you." Claire elbowed him.

"I was amazed at how well we hit it off yesterday. He must've forgotten that he didn't have the time of day for me before the accident."

"Or he realized how much he's missed you and wants a fresh start," Maggie suggested.

Claire was thankful Chase heard this from someone besides her. *Hopefully, he'll realize how much he's loved.* With a nod, she asked, "What time are they coming?"

"Jack said they could get here by 7:00. I've invited Roger and Michelle for dinner, and they said yes."

"Do they know Jack is coming?" Chase asked.

"No. I suggested we make it a surprise, especially now that I know Jack will recognize them. I also hoped the two of you could join us for dinner. Chase, don't you think it's time to introduce Claire to your mom?"

He looked at Claire. "Are you up for all this craziness?"

"Hey, I already accepted my invitation to dinner a few hours ago." With a broad smile, she winked at Maggie and then turned back to Chase. "So the question is, will *you* join us?"

Chase laughed. "You two are in cahoots against me, forcing me to face my fears."

Claire put a finger on his lips and looked playfully into his eyes. "And maybe you'll find out there is nothing to be afraid of. This could be the beginning of a beautiful future."

"Is that a promise?" He raised his eyebrows at her a few times.

"I meant for your family, but hey, if you play your cards right, it's certainly a possibility."

Without warning, he picked her up and spun her around the kitchen. They were both laughing when he put her down.

Claire briefly covered her lips. "Ahem, sorry about that Maggie. What can I do to help?"

"You two are so cute together." Maggie waved at them. "No apology necessary. Now, how about you roll out the pie dough. I need to finish cutting the apples."

"Okay."

"While you do that, I'll go finish the chores. What time's dinner?" Chase asked.

"Brad and Roger went to town on business; I told them 6:00. I'm guessing your mom will be here closer to 5:30 so unless you want Claire to meet her without you, be here before then."

Chase looked at his watch. "Got it." He grabbed his hat and left through the back door.

"I love seeing the change in him since he's met you."

"I wouldn't know how he's changed, but yeah, he's pretty great. On a different note, did you tell his parents about the paintings, and how we found Jack?"

"Not last night, but Michelle and I got together for coffee this morning, and I explained everything."

"Does she know that I'm the artist?"

"No, I thought it would be better if the two of you met first. Believe it or not, she's upset about the paintings."

"Wait—" Claire stopped rolling out the dough. The crease in her brow grew. "But why?"

"Because if God could do all these miraculous things, which she *does* believe, then why'd He wait ten years and allow their lives to be destroyed?"

"Hmm, I hadn't thought of that." Claire went back to working on the pie crusts and got the bottoms put into the glass dishes before saying, "Michelle has a valid point for sure, but from what we've learned, it seems that God's plan reached further than their pain and loss."

"Are you talking about Freddie?"

"Yeah, remember how he said, 'It was like God brought me to the river that day in time to save Zac—'"

"'When in reality, He brought Zac along in time to save me.' Yes, I remember." Maggie smiled. "And truth be told, if Freddie wasn't there, Zac would be dead, and we wouldn't be having this conversation."

"That's certainly one way to look at it, even though I'm sure Michelle is wondering why God allowed the accident to happen at all."

Maggie brought the bowl of sweetened apples and poured them into the pie plates. "You know, Claire, bad things happen to good, and even God-fearing, people. That doesn't mean He doesn't love them. And to be fair, God didn't *make* them put the kayaks in the river that day. Roger should have known better. Unfortunately, he's been angry with God ever since."

Maggie started helping Claire with the lattice tops, both were lost in their own thoughts.

When they finished, Claire said, "I was excited to hear that Zac and Emma had been praying about finding his family. I hope Roger and Michelle's anger, along with their sorrow, will be turned to joy tonight when they embrace."

"I hope so too." Maggie put the pies in the oven. "Now, if you don't mind, you could end and snap the beans while I clean up the mess from the pies. I already have a pot roast in the crockpot with potatoes and carrots."

"Yum, sounds delicious." Claire got a bowl and the basket of green beans and set to work. After a bit she asked, "Michelle isn't really mad at God, is she?"

"No, but she's been through a lot, more than most people realize. Getting the word that Zac's alive was like the story of Pilgrim's Progress. It was a beautiful sight to watch as the weight of the world seemed to roll off her shoulders."

"Aww, I'm so glad to hear that."

"Me too. You know how you care for Chase and want to help him through this transition?"

Claire nodded.

"Well, I feel the same way for my big sister. It was devastating that Roger made her choose him over Chase."

"That's so wrong," Claire said. "I guess I'm going to have to guard my attitude because I'm feeling a lot of anger toward Roger myself."

Maggie dried her hands and came to the table where Claire was sitting. "My dear, none of us know how we will act in difficult situations until we have to face them. So please don't allow these past events to cloud what we all hope will be, as you said to Chase, a beautiful future."

"Amen to that. I'm glad it worked out that I can be here when Zac comes. It should be a wonderful evening for everyone."

Chapter 33

MICHELLE

At 5:20, Claire heard a car door shut. "Now what? Chase isn't here yet. Should I sneak out the back door to wait for him?"

Maggie looked out the kitchen window. "That won't be necessary. Chase is walking from his place now. He'll be here shortly."

"Oh good." Claire quickly took out her ponytail and fluffed her long, wavy hair a few times before letting it fall around her shoulders. "How do I look?"

"Seriously?" Maggie stifled a laugh.

"I wasn't trying to be funny. I want to make a good first impression."

"My dear Claire, you've already done that." She patted her arm. "You can stay here and wait for Chase. I need to go greet Michelle."

There was a knock at the front door just as Chase slipped in through the back. "Wow, my mom got here sooner than I expected." He had changed out of his work clothes and was wearing a button-down, plaid shirt that was tucked into stonewashed jeans.

"Yeah, I was getting nervous that you weren't going to make it on time." She kissed his smooth cheek before adding, "By the way, you clean up nicely." It was the first time Claire had seen him cleanly shaven.

Chase rubbed his chin. "So, does that mean you like it?"

"I do." She smiled and took his hand. "Now, we need to go say hello."

Michelle was taller and thinner than Maggie, and though she was only a few years older, the lines of stress and sadness had aged her badly. Chase favored his mother's side of the family with the dark eyes and sharp facial features.

Chase and Claire joined the ladies on the front porch. When Michelle saw them, he said, "Um, hi Mom, this is Claire."

She smiled and put out her hand to take Claire's. "It's nice to finally meet you."

"Likewise," Claire said with a confident grip and a sweet smile.

Pain emanated from Michelle's eyes as she looked from Claire to Chase and back again. "Not like this one tells us anything. Roger did mention that you were a great help with the cattle drive a while back."

"Actually, ma'am, that was the first day we spent together." She nudged Chase, but he didn't smile. "Now that I've gotten to know him better, I think it would be safe to say you have a pretty amazing son."

To Claire's surprise, Michelle's dark eyes turned into a sea of glass. Her lips quivered as she murmured, "I never wanted things to be like this."

In that moment, time stood still. No one knew how to act or what to say. Claire began to wonder just how much of this story she still didn't know.

Michelle locked eyes with Chase as if pleading for him to reply but he didn't. Claire watched him struggle, wishing he would say something for Michelle's sake. No words came.

Maggie must have felt the tension too, because after giving them time to start some form of discourse, she said, "I have freshly brewed coffee in the kitchen. Anyone want some?"

Michelle held her gaze for a moment longer, flicked a tear away with her index finger, and left the porch. Maggie poured them both a mug of coffee, and they sat at the kitchen table talking in undertones.

Claire followed Chase to the living room, where he exhaled and took a few deep breaths. She gently touched his arm and whispered, "Hey, what am I supposed to do?"

He shrugged. "What do you want to do?"

"Stay in here with you of course, but I thought I should visit with your mom. Aren't you going to join us?"

"You just saw how awkward that was, so no, I'm not coming. I haven't been to the house since Christmas, and my mom only comes to the barns on the day she lost her sons. Brad always gives me the day off, so I make sure I'm nowhere near the ranch."

Claire frowned. "You're telling me that you haven't spoken to your mom in like eight months?"

"Sounds about right."

"Is the lack of communication your fault or hers?" Claire asked, but then quickly said, "Never mind; I'm going to the kitchen."

Chase took a seat at the piano and started playing.

Claire got a cup of coffee and joined the women. "I didn't know Chase could play the piano."

"Neither did I," Michelle said. "He's good."

Claire furrowed her brow. "But how do you not know that?"

"Ever since the accident . . . I assume you *know* about the accident."

Claire nodded.

"We've not been close."

Claire hoped this would be her opportunity to find out what really happened. She knew Chase's side of the story, but was he keeping something from her? "That's the part I don't get. Why wouldn't you love and adore your living son even more? It seems only natural to overcompensate for your loss."

Michelle squeezed her coffee mug. Claire saw her knuckles turn white, though her face remained stoic.

"I mean no offense, I just—"

This time Michelle cut her off. "Stop. Just stop. You have no idea of the pain and loss I've endured. I don't think you're in a

262

place to lecture me about whom or how I should show my affection." She started to stand, but Maggie grabbed her arm.

"You're not leaving. No one's throwing stones here. To put things in perspective, Claire hasn't known Chase for long, so she's only heard his side—"

"Right, but I don't know yours. Has Chase done something terrible that I ought to be concerned about? Should I walk away before it's too late?"

"Oh no, please don't do that. Roger actually likes you, which is rare, especially because you're with Chase. We're the ones at fault here. Roger always catered to Zac and even bought him a horse that we couldn't afford. I seemed to gravitate toward Johnny, who was young enough to still like spending time with me. Chase, unwittingly, got overlooked in the process. After the accident, we were so lost in our own grief that we didn't notice his. It wasn't until I saw Roger's disdain for Chase that I realized our mistake. The thing that fueled Roger's bitterness more than anything else was the fact that Chase couldn't compete at the same level as Zac—"

"But he was two years younger." Now it was Claire's knuckles that had turned white. "Why didn't Roger help him get better instead of bailing on him?"

"I thought if I worked toward saving our marriage and helping Roger get through his depression that his attitude toward Chase would improve." Michelle paused and let out a heavy sigh. Her eyes narrowed. "I suppose, in some ways, Chase was to blame. After Roger sold Zac's horse, Chase became resentful and—"

"Can you blame him?" Claire blurted out. Her face flushed.

Maggie gasped. "Claire, hold your tongue. You know better."

Claire's gaze went from Maggie to the table, but only for a moment. She knew she needed to fix this, or the evening would be ruined before it got started. She cleared her voice, "Ahem, Michelle, my outburst was uncalled for. I'm sorry."

"It's nice to see that you're so protective, but no matter what Roger asked Chase to do, he took it as a punishment . . . or in a negative way . . . which caused him to treat his father with disdain. I hope you can see how this made things worse for both of them."

Claire nodded but bit back a reply.

Michelle continued, "Chase was as lost as Roger, but I didn't know how to fix it. I pushed for counseling but neither of them would go. By the time Chase moved out, the relationship between them was pretty much destroyed."

Huh, it makes sense that the road would go both ways. Claire took another sip of coffee while trying to decide if the one question she still had was worth asking. *Yes, I need to know.* Barely above a whisper, she asked, "But why has Roger's attitude affected how *you* treated Chase?"

"When Chase moved out, I reached out to him and tried to rebuild our relationship, but Roger found out and got jealous. He told me I had to choose. I pleaded with him to reconsider but to no avail. I love my husband and have prayed for years that things would change. Now that we know Zac's alive, maybe things will finally improve."

"Let's hope so, for all of your sakes," Claire said.

"Maggie has been my lifesaver. Even though I didn't have permission to come visit, we would occasionally meet up at the local diner for lunch."

"And I would text Michelle pictures of Chase and give her updates—"

"Which I had to promptly delete so Roger wouldn't find out."

"But Michelle, why didn't you do the same for Chase?" Claire asked feeling slighted for his sake.

"I did in the early years, but the harder Roger became on him, the more closed off he became. Maggie tells me that your relationship with Chase has brought him back to life."

Claire's eyes sparkled as a broad smile swept across her face. "I'm glad I could help. And I'm also relieved to know Chase hasn't kept some deep, dark secret from me."

"You seem to be the one person who can penetrate that tough façade of his," Maggie said. "For that, we're all grateful."

"And I hope I can get to know you better," Michelle added.

"I'd like that." Claire reached across the table to squeeze her hand. It was then that she saw the slightest trace of a smile curl at the corner of Michelle's lips.

The music abruptly stopped when the back door opened, and Brad and Roger walked in.

Maggie got to her feet. "What perfect timing, if either of you would like coffee with dinner, serve yourselves. Now that you're here, we'll set the food out."

"Sounds good," Roger said. "I'm starving." He rubbed Michelle's shoulder as he passed her. "Hi, Claire. I thought that looked like your car in the driveway. Does that mean Chase is here?"

"Yes, sir. We stopped to see Maggie earlier, and she invited us for dinner." Claire joined Chase in the doorway.

He draped his arm over her shoulder and dryly said, "Dad."

"Claire, have you heard our marvelous news?" Roger asked, with baited enthusiasm.

She decided to play dumb, simply to see what would happen. "What news is that?"

"Figures Chase wouldn't tell you, he's probably too jealous."

"Seriously?" Chase snapped. "You're ridiculous."

Claire stepped in front of him. "Oh, do you mean the news about Zac? Of course, Chase told me." She beamed and spoke way too fast, not wanting a feud to break out before Jack arrived in an hour. "I mean for real, how amazing is that? We're both very excited."

Chase left Claire and her rambling with his dad and went to see how he could help Maggie.

She handed him some tongs, a knife, and a platter. "Here, pull the roast from the crockpot and cut it into strips. Claire, while Chase does that, can you please fill the water glasses?"

These activities helped alleviate the tension and Claire was thankful for a diversion. *Dang, I won't make that mistake again . . . I had no idea I was throwing Roger a bone that he would hurl at Chase.*

Small talk ensued while everyone got seated and dished. Then Roger started speaking loud enough that all other conversation ceased. Zac was the topic. How amazing he was to watch at rodeos, and how he couldn't wait to see him. At first, no one interrupted him because they were glad he was in a good mood. Eventually, Brad tried to get in a few words but to no avail.

When Michelle finished eating, she gently touched Roger's arm. "Um, this is the first time we've had a chance to see Chase in a long time, and I've just met Claire. Don't you think we could talk with them for a while?"

"Didn't they just say they were excited about Zac, so what's the problem?"

"We don't even know if Zac will remember us. Chase is right here."

"He's always been right here, it's not our fault he moved out and won't come visit," Roger answered.

Claire cringed. *Ah, so this is how he justifies his actions, putting all the blame on Chase.* She quickly reached her hand under the table and squeezed Chase's knee. He must have gotten her meaning because he didn't reply to that comment, but he did say in a tone that amazed her, "Fun fact, Claire's dad is Paul Patterson, the one who trains horses over in Buffalo. That's where you bought Zac's horse about eleven years ago, remember?"

Roger didn't acknowledge Chase, but looked at Claire and said, "No wonder you're so good on a horse."

It miffed Claire that Roger didn't answer Chase's question, but she did well not to let her frustrations show. "Yes, I was raised on a horse ranch, and even now I work part-time for my dad."

Again, Chase impressed her by saying, "Yeah, you should see her maneuver a horse around the barrels. This girl has skills."

Must be he's made up his mind not to let his dad win by getting under his skin. Claire nudged his shoulder with a huge grin plastered on her face. "You're too kind."

"The epitome of chivalry, right?" They both laughed.

Claire put an elbow on the table and lightly covered her lips. "Sorry, inside joke."

Roger speared a potato and shoved it into his mouth, leaving time for Michelle to ask, "So how did you two meet?"

"Well, it started when I met Maggie at Frontier Days."

"Yes," Maggie said. "Remind me after dinner, and I'll show you the portrait she painted for us. It's hanging in the living room."

"Oh, so you're an artist?"

"Yes. When I'm not working with the horses, I paint and sell my work at festivals and arts and crafts fairs."

"Yeah, well, I'd like to get my hands on the person who did that." Roger pointed his fork at the painting of the boys.

"Why? So you can thank them?" Brad asked.

"Ha-ha, very funny. It was wrong to have that painting for sale at a public event and you know it."

"I don't see why," Maggie said. "As far as I'm concerned, it was a way for me to find the painting and buy it for you."

Roger hit the table. "But this is none of your concern."

Michelle flinched, but must have found confidence in numbers because she said, "Enough already." She pushed her chair back and stood. "I love that painting, and it breaks my heart that we don't have it hanging in our house."

She started to leave the room but collapsed. Brad was sitting at that end of the table and was able to catch her before she hit the floor. Roger jumped to his feet and helped Brad carry Michelle to the couch in the living room.

"Should I call 9-1-1?" Claire asked.

"No, this has happened before," Roger said, his voice now softer. "She'll be okay in a minute. Maggie, can you please get a damp cloth?"

Chase leaned toward Claire and whispered in her ear, "He makes me so angry."

"I know, but you've done well not to show it and for your mom's sake, please don't blow it now." She leaned over and kissed his cheek before getting to her feet. "How about you help me clear the table; they'll be here soon."

She gathered up the dishes, while Chase brought the food back to the kitchen. They didn't bother to talk while they worked, even though Claire brushed playfully against him when they passed each other. By the time they finished, he was smiling and seemed to be in good spirits.

When they joined the others in the living room, Michelle was sitting up. "Sorry, you had to see our dysfunctional family in action, Claire."

"We aren't dysfunctional and don't owe anyone an apology." Roger snorted.

Claire ignored him and looked at Michelle. "What do you think of the portrait of Maggie and Brad?"

"Oh, I hadn't remembered to look." She got to her feet and walked to the mantle. "Wow, you do fantastic work. When Maggie said she commissioned a painting, I was surprised because she's quite the painter in her own right."

"I've seen a few of her pieces, and I agree. However, I had to do a self-portrait in college, and I'd much rather paint other people."

Then there was a knock at the front door.

"Are you expecting company?" Roger asked.

Chapter 34

THE PAINTINGS

Maggie got to her feet with a mischievous grin on her face. "Yes, we're expecting company."

Chase had already left the room so he could greet their guest. "Hey man, come on in." He shook Zac's hand and pulled him close so he could whisper, "They don't know it's you, so have fun with that." Then he gave Emma and Zoe a hug. "Great to see you again. Everyone's in here." He pointed to his left.

As soon as they came into the living room, Zoe ran to Claire, who bent down and scooped her up. "Hi, Zoe."

"Hi, Cwaire."

All eyes went from Zoe to Zac and Emma. "Hi Mom, Dad, it's been way too long."

"You know us?" Michelle asked, but didn't wait for an answer. She engulfed Zac in her embrace and wouldn't let go. "You recognize us! Thank God, you recognize us!"

They both cried.

Roger froze, too dumbfounded to speak. Claire broke the spell by stepping toward him with Zoe still in her arms. Emma followed. "Emma, this is Roger, Roger, Emma."

She reached to take his hand. "I'm Zac's wife, and this is your granddaughter—"

"I'm Zoe."

Claire laughed. "And you're not shy either, are you?" She gave her a kiss and put her down.

Zoe went to pull on Zac's leg. "Daddy, daddy, it's grandpa, and grandma."

Zac let go of his mom, wiped his cheeks on his shirt sleeves and knelt next to Zoe. "I know, sweetie. You want to say hello?"

She nodded. As soon as Zac picked Zoe up, she waved and said, "Hi."

"Hi, Zoe." Michelle reached out her hands. "Do you want to come to grandma?" Zoe immediately went to her and wrapped her little arms around her neck. Fighting back tears, Michelle held her close and said, "What a precious child."

"And Mom, this is Emma."

"It's nice to meet you." Emma rubbed her shoulder. "We're so incredibly grateful to have finally found you."

"And you don't know how relieved we are that Zac remembers us." Michelle, still holding Zoe, gave her a sidelong hug before they continued to talk.

In the meantime, Zac went to greet his dad. "Hey, it's so good to see you." He reached to shake his hand but instead Roger pulled him into his embrace.

"Thank goodness you're alive."

After everyone finished introductions, Zac sat on the couch with Zoe on his lap and a parent on each side of him. Chase and Claire nestled onto the piano bench, which left enough room for everyone else to have a comfortable seat.

Michelle tightly squeezed Zac's strong and callused hand. "I still can't believe it's you."

"Grandma, why are you sad?"

"Oh, but Zoe, I'm not sad."

"Ten why are you crying?"

"Have you ever heard of happy tears?"

Zoe shook her head and then snuggled into her dad's chest.

"Should we call you Zac or Jack?" Michelle asked.

"If you don't mind, I'd prefer Jack. It would just be easier." He looked from his mom to his dad.

Michelle started to answer, but Roger cut her off. "Jack it is. I do have a question, though. You and Chase act as you've already seen each other. When did that happen?"

"Yeah, we met up by chance yesterday at Claire's dad's place. I needed a horse for the rodeo this weekend."

"So you see, Roger," Claire said, with a mischievous glint in her eye, "Chase hadn't kept this wonderful news from me, but we didn't tell you because we thought it would be nice for Jack to surprise you."

"We were surprised alright," Michelle said cheerfully. "But Maggie, I talked to you this morning. When I expressed my concerns about Jack not recognizing us, why did you leave me in the dark?"

"That's because I didn't know."

"Yeah, Mom, she didn't know until a few hours ago. I called Claire to get your numbers, but she only had Aunt Maggie's. Once I talked to her, we worked out this plan to meet you here." Jack winked at Maggie.

"It's perfect," Michelle said, "just perfect."

Claire noticed the strain that had taken up residence in Michelle's eyes was gone. In its place was a peace that seemed to pass understanding. Even the sharp lines of strain etched within her brow looked softer. The transformation was a beautiful sight to behold.

"I hope I don't wake up and find out that this was all a dream."

"It's no dream, Mom, and you have Claire to thank for that."

"Claire? What does Claire have to do with anything?" Roger countered.

"She's the painter God used to bring us all together."

Roger clasped his hands together over his knees. "I'm not following."

Michelle's eyes widened. "You're the artist, who did the painting of our boys, aren't you?"

She nodded.

Roger jumped to his feet and started pointing a finger in her face. "You mean to tell me you did the painting? Why didn't you admit it?"

Zoe climbed off Jack's lap, stepped between them, and pulled on Roger's jeans. "Hey Grandpa, why are you yewwing at Cwaire?"

"It's okay, Zoe," Claire said. "We're just having a big people conversation."

"K." She scampered over to her mother and leaned against her knee.

"Roger, do you see the irony in your anger?" Claire asked. "Your beloved son is sitting in our midst because of that painting. Besides, how did you expect me to admit it when I knew how mad it made you? I was hoping that once you saw Jack, you'd lighten up about it."

"Wait, Dad, why does the painting make you mad?" Jack asked.

Roger took a step back and looked his way with a blank expression on his face. "I, uh . . ." He shoved his hands into his pockets and said no more.

"If it weren't for Claire, I never would've found you. She did a painting of Zoe, too, and had it set up as a sample of her work. We saw it at her booth at the Beartrap Festival a few weeks ago."

"That's how we met," Emma added, "but at that point, we didn't know anything about the supernatural paintings, or that there was any connection to you."

Jack nodded at his wife. "Right, and since then, Claire did a painting of Freddie, the man who pulled me from the river and saved my life. That painting is how she found him and after recognizing a few letters on the bottom of a carving I did, she connected the dots and discovered that I was alive. I, for one, am extremely grateful for all the paintings. They were how God answered my prayers to find you. The fact that she's dating Chase is a perk for us all."

"Thanks, Jack. I like the way you think." Claire nudged Chase's shoulder, and they both smiled.

Michelle interrupted them, "But I don't get it, how did you do the paintings?"

"Maggie, why don't you make more coffee, and I'll cut the pies. Then we can take turns explaining the miraculous events of the last two months over dessert," Claire suggested.

"That's a great idea. And Jack, the painting that started it all is hanging in our dining room if you'd like to see it."

Chase went with Jack to show him the painting. On the way, he whispered, "Please don't ask why it's here and not where it belongs, okay?"

Jack nodded and said, "Wow, this is too funny. You're on your toes, trying to look taller." He looked up at Chase. "You have me by at least two inches now."

"That's right." Chase smirked. "Now you can be my little, big brother." He punched his arm.

Claire kept an eye on the brothers while she cut the pies. Their interaction with each other made her happy. She saw it made Michelle happy, too. Yet Roger, for reasons she couldn't understand, still looked miffed.

Maggie came with a stack of plates and set them on the kitchen table.

"Look." Claire nudged her arm and tipped her head toward Roger. "This could get ugly."

"You're so perceptive," Maggie whispered, and then she called everyone to come to the kitchen. "It'd be easier if you served yourselves."

"We're going home." Roger pulled on Michelle's arm. "If you want to see us, you know where we live. Let's go."

"I'm not going anywhere." Michelle forcefully pulled her arm away and dropped into a kitchen chair.

Roger glared at her. "How dare you?"

Both boys turned, Chase cringed.

"Hey," Jack yelled from the dining room. He skirted the table in lightning speed and stepped between his parents. "I know I've missed the last ten years, but what's the problem?" He looked from his dad to his mom.

"This is nothing new, but I'm sick of it," Michelle said. Her eyes were no longer happy or sad; instead, they blazed with intense anger. Her hands started to shake, so she squeezed them together. "I've catered to your father for those same ten years, doing everything I could to make him happy, but nothing was ever good enough." She turned to face Roger. "Technically, I lost all three of my sons because you wouldn't even let me love Chase." She buried her face in her hands and began to weep uncontrollably.

Everyone was at a loss. To Claire's surprise, Roger looked more shocked than embarrassed.

Then through heaves and muffled sobs, Michelle looked up and said, "Now that Jack has come home, you're going to deprive me of him, too?"

Jack knelt and held her close. "Mom, you're not going to lose me again, I promise."

She grabbed hold of him and pressed her face into his neck, her moans becoming louder by the second. Years of pent-up frustration and pain had finally hit a breaking point. The flood of grief was working its way out of her system, and no one planned to deprive her of that. Except Roger.

He grabbed his hat and headed for the back door. Jack continued to hold his mom while he called after him. "Dad, please wait. Why are you leaving?"

Roger didn't acknowledge the question or bother to answer. Instead, he slammed the door on his way out. The noise made Michelle flinch and look up. Maggie had already grabbed a box of tissues and put it on the table in front of her.

Michelle used one and then said, "I'm so sorry." She got to her feet. "I need to go."

Brad stepped in front of her. "You're not going anywhere. We've all made sacrifices for him, and for once, we're not going to give in to his manipulation."

"But I'm afraid he could hurt me when I get home if I don't go right now."

"Has he ever hit you?" Jack turned white and then flushed all within a matter of seconds.

"He did in the early years, but over time I learned how *not* to make him angry." She tried to pass Brad.

"I'm not letting you leave this house," he said firmly. "Especially after what just happened. Roger's not a little mad, he's furious!"

They all heard the truck rev loudly and spin out of the driveway.

Michelle cringed. "Oh, Brad, what am I supposed to do?"

"My dear, this all spun out of control rather quickly. Now we need to take a minute and breathe."

Emma picked up Zoe, who had been hiding behind her ever since the tumult started. She gave her a hug and looked at Brad. "But we thought our coming would be a blessing to everyone."

Jack still looked bewildered. He shook his head and said, "Me too, so can someone please explain?"

Claire stepped forward. "I know I'm an outsider looking in, but from what I just saw, before the blowup that is, your dad got jealous watching you and Chase joke about the painting."

"That's what I thought, too," Maggie said.

"But what's there to be jealous of?" Jack asked. "I don't get it."

Chase, who until now had stayed out of the conversation said, "Me. Apparently, you don't remember that you were always Dad's favorite."

Jack shrugged, "I guess not, but then why isn't he glad to see me?"

"He's thrilled. You were all he would talk about at dinner, but he doesn't want to share you with anyone, especially with me."

"Chase, if you don't mind, I'd like to explain," Michelle said, stepping closer to him. "But first, can I please have a hug?" Without waiting for his answer, she threw her arms around him. "I love you." Tears again began to flow. "I'm sorry that you don't know how much . . . I'm sorry he made me choose . . . I had enough love for both of you. I don't know why he couldn't see that."

Chase melted into her arms. "Oh Mom, I've wanted to love you, too."

"Let's give them a moment," Maggie said as she whisked a tear from her own cheek. "Brad can you please grab the forks and plates?" She picked up the pies and brought them to the dining room. Claire quickly put the mugs on a tray and brought the coffee.

They all took a seat, leaving the two chairs closest to the kitchen empty.

While Maggie was dishing the pie, Claire leaned over and whispered in Brad's ear, "Thanks for not letting Michelle leave."

"This has been a long time coming for both of them, now we need to pray for Roger." He looked at Jack. "He's been like a kid in a candy shop ever since he found out about you. It's sad to say, but I think he's extra giddy because you've been their favorite rider ever since you hit the circuit."

"But why does my dad hate Chase so much?"

"Because he's not *you*," Maggie said.

"Wow, I must have been a real piece of work."

No one had noticed Chase standing next to Michelle in the doorway. When he spoke, everyone looked at him. "That's not why, Jack. You were very good and worked hard to be successful. Dad took pride in that, hence his excitement that you've made the circuit. Mom, do you still have all of Jack's trophies from high school on the mantle?"

"Yes, they're still there." She gave a weak smile.

"But Chase, I thought I remembered that you loved to ride. Why don't you compete?"

Chase winced at the question. "Hmm, I say we save that story for another day." He pulled a chair out for his mother, and they both sat.

"It's a sad story, and I agree it might be better to wait," Michelle said. "There are, however, a few details you need to know to make sense of why your father reacted the way he did. As I'm sure you've been told, Johnny died in his arms."

Jack nodded.

"That was devastating for all of us, but even more so for him. Then to add to our pain, the search and rescue teams couldn't find you. We held out hope for days that you had made it to land. Authorities put out a missing person report; it was on the news, the radio, and in the papers south of where the accident happened. After two weeks of looking and no one reported seeing you, or finding your body, the rescue team gave up because they assumed you got tangled under some rocks below the water and had drowned.

"They said if we wanted to wait to have your funeral until after the high spring waters subsided, they still might be able to find your body. By fall, all hope was gone." A single tear escaped as she said, "We even had a headstone made. Your empty grave sits right next to Johnny's at the Hillside Cemetery where your dad and I still visit almost every week."

"I'm so sorry that I couldn't remember my name, that I couldn't find my way back to you sooner."

She waved off his reply. "We're not blaming you. Maggie told us how Freddie saved you, and we hold no animosity toward him. We're so grateful that you're alive and here with us. Yet all of our relief and joy can't change the fact that those events stole the last ten years of our lives."

With a shake of the head, Emma said, "I can't even imagine."

"We all dealt with this pain and sorrow in different ways. Roger fought with depression and became angry at God; he even quit going to church. He also became possessive of me but pushed Chase away. As Brad said, this day was way overdue even if you never returned to us."

"But what are we going to do about Dad?"

Chapter 35

THE VOICEMAIL

"I don't know," Michelle said. Everyone noticed the tremble in her voice and how her hands shook when she took a sip of coffee.

Chase touched her arm. "We'll figure something out, Mom."

"I've gained two sons today, which fills my heart to overflowing. I just hope after all we've been through that it doesn't cost me my marriage because I love your father very much."

"Hey, Mom, let's not prematurely worry about that," Jack said. "I don't think God would bring me back into your lives, especially the way it happened with Claire's paintings, simply to cause you more pain."

"I hope you're right." She gave a quick shake of the head as if to ward off the pending doom. "But now, I haven't heard about your lives. Emma, how did you meet Jack?"

"He came to work at my Grandpa Bobbie's Ranch about nine years ago."

Jack held up a hand. "For those of you that don't know, Bobbie is Freddie's younger brother."

Emma giggled. "Right. That *is* an important detail because if Freddie didn't bring you to the ranch, I wouldn't have had an opportunity to lay eyes on the hot new cowboy." She winked at him.

"Seriously though, before I met Jack, and even now—well, when I'm not in baby making mode—I help with the horses on my Grandpa's ranch. I'm actually the one who retaught Jack how to do some of the more difficult maneuvers, ones he's now perfected and uses in competitions."

"She's a very good teacher." Jack grinned. "The rest is history. We got married almost seven years ago."

Claire nodded her approval to Emma and said, "It's nice to know that you can ride too." Then she smirked at Chase who was sitting across the table from her.

He set down his fork and leaned on his left elbow. "Funny story, when I first met Claire, all I knew about her was that she could paint. Emma, you would've been impressed with how determined she was to prove she could ride."

Claire bobbed her head at him but didn't interrupt his story.

"It worked out well for me because we got to spend the day together. It wasn't until a week later that I learned about her father's horse ranch. She hasn't let me live that down since."

"Nor should she." Emma laughed and gave Claire a high five.

"And this is what we've been missing," Michelle said. "You all have such fun and outgoing personalities. I wish Roger had stayed. He would've seen that there's no reason to be jealous and every reason to be grateful and happy."

"Speaking of Dad, do you think it would help if we come to your house for a while?" Jack asked. "That way we can spend some quality time with just the two of you."

"And we can also get a sense if you'll be okay before we leave," Emma added thoughtfully.

"Oh, I would love nothing better." Michelle stood and turned to Brad. "We should probably go. As you well know, I've already pressed my luck by staying this long."

He nodded and this time he didn't try to stop her.

She gave Maggie a hug. "Thanks for dinner and opening your home for such a special occasion."

"It was our pleasure."

Jack came around the end of the table to join his mom. "And thanks, Uncle Brad, for saving the ranch."

"Now that hasn't always been a pleasure," he admitted. "But for Chase's sake," he looked his way, "it's always been worth it." It was then that Brad finally smiled.

With a set jaw, Chase nodded.

"I know I've made some poor choices, especially concerning you, Chase," Michelle said. "And I know this doesn't fix things, but it did bring me comfort to know that your Aunt Maggie and Uncle Brad have been here for you."

This time, he smiled.

Claire watched in silence as each of them added to a dialogue that could barely scratch the surface of a decade's worth of pain. It was honest, but not spiteful. Raw, but no longer festering. Each was desperate, in their own way, to find healing.

Chase stood and reached to shake Jack's hand. "See you at the rodeo on Saturday. It will be extra fun to watch you, now that we know who you are."

"Absolutely!" Claire said. "And be sure Freddie still comes. Now that he knows you recognize everyone, he might not want to risk Roger's wrath."

"Let's see how things go after we spend some time with Dad. I'll keep you posted."

Once the others had left, Brad said, "To be honest, Roger disappoints me. When we went to town earlier, he seemed whole, like life had returned to him."

"Yeah, I was surprised that he would just leave," Chase said.

Maggie had already started gathering up the pie plates, but stopped to join in the conversation, "I think that move backfired on him. When Michelle wouldn't leave, he was too embarrassed at that point to stay."

"What?" Claire asked. "Do you think he thought if they left that Jack would just follow them home, so he could have him all to themselves?"

"Sounds about right," Brad said.

Everyone helped clear the table and Maggie started putting the leftovers away while Claire loaded the dishwasher. Chase rinsed a cloth and began wiping the counters. Brad looked lost, so he poured another cup of coffee and took a seat at the kitchen table.

A few minutes passed without conversation. Finally, Chase spoke. "Technically, Dad still won because instead of spending the rest of the evening here, all together, Jack felt obligated to leave early."

Claire loaded the last of the glasses into the dishwasher and turned toward Chase. "Yeah, but if you think about it, Jack's caught between a rock and a hard place. I believe he left more to protect your mom than to cater to your dad."

"Again, that sounds about right." Brad set down his mug. "Yet it shouldn't be about winning and losing. Why can't Roger count his blessings and move forward?"

"From what I've seen, Roger's behaviors ebb and flow. One minute he's happy and seems like a great guy and then the next he's selfish and petty. Just because Jack is back, that's not going to magically put Roger completely on an even keel. But there is one thing I'd like to know. How do *we* move forward from here so that we don't expect too much too soon and exacerbate the problem?"

Maggie finished putting the food away and joined Brad at the table. "That's a good question, Claire. I think we'll probably have to wait for Jack to fill us in when he calls later tonight."

"Right," Brad said, "and for now, I don't see where we have many options other than staying the course like nothing's changed."

"What, and hope for the best?" Chase snapped. "I'm sick of his selfishness and how he always gets his way. You heard Mom. I can't even imagine the crap she's had to put up with just to keep the peace." He came to the table and put his hands on the back of an empty chair. "Maybe we should let the ranch fall apart and see if his precious Jack can save the day."

"Chase, stop!" Maggie held up a hand, similar to how she did the day Claire brought their painting. "None of this is Jack's fault, so it would be wrong to take it out on him."

Chase crossed his arms and started tapping his fingers on his bicep. "Do you have any idea how badly I've wanted to leave this place? To leave him? Well, here's my chance."

"And what would that accomplish?" Brad countered, raising his voice ever so slightly. He pushed away from the table and stood. "It's not like Jack's going to move his family here and start helping on the ranch."

Though Chase glared, spewing words that weren't spoken, he set his jaw and didn't answer. No one did.

Claire was impressed with the way Brad handled that, even though she didn't like the uncomfortable silence. There was no point in adding to the conversation; she'd already given Chase her pep talk earlier. If he still wanted to leave, she wasn't going to stop him.

Brad and Chase stood as marble pillars, with eyes locked, neither conceding. Maggie fidgeted with the white doily that sat under a vase of fresh cut flowers.

Not knowing what else to do, Claire skirted the table, whispered a thank you in Maggie's ear, and then promptly walked toward the front door.

This must have broken the spell because Chase called after her, "Hey, hold up, where are you going?"

"Home. I can't fix this, and if you still need to get out of here that badly, far be it from me to stand in your way. Good night." With that, she left the house.

Chase didn't follow her initially, but a moment later he called from the porch, "Hey, do you want to go for a ride or something?"

"No." With arms crossed, Claire turned to look at him. "What do you want from me anyway?"

He came down the steps and walked toward her. "What do you mean?"

"Sure, we could go for a romantic ride in the moonlight. Under normal circumstances, I would think that was a great idea, but where do we go from there?" She flipped her palms upward. "I'm not following you to Texas, so if you're seriously leaving, you need to know that you'll be going alone."

She opened the door, but before she got in, she said, "If you change your mind and decide to stay, give me a call." The tears burned as they ran down her cheeks. "Good night, Chase." She jumped in her SUV and started to pull away.

Chase darted in front of the vehicle to stop her. "Please wait."

She threw the shift into park and stuck her head out the window. "You need to move. Go have your pity party and figure out what it is that you really want."

He held up his hands, took a step back, and started to walk toward her.

Instead of waiting for him, she threw the shift into drive and pulled away. She saw him run after her in the rearview mirror and heard him yell, "Claire wait, I need you." But she wasn't in the mood to deal with this right now, even though her heart ached for him.

It was close to 10:00 by the time Claire got home and saw that she had three missed calls and one new voicemail from Chase. Before listening to it, she went inside and got ready for bed. Fifteen minutes later, she stuffed a few pillows under her left arm, curled up under the blankets, and hit the play button.

"Hey, um, I really can't believe you left like that. It sucks to know that you don't think I'm worth fighting for. You said you loved me . . . no matter what I chose . . . but apparently, those were empty words."

A twinge of pain shot through Claire's chest.

The message continued, "Am I perfect? Far from it. Do I have hang-ups? Absolutely. I'm sorry that I have baggage and that . . ." She heard him stifle a cry. "And that I can't live up to your expectations. There's no sense in prolonging the agony for either of us any further. This will be the last time you hear my voice, so sweet dreams my dearest Claire."

She lowered the phone and squeezed her hand over her mouth. This wasn't how she wanted things to end. She just supposed Chase needed some time to cool off and to start thinking rationally about his future, especially after what Brad had said to him. His emotions were as capricious as Roger's, though Claire realized he probably couldn't see that. She played the message again before burying her head under the pillows and crying herself to sleep.

The ringing of her phone woke her. Before answering, she looked to see the time; it was now close to midnight. When she saw it was Maggie, she sat up and cleared her voice. "Hello." Instead of saying more, she thought it best to see what Maggie had to say first. She half expected to get the riot act for leaving Chase like that, but then maybe she'd heard back from Jack.

"Sorry to call you so late but I thought you should know that Emma called. She said everything went very smoothly. Jack and Roger hit it off really well, and Michelle didn't seem to be in any danger when they left."

"So now what?"

"Emma was concerned, because like we said before you left, Jack feels trapped, but for now, he believes he should build his relationship with his parents and try to connect with Chase separately."

"Have you told Chase this?"

"Not yet. He sat on our front porch for close to an hour after you left. Brad tried to talk to him, but he just stared off into the darkness and didn't say a word."

"Huh, Chase left me a voicemail, basically saying goodbye . . . like it's over between us forever."

"Is that what you want?" Maggie asked.

"Of course not, but I can't stay with him simply to be his crutch either."

"Oh, Claire, what you have with Chase is far more than a crutch. If you don't count the rollercoaster of reactions because of these recent events, I've never seen Chase happier." She hesitated. "It's probably not my place to tell you this, but you're all he talks about, even with Brad. He's clearly in love with you."

Claire climbed out of bed, grabbed an afghan off the back of the couch, and wandered onto the porch. "Then why is he calling it quits? You know as well as I do that we've not been together that long. How does he expect me to drop everything and move to Texas with him?"

"I didn't say you should move to Texas, but maybe you could convince him to stay."

"But I've already tried. He told me he was leaving earlier. We had a long talk in the barn before I came to help you with the pies. He seemed good, remember?"

"I do."

"And I'm sure you noticed how he behaved at dinner, not reacting negatively when Roger tried to goad him. I was impressed, but then, like out of the blue, he says he's leaving again and that it's over between us. I don't get it." She flopped into one of the wicker chairs.

"Yes, he can be pretty stubborn." Maggie stifled a laugh before asking, "But don't you see the same stubbornness in yourself? It's what makes you two a good match."

"If these were happier times, I'd be amused, but my heart feels like a vase that's been dropped on the floor and has shattered into a thousand tiny fragments."

"Oh, my dear, I meant no harm."

"I know." Claire pulled her legs up to her chest and wrapped her arms around her knees. "I also know you think I'm wrong, but I'm not going to beg him to stay."

"I don't think you're wrong. It's just hard because Brad and I both know that if Chase does go, he won't put forth the effort to keep in touch. We don't want to lose him . . . and truthfully, we don't want to lose you either. You've become a good friend to me, and Brad adores you."

"And I thought you weren't going to beg? Tell you what; I'm still coming to the rodeo. We had plans to meet up with Freddie, so I'll see you on Saturday."

"Sounds good. Thank you."

"Bye." Claire turned her gaze toward heaven, but the serenity of a million stars couldn't begin to calm the turmoil within her. Minutes turned into an hour. Finally, she got out her phone and sent Chase this text.

Chapter 36

GUIDANCE

'I never said I wanted to break up, or that I wasn't willing to fight for you. What I said was, 'I'm not going with you to Texas.' If you choose to stay, then I'll know you chose me. I'm glad your voice is the last one I'll hear before going to sleep. ☺'

Claire reread the text, making sure it was exactly what she wanted Chase to know and then she hit the send button. *If this doesn't make him see reason, then it really is over.* By the time she went back inside and snuggled underneath her blankets, it was very late, but not too late to listen to Chase's message one more time. A sigh escaped her lips. *Hopefully, in the morning, we'll both see things more clearly.*

Claire woke exhausted, but she had an 8:00 o'clock appointment with clients that she couldn't pass off to Trevor. The horse they were selling was her responsibility and she needed to be present.

Trevor was already at the barn when Claire arrived at 7:15, so she jumped in and helped him finish the morning chores. At first, they were both doing different things and not close enough to carry on a conversation. Claire didn't mind though, she wasn't really in the mood to talk.

At 7:40, she brought the horse that was being sold to the center aisle and started brushing it down.

It wasn't long before Trevor grabbed another brush and came to help. "No offense, Sis, but you look awful."

"Probably not any worse than I feel."

"Are you sick?"

"No, I'm just . . . truth be told, I don't know how I am. Jack came to see his parents last night. They met up at Maggie's house while I was there."

"Oh yeah, how'd that go?"

"Not as well as we hoped."

"But I thought Jack remembered them."

"He did, and his parents got to meet Emma and Zoe. It was perfect."

"Okay, um . . ." Trevor stopped brushing his side of the horse and rested his arms on its back. "What am I missing?"

Claire continued to brush. "Time's a-ticking, get back to work, and I'll tell you."

"It's not like we don't have a minute. What's going on?"

She finally quit and looked his way. "Instead of Jack's return bringing healing to the family, this reunion has actually made things worse between Chase and his dad. Now he's talking about moving to Texas and he basically broke up with me when I said I wouldn't go with him."

"That stinks. I liked Chase and thought the two of you looked good together."

"Me too, but there's not much I can do about it." Claire blew out a heavy breath and started brushing the horse again.

"He's not gone yet, and who knows, maybe he'll change his mind."

"Doubt it. What makes this even harder is the fact that I don't blame him a bit for wanting to leave."

"Who's leaving?" Paul asked as he came to join them.

"Chase," Trevor said. He reddened as he realized he wasn't the one who was supposed to answer. "Sorry, Sis."

Claire only shrugged.

"How long have you known about this, Claire?" Paul asked.

"Since last night. It's more like he's running away from his problems, not so much from me."

"I don't know if you like him enough to keep him around, but after work yesterday, Rodney gave me his two weeks' notice. His apartment will be available, too, so Chase could come work for me and even have a place to live while the two of you figure things out."

Claire tipped her head in astonishment. "You'd offer him the job without an interview or references?"

"Of course. You wouldn't be with him if he wasn't a hard worker, and I was impressed with the way he handled Trev's horse the other day when he rode with Jack."

"Um, do you need your answer right now?" she asked. "We're not exactly speaking to each other at the moment, and I think I'd like to see how things play out Saturday at the rodeo if you don't mind."

A father and his son walked into the barn and the conversation was dropped.

Chase wasn't mentioned again that morning.

After work, Claire went to have lunch with her mom and told her about the grand reunion and her quarrel with Chase. She opened the text that she sent him and handed her phone to her mom.

"Aww, how sweet."

"Well, it didn't help. He hasn't replied."

Helen slid the phone back. "That doesn't mean he won't."

Claire thought her mother sounded quite convincing, but she wasn't so sure, especially after his voicemail. "Yeah, but I assumed he was only mad at me last night because I left. How is that any different than when he took off on us a few nights ago?"

Helen shook her head. "It's not different, and yet, you have to remember that he hasn't just hit a rough patch. It's more like an untended field where briers and thistles have taken over. The land is still good; he's just having a hard time seeing past all the weeds and debris." She took a sip of iced tea and continued, "Be willing to give him some time and space to come to that conclusion on his own. I'm confident that he'll find his way through."

"Wow, Mom, when did you become a philosopher?"

"Since the painting fiasco started making sense." She let out a little laugh before adding with a straight face, "You also need to keep in mind that you threw a wrinkle into his exciting new plans when you said you wouldn't go with him. That makes his choice to leave far less appealing than it would've been."

Claire put her elbows on the table and joined her hands with her thumbs under her chin. "You've seriously thought this through, haven't you?"

"It's not rocket science. Sometimes we just need to see things from a different perspective, that's all."

"I was stuck in my own bubble of pain and self-pity before you gently burst it. Thanks." Claire smiled as she got to her feet. "I need to get going, but now with a fresh perspective, the waiting will hopefully be a little easier."

By the time Claire got home it was mid-afternoon. She was still exhausted from a lack of sleep and tired of fighting with her own emotions, so she took a shower and then crawled into bed. Before falling asleep, she listened to Chase's message again. She needed to hear his voice.

Claire's alarm woke her from a deep sleep. Coming into consciousness, her first thought was of Chase, so she scooped up her phone to see if he had sent a text. "Nothing!" In a huff, she threw the covers back over her head. A minute later, her phone dinged with a new text. It was Paul.

'Hey. Rodney called in sick. Can you come early to help with the chores?'

'Sure.'

She crawled out of bed and got dressed. On her way to the kitchen, she decided to give Chase a call. *Hopefully, he'll think it's cute that I'll be the first voice he hears this morning.* He didn't answer. *Huh, maybe he's in the shower.*

The quickest option for breakfast was to toast a bagel while the coffee brewed. She could bring both with her. Chase had not returned her call, so once she was ready and on her way off the mountain, she tried again with the same result. "This is ridiculous. Maybe I jumped the gun in telling him that I loved him. At the moment, I'm not even sure if I like him."

Her emotions were vacillating between anger and sadness. About five minutes later, she hit the brake and threw the shift into park. *Ugh, why does this have to be so complicated?* She couldn't call her dad and say she wasn't coming to work, especially after he'd already asked for her help, but she needed to talk to someone, so she called Maggie. "Hey."

"Good morning, Claire."

"I told myself I wouldn't call you to see how Chase is doing, but he won't answer his phone."

"I'm not surprised."

"But why? I sent him a sweet text after you called the other night and I thought surely by yesterday afternoon or evening he would've replied."

"It's not you, it's Roger. Brad came home from work last night and told me how smug and condescending he was to Chase. For the first time, in probably eight years, Brad is even talking about leaving the ranch. Unfortunately, he's been out of the corporate world for so long he doesn't know who'd hire him."

"None of this seems right. Why would my paintings change, and all the pieces fit perfectly together, just to have the rest of the family fall apart?"

"Now that's a good question, but it's also one I don't have an answer for."

"Okay then. If you happen to see Chase, maybe you could encourage him to call me. Either way, I'll see you tomorrow."

Later that morning Paul brought a Warmblood to the arena where Claire was already working with a Thoroughbred. "Hey, Claire, Trev and I are planning on going to the rodeo tomorrow. Do you want to come with us?"

Claire rode closer. "No thanks. I want to have a vehicle there so depending on how things go, I can stay."

"Makes sense." Paul retightened the girth and then looked at Claire. "I'll need an answer from you or Chase by tomorrow night. If he's not going to take the job, I'll need to advertise for a new ranch hand."

"It's looking less likely. He won't even answer my calls. I do appreciate you giving us until tomorrow though . . . hopefully, we can work things out."

"That'd be nice."

"And Dad, thanks for taking *me* into consideration on your decision."

"You got it kiddo. I really think having Chase work here would be a good option for him, but only if it's a good option for you, too." He looped the reigns through a hook and went to set up some barrels.

Claire took her horse over a few jumps and returned just as Paul was mounting his. "I know none of us kids died, but how were you and Mom able to treat us all equally?"

He removed his baseball cap and rubbed his head a few times before answering. "That's a deep question for a worktime conversation, don't you think?"

Claire shrugged, "We can keep working."

"Okay, we can talk while I get this horse's legs warmed up."

They both eased their horses into a walk before Claire said, "I found out recently that Chase's parents always favored the other two boys, even before the accident. Me, on the other hand, being the only girl, I never felt like you treated me better or worse than my brothers."

"Yeah, if anything, we treated you too much like the boys."

"That's for sure," Claire laughed.

They stepped up the pace.

"But Dad, I need some of your wisdom. I talked to Maggie this morning and found out now that Jack's back, Roger is more unreasonable toward Chase than ever."

"Huh, that's a tough one because I've discovered that once you have an attitude toward someone, it can get to the point where the other person can't do anything right . . . even when they haven't done anything else wrong."

Claire nodded. "I'm sure that's what happened here."

"All the more reason it'd be nice if Chase could come work with us for a while. It's closer to the family who still loves him and wants him in their lives, but far enough away that it gives time and space between him and his dad—"

"Without cutting off all opportunity for reconciliation."

"Exactly."

"Thanks. I knew talking to you would help." She brought her horse to a stop and looked thoughtfully into his eyes. "I'm so grateful I have a loving support system. I couldn't imagine having to go it alone."

"Well on that note, I owe you an apology."

Claire started fidgeting with the reins. "But I thought you already apologized."

"Kind of, yet the more I see how this is all playing out, the more I realize how hard I was on you about your painting story. It frustrated me the night you told us how you met Chase because all I was trying to do was to protect your mom. It wasn't until then that I noticed the wall I had built between us."

"It's okay, Dad, those paintings were hard to fathom for all of us, until they started making sense."

"True but let me finish. That night I found myself on the outside looking in. I felt angry and jealous and even betrayed by your mom and Trev because neither of them had filled me in. Yet, my reaction was no more their fault than yours. It was something I had to come to grips with. I could choose to stay on the outside and be miserable or I could rip down my walls. Thankfully I did. Not just for your mom's sake, but for you and Trev, too."

"This sounds exactly like what happened between Chase and Roger; except *their wall* seems insurmountable."

"And in a small way, I can see how that happened. It's not a good place to be."

"I hope you know that I hated being at odds with you." Claire's countenance brightened. "I'm thankful it was short-lived."

"Me too. I also noticed that you didn't hold it against me, and for that, I'm the one who's grateful."

"I can't even imagine the pain Chase has endured. I just hope it doesn't take another ten years for Roger to recognize what he's thrown away—"

"And that Chase realizes he needs to forgive his dad if there's ever going to be reconciliation," Paul said. "Now, we need to get back to work."

Chapter 37

FOUR LETTERS

Claire wasn't ready to give up on Chase, even though it appeared that he was serious about her never hearing from him again. Her hands shook as she hit his number and held the phone to her ear. *Come on, Chase, pick up already.* When he didn't answer, she left a voicemail. "Hi, Chase. I talked to Emma last night and she said that Freddie will be at the rodeo today. They're all coming early to have breakfast with your parents in town. You probably already know that. I hope you plan on joining them. I'll meet you and Freddie near the east end of the grandstand around 11:00." She paused before adding, "I've missed you."

Her cheeks flushed with anger as she hung up the phone. She didn't understand how one disagreement could end everything, especially after all the texts and long phone conversations they had almost every day until recently. Even if she didn't go with him to Texas right now, that didn't mean she wouldn't be willing to join him down the road. What frustrated her, even more, was the fact she couldn't tell him about her dad's job offer. If he wouldn't even speak to her on the phone, she didn't want to see him every day at work.

Before she left for Ten Sleep, Claire went to the loft to get her 35mm camera. It had been over a year since she'd attended a rodeo and now that she was selling her paintings at shows, she wanted to get some quality digital shots of the riders in action. Those kinds of paintings were a good money maker for her.

On her way back to the stairs, she stopped at her art desk and started reading the different notes that she had pinned to the corkboard. The one that held her attention this morning was: 'There's a story yet to be told. When you hear it, pursue.' Because of the way everything came together with the paintings and the reunion, she assumed there were no more stories to tell.

As far as Chase was concerned, she couldn't make him talk to her, and if it weren't for Freddie coming to the rodeo, she would have stayed home.

Claire's original plan was to leave early so she could swing by Chase's house, but when he didn't answer her call, she decided to go straight to the rodeo. At least Freddie would be there, and though it seemed unlikely, she hoped Chase would be with him.

After finding a place to park, she started walking toward the grandstand. It wasn't long before she saw a group of familiar faces, which included Maggie and Brad, Roger and Michelle, and Emma and Zoe. They were standing around Freddie's 1958 Chevy pickup, so she joined them. "Well look at you Freddie, all spiffed up and showing off your truck."

Everyone looked her way.

Freddie did a one-eighty so he could see her. "Hey Claire, I made it. This is the furthest I've been from home in over forty years."

"I'm so proud of you." Then, without warning, she kissed his scarred cheek and gave him a big hug.

"I knew I liked you right from the start but now I appreciate you even more." He laughed. "Most people don't even want to be seen with me in public. Let alone show me affection."

"Hey, the war wasn't your fault, so there's nothing to be ashamed of. Besides, we're family now." She winked.

"Speaking of family, where's Chase?" Freddie looked over her shoulder.

"Um, I don't know. I thought he would be here with you."

"He's probably off sulking somewhere," Roger snipped. His new outfit matched the sharpness of his reply. "He's been jealous of Jack ever since he's been back."

"That's not true and you know it!" Emma snapped.

Taken aback by her pert reply, Claire quickly pulled her close and whispered, "For Jack's sake, it's not worth getting on Roger's bad side. We all know the truth."

"What's that, Claire? Speak up so we can all hear." Roger's sarcasm wasn't missed on her.

Neither did the panic in Michelle's eyes escape her notice. "I've had my paintings on display at arts and crafts shows all summer, so this is my first rodeo of the season. I can't wait to see Jack ride." She forced a smile.

Roger started to counter, but Zoe broke the tension by pulling on Claire's leg. "Hey Cwaire, see my new dow?" She held it out.

Claire knelt by her to take a better look. The 14-inch doll had long, curly, blond hair and an outfit that matched Zoe's. "She's beautiful; almost as pretty as you."

Then Zoe put her little hands around Claire's neck, knocking off her cowgirl hat. She giggled and Claire helped her get it back on and tucked her curls behind her ears. "Tank you, Cwaire."

"And thanks for showing me your doll. You take good care of her now, okay?" Zoe nodded and squeezed her tight. When Claire stood, she faced Freddie. "I said we'd show you the sights. Are you ready?"

"I sure am, my dear. Let's take my truck. Do you want to drive?"

"For real? Of course, I do." Claire's smile came naturally this time. "Hey, Emma, save us three seats, we'll be back before the rodeo starts."

"You got it. Have fun."

Freddie tossed her the keys, and they both climbed into the truck.

"Just so you know, it's been a while since I've driven a stick. I hope I don't embarrass you pulling out of here."

"You could pop the clutch all the way through town and it wouldn't bother me a bit."

"Well then, let's go." She put the shift into low and jerked the truck forward but not enough to make a scene. It wasn't until they were out of the parking lot that she asked, "How did your meeting with Roger and Michelle go?"

"It went well. Jack helped me answer the few questions his parents still had. Everything went much smoother than I expected."

"That's great. I'm so glad to hear it," Claire said.

"When I asked you about Chase back there," he motioned with his thumb, "Roger's snarky reply surprised me, especially after he treated me with the utmost civility."

"I think it helped that Jack had already spent time with his parents and that he was with you. They are so grateful that he's alive. For now, that's all that seems to matter."

When Claire reached 2nd Street, she said, "Because Chase isn't with me, I really don't know what to show you. All I knew was that I couldn't stay there with Roger and risk saying something I'd regret."

"Yeah, I was flabbergasted by Emma's reaction," Freddie said. "She's always been honest, but that was too raw for me not to be concerned. What's really going on?"

"It's a long story, but the easiest way to explain it would be that Roger has always wished it would've been Chase to die and *not* Jack. Now that he has his favorite son back—"

"That's just wrong! But why is Chase jealous of Jack? I know I only met him once, but the brothers' personalities are so much alike."

"And the day they met at our ranch, they hit it off amazingly well," Claire said. "Chase isn't jealous; he's just trying to navigate through this new reality and give Jack time to build a relationship with his parents. Regrettably, his absence has caused Roger to interpret his actions in a negative light."

"I don't understand why Jack can't build a relationship with them both."

"Like I said, it's a long and sad story." Claire started driving to the ranch; she wanted to see if she could find Chase. "I thought Jack's return would bring healing to the family, but in some regards, things have gotten worse. Even Brad is frustrated with Roger."

Freddie leaned against the passenger door and shifted his weight so he could see Claire better. "There's still one thing I don't get though. Why isn't Chase with you? I don't see how Jack's return would affect your relationship."

"It's complicated. Chase said he was leaving. That he's had enough of his dad's condescension. A friend of his has a job waiting for him in Texas. I told him Wednesday that I wouldn't go with him. He hasn't spoken to me since."

"But I thought you two were in love."

"I thought so too, but we haven't dated for that long and moving is a bigger jump than I'm willing to make at this point. The bigger issue is that I don't think Chase should run from his problems. His dad won't care if he leaves, but what about his mom and Jack, or his Aunt Maggie and Uncle Brad. They gave up good paying jobs in Denver to come save the ranch and in a roundabout way, they saved Chase too."

"*I'm not* a good one to give advice on that score. I've hidden for over half my life because of rejection. I can't blame Chase for saying enough is enough and wanting to get out of here. Yet, I agree with you my dear Claire, moving right now would only make the chasm between him and his father wider. Unfortunately, it would fuel Roger's argument that Chase is jealous. Don't you think you and Jack could convince him to stay? You could help him see that things will eventually work themselves out with his dad."

"I've already tried, and who knows, he could be halfway to Texas by now."

"Let's hope not."

Claire pulled up the driveway, passed Maggie's house and parked in front of Justin's place. No vehicles were in sight. "Hey, I'm going inside to see if Chase's things are gone." She patted Freddie's arm and hurried around the house to his back entrance.

When he didn't come to the door after a robust knock, she tried the handle. It wasn't locked so she opened the door far enough to stick her head through. "Hey, Chase, are you here?" She waited for only a second before stepping inside.

Wads of paper were strewn across the kitchen floor and on the table, placed neatly in order, were four sealed envelopes. The first had Aunt Maggie and Uncle Brad's names on it. The second was for Roger and Michelle. The third was for Jack and Emma. And the forth was for Claire. She picked it up and held it close to her heart. *So he really left. I honestly didn't think he'd go without me.*

Claire took a seat and slowly opened the envelope. Inhaling a deep breath of his scent, she began to read the letter.

'My dearest Claire, thanks for showing me what it feels like to fall in love. You are beautiful, talented, and fun to be around. Under different circumstances, I would have liked to grow old with you. It's great that you found Jack and showed him his way home. I'm so proud of the man he's become. I find comfort in knowing that my dad is finally going to be okay now that they have been reunited. I'm sorry to admit this, but I've hit my breaking point. I decided not to go to Texas; I'm going to see Johnny. Chase.'

Claire gasped and covered her mouth. Then, without thinking, she scooped up the other letters and ran out of the house. She jumped in the truck and tossed the letters to Freddie. "We have to find Chase before it's too late." She started the truck, spun it out of the driveway, and gunned it toward the barn, leaving clouds of dust in her wake.

Freddie banged against the door. "Whoa, what's going on?"

She didn't answer until she reached the barn and threw the shift into park. "Here, read this." She handed him her letter. "I don't see Chase's truck, but I want to make sure his horse is here before checking anywhere else."

Claire again left Freddie, this time running into the barn.

As she hurried toward Mingo's stall, she saw the door was open. The bridle and saddle were not on their hooks either. Instead of continuing in that direction, she made an about face and ran to Brad's office. His door was ajar, so she burst through and screamed when she saw one of the shotguns was missing from the case that was usually locked.

With her heart pounding in her ears, she rushed back outside. Freddie had already gotten out of his truck and was coming toward her with the letter. "Claire, what is it?"

"Chase's horse is gone, and a shotgun is missing, which means he's within riding distance. Can you find your way back to the rodeo?"

"Yes."

"Here, give me my letter." She reached to take it and shoved it into her vest pocket. There was no time to read it again. "Now, take the other letters with you and give them to his family."

"Shouldn't you call Maggie?"

"No. It's either too late or it's not. Tell them Chase is missing and have them read their letters before you tell Maggie and Brad that I'm taking Chicory and heading to the memorial. She'll understand."

Chapter 38

A PRAYER

This can't be happening. Not now. Not after all Chase has been through. In all of Claire's frustrations with Chase over the past few days, never once did she imagine he would consider suicide to be an option. Leaving was one thing. Quitting all together was unfathomable. What made it even harder to comprehend was his heartfelt note. Panic-stricken, but not paralyzed, she ran back into the barn and hurried to saddle Chicory.

I hope I'm right in assuming he's gone to the memorial.

"Dear Jesus, please don't let me be too late," Claire prayed aloud as she tightened the girth and quickly mounted the horse. With adrenaline coursing through her, she and Chicory dashed out, leaving the barn door open and doubt behind them. They had just passed the workshop when Claire spotted Chases) truck parked behind it. Fresh anxiety pierced her heart as she knew she needed to check inside before they went any further.

"Whoa, girl." Claire jumped down and blew out a long heavy breath when she realized the truck was empty, but her relief faded fast when she saw his cell phone sitting on the seat. *That means I won't be able to distract him by calling.*

She mounted Chicory again, flicked the reins, and gave one thunderous kick to the horse's ribs. They were off, racing toward the eastern gate. At first, all she could picture was the dark empty stare in Chase's eyes while blood ran down his face. With a quick shake of her head, she pushed her thoughts to the first time they rode together through this very field and how she was so taken with him. His smile. His manners. The way he said, 'Ma'am, let me assure you that I am the epitome of chivalry' . . . She smiled at the recollection. She wanted that guy back. But even if she got to him on time, would he be able to find his way home?

"Come on, Chicory, I need you to fly." She kicked her again and they reached the gate in less than ten minutes. It was already open, so she urged her horse forward without bothering to shut it.

Bam!

Claire instinctively ducked at the sound. A single shot echoed off the mountains. "No!" she cried and pushed Chicory deeper into the woods. They made good time on the first part of the trail, but when it narrowed and got steeper, they had no choice but to slow down. She was half tempted to run but then realized once they got by this steep part, the horse would be faster.

Ahead of them was the sound of breaking branches and tumbling stones. Claire brought Chicory to a stop when she saw Mingo. He was not on the path but was frantically working his way down the mountain with no rider on his back. Claire gasped and covered her mouth.

I can't believe he would actually do it. Hope was fading fast.

Every tick of the clock, every moment of delay, brought more anxiety. "Come on, Chicory, we have to keep going." She could no longer hold back the tears as they continued to climb.

A few minutes later the path opened, and they could move faster again. Her heart seemed to keep pace. She tried not to think of the reality that awaited her because it made her feel nauseous.

Smoke. Claire didn't expect to smell smoke. As they got closer, she could see the flames through the trees. *I hope he didn't set the memorial on fire, and then shoot himself inside it. That will be more than I can bear.*

Claire impulsively started screaming Chase's name over and over. He didn't answer. Finally, she reached the clearing. The shed was engulfed with fire. Chase was not in sight.

Chicory balked and reared at the flames, so Claire jumped off the horse and tied her to a tree out of harm's way. Then she ran toward the shed.

The sound of the sizzling kayaks melting under the intense heat caused Claire to shudder. Without warning, the roof collapsed, and the building came down, throwing sparks and debris toward her. Black smoke reeled outward, invading her lungs and burning her eyes. She couldn't breathe, but she couldn't stop either. She had to at least save Chase's body. With the corner of her sleeve, she covered her mouth and ran to her left, around the remains of the burning structure.

That was when she saw him. Chase sat cross-legged with the rifle lying across his knees. He looked like a stone statue, staring expressionlessly at the fire.

His lack of movement caused her to wonder if he even realized she was there, even though she'd been calling his name. She ran toward him, grabbed the shotgun, and emptied the other shell from the barrel before tossing it behind her.

Even then, Chase didn't move.

Claire knelt in front of him and put her hands on his face. "You're alive." She pulled him into her embrace. "Thank God, you're alive!"

When Chase didn't move or acknowledge that she was there, she sat back on her heels and looked into his bloodshot eyes. To her surprise, his expression hadn't changed. His body was still rigid. Her relief of finding him alive started to vanish . . . it was like Chase was trapped in some distant place where she couldn't reach him.

"Come back to me. Please, come back to me." In desperation, she started shaking him. "Chase! Snap out of it! I'm here. You're safe. I love you."

Nothing registered. She wanted him to come back to her. To acknowledge she was there. To know that she had made it in time.

Again, she gently pulled him close and started rocking him in her arms. She leaned her face next to his and in a softer, calmer tone, she whispered, "I can't lose you. Not now. Not like this."

Still, no response.

Tears ran from Claire's eyes and between their cheeks as she prayed for Chase to revive.

His body began to shake, his lips to quiver.

Then, as if consciousness had returned, he pulled away from her and buried his face in his hands. "Why couldn't I pull the damn trigger? I'm such a chicken." His heaves rose and fell like the giant arms of a wind turbine. Through muffled sobs, he added, "I'm not worth saving."

"You're worth saving to me." Claire lifted his chin, pleading for him to make eye contact. "I was scared out of my mind when I heard the shot. What happened? Did the rifle fire by accident?"

With a tight jaw he shook his head, but no explanation came. "Chase, what is it? I'm here for you."

He finally looked at Claire just long enough to say, "But I didn't ask you to come." Pulling his knees to his chest, he wrapped his arms around them and moved his gaze toward the fire. The kayaks still sizzled, black smoke filled the air.

Claire's cheeks burned at that comment. Everything within her wanted to run, to get on Chicory, and leave. Yet, the personal sting was nothing in comparison to saving a man's life, even if things didn't work out between them. She took a seat next to Chase and watched as the smoke swirled upward. The flames were all but gone and the spark of hope that she held for their relationship was dying with the fire. The unwelcomed reality caused her heart to hurt.

It was Chase who broke the silence, "I'm so sorry, Claire, that was uncalled for. I'm obviously glad you came."

As far as I see it, nothing is obvious. She did well to keep that thought to herself, knowing it would have come out harsher than the volatile situation could handle. With clenched teeth and eyes narrowed, she turned to face him.

For the first time since she arrived, his breaths were steady, and his mind seemed clear. He reached to take her hand. "I don't blame you for being angry with me. I didn't think I'd be here to have to deal with the aftermath, but I couldn't bring myself to pull the trigger."

"But I heard the shot." Another tear rolled down her cheek.

"That's because I fired a frustration shot into the air. I thought it would help calm my nerves so I could pull the trigger a second time and end my agony. Instead, it woke me to the reality that I didn't want to die. But then I remembered my letters. I still had to end it because I couldn't bear to face my dad or Uncle Brad."

"Is that when you set the memorial on fire?"

"Yes. As I watched it burn, the pain became so intense that I knew it was now or never. My courage rose with the flames. I raised the rifle to my mouth, and just as I went to pull the trigger, I heard you calling my name. I dropped to the ground right here, knowing my opportunity had passed." He turned to face Claire. "In that moment, it was like I died and yet I lived. You saved my life." He crumpled into her lap and started crying again.

Claire leaned over him and rested her face on his shoulders. *Dear Jesus, please help Chase find his way back to you. Help him to realize true peace and happiness ultimately come from surrendering to you and not from his dad's approval.*

The ringing of Claire's phone startled them both.

"It's your Aunt Maggie. I need to let her know I found you." She put it on speaker so Chase could hear the frightened anxiety in her voice.

"Have you found Chase? Is he alive? Please tell me he's alive."

"Yes, Maggie, he's alive."

"Oh, thank God! Tell him that I love him. That we all love him and that somehow we'll figure this out. Tell him."

"I will." Claire patted Chase's back. He sat up and started rubbing his lips with the back of his index finger. That dark, lost look had once again invaded his eyes and it had her worried, but Maggie's barrage of words didn't give her time to contemplate its meaning.

"Is he hurt? We saw Mingo running through the field with no rider, and then we saw the smoke. The guys are saddling their horses now. They'll get Mingo and come to bring Chase home."

"Maggie, slow down. I just found him. We need a minute to get our heads around all of this. Let everyone know that he's okay and that there's no need to hurry."

"I will, and Claire, thank you for saving our family yet again. We love you too, you know?"

"I know. Thanks."

As soon as Claire ended the call, Chase scrambled to his feet and started pacing. "I can't go back to the house. My dad will mock me and say I only did this to get attention. He'll tell everyone that I'm jealous and petty and worthless. I can't do it. You shouldn't have found me."

"Chase, stop!" Claire grabbed his arm and got right in his face. "Didn't you just hear the relief in Maggie's voice? She was speaking for all of them, not just for her and Brad. Can't you see that? They love you and want this conflict between you and your dad to be reconciled."

No longer able to hold her gaze, he walked to the memorial where there was nothing left but ash and molten plastic. Without warning, he dropped to his knees, buried his face in his hands and started praying for forgiveness . . . and for help to face his dad.

Joy flooded Claire's heart as she came closer and silently joined him. Eventually, the sound of voices in the distance caused her to look up. When she did, she noticed a part of the Bible sandwiched in between melted pieces of Roger's kayak. She cast a quick look around for something strong enough to pry with and caught sight of the rifle. *That will work.* Rushing to get it, she immediately shoved the barrel into a small crack and forced the plastic apart.

Chase had gotten to his feet and was wiping his face with the corner of his sleeve when he asked, "What are you doing?"

"Rescuing your dad's Bible. I have a feeling that he's going to want it again." She made the opening wider. "There, is the plastic too hot to pull it out?"

Chase kicked some of the hot coals out of the way and stepped close enough to reach the Bible. Some of the edges were burned but it was mostly still intact. "It seems fitting that the Bible would be the only thing to survive."

"Well, I dare say it wasn't the only thing."

Chapter 39

ROGER AND CHASE

Three horses and two riders came into view. Roger rode beside Brad, and Mingo brought up the rear.

Claire felt Chase tense, so she squeezed his arm. "I'm here for you, no matter how your dad responds."

"I know and if he's harsh, this time I deserve it." He handed her the Bible, brushed the ashes from his hands and walked around the smoldering kayaks to greet them.

Claire stayed put; she knew this was something he had to face alone.

Roger jumped off his horse with the letter clutched in his hand and started running to Chase. At first, Chase stepped back and looked at Claire. She waved him on and mouthed, "You've got this."

He took a deep breath, exhaled quickly, and turned to face his father.

"My son." Roger grabbed his shoulders and shook him. Tears ran down his reddened cheeks. "You're alive. Thank God, you're alive!" He flung his arms around Chase and through the intensity of fresh moans he said, "I'm so sorry, my son, I'm so sorry."

Chase didn't answer, though he held on tight.

When they did separate, Roger choked out, "I've been a damn fool and incredibly selfish. Yet, my pain and loss are no excuse for how I've treated you, or your mother, all these years." He shook his head. His voice, now raspy and broken. "You've been right here, fighting your own demons, but instead of helping you . . ." He clasped a hand over his mouth as fresh tears ran down his cheeks. Unable to keep his composure, he turned away. A moan escaped his lips before he continued. "With bitterness consuming my own soul, I purposed to let you die along with your brothers so that I wouldn't miss Zac so much." He turned back, shaking the crumpled letter toward Chase. "Reading this, ahem . . . pierced my heart."

Chase started to speak, "But—"

Roger put out his hand. "Please, let me finish. This snapped me back into reality. I don't want to lose you. I'm not sure if you can forgive me . . . and I won't blame you if you can't ... but maybe we could start over. I've missed you and I'm asking you to give me a chance to be your father and your friend."

Chase stepped back, not in fear or anger, but so he could look into his father's bloodshot eyes.

Claire had moved closer so she could hear and see. Roger's face contorted with a mixture of regret and sadness. They couldn't get back the last ten years, but she knew their future depended on Chase's reply. Would he choose life and family, or would he hold on to his bitterness and continue to walk through life alone?

The moment was raw and messy, the turmoil deep. Only time could bring true and lasting healing. Yet, it had to start somewhere, and here amidst the ashes of a smoldering memorial was as good a place as any. Yes, what was erected in the honor of the dead was gone. In its place stood the living. The two men whom those events had all but destroyed.

Claire held her breath as she waited for his answer.

Suddenly, Chase fell into his father's arms, desperately grabbing handfuls of his shirt and pulling him closer. "I've missed you too, Dad. More than you could ever know." Their groans echoed off the mountains and were carried away by the winds of regret. They embraced for a long time.

Brad left the horses and came to where Claire was standing. "You know, just as saying sorry doesn't seem like enough at the moment, neither does saying thank you. But thank you for saving our family."

Claire met his gaze. "Oh Brad, God is the one you really need to thank. I'm simply the painter . . . the one He chose to use." She held out the Bible. "It seems right that this survived, don't you think?"

He nodded and took it.

Epilogue

THE PAINTING

Later that day, Chase asked Claire if she would take a walk with him. They started across the lawn, leaving the chatter of a houseful of happy people behind them.

Roger must have seen them leave because he came with Michelle to the porch and called, "Hey son, you take good care of her; she's a keeper."

"I'll try, sir."

"And please, call me Dad."

"Dad it is." Chase tipped his hat toward him and smiled.

"And Claire, the painting is coming home with us tonight."

"That's great. I can't wait to see where you hang it."

"It's going above the fireplace. I'm going to box up all of Jack's old trophies. I want that painting hanging right where we can see all three of our boys every single day."

Michelle squealed and squeezed his arm. "Oh Roger, thank you."

Zoe ran onto the porch and grabbed Roger's hand, "Hey Grampa, come see pictures of my horse."

He scooped Zoe up and said, "You two enjoy your walk. We can talk later."

"Wow," Chase said as they turned and continued toward the barns. "My dad is scaring me."

"He's on an emotional high right now. That's not to say he'll crash, just don't expect this to be the new normal."

"On that note, I look forward to seeing what our new normal will look like."

"Well, if you still need to move to Texas, I'm not coming with you; but my dad has a job opening, and we want you to be the guy to fill it."

"Oh yeah? How long have you known about this?" He stopped to face her.

"Since Thursday." Sadness suddenly shrouded her joy. "But you wouldn't answer my calls."

He grimaced. "I was so lost and broken . . . I hid from everyone that I loved, including you. Then, to my amazement, you pushed past your own feelings of rejection and came to save me from myself." Fresh pain emanated from his eyes. "I'm sorry I hurt you, Claire." He reached to tuck some loose strands of hair behind her ear, allowing the backs of his fingers to brush across her cheek. "Would you be willing to give me another chance?"

She took a step back. Her answer was calculated and bold. "On two conditions."

"Do I dare ask what those might be?"

"First, that you always remember this day as a day of hope and reconciliation. I know the pain that brought you to this point has been years in the making, and there will still be challenges ahead of you." She took his hands. "Let this day be a reminder that no matter what you go through, there are people who love you deeply."

He nodded thoughtfully.

"Second, I need *you* to start believing in that strong and charming guy who opened the gate. The guy whose aunt and uncle thought he was worth staying for."

"I promise to work on that." A smile crept into the corner of his lips, though it didn't reach his eyes.

"Oh, and one more thing." Her face lit up. "I want the guy back who calls to tell me good night so that he's the last person on my mind when I fall asleep, and then calls again in the morning so he's the first thing on my mind when I wake."

"Now, that I can do!" With hope renewed, he drew her into his embrace.

She nestled her face against his chest, heard his strong but steady heartbeat and thought, 'Love gained, love lost . . . calamity makes or breaks a man . . . and yet, sometimes it's both.' *Yes, sometimes it's both.*

THE END

Acknowledgments

Thanks first to the Lord Jesus who put this story in my heart and then helped me in my efforts to let it spill out onto these pages. I am forever grateful.

To my team of beta readers: Colleen Frasier, Jessica Jennings, Emma Joy Hill (author of: ASHES OF GLASS) and Stephanie Dean. Each of you found different elements that needed improvement. Your attention to detail and your pointing out of plot or character inconsistencies strengthened the story and have made me a better writer. You were all fantastic and deserve praise. Thank you!

Many thanks to Nancy Vossman, Brenda Riehle, and Carol Bush. You all played a special part, not only with editing, but also with affirmation at critical points in the process that helped me get across the finish line.

To my beloved, Ron. Your support and input, from beta reading to editing to publishing, have been invaluable. I would not have gotten this book to publication without you. Thank you so much!

To Jessica for your input and creative eye in helping me with my book cover design.

www.arleenjennings.com

Twitter: @ArleenSJennings

Made in USA - Kendallville, IN
45052_9781090711823
07.14.2022 1337